STARVE

A J MERLIN

Cover Design by Daqri Designs

EBOOK ISBN: 978-1-955540-74-2

PAPERBACK ISBN: 978-1-955540-75-9

May your survival be worth the sacrifice

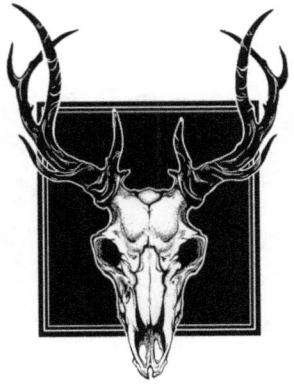

AUTHOR'S NOTE

To my lovely readers-

Starve marks the first time I've delved into my love of folklore-esque horror, and my interpretation of a combination of myths. It's a dark, brutal standalone where the **horror** is just as important as the **romance**.

A few things to note - the ending is happy, in its way. The dog doesn't die, but you will want justice for her. This has more visceral gore than you may be used to from my work, but it's necessary and (hopefully) you won't find it too hard to stomach. It contains cannibalism, mental health and illness rep, and gore.

CHAPTER ONE

EVERYTHING IS TOO LOUD.

The talking in the coffee shop.

The sound of chairs scraping against the floor.

And worst of all, the thoughts that are racing and chasing each other in my head.

My fingers tap on the cheap cardboard cup in front of me. I stare down at it as if the cooling caramel latte is going to grow arms, pick up a chair, and smash it across my face. Though maybe that would be a mercy if it could distract me from the noise of pure existence around me.

How dramatic of me, I tell myself silently, my gaze flicking up to a large, round man as he drags his chair back across the floor and stumbles to his feet. I can't tell how much of his shape is him, and how much are his clothes, but I'm willing to bet it's a solid sixty-forty split.

If he's this cold in a coffee shop, he should really find a better place to live than Whippoorwill Gap, Washington. My eyes track him as he leaves, and I can't help the small flicker of a smile at the way he literally crosses himself once he gets to the door. Like the cold is a sentient entity dead set on tearing him limb from limb.

And maybe it is. Sometimes when I don't put on enough layers in the winter, I definitely take the weather personally. But this isn't winter, and he won't make it if this is him now.

But my smile fades as the noise filters back in, and my fingers tap a bit more insistently on the cup in front of me.

I can't do this.

The thought is abrupt and the sentiment is immediate. Before I can really think about what I'm doing, I jump to my feet, sending my chair clattering back from the table with my jerky, too-quick movement. Luckily, I catch it before it falls, but my stomach still clenches as it teeters on its rear legs and my fingers grip the fake wood of the backrest.

Are my hands shaking?

Yeah, they're shaking. But I hope it's only obvious to me, as I very carefully slide the chair back under the table where it belongs. I know I'm putting too much time, too much care into the action. But I can't help it. Nor can I help the way it feels like every pair of eyes in the coffee shop are on me. From the teenagers in the corner to the person in the drive-thru window talking away at the bored-looking barista.

It's hard not to look at every single one of them, and impossible not to wince at each laugh, snort, and every smile I see. My brain tells me they're all directed at me, so whenever someone leans over to say something to the person next to them, I'm convinced the quiet mutterings are about me.

Maybe I'm walking too quickly. Or perhaps my paranoia is showing on my face. They heard my chair, or they're mocking my black fleece-lined leggings that are just a touch loose under my thick red hoodie that's too long but so comfortable.

But I'm so close to the door, even as my heart pounds in my chest over *nothing at all*. I can go have this breakdown in my car, then another one in the comfort of my home instead of in the public loudness of this too-bright coffee shop.

This was a bad idea.

But lately, bad ideas are the one thing I'm good at.

"What?" Words filter through my brain, louder than the others. I stop so quickly that I stumble with my hand close to the trash by the door where I intend to throw my full, gone-cold coffee.

A young girl, maybe nineteen, stands in front of the glass door, a rag and bottle of cleaner in her hands as she looks at me. Her expression falls to confusion, and she glances down at my cup, then at me. "I just said have a good day," she repeats calmly, slowly, like maybe I'm hard of hearing.

In reality, my brain is just too full and too busy processing everything around me to take in anything else.

"Right. Umm. Sorry. Thanks." My voice comes out stilted and almost panicked, no matter how much I will myself to at least pretend to be okay today.

Fuck, I'm really not okay. That's the problem, and I've never been a very good liar. A smile twitches on my face, though it quickly withers and dies. "Sorry," I say again, splashing my fingers with cold coffee as I toss my drink into the trash.

"You didn't do anything to be sorry for," the girl promises me, pushing open the glass door for me. "But if you didn't like that, we could totally make you something else," she adds, probably having heard the loud *thump* of my cup in the trash and realizing just how full it had been.

Embarrassment surges through me, and I remember how horrified my mom was anytime I tried to throw a half full bottle of liquid into the trashcan back home. But I remind myself it's not that uncommon. That people definitely do it all the time.

"No, it was good," I insist quickly to reassure her. "I'm just not feeling so great." Truthfully, I don't think I even tried my drink. I was too busy fighting down the panic crawling up my throat and failing gloriously, given my current vibrating nerves and the blood I can hear rushing in my ears.

She says something else, but I don't hear it enough to do more than respond with a distracted smile. I murmur something I hope is a polite thank you, and press my hand against the cold glass of the door before slipping outside, already counting the steps between me and my unobtrusive black car in the second row of the small parking lot.

While the sidewalk is the easier option, given the icy parking lot, after three steps I realize it's no longer a possibility for me. Not with the way my brain is telling me that all the people at the window tables are watching me, waiting for me to slip and smash my face against the concrete.

They're judging me, I think as I see a woman frown at her phone and say something to her companion.

They're making fun of me, my mind promises me, when a man snickers and covers his smile with his hand.

"Fern, you're fine," I breathe, stepping off of the sidewalk into a patch of asphalt wet from last night's rain. "You're fine; your brain is just being a dick. You're used to this." At least out here, alone in the parking lot, there's no one around to notice my one-sided conversation.

Nevertheless, every inch of me seems hyperaware. My skin prickles, the hairs on my neck standing up, and it's so hard not to constantly turn to look behind me, with only the threat of looking like I'm seizing and giving myself whiplash stopping me from doing so.

"No one is looking at you," I tell myself, repeating the words my therapist had told me so many times. "You're not that important. They're living their lives, just like you're living yours, Fern."

The words feel like ash on my tongue, losing their efficacy almost immediately. Thankfully, when I slip a few steps later, I'm at my car and can easily catch myself on my door even as a soft, embarrassing yelp leaves me at my stumble.

As fast as humanly possible, I slide into the driver's seat and close the door. My finger hits the ignition button just as my boot jams the brake pedal, and my car whirrs to life with all the surprisingly subtle noise of a hybrid. Admittedly, the electric side of it isn't a sound I hear very often, given the frequency of me forgetting to plug it into the charger when I get to my house. But today, I'm happy about the softness of the battery and the soft whirring that lets me know it's on while I settle back against my seat and just focus on breathing.

That's all.

In and out. Over and over, until I feel just a little bit more human. All I have to do is get myself home. The quiet of my little home in the woods is beckoning me like a lullaby, and I know that once I get there and can decompress by myself, maybe scream into a pillow or cry in the shower, I'll be fine. Or at least closer to fine than I am right now. I just need to get there first, while my brain screams *danger* at me like the wail of an ambulance siren.

"You can so do this." I sigh, shifting to sit up properly. Next comes my seatbelt, and I'm careful while I reverse out of the parking lot to make sure I don't accidentally hit someone else's car. Which would be more than a little traumatizing, given my current proximity to a full-blown panic attack caused by overstimulation and poor life choices.

I really don't need a vehicular incident added to my tally today, truth be told.

The twenty-one minute drive feels more like triple that,

but somehow I finally pull onto my narrow, winding street. In the distance, through a veritable sea of trees, I can see some bits of the Cascade Mountains. Not for the first time, I applaud myself for buying a home so far out in the middle of nowhere so I don't have to see another person for days if I don't want to.

Though I guess if I were to have a slip and fall, it would take a long time for the paramedics to come get me. And my road is creepy enough as it winds through spindly trees that smarter people might turn back after claiming to see a ghost in the woods.

The thought makes me sigh when I see my neighbor's driveway and the flapping sheets he puts up in his trees to drive home that point, to scare anyone who might come back here to bother them, or so he claims. Even though I told the eighty-year-old one-eyed lumberjack there's very little reason for anyone to come this far back in rural Washington to fuck with him.

But what do I know?

The road narrows, becoming barely two lanes wide as my cabin-style house finally comes into view. The trees part to show my gravel driveway and the solitude I've been seeking ever since this panic set in.

Or what *should* be the start of my solitude and peace today.

But my hands grow cold when I see a shiny red car parked in my driveway. I can't help the urge to just drive on past instead of park beside it, already a little frustrated at seeing my mom's car.

Please, I beg the universe. *Please don't let her husband be here.* I can barely handle my mom on the best of days. I absolutely can't handle her husband today, too.

But as soon as I park, all four doors of the sedan launch open. As the two adults in the front seats get out and stretch, my step-dad's kids, Noel and Noah, jump out like mini nukes set on destroying my entire life.

"Finally!" Noel complains, rolling her eyes at me. "We asked if Mom could just let us in, since she has a key. But she said we had to *wait*." God forbid someone tell either of them to wait, I suppose, though I manage to give something like an apologetic smile. Or at least an approximation of one.

"Hey, Mom. Hi...Nathaniel," I greet with a wan, clearly distressed smile. "What, umm... What are you doing here?" *Please say leaving.*

"We thought we'd come pay you a visit. We were in the area, Nathaniel took us to lunch over in Mazama," she explains, and I realize he must be in the middle of a big contract if he's taking her to some fancy tourist restaurant over there.

But clearly the point was to come see me, since there are plenty of closer, better restaurants back in Spokane.

"I'm really happy to see you—" She hugs me without pausing outside of my personal bubble, and I set my jaw hard so I don't lose my grin. "But umm, I wish you would've called? I'm sort of—"

"Oh, we won't be here long. And we won't be any trouble. The kids have been asking about you lately, and I've missed you," my mom says, flapping a hand at me. Nathaniel gives me a bored grin, leaning on the car with his phone in his hand.

None of them had asked about me. My mother's just a nosy busybody, is what I want to say. But I know better than to make this an issue when it doesn't have to be one. All I need to do is—

One of the twins runs into me, hard enough to send me stumbling to the gravel in my driveway. There's a giggled, distracted apology, but they don't stop to help as I pick myself up and sigh at my now skinned up palms.

I can't do this.

"Gosh, Fern," my mom sighs with her tone that makes it seem like I did this to myself.

"It's fine." I stare down at my stinging hands, palms welling with blood. "It's, umm...it's fine." Fuck, it's really not fine. I'm at the end of my rope, and the twins are cutting through it until I'm stuck with fraying threads of nervous frustration. "I-I'm going to go get cleaned up. But Mom, I really don't have time for this today. I just came home to pick some stuff up." It's a lie, but I can't help it.

I need them *gone*.

Without listening to her reply, I stumble toward my front door, fishing my keys out of my pocket and getting blood on my shirt as I do. Every beat of my heart seems to make the blood flow a little faster, and I don't bother putting my keys away as I walk inside. I just...drop them.

That feeling is back, the one I've been trying all day to push aside.

It's all *too much*. Everything is too loud again, from the heater to the fridge, to the electricity in the walls.

Noel or Noah shrieks and I trip at the noise, reminding myself that it's fine.

I'm fine.

I'm.

Fine.

Somehow, I make it to the bathroom without really being conscious of the route my feet take. Somehow I do it without falling over something, though once I do I just stand there, watching my pale reflection in the mirror. My blonde hair is limp, and my light blue eyes are so pale, they look like the panic and loudness have pulled out all the color until I'm just a ghost.

God, I wish I was a ghost right now.

I'm fine, I'm fine—

This isn't the end of the world, I tell myself as panic crawls up my throat. My palms ache, the electricity whirs, and every breath seems to thrust my heart into overdrive. I need to be alone, but I know from experience it'll take an hour or more to get rid of my mom, my step-dad, and their terrible children.

I know they'll want to stay. They'll want to chat. They'll try to talk about all the things I'm doing wrong while the twins run through my little house like bulls in a china shop.

I'm fine, I'm fine, I'm—

The front door closes and distantly I hear my mom saying something, calling something that might be my name. But I can't pull my eyes from my reflection in the mirror. My hands hurt more than they did earlier, but I'm not looking at them. Dimly, I remember getting the first aid kit from under the cabinet.

I think.

I swear I did at some point in the last minute.

Maybe they hurt because I'm bandaging them, even though something feels wrong with that statement.

Why do my hands hurt so badly?

"Fern?" Mom's voice echoes in the hallway, making me wince. The sound wars with the buzzing electricity that's oppressive in my ears, and the way my hands just hurt so badly that it makes me grit my teeth.

I'm fine. I'm fine.

I'm fine—

"FERN!" My mom's scream drags me out of my thoughts, and I stare at her, puzzled by the sudden draining of color from her face, and the way her eyes aren't fixed on my face, but on my hands. "Oh my god, Fern. *What did you do?*"

Finally I look down, seeing the small scissors clutched in one hand. My knuckles are white from being curled tightly around them while my other hand lies flat against the sink as I dig, dig, *dig*—

The blood is the last thing I notice before my mom suddenly grabs me, already yelling for Nathaniel as she chucks the scissors against the far wall and covers my hand in a sage green hand towel.

Rather than being worried about what I've done, all I can think of is how the blood isn't going to come out, that it'll ruin the color scheme of my bathroom if it stains.

Priorities, after all, are important.

CHAPTER TWO

F ERN H OLLIS.

Twenty-three.

Right? My mom questions my age as she repeats it to the nurse for my record, but I'm too busy staring at my hand to really notice. It doesn't even hurt. At least, not like it probably should.

She's twenty-three. Yes.

I am twenty-three. Thanks for noticing, mom. But then again, I suppose I should just be thrilled she knows I'm older than eighteen and younger than twenty-five. Anything else is really just gravy, since she normally doesn't worry herself with details when it comes to me.

After all, for the first year after I moved, she didn't know the name of the town I live in. Though in her defense, she was busy.

With a new husband, new kids, and a new life.

The words from the nurse sound hesitant. Apologetic. When something in them makes me realize I should be listening, my mind urges me to come to the surface instead of drowning in the comfortable, fluffy blackness I've been in since the incident in my bathroom.

"No." I cut off the nurse, blinking up at her, and she gives me a sympathetic look just as my mother stares between us, obviously confused. "There's no way you're serious."

The nurse bites her lip, looking back at her computer with obvious distress on her face. "I see you've heard about our sister facility," she says, her voice stilted. "I can promise you, Miss Hollis, there's nothing to worry about regarding Bluebone Ridge Mental Hospital."

I fix her with a look, wincing as the pain in my hand makes itself known. Even though they gave me a numbing shot before putting in the three stitches to hold my palm together, it definitely still stings. And now that I'm fully aware again, the pain is here with a vengeance. "I don't need to go anywhere." I sigh, running my other hand through my blonde hair. "It was an accident."

But I don't need to look at either woman to know they're giving me *the look*. "Come on, Mom," I plead, hoping that for once in my damn life, she's on my side about this.

I hadn't been trying to kill myself, or really even hurt myself. I was overwhelmed, overstimulated, and just unable to think straight. Even if she hadn't shown up, I would've been fine.

She owes me this.

"I...I don't know, Fern," my mom argues gently, reaching out to touch my arm. "You were standing there in the bathroom digging a pair of scissors into your hand like you didn't even feel it." She says the words carefully, like she's afraid of saying the thing that'll set me off again. Something that will mean she has to stick around longer instead of going home to Spokane with her newer, shinier, less mentally unstable family.

"I understand your uncertainty, but our doctors have determined you need to be evaluated," the nurse tells me gently, setting her iPad down on the counter beside her. "Unfortunately, we're past a discussion about the matter, Fern." I hate the way they both say my name, and I close my eyes with a sigh, refusing to let myself freak out even more.

Crying apparently won't get me out of this, but...

"Not Bluebone Ridge," I try this time, with more conviction in my tone. "There's no way you're sending me there."

The nurse frowns again, looking at the door as if she'd rather be anywhere but here. But really, that just makes two of us. Every tired, stressed nerve in me prickles at the idea of being shipped up the mountain to the place where all local horror stories are born, but my mom just looks confused.

"What's the problem with Bluebone Ridge?" she finally asks, a touch of irritation in her tone when neither the nurse nor I volunteer the information. "We have insurance. If the care there is subpar—"

"That's not the case at all, Mrs. Hollis," the nurse assures my mother with a tight smile.

"Whittier," I correct without thinking. "Her name is Whittier."

"My mistake, Mrs. Whittier. The hospital is up in the mountains. It's a very nice facility—"

"It's haunted," I mutter with a sigh, interrupting her. "Those are code words for 'it's haunted and in a deserted place.'"

"It's rural," the nurse clarifies tightly. "It was rebuilt several years ago, but there are unfortunately local legends about it that paint Bluebone in a less-than-favorable light. I can promise you, truly, that I wouldn't be sending your daughter there if I—"

"If I offer you one hundred thousand dollars, will you go

with me as my nurse?" I interrupt again, rolling my eyes up at her. When she doesn't answer right away, I grin in an unfriendly manner. "Haunted. Deserted. Where dreams go to die and where local horror stories are born, Mom. The creepy ambient music kicks in about a quarter of the way up, where the road gets all windy and the wind starts howling."

"Well..." My mom looks a bit troubled. Like she's maybe regretting her decision to agree with the doctors about me needing help. At least, that's my hope until she looks at me with that guilty, self-serving expression I know all too well.

"You're being a bit dramatic, Fern," she tells me softly. "And if they think this is for the best, then I have to agree with the doctor."

"You mean the doctor who talked to me for all of five minutes while focused on an iPad, whose signal cut out three times? That doctor?"

Both women just look at me, expressions flat and making it clear they're over my shit. But if I'm going to Bluebone Ridge, I'm going to make sure their days are as shitty as possible, since I'm sure it won't compare to mine.

Fuck... Getting committed really wasn't part of my plan today. But focusing on old ghost stories really is helping me not focus on the idea of being committed *against my will.* "What if I say I'm fine?" I sigh, running a hand through my hair again and hating the burn of tears in my eyes. "What if I sign a paper saying if I stab myself with scissors again, it's no one's fault but my own?"

"Unfortunately, that's not how it works, Miss Hollis," the nurse informs me, her smile still tight and unamused. "But you're welcome to disagree with our assessment and say no to a seventy-two hour evaluation."

I perk up, brows raised. "Really?"

"Sure," she deadpans, the sarcasm winning out over

professionalism. "And then I'll get a hold of a judge, have your rights stripped, and you'll end up in Bluebone either way. So it's your choice on whether you want this to take two hours or four. If I were you, I'd rather get there sooner so you don't miss dinner."

"Oh." I settle back against the bed, rolling my eyes up to the ceiling. "You're right, obviously." When I flex my fingers, my palm twinges. "Wouldn't want to miss dinner in the haunted, half-abandoned, crumbling asylum in the mountains. Silly me."

My mom seems surprised when she's informed I can't drive myself, and looks at me like I'm the problem, as if I'm causing the medical system to do more work than necessary. As if I *want* to ride in an ambulance up a winding mountain, to a mental hospital with more horror stories than any house in Texas full of dead bodies.

But I can sense the vibes change in the room when the nurse leaves, and my mom glances at her phone more than usual, tipping me off about what's wrong.

She wants to leave. Because of my little incident, her mandated parental time is long over, and her internal alarm is going off for her to get back to the life she prefers living. The one where I'm a phone call and a hundred miles away, instead of in her face and taking up her time.

"I'm fine, mom." The well-rehearsed words are out of my mouth before I can stop myself, followed by the usual pang of disappointment that twists in my chest. She's always been this way, so I can't exactly be surprised. "You can go home." I give her a wan, forced smile, which she returns too quickly, showing me she was just waiting for this; waiting for me to release her from motherly duties.

"I can stay." But there's no conviction in my mom's words. And when she pushes her dark brown hair back behind her ear, it occurs to me, not for the first time, how different we look. I can't help but wonder if she'd care more if she saw some of herself in me.

But it's twenty-three years too late for that, so I file the thought away and force myself not to look needy and scared.

Which is hard, since I'm both of those things right now. Being thrown into a mental hospital for a mandatory seventy-two hour psych hold really wasn't on my schedule or my bucket list. Especially Bluebone fucking Ridge asylum.

My brain goes through options, frantic in the last few minutes of relative freedom that I have. *Relative,* because I was already informed there's a security guard outside, just in case I do something stupid like try to run the fuck away like a psycho.

Which, honestly, is pretty tempting.

"I can stay," Mom says again, like I hadn't heard her the first time. But there's even less conviction, if that's possible, and everything in her words hints that she'd really rather not. "I can't really do anything. But I can stay until the EMTs get here to transport you—"

"You're fine." Cutting her off before she can turn the conversation into the suffering Olympics. I don't need to hear about how she's been in worse situations with less support, or how she never would've expected anyone to hold her hand. I know this song and dance, and I'm not interested in repeating it today. "It's okay, Mom." I give her a reassuring smile, like she's the one going through a hard time instead of just the one mildly inconvenienced after showing up at my house unin-vited and letting her step-kids shove me to the ground.

In a way, this is sort of her fault. God forbid she fucking *calls me* before busting into my life.

I miss her next words, but I blink when she gets to her feet with her purse slung over her shoulder. She walks forward and hugs me awkwardly, radiating discomfort at the situation.

"Call me if you need anything, okay? I can stay. I could get Nathaniel to take the kids—"

"Nah, it's all good, Mom." I try not to sigh the words, but fail miserably. "It's...fine. It's always fine."

She gives me a look. *The* look, if I'm being honest, and I know my words have had the effect they always do. They chase her away, sending her out the door with one last well-wishing statement coming from her mouth.

"Take care of yourself, Fern. Call me if you need anything." Then she's gone, just like always. Except this time she's leaving me in a hospital bed, alone, as I wait for EMTs to take me to a probably haunted asylum.

But then again, I can't really be surprised.

Things never change with my mom.

CHAPTER THREE

THE MOMENT THE AMBULANCE MAKES ITS WOBBLING WAY INTO THE main parking lot of Bluebone Ridge, I'm ready to commit a war crime to escape. Never before have I ever considered myself someone who gets carsick, but then again, I've never ridden in the back of an ambulance up winding mountain roads so narrow that I was sure on no less than eighteen occasions we were going to go plummeting over the cliff.

And judging by the look on the female paramedic's face who sits beside me on the seat, I'm not the only one; which brings me at least a little comfort. She takes deep, shuddering breaths as I watch with my legs curled up under me on the stupid stretcher I was wheeled out on.

Stupidly.

All of this is a joke, in my opinion. No matter how much I tried to describe that I'd dissociated—that it's something I do sometimes—the nurses just looked at me as if I were about to start shrieking like a banshee and running into walls. The doctor, of course, had been exempt from my pleas to go back home, seeing as he only met with me over an iPad with a shitty connection.

"You good?" I ask the paramedic, who looks at me with what I'm sure she's hoping is a reassuring glance. "Is it your first time to the cursed asylum on the mountain?" Given that she's from the area too, I have no doubt she knows the stories of this place.

"Unfortunately not," she replies with a sigh. She sits up straight, gulping in deep breaths. "But the drive is awful every time. I get sick on the mountain roads."

I give her a few seconds, and then say in my most reasonable tone, "Tell you what. We could just turn around and go back now. I'll hold your hand on the way down, and we'll count the near-falls together. Seems like company would make the drive better, you know?"

My not-so-subtle bid for freedom gets a chuckle out of her, and the next smile she gives me is more genuine than her earlier glance. "Would if I could, hon," she promises. "But that would break a couple of laws, and I like my job. Look, it won't be that bad, okay? Most likely, they'll evaluate you and you'll be home within three days. I won't be your ride then; they have driver services for that. But seventy-two hours and you're home."

"Or I die because Bluebone ridge is haunted, cursed, and probably falling apart," I reply sweetly, unable to help myself. "And the fact you didn't immediately refute my statement tells me you don't think I'm wrong."

"I think there are places I'd rather be than the top of the mountain, but if I had to be on a mountain, there are worse ones than this one." Her tone is just as overly friendly as earlier, and it makes my lips twitch into a reluctant smile. Though her grin falls as she looks down, and reaches forward to snatch my fingers away from my palm. "You've got to leave that alone," she scolds gently, then sighs worriedly.

"Oh." I look down and belatedly realize I'd been messing with the cut in my palm that's now stitched up and still half-numb. "I didn't realize..." I trail off, not wanting to admit I hadn't realized I was doing it. Just like I didn't realize I was cutting myself earlier.

But I guess that's why I'm here.

Because I'm stuck with a case of *I didn't realize* in the worst way imaginable.

"Yeah. I'll uh, I'll work on that. I wouldn't want them to strap me into a wheelchair with oven mitts on my hands so I can't poke at it." My retort is a bit lame, and a little rambling, but I'm not at my best right now. Truthfully, I'm proud of myself for not being a toddler-like mess on the floor, refusing to go anywhere and clutching onto any nailed down fixture in the ambulance.

The only thing stopping me is how embarrassing that would be, and the fact that the EMT beside me looks like she could bodily remove me from the ambulance without a problem.

I didn't realize we stopped moving while we chatted, so the doors opening make me jerk. But I recover quickly and am about to get to my feet when I see the orderly outside with her hands clasped around the handles of a wheelchair. "I don't need that," I'm quick to say, wanting to keep whatever dignity I have left semi-intact.

But the woman gives me a withering look, not bothering to smile. "Sorry, sweetie," she tells me in a voice bordering on condescending. "I hate to tell you, but everybody has to come in here the same way."

"Even though I can use my legs just fine?"

"Especially then." She makes a gesture toward the wheelchair, and I glance back at the EMT like she's suddenly my ally in this situation. But one look at her apologetic smile tells me that's not happening.

And it hits me again how much I don't want to do this. How I'd really rather be absolutely anywhere but here at Bluebone Ridge.

I don't want to do this.

More than that, I'm *terrified* of those doors closing behind me and some doctor making the decision that I'll never be fit to leave.

There's no way I can stay here.

I can't—

I'm pulled from my spiral when the paramedic grabs my hand suddenly. When I look down in surprise, I see she's holding my fingers in hers, keeping it away from my injured palm. A glance at her face shows me a silent warning there, and I ruefully remind myself that pulling out the stitches in my palm certainly won't make my stay here any shorter.

Taking a breath, I force myself to climb out of the ambulance. With the help of the driver, who grabs my uninjured hand to support me, I jump to the gravel that crunches under my feet. The air up here is somehow colder, even though we're only about thirty miles away from Whippoorwill Gap. But I guess being this much "closer to God" will do that to a place. In my hoodie, I shudder and draw my arms around myself to glare dubiously at the wheelchair, unable to stop myself from going through every option in my brain to get out of sitting down.

"Not going to work," the orderly says, not unkindly. "Though I can't blame you for trying. But the sooner you sit, the sooner we can be done and you can be out again. Okay?" There's something convincingly gentle in her words that I believe, and even though I'd absolutely prefer to be doing anything else, I force myself to sit gingerly in the wheelchair.

Immediately, I hate it. I feel small, and awkward, and inept as she talks to the paramedics, and I can feel my shoulders hunching protectively while I take a minute to look around the courtyard.

I don't expect to see a *wolf*.

On further inspection—since I have nothing better to do—I realize it's not a wolf, but a very convincingly wolf-like dog. With a mix of grey and red-brown fur on its head and shoulders, it looks regal and wild in the courtyard. It takes a moment longer for me to notice the leash tied to a nearby railing, and the way the dog stares at a nearby door makes me think its owner is there.

Seconds later, the door opens, admitting a scowling man into the courtyard. The dog scrambles up, though when the man unties its leash and yanks on it, the dog hunches, reminding me of my defensiveness. A bitter taste rises in my throat, and I watch as he jerks again on the leash, not bothering to give the dog any kind of verbal command but expecting it to know what he wants, anyway. And judging by the flinch anytime the man looks at him, I can't imagine the dog is very fond of the man.

I want to look away.

I want to look anywhere else, because I hate seeing animals mistreated, but I can't help watching. Even when the orderly starts pushing the wheelchair over the sidewalk toward the double doors of Bluebone Ridge, my gaze stays glued to the sight of the man dragging the dog toward the gates.

"Why is there a dog?" I find myself asking, though in a few seconds I can no longer see either the dog or its handler.

"Oh, Moro?" The orderly doesn't look back, though her voice is a little tense, like this is a subject she wants to avoid.

"She's not a pet, if that's what you're thinking. Or a therapy dog. We get predators up here sometimes, so having a dog around can help scare off unwanted four-legged visitors." She laughs weakly at her own words, though I don't give her the benefit of doing the same.

Even though she never did anything to me, I can't help being resentful of the orderly and everyone here. Well, everyone except Moro. There's no way I could ever hate a dog, and my heart hurts for her.

I cross and uncross my ankles in the wheelchair, feeling prickly and fidgety the whole time. The doors to the building are automatic, and I can't help wanting to curl up into a ball and die as she wheels me to a large front desk where she stops to chat about my file with the man behind the desk.

But now, we're not alone. Not just because of the desk attendants, but also because of the other patients here—a few of whom glance my way. Some of them are in street clothes like me, and some in light blue outfits that remind me of scrubs. Most are wearing light jackets or long-sleeved shirts under the short-sleeves of the powder blue outfits.

But I know I shouldn't be surprised, so I remind myself my arrival isn't exactly a shock or a spectacle to them. People come through these doors all the time. My eyes flick from person to person, and I force myself to focus on little details, instead of faces. Tattoos on fingers and necks. Blue and purple poorly dyed hair. The tap-tap-tap of someone's fingers that has me wanting to do the same thing.

Tap-tap-tap. Then I realize I'm doing it too, matching the movement of the girl leaning against the corner. She's not looking at me, but is instead staring up at the high ceiling above us, murmuring soundlessly.

Tap-tap-tap.

Our movements are in unison now, and I find I can't quite

stop the movement of my fingers on my leg. It's comforting, especially when, on every tap, the gash on my palm twinges just a little bit. Curious, I look up too, though all I see is a corner of the room that looks like it hasn't been dusted in too long of a time.

"*Fern Hollis.*" I hear my name spoken by the desk attendant.

"*Twenty-three.*"

"*Sent by Whippoorwill Baptist.*"

My new least favorite hospital, and one I will definitely never be patronizing again, even if I'm in danger of dying. Especially then, quite frankly, since I'm not sure how a doctor on an iPad could help me at all.

"*Seventy-two hour hold.*"

Fuck, that sounds worse every time I hear it.

Tap-tap-tap.

When I blink, I realize the girl is looking at me, though with a jolt it occurs to me that I have no idea when she turned away from staring at the ceiling. She hasn't stopped tapping her arm, and neither do I. It's like some inpatient morse code that I don't understand, but I can't stop doing it now.

Her head tilts, and she looks almost...concerned. She mouths something I can't understand, and mouths it again, then again, until finally it hits me what she's trying to say.

Go home.

As if I fucking can, I wish I could howl back. I bite my lip and frown, glancing up in an exaggerated way at the orderly as if to remind her of where we are. I doubt an escape attempt would go well here, and I don't want my seventy-two hours to be extended to seventy-two *days.*

But she mouths it again.

And again.

Then finally the shape of her words change, and again it takes me a few tries to read her lips.

They're coming.
They're here.
They're coming.
They're here.

Suddenly, my view of her is blocked by the orderly, who grins down at me with the obliviousness only the neurotypical can achieve. She doesn't even notice the tapping of my fingers, or if she does, she doesn't remark on it.

"Ready to get out of that chair?" she asks, reaching out one hand like a benevolent deity offering me sacrament. I sit up immediately without waiting for her to actually give me permission, though I duck away from her offered hand.

I don't need help. Especially from Bluebone Ridge, and I can't help but be resentful of my situation. The orderly gives a small frown, which she quickly hides, before smiling at me again. This time, however, it's a little forced. Not that I care. Her feelings aren't on my list of things to give a damn about today. All I care about is her approval of me so I don't end up somewhere worse.

If there even is somewhere worse...

"I'll explain everything while we walk, if that's all right with you. You can call me Esther, by the way." Her smile feels even a little less genuine now, and almost a bit wooden. But I only return it politely as I glance back at the corner where the strange tapping girl was.

But she's not there anymore. No matter where I look in the large room with benches and an almost cathedral-like appearance, I can't find any trace of her at all.

"Is this place meant to look like a replica of a hospital from the 1800s?" I murmur, following the orderly, *Esther*, away from the desk.

"Oh, it isn't a replica," she assures me. "While there have been updates made and conveniences put in, this building is almost just as it was when it was originally built. Though it's not from that long ago. It was built in 1924 and has always been a wellness center."

Wellness Center is a new one for me, but I keep my mouth shut.

"So I should be on the lookout for flapper-era ghosts, instead of pre-colonial ones?" I can't help but ask mildly. Esther stops in front of me, turning that wooden smile in my direction that I meet with slightly narrowed eyes and a plastic grin of my own. "It's nervous humor," I assure her.

Somehow, that seems to mollify her a little bit, even though it's a lie. While I'm terrified as hell, I've always had opinions about Bluebone Ridge, ever since I first heard the stories. "There are no ghosts here, Fern," she assures me. "Especially any that are out to hurt you. No matter what rumors float around about this place, there's nothing harmful about Bluebone Ridge, all right?"

She turns suddenly, reaching out to grip my shoulders in a way that's probably supposed to be comforting. I see her smile, though I look away, over her shoulder to stare down the hallway lined with thick-glassed windows casting wavering shapes on the floor from the light outside.

But that's not what holds my attention.

At the end of the hall—dressed in the plain powder blue outfit of a Bluebone Ridge patient—a man leans against the doorframe, his hair black enough to soak up the sun from outside as it falls across him.

He meets my gaze, though from this far, I can't tell what color his eyes are. And the whole time that Esther talks, he seems unnaturally still and almost not breathing.

"There's nothing here to hurt you, all right?" the older woman promises, her smile still so fake it hurts. "We're here to help you, Fern." Her fingers tighten, then loosen on my shoulders, but I still don't look at her. I'm too focused on the man. There's nothing particularly special about him, save that he's olive-skinned and good looking as hell. So I don't know why I'm so interested.

A smile twitches at his lips, though it isn't quite a friendly look. Slowly, he reaches up to press a finger to his lips, nodding at the orderly before stepping away from the door and disappearing down the far hallway, just as Esther turns to see where I'm gazing.

"What are you looking at?" she asks, interested rather than accusatory.

"Nothing," I murmur, not hesitating to lie even for a second. "Just the sunlight through the windows." Blinking, I snap myself out of it, offering her a smile that probably doesn't look very genuine. "Is that glass from the 1920s too? It looks weirdly thick and wavy."

Her suspicion fades, and she immediately launches into an explanation about glassmaking that I couldn't care less about, before leading me on this nonconsensual guided tour through the totally haunted asylum up in the mountains where it's already feeling like someone is watching.

CHAPTER FOUR

THE REST OF THE 'TOUR' PASSES WITH ME THINKING OF APPROXIMATELY two things that I can't get out of my head.

The man in the hall with the small smirk as he pressed a finger to his lips.

And, predictably, the dog.

It's like a game of Pong in my brain as both topics battle for supremacy, though I'm sure Esther won't want to hear about either as she shows me the hall of therapists' offices, the rec center, both back courtyards where a sea of blue-clothed people exist in varying degrees of displeasure, and finally the dining hall. My stomach twists as I remember I haven't really eaten today, though not for lack of my mother trying to get food at the hospital.

When she'd offered to bring me something, the nurse jumped down her throat and told her it wasn't protocol, and to my mom's credit, she tried to argue. She told the nurse I'm quick to get nauseating headaches from hunger, but the nurse only shrugged.

Really, Whippoorwill Baptist will forever be on my shit list,

I've decided. And the idea of making an account online just to leave them a strongly worded poor review is incredibly appealing.

"Any questions?" Esther asks, stopping outside of a room in the women's residential wing. She already told me in stern terms that women are not allowed in the men's wing and vice-versa, as if I'm an unruly, sex crazed teenager looking to bang every eligible inpatient in my seventy-two hour stay.

Not that I'd let that comparison slip out loud, of course.

"Uh, no," I murmur, stroking my fingers over the sterile blue cotton of the clothes she gave me to change into. They're unappealing at best. At worst...well, at least I'm in good company, I suppose. After all, not everyone in residence can be a serial killer, statistically speaking.

Probably.

"You have four hours until dinner. In two hours, you'll need to be at Dr. Hallman's office. You remember where that is?" she asks, putting that stern edge into her voice. I nod in agreement, and graciously accept my sneakers back on top of my new outfit, now bereft of their dirty white laces that I clearly could've used to strangle myself.

"I suggest you spend some time in your room, or if you like, you could head to one of the courtyards. Any closed door with a STAFF ONLY sign is off limits, and going in won't win you any favors." I nod again, and this time Esther steps up, her hands coming up to embrace me in what I'm sure she thinks is a warm, convincing way.

Not that I believe it.

"I know the stories that go around about Bluebone Ridge..." She sighs, giving me her best understanding smile. "I know you really don't want to be here. You're taking this really well." She offers me another kind look that feels just as put on as the rest of her current speech. But I give her my own smile, hoping I look appropriately reassured.

Which I am not.

When she leaves, I walk into the room Esther showed me, changing quickly into the stretchy, powder blue outfit. It's certainly not that flattering, and with my pale blonde hair, it just serves to make me look more washed out than usual. Not that I can see much of myself in the small, bolted down bathroom mirror.

Touching it proves that it's definitely safety glass, and it occurs to me that it has to be. After all, wouldn't want those of us with suicidal natures offing ourselves, I suppose. But the reality of it only makes me feel worse.

I'm not fucking suicidal.

I don't want to kill myself.

How do I explain that I just get overwhelmed? That sometimes I can't help how I feel, and how nothing seems real?

"Fuck," I murmur, reaching up to run my fingers through my hair. Leaving the bathroom, I take a moment to look around the small room with its two twin-sized beds. It's not freezing, at least. The door is heavy, with a small window at face level that looks way too much like a cell for me. So I don't look at it. Instead I go to the window, pressing my nose against the cold, thick glass to look at the wavy mountain outside.

Not that I can see much, given that the treeline starts only a few feet from the window. Tall and thick, they look like they've been left to grow untamed since this place was built. And honestly, they probably have. Looking up shows me the sight of other, taller mountains in the range, and I lean back just to breathe against the window, fogging it up.

With a small smile on my face, I reach up with my index finger, dragging it up and down until the word *hi* stares back at me in the fog. When it starts to fade, I breathe on the glass again, a stupid, rueful grin on my face.

Until something outside in the woods catches my gaze through the foggy glass. I jump in surprise, going up on my toes to look through the trees, expecting to see an elk or something similar.

But there's nothing.

No movement in the dark pine needles, or anywhere else on the grounds. There's no movement, though from somewhere far away I hear the sound of barking that I assume must be Moro. It fades after a few moments, leaving me standing there, staring through the thick glass and looking at nothing again.

"You won't be able to open it." The voice makes me jump, and I whirl around to look at the open door behind me. Standing there is a girl probably around my age, with dark circles prominent under her eyes and a frown on her lips. She tilts her head to look at me, surveying my face for a few moments as I just stare back at her.

"You get your own room," she goes on, stepping inside and glancing at both made beds. "That's pretty nice. Well, I don't know actually..." She looks thoughtfully out the window behind my head, then back at me. "It gets a little creepy up here in the mountains. I'm Sam."

"Fern," I reply automatically, clutching my fingers against my injured hand reflexively. It hurts enough to be grounding, but not enough to really distract myself from the situation. I look her over, trying to see past the exhaustion and the dark circles to something other than her dry grin. But really, that's the most noticeable thing about her, apart from us matching in our powder blue 'client' uniforms.

"Are you here for a while, or...?" she trails off, leaning against the doorframe with her arms folded. My stomach twists around nothing, reminding me not for the first time that I haven't eaten today, and I threw away my one source of sustenance this morning at the coffee shop.

Was that really only this morning?

It seems so much longer than that, though realistically I know it was only maybe nine hours ago now since I left the coffee shop to go home. Yet another strike against Whippoorwill Baptist is that I was in a room, starving, trying to doze for a good five hours of my day, at least. Probably closer to six.

They really will be getting a strongly worded review from me, whenever I'm free from Bluebone's haunted halls. "Hopefully not." I sigh, reaching up to run my fingers through my blonde hair. "From what I've heard, it's just a seventy-two hour thing."

"Ah." Sam nods, seemingly reading between the lines. "Tried to kill yourself? Hurt yourself? Mentioned around someone that you might be a little depressed?" Her eyes lock onto my hand, and I rush to link my fingers behind my back a little self-consciously.

"Something like that." She's a little too close for comfort to the truth, though I don't know why I care. After all, I doubt she's in a better situation. "What about you?"

"This is my third stay. I've been here a month so far, this time." Sam seems so cavalier about it that I glance up at her, surprised, only to see her dry, humorless grin widen. "I meant it, when I did it." She shows me her wrists, which are scarred with tally marks that stand out, stark against her skin.

I find myself biting my lip, and I gaze up at her, seeing more than the dark circles and the unhappy smile. "Sorry," I murmur, which seems to surprise her.

"Why?"

But I'm unsure how to respond to her, so I look down, unable to meet her eyes. "Because you deserve better."

"You don't know me." I can hear the confusion in her words, but I only shrug, unable to really explain better. I can't help the sympathy that twists my heart like a wet rag, or how I suddenly want the best for this girl who I've only known for five minutes.

"Hey, umm." Seeking to change the subject, I latch onto the first thing I can think of. "When I got here, I saw this other woman. She looked sort of...unwell." My arms cross in front of my chest, and I can't help repeating the tapping motion of my fingers on my arm as I think about her.

Sam snorts and relaxes, then walks into my room to sit on the bed closest to the door. The one I haven't touched. She curls her legs up under her, feet bare. I follow suit, figuring I don't really need my shoes on floors that are surprisingly not as cold as I expected.

It feels better immediately, without my laceless sneakers threatening to slip off at any moment, and I mirror her on the other bed as she says with a little smirk, "We're all sort of unwell here. I'll need a little more than that to know who you mean."

Again I bite my lip, wondering if I should just laugh it off instead. I don't want her thinking I'm worse off than I am. But then again, what exactly can Sam really do, when she's in a shittier situation than I am?

"She was tapping." I emulate the motion on my arm, tapping out in counts of three. "And when I first saw her, she was looking up at the corner of the room, like there was something there. There wasn't," I add, just to be clear. "Then she looked at me and said—"

"That's Hattie." Sam cuts me off quickly, not needing me to finish. "Curly brown hair?" At my nod she goes on with a sigh. "Yeah. Hattie is, uh, she's not leaving Bluebone Ridge anytime soon. Her and Tyler are probably going to be here for life, if I had to guess."

"Tyler?"

But Sam just shakes her head. "Look, don't take anything she says seriously. She's had a hard time. I'm not saying you should be mean to her—please don't do that either—just you know. Nod and ask if she needs anything. Get an orderly if you think you need to. She's not going to give you anything that makes sense." Sam gets up, surprising me as she rubs over her wrists. "You'll be fine. I know the rumors about this place, but you don't have anything to worry about. Seventy-two hours isn't the worst thing ever."

"Right," I agree dryly. "There are definitely worse things. Like being stabbed, or getting hit by a car." Sam snorts at my words, and shakes her head, though there's a small grin on her lips.

"Just show up for therapy and don't act like you need to stay longer than you're in for. Then you can go home and forget any of this ever happened." She studies me for a few seconds longer, looking down at my bandaged palm. "I'm two rooms down to the right," she adds. "So, if you need anything, just come find me. I don't have my own room, though, so maybe don't come in yelling."

"I don't really yell, so you're safe on that end. Unless I'm being murdered by the ghosts here." I can't help the sarcastic tone of my words, and they make Sam snort as she leaves, without giving me another word.

It's...strange.

But then again, everything here is.

I sit for another few minutes before the stillness becomes too much, but when I get up, it's to head back for the window where I stood before. I look through the thick panes of glass, pressing my nose against the chilly surface, and once more look for any sign of movement outside.

Unsurprisingly, I'm met with absolutely nothing. Leaning away, I sigh against the glass, fogging it up and reinforcing the *hi* I wrote there on the glass. It brings me some stupid, childish pleasure, but I don't push that away.

Right now, I sort of need it.

It's my stomach clenching and twisting, reminding me that it's about to eat itself in displeasure, that finally makes me push away from the window. I could nap, I think to myself, but I don't end up stopping at the bed I refuse to call *mine*.

Before I can really think about it, I'm out in the hallway. It's mostly quiet, with only two women at the end of it standing near a window, talking in muffled voices. They don't look up at me, and I curl my toes against the hardwood floor under me, pressing my fingers against my bandaged palm.

"It's never going to heal if you don't let it," I breathe softly to myself, shifting from one foot to the other. I automatically move to put my hair up, only to remember belatedly that my elastics were summarily confiscated back at the hospital. I doubt I'll even be allowed to use a shoelace, or part of one, since I could obviously strangle myself with it. Even if it won't fit around my throat, since an elastic wouldn't either.

I groan as I walk down the side of the hallway I hadn't come in by, running my fingers through my slightly tangled, limp blonde hair. I want to shower, but I've seen the bathroom. Nothing in me wants to shower in an open room, with only a half curtain for privacy, within the time limit of precisely six minutes set by the orderlies.

I'll just be gross and grimy for the next seventy-two hours, and gladly at that.

Instead of following any set path, I follow the line of windows down a few different hallways, keeping an eye out for

STAFF ONLY signs. Even inadvertently, I don't want to end up breaking any rules over the next three days, though I don't know what the consequences for doing so would entail. Another sigh leaves me, and I can't help feeling like I'm slouching as my stomach clenches, once again—

Movement outside of a window, in the trees beyond, catches my gaze and makes me stop. But this time, it doesn't disappear. A blur of something larger than a dog moves through the trees in graceful, almost jerky movements. I follow it, picking up into a fast walk to watch through the thick glass. It's impossible to tell what it is, though it certainly doesn't look like an elk.

Curiosity wins out over caution as I follow the outer halls, nearly having to run to keep up with the figure outside. Distantly I hear the sound of arguing, but I ignore it. I can't help the way I'm fixated, on the way I *need to know* what's running in the woods outside.

Surely, ghosts don't run through the trees.

"—I said *stop*—"

"You don't get to tell me to stop. You don't get to—"

"You think this will fix anything? Do you really, honestly think—"

I turn the corner just as the voices filter into my head and the words start to make sense. But I'm too late to stop or even slow down, and too late to do anything when I veer into the small stairwell where two men are squared off against one another.

All I have time for is to recognize the surprised face of the man I saw earlier, before I crash into whoever he's arguing with, nearly knocking both of us over.

The man I haven't seen before saves me from falling down the stairs, gripping my forearms in his hands with remarkable reflexes. "Oh, hello," the man greets, a wolfish grin on his lips. "And what do we have here?"

CHAPTER FIVE

THE MAN HOLDING MY ARMS IN HIS FIRM GRIP IS ATTRACTIVE, WHICH perhaps shouldn't be the first thing I notice. But of course, it is. His dark hair is brown, rather than black like the other man I saw earlier in the hallway, who now is scowling and nearly seething with frustration. But my savior's dark, nearly black eyes seem to glitter brighter at his obvious discomfort. His grip tightens to the point of being painful, and I can't help the soft breath that leaves me.

"Let her go." The other man steps between us and gives him a shove, forcing him to release his hold on me. Not that he seems to mind. Instead, he grins and lifts his hands in clear surrender while looking barely apologetic. Just...amused.

"I'm sorry," he says with a small laugh, looking at me instead of his companion. "I wasn't expecting you to run into me. You're new here." It's not a question, and it throws me a little off guard.

"Yeah, umm..." My eyes go to the window instead, where I search in vain for the movement I saw before. "Did you see something outside?" I can't help my curiosity, and my desire to figure out what in the world is running through the woods outside.

"Did *you?*" the smiling man is quick to challenge. He links his hands behind his back, head tilting to the side in a strange way that makes me give him a second glance. "I'm sorry I'm being so weird. I'll be honest with you; they changed my meds a few days ago and I'm feeling really off."

That makes me feel a little bad, and I finally give him my full attention. Or at least, as much of it as I'm willing to spare. Behind him, I can't stop glancing at the black-haired man with eyes as dark as vintage emeralds. Between the two of them, I've never seen anyone with such dark eyes.

"I'm Tyler," he adds, a little belatedly. "This is my friend, Cairo."

"You guys don't really seem like friends," I point out, crossing my arms over my chest. I glance out the window again, but quickly give up on the idea of seeing where whatever was in the trees went. "And you really didn't see anything?"

"No." It's Cairo's turn to actually contribute, and he glances toward the window with dismissive disdain. "But we were a little busy. And you're right, we're not friends." He gives Tyler a brief, very unfriendly frown.

"This is the part where you tell us who you are." Tyler isn't exactly subtle, and he grins mischievously when I give him my attention again. "Unless you want me to give you a nickname. A really embarrassing—"

"You're acting like such an ass." Cairo's words and sigh cut him off, and he rolls his eyes up at the stairs above us. "We didn't see anything," he says in a firm voice, finally looking back at me. It occurs to me he looks tired. *Both* of them are sporting dark circles under their eyes and there's a pale undertone to their skin that makes me think they haven't seen the backs of their eyelids in weeks.

"You really didn't?" I can't help pushing the question, glancing toward the window again. "I followed something here from the women's hall. Something was running through the trees, but I couldn't really tell what. It definitely wasn't an elk. It moved more like—"

"So you want me to give you a nickname? Because I can come up with one on the spot," Tyler assures me, breaking in like I haven't been talking. It's irritating as hell, and I glance his way to give him a withering look. I don't love being interrupted, especially when I'm trying to explain something or ask a question. So far, Tyler isn't on the top five list of people I've met here. He's somewhere below the orderly and Hattie.

But I don't want a weird nickname to start circulating, and I suppose there's not exactly a reason for me to keep my name a secret. What am I hiding, except that I, like everyone else here, have a few issues? "Fern," I admit finally with a sigh. "Just Fern." Though I feel stupid, since it's not like Fern could be short for something reasonable.

Fernatility?

Fernalicious?

God, I really am hungry, and clearly my stomach is pulling calories from my higher brain function for me to be thinking up stupid names like *Fernalicious*. Raking my injured hand through my hair, I still can't help yet another pointless look through the window.

But this time, I swear I see something in the trees. It isn't running. It just shifts a little, trying to conceal itself behind a large tree. "Look—" I dart to the window, pressing my face against the heavy, thick glass there. "See? That's what I'm talking about."

From what I can see of our reflections, I notice Tyler starts moving first. He steps toward me, mouth open, but suddenly he's intercepted by Cairo, who presses close enough behind me that I can feel his warmth radiating against my skin through the powder blue cotton. "I don't see anything," he breathes quietly, his hand coming up to press against the window. He's tall, so he blocks me from anything else in the space, and I can't help feeling my heart race a little in reaction to his nearness.

I don't know him.

This definitely isn't safe.

Biting my lip, I go back to searching the trees, ready to argue that it's *right there*. But instead, all I see is a smaller tree waving in the woods amid the bigger trunks and branches. Suddenly I feel stupid. There's obviously nothing here, and the more I think about it, the more I tell myself that whatever I saw moving around before probably *was* a deer, or a wolf, or an elk. Even though I was so sure before it wasn't.

It's not like I've seen any of those animals up close, after all.

"You don't look so good." Cairo's voice is quiet, and a little unsure. As he gazes at me from so close, the dark circles under his eyes are so prominent that I have to wonder what his definition of not looking so good is.

"Says the guy with veritable bruising under both eyes." I sigh, rolling my eyes up at him in my exhaustion. Though I swear I see a flicker of a smile across his full lips, he pulls away. "I'm uh. I'm hungry," I admit.

"I know the feeling," Tyler mutters, which only makes Cairo shoot him a look of irritation. He stops backing up and remains between Tyler and me, like he's calling dibs or just generally being weird.

I'm willing to bet it's the second.

"The...uh...hospital wouldn't let me eat before coming here.

So the last thing I had was muffin crumbs this morning." This is a safer topic, it seems to me, than whatever they were fighting about. And definitely safer than my hallucinations and delusions of things in the woods. Clearly I'm reading too far into the stories about this place being haunted.

Or I really, *really* just need a sandwich.

"Yeah, that sort of happens when you end up in the ER for..." Cairo trails off, his eyes darting to my hand. From the corner of my eye, I see Tyler step a little closer, but then Cairo continues. "I can take you to get something to eat. At least enough to hold you over until dinner. If you want?"

Normally, I'd refuse. My stranger danger sense has been going off nonstop ever since the ambulance stopped here at Bluebone Ridge and I'd rather hold everyone at arm's length until I figure my shit out...which probably won't happen until I'm safely back home and buried under my blankets.

Three days, probably, I tell myself, and cross my fingers the doctor will agree with that assessment. Maybe with our meeting being in person instead of over a fucking iPad, I'll get the chance to actually plead my case and explain what's wrong with me, instead of retaining the label of suicidal and being stuck on the haunted mountain.

"Isn't dinner in like four hours?" I ask, my stomach silently threatening to eat my other organs even as I question Cairo's offer. "I didn't take it as having a free schedule while I was here."

"Depends on..." Tyler trails off, though he'd clearly been waiting to leap on answering the question. His voice changes, sounding a little strange, and both Cairo and I turn to look at him. Though my look of concern isn't mirrored in the black-haired man's face. Without another word, Tyler just leaves. He walks out the same way I came in, without a backward look at either of us or *anything* to explain where he's going or why.

Not that I warrant an explanation, I guess. But he seems to know Cairo well enough, judging by their familiarity and shouting match from minutes before.

"Fucker," Cairo mutters unexpectedly, though immediately his attention is back on me. "This place could be worse." He offers me a tiny, mischievous smile, then offers his hand to me. It takes a moment for me to understand he really wants me to take it, and I do. I let him wrap his fingers around mine, and I notice his palm is cool, rather than warm like mine. It's a relief, as someone who's always looking for a way to cool down and runs hot enough to want to bury herself naked in the snow sometimes.

But his touch also sends a strange, almost electric sensation through me that has the hair on the back of my neck standing up, even though I've never experienced a feeling quite like it. Before I can stop myself, I jerk my hand back, and Cairo lets me. "Sorry." The word is out of my mouth quickly, apologetic and breathy. "I didn't mean—"

Cairo shakes his head, and his lips twist in a very amused smile. "You don't need to be sorry," he tells me, in that soft, drawling voice he seems to have when he's not yelling at Tyler. "Seriously, it's probably better that you aren't so trusting of any stranger you meet. Especially in a mental hospital." He gestures faintly at the walls surrounding us, reminding me yet again that our matching powder blue uniforms aren't by choice or necessitated by fashion.

"And I'm not offended, so I'll still take you to go find food. Esther gave you the official tour, right?" He rolls his eyes as he asks, showing me exactly what he thinks of the orderly from earlier.

"Why don't you like her?" I follow him as he turns, trudging down the stairs as our steps echo in the narrow stairwell. I have no idea where we're going, obviously. And when

Cairo pushes open a door at the bottom of the steps, I'm still not sure what part of the sanitarium we're in.

He shrugs, gesturing for me to walk through. I do, once again taking a moment to study his face while he's busy shutting the door just enough to look closed, but not quite. When I glance down, I see a piece of something at the bottom, creating just a bit of a barrier to stop it from locking.

Interesting.

When Cairo looks up, I do too, at precisely the right time for our eyes to meet. His dark, emerald eyes are deep set in an angular face that speaks volumes of his shrewdness. there's a dark glint in his gaze telling me he sees more than I'd ever know. If I had to guess an age, I'd say he's maybe thirty, at most. Though I definitely can't say for sure.

I've never been very good at judging ages. And considering the tired lines and dark circles under his eyes, I really could be pretty off the mark.

"It isn't personal," he says finally, leading me down a quiet hallway. I hear talking behind some of the doors, but he doesn't seem particularly bothered by it. In fact, when he turns down another hallway, it's just in time for me to see a woman push through a set of swinging double doors ahead of us. Judging by the smell in the hallway, it has to be the kitchen. Or *a* kitchen. This place is big enough that it could easily have more than one.

For a few moments, I follow him, surprised that he's so quiet. When we were still with Tyler, he seemed more talkative around me, making me wonder if that was bravado or to prove a point. Hell, maybe he really just doesn't like me either, for all that he doesn't know me. He pushes into the kitchen easily, without hesitation, and when I follow behind him, it's with hunched shoulders. I can't imagine we're just allowed to be in here.

"Hi Cairo!" The woman who just went in stops cutting vegetables, and looks up at him with a wide, friendly smile. "You missed dinner last night. Again. Should I be concerned?" She doesn't sound like she is, though. She just seems friendly, and belatedly her eyes fall on me. "You're new here." It's not a question, and I bite my lip at the unexpected observation.

"I'm Fern," I greet, and I lift a hand to give her a lame little wave. "Sorry. Uh, I haven't eaten all day and Cairo said—"

"Oh, it's no problem!" The woman looks to be in her mid thirties, I decide as she bustles around the kitchen. "Any allergies?" At my head shake, she goes to the fridge and opens it, grabbing things out to put in a bowl. Then she snags a bottle of water from it and closes the large industrial appliance with her hip before turning on me again.

"I have a few leftovers from lunch. It's not much, and definitely not a real meal, but it should keep your stomach from protesting too much." I'm still in shock as she hands me a tray with a wrapped sandwich, the bottle of water, and a bowl of fruit on it.

This is definitely a better meal than I manage to fix for myself about fifty percent of the time. I look up at her, my first actual smile showing for the first time today. "Thank you so much," I tell her, meaning every word. "Maybe now my stomach won't eat my organs."

That gets a snort from Cairo. "You can eat in the dining hall. If that's okay?" Though the suggestion is for me, he addresses the question to the woman, who nods her head and waves at us dismissively. She already seems back in her little world when she starts cutting up vegetables again and only offers me one last smile as Cairo guides me out of another door in the small kitchen.

"She's not the only one who works in there, right?" I ask, glancing back at her as the door swings closed behind me.

"This is the staff kitchen and dining hall. I usually eat here because I like to avoid..." he trails off. "Well, everyone I guess. So yeah, she's the only one who works in this kitchen."

Without hesitation, he sits across from me at a small table by the window, and I can't help gazing outside, searching the trees for whatever I swear I saw before. But I must take too long, because Cairo taps the tray pointedly, and when I look at him, he tilts his head to give me a rather unimpressed look.

"You're supposed to be eating, remember?" he asks me, prompting me to roll my eyes.

"Yes, *Father.*" I crack open the water bottle, taking a drink as I study him. For a moment, I'm not sure where he's looking, as his eyes are on the table between us, but when it hits me, I move to draw my other hand back, suddenly self-conscious of the bandage on my palm and the stitches underneath.

"Wait." He reaches out quickly, too quickly for me to beat, and his fingers gently encircle my wrist, careful about where he touches. "Can I ask what happened?"

"Depends," I challenge unintentionally. My fingers flex in his grip, and I make myself meet his gaze as I set the bottle back down. With only one hand, I can't unwrap the sandwich, so I instead pick up the plastic fork and stab a piece of strawberry. "What will you tell me if I tell you?"

"What do you want to know?" A small, grudging smile flickers over his lips, and I realize he's the master of micro-expressions. He never seems to react strongly to anything, and if I'm not watching, I'll miss his reactions entirely.

"Why are you here?" It's a bold question, and not one I feel like I should be asking. But that's the equivalent of what he's asking me, so it feels fair.

"Oh, we're going straight for the kill, are we?" He lets go of my hand and I unwrap the half of a sandwich, noting with relief that it's chicken salad instead of tuna.

God, I hate tuna.

I only shrug my shoulders and pick up the sandwich, biting into it cautiously in case there's something that will have me spewing out the contents at Cairo and ruining our little budding, temporary friendship for good. But it's mild, not too wet, and with a crunch I identify as celery. All I could really ask for if I was being picky are grapes or curry, but I'm more than happy with this.

So is my stomach, more importantly, meaning that my liver and kidneys will live to see another day instead of being feasted upon in tribute.

Cairo doesn't answer. He sits back and just looks at me, with his head tilting one way, then another. "Fine. You don't have to tell me. I could guess, probably." His eyes flicker down to my hand, making me feel more than a little self-conscious. "But I figure you'll get tired of rehearsing the explanation you'll give to the therapist, anyway. I'll save you the trouble. How about you tell me what you think of this place so far, Fern?"

"It's creepy," I reply automatically, swallowing my food. My sandwich is gone in four bites, though I'm too tired and over this to be embarrassed by looking like a starving, feral creature in front of this gorgeous stranger. He's probably not available anyway, I tell myself. And even if he is, I don't know enough about his particular brand of fucked up to know if I'd even be able to handle that. "There was a girl when I got here —Hattie?—who was like, staring at the ceiling and muttering weird shit. It wasn't the best introduction to a new place I've ever had."

Now that I've basically swallowed the sandwich whole, like a snake that can unhinge its jaw, I find I'm not nearly as hungry. I roll the blueberries in the bowl around, instead of actually committing to eating them. "Do you want some?" I ask, remembering what the kitchen manager said about Cairo skipping meals.

"Nah, I'm not really a fan of fruit." Cairo is quick to brush off my offer. But he's not looking at me as he says it. Instead, he's studying the thick-paned window, much like I did earlier. "What did she say?" he asks, mildly, as if he's not very interested. I study him in return, and for the life of me, I can't decide if he's faking it, or he really just doesn't care that much.

"They're coming," I say, repeating her words. "And uh, they're already here. I think. She was sort of mouthing the words, so I might be wrong. But that's what it looked like." I watch him for any reaction to my words, but Cairo doesn't give me anything at all to figure out his intentions.

Maybe he really just isn't that interested, and I'm thinking too much into this. "Can I ask you something, then?"

"Not if it's about me." His words are plain and honest, and he gives me another one of those tiny, soft smiles. "Otherwise, sure."

"I'm over asking about you. You know the dog? The one that was tied up to a railing outside?"

His face hardens, and he goes right back to looking out the window. "Moro..." He sighs. "Yeah, I know her. Well, I know *of* her. Jeremy doesn't let anyone touch her."

"Is she...okay? Like, I don't know, it just seemed..." I trail off, not sure how to really say what I mean.

"You'll work yourself into a fit worrying about things you can't change, Fern." He gets to his feet suddenly, startling me. "Sorry. I want to make sure you know how to get to your therapist's office. Are you done?" He glances down at my food, which I haven't touched in the past minute or so after I managed to eat a few more bites of fruit.

"Yeah." I get up as well, but before I can take my tray, Cairo swipes it from the table. I follow him to the trash, hands behind me and feeling like I'm just hovering awkwardly while he tosses my garbage and sets the tray on top of the counter. "Thank you," I offer, just as he moves to brush past me, aloof once more.

"You don't need to thank me." His eyes dart back to mine, and he looks so very tired. "I haven't done anything to be thanked for."

"What were you feeling?" Dr. Radley's words are kind, and said in the same tone they've been all session. But that doesn't really make me any less on edge. Sunk deep in my overstuffed leather armchair that sits across from hers, I glance up at her, a little confused.

"What was I...?" My fingers trail over the bandage on my palm, though I make an effort not to pick at it or pull at the ends of the adhesive like I really *do* need to be kept here for the long haul. "What do you mean?"

"You were standing in the bathroom and you didn't know you were cutting yourself with the scissors. Are you telling me you didn't feel the pain?" She sits in her chair like it's a throne, with her legs crossed and her brown hair pulled into a tight bun. Her black glasses only add to her appearance, making her look elegant and refined even in the casual slacks and shirt she's wearing.

I wish I knew how to look half as good.

"I guess...I felt it a little. But I couldn't break out of it. I was just overstimulated. Sometimes I get that way. It's not like I was trying to kill myself, or actually hurt myself—" I can tell my words are getting faster from my anxiety, but now that I'm rambling, there's no cure for it. "I just get overwhelmed," I say, trying to come at it from a different way. "I didn't mean to—"

"I'm not saying you meant to," Dr. Radley cuts in patiently.

She offers me a reassuring smile and sets down her iPad on the small table beside her. When I look up at the clock, I notice in surprise that it's already been close to forty minutes. I'm basically almost done with our 'evaluation' meeting. "I know things can get hard. And you don't seem like someone looking to end your life, from what I can tell. I agree with the seventy-two hour temporary hold, unless something changes. I'd like to see you daily while you're here, and also I'd like you to participate in group therapy at least once. Does that seem agreeable to you?"

I don't really have a choice, so I nod my head a few times, grateful. "Y-yeah. Thank you. I'm sorry." The differing reactions come out quickly, and I sit back a little, sinking slightly deeper into my trap of a chair.

"You don't have anything to be sorry for. If nothing changes, you can go home on Sunday's morning bus." With relief, I realize that'll technically be a few hours short of seventy-two, and while it isn't much, it still makes me damn relieved. I hadn't realized until now just how terrified I'd been that she would decide to keep me here, and the assurance that I'll get to go home instead is enough to make me want to just go limp in this chair and fall asleep.

"Thank you. I'm glad you don't think I'm...something I'm not." Not knowing how to express it more than that, but Dr. Radley just offers me that same kind smile she's offered throughout the session. I get up when she does, though much less gracefully, and follow her to the door. She opens it, once again causing the heavy, intricate wood and glass to creak open on its hinges, making me wince.

"Sorry about that," she says with a sigh, grimacing at the thing. "I can't bring myself to let them replace it. It's original to Bluebone Ridge, and I can admit I love so many of the things that still exist up here after all this time."

"Oh, really?" I leave, glancing at the door and the different shades of wood that make it up, plus the stained glass panels. "It really is pretty." And heavy. And creaky. "Most stuff up here is just sort of creepy."

"Only because you don't understand things up here," Dr. Radley is quick to disagree, though she doesn't look upset. "I can promise you, Fern. That if you were to spend time actually studying the history of this place and the relevance behind it, you'd find it just as interesting as I do."

I can't help but disagree, but I definitely won't say that. Instead I laugh it off, trying to sound friendly and more importantly *sane*, before making my escape with the intent of going to my room and taking a sixty-four hour nap.

CHAPTER SIX

Group therapy is much worse than how it's portrayed in any movie I've ever seen it in, and at the ungodly hour of eight am, I'm barely awake enough for it. Both Sam and Hattie are part of the group, with the other seven women being ones I haven't met, though I saw a few of them at dinner last night.

Sitting with my styrofoam cup of steaming coffee, I sip at the burned, not sweet enough liquid, my nose wrinkling with displeasure. It really is not great, but I sigh and suffer with it anyway. After all, what else am I going to do while the therapist—who is younger and less patient than Dr. Radley—tries to get Hattie to talk.

Again.

So far all Hattie has done is stare at the ceiling and mouth things I can't quite make out, and whenever the woman next to her touches her arm, she flinches and pulls back, looking like she's seen a ghost. That ends the situation quickly, and the therapist, whose name I think might rhyme with *Rat* but really could be anything, turns her eyes on me. "What about you,

Miss..." She glances down at her clipboard, and I wait for her to go through the names.

I suppose I could help her out, but the last time someone interrupted her this morning, she seemed less than pleased. So we all just sit there while she counts through names until she finds mine penciled in somewhere near the bottom. "Fern? You're Fern, right?"

I press my lips together to avoid asking who else would be the person she added hastily this morning to her group, but I force it to look more like a smile and nod. "Yep. That's me. I'm Fern. And uh, could you repeat the question?" I ask, having forgotten what we're talking about while she focused on getting through Hattie's haze and figuring out my name.

"I want to know if any of your memories, any past events of your life, are really affecting you right now. I want to know what things you think of the most, or memories you reflect on more often than others. Do you still feel the effects of any past events on you now? Especially now that you're here?" She repeats the question by reading it off of her clipboard, giving it a false, plastic quality that doesn't make me more inclined to answer.

But I don't respond right away. I fiddle with my nails, hands still wrapped around the cheap styrofoam while my coffee steams in the cool air of the room. My toes curl in my sneakers, and again I get the feeling of not being comfortable in my shoes without the laces. But I hadn't wanted to accept the 'gift' of grippy socks, like most of the other women in here are wearing.

"I'm not sure," I admit. "I mean, I'm pretty happy most of the time." That's not quite true. But it's not something I really want to whine about here. "I live on my own down in Whippoorwill. I have a nice little house, and my mom comes to visit sometimes." Though I wish she wouldn't.

"Really?" She writes something down, though I can't read it from this far away. "And what would child-you think of where you are now, Fern?"

The question catches me off guard. My smile fades, and I'm hit with memories of learning to play the piano with my dad and trying everything to gain my mom's approval. Not that I ever succeeded. Sinking back in the chair, I have to fight off the white noise in my head of them fighting at night, when they thought I was asleep and couldn't hear them.

I remember my father begging my mother to at least try to love me, but thankfully I snap out of it before her response plays out like a bad record in my head. Not that it would be the first time.

Child me just wanted to be loved unconditionally.

Now I know better.

"I think she'd be interested to know where I live. And a bit disappointed that I didn't move to Alaska." I offer the therapist a small smile, and before she can ask me to go on, I explain, "When I was younger, I watched *Balto* a few too many times. I could probably recite the whole movie by now, and I thought I could grow up to train sled dogs. Child me thought for sure I would've won the Iditarod at least twice by now, and live with my thousand huskies up in Wasilla."

A few of the women, including Sam, snort or chuckle. At least my story is good for that much, I figure. The therapist seems satisfied as well, and moves on to her next victim. She goes through everyone with varying degrees of success and even asks Hattie again to say something; trying to rephrase the question to get through to her. But Hattie only shakes her head, staring at nothing.

By the time she gives up, it's almost ten. While I ate before group therapy, I still wish there were better options here than tasteless scrambled eggs and burnt bacon. The coffee in my cup is mostly gone, since desperation meant I drank it all, and as we're dismissed, I move to the side of the room with the trash can to chuck it away.

Still, I'm not the last out of the room. Sam stays, talking to the therapist about God knows what, and when I'm out in the hallway, the reality of drinking way too much coffee hits me. Or more specifically, hits my bladder. Hard. The bathroom is only a few yards away, down the other end of the hallway from where I intend to head down next to check out the library or the outside courtyard. Such is the advantage of wearing shoes instead of grippy socks, is how I'm choosing to look at things. I can go where others cannot.

The bathroom is empty, and just as hollow-feeling as every other part of Bluebone Ridge. The shower stalls have no curtains and limited privacy, explained to me as a way for us to be checked on at all times. Already I've decided I will *not* be showering here. There's no way I want to be worried about the possibility of an orderly strolling by to make sure none of us are drowning ourselves under the shower head while I'm naked.

When I go to leave the bathroom, the door suddenly opens inward, forcing me to stumble backward and nearly trip over myself. I gasp, arms flailing, and catch myself on a stall, though I end up jabbing myself in the shoulder with the door painfully.

"What—*Hattie?!*" I yelp as the woman steps inside; when she registers my presence, her eyes focus on my face in a more lucid way than she could manage earlier.

Without warning, the woman hugs me. Her arms wrap around my shoulders and she drags me tight against her, with a grip strong enough that I can't pry her off.

"It's okay," she coos with a sigh, her head on my shoulder. She's acting like she's comforting me, and I have no idea why.

But she's holding onto me strongly enough to choke out an elephant, if she really wanted to, and my flailing arms seem to have no effect on her, nor do my staggering attempts to keep us both upright.

"It's okay," Hattie says again. "I know it hurts, but it's not that bad. You're okay." Something in her voice is so genuinely kind and caring that it makes me more confused than afraid. Any thoughts of screaming for an orderly immediately fade, and I force myself to go still until I'm leaning against the stall behind me. It isn't like she's trying to hurt me, after all.

"Are *you* okay?" I ask, my voice soft. I hope it's clear that I'm asking her in a genuine way, and not to make fun of her.

She hums a reply, and I feel her shake her head against my shoulder. "I'm so tired," she tells me in a quiet, conspiring way. "I'm always so tired these days. But that's not important, Fern." It surprises me that she knows my name, since I'm not sure how much the things going on around her really sink in. Most of the time, it seems like she's not really here at all.

But apparently I was wrong to think that.

We stand still in our awkward, one-sided embrace for another minute, my arms coming up to brace her elbows just in case she suddenly falls. I have no idea what to expect, but it isn't for her to draw back to press her forehead to mine. "They're coming," she whispers, her eyes on mine. "You understand that, right? They're coming, and they're already here."

Suddenly my whole being goes cold, and the bathroom seems so unsafe and empty. I draw away from her as much as she lets me, and I shake my head. "I don't know what you mean," I whisper, at the same volume as she spoke. "Hattie, what are you talking about? Who's—"

The bathroom door opens, admitting another patient in blue scrubs I've never seen before. She gives us a quick, surprised look, then mentally shrugs it off and heads for a stall.

I watch her go, wondering if I should try to explain the situation before she gets the wrong idea. But then again, I'm not even sure what the *right* idea is. Instead, I right myself, prepared to ask Hattie again what she means, so I can puzzle out her answer.

But she's no longer in front of me. Just before the door swings shut, I see the hint of her blue shirt as she goes off to terrorize some other part of the sanitarium or do whatever it is she does.

Leaving me confused and shaken in the third floor bathroom, wishing I could be anywhere but here.

When I finally make my way outside, the courtyard proves to be anything but the refuge that I hope it would be. How can it be, with Moro the wolf dog being neglected nearby and me just sitting here, not helping?

I sigh with my head in my hands, sitting on a staircase that's invisible to the rest of the courtyard thanks to its solid stone wall. But that doesn't help block out any of the noise. Moro whines about twenty feet away from me, once again tied up and left next to a railing. I saw an empty water bowl beside her, which has my teeth gritted together and my entire being on edge. I hate how Jeremy treats her, though I've only seen glimpses of the blond security guard who appears to be in his mid thirties.

And ugly, with a sneer that constantly adorns his long features. I watched subtly for twenty minutes as he chatted with his friend, while Moro nosed at him more than once to get attention or probably *water* since her bowl has been empty since I came out here. But every time he shoved her away with one foot, not caring at all, until she eventually crept back along the precarious slack in her leash to lie down heavily against the stone wall.

It's disgusting, and I have no idea how it's allowed or okay.

But I have to remind myself over and over *and over* that I cannot make this my business. Especially since I can't risk staying here longer than I have to. I don't want to piss off a guard enough that he finds a way to get my stay extended. Or, even worse, so he ends up treating Moro with less care than he already does, though that would be outright abuse. Not that it isn't already.

Finally, I hear her sigh, and her whining stops, as if she's given up and resigned herself to being treated like crap for the rest of the day. It causes my heart to twist in my chest, and I feel sick enough to know I have to get up and go somewhere else. Anywhere else, actually. Somewhere that I can't see or hear her. Otherwise, I'll do something stupid like break her out and punch her handler in the face.

Which *definitely* would not help my cause.

I walk around the perimeter of the courtyard, walled in by a thick iron fence, and go up on my toes a few times to look through the fence into the trees beyond. It's chilly for late summer, but then again, it's always chilly up in the mountains. Even my thermal base layer under the short sleeve blue shirt isn't quite enough to keep me warm, and when I exhale, my breath puffs into the air in front of me while I drop back down from the balls of my feet, once more seeing nothing in the woods beyond.

Honestly, I need to get over this feeling of having seen something in the trees. It was either an animal or my starving delusions, nothing more. And if I get too fixated on it, someone is going to notice and think I belong here for longer than the prescribed seventy-two hours, which I've decided I would not survive.

My steps take me along the abandoned gardens that apparently once grew food for both the patients and staff, back when this place was more than just a mental hospital and before it was so easy to have things shipped here. Now the stone planters and rows in the dirt just look sad, with their cracked and unkept edges. There are only a few other patients here, and two of them talk to each other like their conversation might get heated; because of that, the orderly sitting on the stairs and reading her book has her eyes on them.

Though she spares me a quick warning glance, as if to remind me any shenanigans won't be tolerated. But she's quick to put her attention back on the two arguing men, who are starting to get just a little louder, though nothing extreme. I keep walking, uninterested in their problems, until I come to the dilapidated old garden shed.

Naturally, it says STAFF ONLY on the door. But when I look back at the stairs, I see the orderly is up and marching toward the men, her back to me, and I take that moment to slip inside, though I know I could get in a lot of trouble for doing so.

I decide quickly that my defense, if I'm caught, will be that the sign on the door was barely legible and falling apart, so maybe I just hadn't seen it or realized what it said. It's the best I've got, and with my curiosity about the small space winning out, I push it to the back of my mind to focus on the small shed that's about the size of my bedroom back home.

But really, it's underwhelming. I don't know what I expected, but storage should've been at the top of my list. A few boards and screws litter the floor on one side of the room, along with an old toolbox. The windows are cracked and so dirty they look solid grey, with no transparency to be found.

Still, I figure that since I've gone to the trouble of sneaking in here, I might as well make the most of it. I work my way along the shelves, studying every piece of discarded junk I can, and eventually make it to a stack of newspapers that are yellow with age and falling apart.

ATTACK NEAR BLUEBONE RIDGE SANITARIUM LEAVES
TOWN PARANOID.

The headline jumps out at me, and I very carefully pick up
the top newspaper, noting the way it starts to almost disinte-
grate in my fingers. My mission is thwarted instantly, however,
when I realize that so many of the words are distorted from
water damage and time that the article itself is unreadable.
The only thing I can see is the top of a picture of someone with
dark hair, though I can't tell if that person is supposed to be a
suspect, a victim, or a witness. Eyeing the title again, I run my
fingers over the old paper, feeling the way it gives under the
pads of my fingers. I've definitely never held a newspaper this
old, or in this bad of shape.

It's interesting, and I wish so badly that I could read the
article, instead of just the headline. I try again anyway, finding
only a few legible passages that make no sense out of context. I
don't know what kind of attack it supposedly was, though I
manage to find the date at the top of the paper, almost washed
out as well.

August 6, 1988.

Nearly forty years ago, but only a week away from now, in
terms of month and day. I have no idea how in the world this
paper has survived so long, or what in the world it's doing out
here, of all places. Still, it's interesting, and I give it one last
glance, wishing again there was some way for me to see
anything else.

It takes only a moment for me to decide to go through the
rest of the papers as well, so I set the first aside, my fingers
brushing against the others in the messy stack. The next few
are so faded that I can't make out anything at all, and yellowed
beyond belief, and when I grab for one near the bottom of the
stack, I'm shocked into nearly dropping it by an amused,
curious voice behind me.

"Didn't you see the sign on the door?" Cairo asks in his usual drawl, so close I can feel his body heat behind me. "This is staff only, Fern. If you get caught in here, you're going to be in trouble."

"Are you going to tell on me?" The words are out of my mouth before I can stop them, and I glare back over my shoulder at the tall, dark-haired man. "Because I'm pretty sure you'd be in just as much trouble as I am."

Cairo rolls his shoulders in a shrug and moves to lean his hip against a nearby table covered in dust and stray pieces of wood and screws. "Sure," he agrees. "I'd be in trouble too. The difference is, I'm not trying to get out of here before Monday, so I have nothing to lose." There's something like a satisfied, mischievous gleam in his eyes as he says it, but he makes no move to follow through on his threat.

He just stands there. *Watching.*

"I was in the courtyard..." I sigh, breaking first in the silence. Though I don't know why I feel the need to explain, I run my fingers over the newspaper in my hands, wincing as it tears as easily as wet tissue paper, no matter how careful I am. "But I hate seeing or hearing Moro. Well, I hate how mistreated she is. She looks to that guy for literally a fucking crumb of attention, and her water bowl had been empty since I got out there." Now that I've gotten going, I can't stop, and my hands tremble a little in my frustration. "How is it okay for him to treat her like that? How does no one else here give a damn?"

When Cairo doesn't answer, I glance up at him, catching a small flicker of surprise on his face. "That's what bothers you?" he asks. "A dog?"

My scowl deepens, but he holds up his hands in surrender just as a real, full grin curls his lips upward in apology. "Whoa, I didn't mean it like that. No need to plan my death behind those pretty eyes, Fern." Cairo steps forward, plucking the newspaper from my hands and tossing it to the shelf behind me. "Most people are too absorbed in their own problems to care about Moro, that's all I'm saying. So I wasn't expecting that to be your first concern." He doesn't move away this time. He stands right in front of me, searching my face with his unreadable expression.

"Do you like dogs?" I don't know why that's what comes out of my mouth, but it is.

Cairo snorts. "Yeah, I like dogs. Who doesn't?"

"Assholes. That's who doesn't." When I try to move away from him, with half a mind to make sure the coast is clear so we can both leave, Cairo suddenly reaches out, grabbing my arm and lightly pushing me against the shelf with the newspapers. It rattles a little, and I nearly stumble, but his grip on my arm keeps me upright easily.

"What happened to your hand?" Cairo's hand runs down my arm until he can pick up my bandaged hand and hold it up between us.

My stomach flutters, though it's not from anticipation or excitement at his closeness. It's anxiety, and the prickle of nerves that signals the whispers of discomfort. "What makes you think I'm going to tell you today, when I wouldn't yesterday?" My voice comes out more confident than I feel, and I mentally pat myself on the back for the act.

His smile isn't particularly kind when he leans forward just a little until he's invading my space enough that I can feel his breath on my skin. "What makes you think I won't be pushy about it?" he parrots back at me, in a voice that sounds a little unnatural. His tone, his intonation, feels almost like a recording of my own.

It's...unsettling.

Glancing down between us, I study his hand on mine. He lets me turn my hand in his grip, and I note with mild interest that he's naturally more tan than I could ever be, due to the olive tone of his skin. There are scars on his knuckles, which draw my attention and my curiosity, but I bite back my question about them.

"If I tell you, will you tell me why you're here?" I challenge at last, looking up to meet his gaze. "That's only fair."

"I wasn't trying to be fair, and if it came across that way..." He shrugs, smiling again. "Well, it wasn't intentional. But yeah, all right. I'll humor you, Fern." The way he's so fixated on me feels different, and overwhelming in some ways. Like every single inch of him is here with *me* instead of in his own thoughts.

It's intense.

It hits me that he could be lying. There's every possibility I'll tell him and he'll just walk away without telling me a goddamn thing. But my curiosity wins out; Cairo doesn't seem like someone who belongs here, from the little bit of conversation I've had with him. If there's a chance of him assuaging my nosiness, then I'll take it.

"I get overwhelmed sometimes," I offer, flexing my fingers against his and looking down at my hand. "My mom came to visit with her new husband and kids." I'm not able to help the way my tone twists to displeasure, though he doesn't remark or make a sound. "I was already overwhelmed, and I just wanted them to leave. I didn't realize what I was doing, but I was...hurting myself. With first aid scissors," I admit, grimacing up at him apologetically, as if he has any care for what I did or my wellbeing.

His gaze doesn't soften. He just watches me with that same look of guarded interest, and finally looks down at my hand. "I did what I had to do to survive," he says at last, a sigh in his words. It takes a second for me to realize he's answering my question about him, rather than remarking on me.

Conversation with Cairo is strange, I observe belatedly. And if I know if I'm not paying close attention, I'll fall behind quickly.

"That doesn't make any sense," I point out, when he doesn't offer any more of an explanation. But Cairo only shrugs and lets go of my hand. When he moves to walk away, my indignation at not receiving a satisfying answer gets the better of me, and I reach for him quickly, intent on demanding more of an answer.

But he's too fast. He whirls back to me just before I can grab his sleeve, pushing me against the shelf so it rattles and dust puffs up before falling to the ground around us, along with one of the nearly desiccated newspapers. "I did what I had to do to survive," Cairo repeats, suddenly only inches from me. His eyes look so dark that I can't tell where his pupils begin, and it gives him a strange, inhuman quality as he pushes even closer, so our faces are only inches apart.

"And sometimes, I do things I shouldn't." His gaze flicks down and I swear he's studying my mouth, and the way I'm panting in sharp surprise from the way he's caging me in against the shelf. I can feel him wavering, and my mind races with every possibility of what he could do. Of the many ways I could regret being in here with a man in an asylum who was clearly committed for a reason. "Do you think you'd do what you have to, in order to survive?" he murmurs, and I look up at him with wide, confused eyes.

But Cairo doesn't wait for an answer. He pushes away from me with a quick exhale, running his fingers through his short black hair. His long stride takes him to the door in a moment, where he hesitates, without looking at me. "The orderly on this side will be in the back courtyard for maybe another five minutes," he tells me, still not turning. "So if I were you, I'd get out of here before then. Otherwise, you're going to be in trouble." He taps the sign on the door pointedly, and even without him facing me, I see a wolfish smile on his lips for barely a second before it fades.

"I wouldn't want you losing out on your chance for early parole from the haunted sanitarium, Fern." His words are dry. Like there's a joke to be had I'm not understanding, but a second later he's gone.

Leaving me in the dark, musty shed with old newspapers as my only companions. The silence seems oppressive and judging, but I don't move. Not yet. Not until I can get my racing heart under control, and not until I've given him enough time to not be anywhere near me when I walk out of here.

After all, I'd rather die than have him read in my face an emotion I refuse to admit to today.

CHAPTER SEVEN

FREE TIME IS BOTH THE BEST AND WORST THING ABOUT THIS PLACE, I've decided. There are enough wandering orderlies and guards that there's not a lot of chance of something traumatic happening. Especially since any object that could be used for self harm or just harm in general is carefully locked up somewhere none of us know about. Plastic utensils included, since they're all disposed of under an employee's careful eye after every meal.

I've never felt more like I'm in prison, and every single hour has me promising myself rather vehemently to never end up in this situation again. No matter what. I'm not sure how being here can help anyone, since it certainly isn't helping me.

Flipping through the book I'm "reading," I realize I'm hardly paying attention to it. There are no good books on the bookshelves of the solarium on the second floor, with most of them being dry non-fiction stories or autobiographies.

God forbid the mental patients get smut or romantasy, I suppose. Who knows what we might do with such clandestine, taboo topics?

A noise makes me glance up from the small alcove I'm sitting in under a window. As a long time floor-sitter, I don't need a chair to make myself comfortable. In fact, I'm curled up with my legs under me, a pillow on my lap to support my arms as I lean against the cool wall behind me and listen to the wind outside as I read. It's nice enough outside that most of the others are using their free time to go outside or at least somewhere more interesting than the empty, and slightly dusty solarium on the second floor.

But I like my alone time, and I like just listening.

I lower my hands and the book to the pillow, stroking my thumb over the cover as I listen again. I'm not sure what the sound could've been, especially since I haven't heard it again. A door, maybe, or just one of the many ancient pipes that groan and pop in this place. It could be anything, and none of the things it could be are any of my business. Especially when I'm trying to keep myself out of anyone else's business, in fear of having to stay here longer.

Two more nights. That's all I need to suffer through. It's already almost nightfall, and I tell myself that it's basically one and a half nights before I'm out of here. Thirty-six hours, if the bus is on time Sunday morning.

Counting down the minutes probably doesn't help very much, truthfully, but I can't seem to get my mind off of it.

With a sigh, I look down at the book I'm holding, disappointed. Out of all the options on the shelves, this one, with a few stories of the history of Bluebone Ridge, felt the most promising. Still, the chronicle of how this place was built and became self-sufficient up in the mountains is drier than I hoped it would be.

Honestly, I'd rather read a shopping list than this. I hoped for something other than factual accounts and explanations on architecture. I wanted stories about how this place came to be. Not—

The solarium door opens, then closes sharply with a flurry of movement. Hattie presses herself against it, sagging, and her shoulders shake as she presses her head to the heavy wood. My heart twists in concern, and I slowly, carefully get to my feet. She hasn't seen me, that much is certain. But I'm not sure if I should involve myself in whatever is happening here.

Please, don't let me regret this, I plead silently. Setting down my pillow and book, I clear my throat so she knows I'm here, but Hattie doesn't turn from the door. She's swaying a little, and her curly red hair obscures her features from me. Like every time I've seen her since my arrival, she looks unkempt and a little unwell.

"Hey..." I greet, creeping closer to her. She's never struck me as someone who's violent, but I still can't help wanting to be careful. My stomach twists a little in concern, and I take a step to the side, giving her more of an opportunity to actually see me. "Hattie?"

At her name, she whirls around, eyes wide, and studies my face with a look of panicked confusion. Once she sees it's me, however, the panic fades, and she slumps back against the door as if she can barely hold up her weight. "Fern," she sighs out, like it's a relief.

"Yeah, it's just me. Are you—"

"What are you doing here?" she asks, as if I hadn't been speaking. Her eyes move rapidly over the medium-sized room, going everywhere like there's some hidden threat to be found.

I try to seem relaxed and at ease, but it's a losing battle. So I smile kindly at her and say, "I'm just reading. I'm sort of tired, and I was just hoping to find—"

"No, no." She shakes her head and runs a hand through her hair, looking frustrated. "No, what are you doing *here?*"

It takes me a moment to guess her meaning. But telling an unwell mental patient who definitely needs to be here the details of my issues isn't what I signed up for today. Then again, it's not like she's going to judge me, and I doubt she's going to tell anyone. "I hurt myself." With a sigh, I show her my bandaged hand. She reaches out with jerky movements, and latches onto my wrist with a surprisingly strong grip.

"Oh...no...you shouldn't—" Her eyes find mine, mournful at my admission. "No, that's not fair. That's not right."

"You're telling me," I agree dryly, trying to grin and mostly failing. Not that she really seems to notice. Her thumb strokes over the bandage, and I swear she seems to fidget without really moving. But I've noticed Hattie is so restless all the time, not just now.

"Do you need me to get you some help?" I ask at last, letting her draw me over to the window where I was reading before. My stomach clenches nervously at not knowing what she's doing, and the sudden fear that she's going to launch forward and gnaw out my throat. But I remind myself I'm being stupid, and feeding into stereotypes. Hattie has never done anything to me, and she seems pretty nice, all things considered.

"No." Her voice is soft as she turns to lean against the window. She brings her hand up, and by extension mine too, until she can press them both to the glass before turning to stare out the thick, wavy pane with thoughtful contemplation. "You saw them." Her words aren't a question.

But somehow, I know exactly what she means. I look out the window as well, worrying my bottom lip between my teeth. "I don't know," I say finally, my words slow and unsure. "What is it you think I saw?" There's nothing out there now. I haven't seen anything strange at all today, except this morning with Cairo in the shed. And not to mention Hattie in the bathroom after group therapy, though I can't be sure she remembers that.

She doesn't answer right away. Instead, her fingers trace shapes in the glass, though without it being foggy, nothing is showing up. She just stands there with both of our hands on the glass, like I haven't asked her anything. But I'm good at being patient when I really need to be. Though I'm sure my mother would disagree with that statement. So I just watch her, hoping she'll be ready to explain.

"They're just so hungry, he says. And I've seen them." I don't know what she's talking about, and it feels like I missed the first half of the conversation. I think back, scanning my brain for any clue at all about what she's trying to say, but I find nothing. *Nothing* echoes back at me, and without an explanation from her, I don't think I'll be able to decipher what the hell she means.

"Who's hungry? And who says? What are you—"

From the corner of my eye, movement in the trees outside catches my attention and I turn to look, just as I hear Moro barking from somewhere in the courtyard, though the sound dwindles after only a few seconds. Not only that, but I now can't see anything in the trees, no matter how hard I look. It makes me wonder if I was just imagining things in my sudden paranoia.

"Hattie, what is going on here?" Stepping closer to her, I reach up with my other hand to lightly grip her arm, hoping I don't scare her away but also striving to get her full attention on me.

It works, in a way.

Hattie looks at me with wide brown eyes, the freckles spattered over her nose looking stark against her paleness. Her hands come up to mirror mine, gripping my sleeves just under my shoulders before she leans in until our foreheads are almost touching. "They're *starving*," she whispers with wide eyes and a tremble in her voice. "You don't understand, Fern, how hungry they are. He showed me what they look like. He told me they deserve to eat."

"Who showed you? *What* did he show you?" More and more, I'm starting to wonder if this is her delusions speaking, rather than something real. I'm almost embarrassed to be so drawn into it when I know she's troubled and really needs help. She's not talking sense, and she's not saying anything I can interpret, I'm sure.

Voices outside catch my attention. When I turn at the sound of frantic footsteps, Hattie grips my arms more tightly. "It's not what you think." Her words are rapid, panicked. "They aren't like us, and they're so hungry. You can't hate them when they did what they had to in order to survive." The words ring familiar, but I'm too distracted by the steps and voices getting nearer.

"Hattie—"

"They've never had someone say hi to them before. They liked the message on your window."

My blood goes cold, and I turn back to her, feeling like the world is spinning under me. "How do you know—"

But I don't get to finish the question. The door snaps open, revealing two women, one of whom is the orderly who showed me around yesterday. "She's in here!" she calls back to the other employees, and Hattie jerks away from me, shoving me hard enough that I stumble.

"I wasn't lost," a confused, slightly hysterical Hattie snaps to them. "I don't need help."

But Esther's smile says otherwise. She doesn't so much coax Hattie out as drag her, with the help of her cohort, though she turns to give me a concerned look over her shoulder before she goes. "Did she hurt you?" Esther asks, looking me over.

I shake my head, not sure what to say. "N-no," I stammer at last, leaning back against the window again with my arms wrapped around myself like I need the support. "No, she just..." But I trail off under Esther's watchful eye before taking a breath to steady myself. "She just wanted to talk."

But even once they're gone and I can no longer hear Hattie arguing with the orderlies, I don't move. I stand there, against the window, feeling suddenly very alone but *not* at the same time, and wondering how the hell Hattie knows what I wrote on my window that faded within a minute, when she hadn't been there to see it.

CHAPTER EIGHT

It's almost impossible to pay attention to Dr. Radley while she talks today. I'm *so close* to getting out of here that all I want to do is bounce off the walls in preparation. Though I'm sure the only place that would get me is here. For a longer period of time, at that. So I manage to force myself to look somewhat calm, as if I'm not vibrating at the seams to get the hell off this mountain and away from the creepy asylum.

They're starving.

I can't get Hattie's words out of my head. I've even considered bringing it up to Dr. Radley, to ask her about those words or about what could be up here that's hungry. But then I risk sounding delusional, and I'd really rather not.

Though I'm nodding along with her, when she makes eye contact with me, I realize with a jolt that I honestly have no idea what she said. So when she stops speaking with an expectant look on her face, all I can do is stare at her and try to recall the last five minutes of conversation.

Which, unfortunately, I can't seem to do.

But Dr. Radley catches on fast, and her lips curl upward in

an indulgent, amused smile. "I won't get mad at you for not paying attention. I know how much you want to go home, Fern." She even eases back in her chair, like she's trying to give me the impression of being relaxed. She definitely doesn't look like she is, however. It seems put on, and I wonder if she's even capable of not looking fully aware at every moment.

"Sorry." I sigh, quick to apologize as I hunch my shoulders in an instinctively guilty reaction, like a child who was caught doing something she shouldn't. "I'm not trying to be rude or anything. It's just that I'm just really...looking forward to going home." I figure it's better not to insult this place by making it clear quite how much I want to get the hell out of Bluebone Ridge. But she only smiles again, still looking indulgent.

"You're not supposed to love it here. It's supposed to be a safe place for you to get the help and coping mechanisms you need to make good choices."

"And to not cut into my palm with first aid scissors?" I ask dryly before I can stop myself. But she only snorts instead of looking disdainful or irritated.

"Yeah, that too. Tell me, do you have anything you want to talk about before you leave in the morning? Any questions or concerns for me? Anything you'd like to bring up? I think it would be a good idea for you to continue seeing someone, but I can't force you to." She puts her iPad to the side and places her hands in her lap, which makes this feel like a much more casual conversation than a mandatory therapy session.

I bite my lip as I watch her, trying to judge her reaction to the question I haven't asked. But hopefully, if she does get mad, I can just backtrack my way out of it. "How long have you worked here?" I inquire finally.

"About six years now," she answers without hesitation. "I also run a practice in town, though. I believe in the same town you're from."

"You have a practice in Whippoorwill?" My brows lift slightly in surprise, but I push that away. I wouldn't have thought the town is big enough for a therapist. But what do I know? Clearly it's big enough to have at least one accidentally self-harming peasant in need of temporary inpatient care.

Emphasis on the *temporary*.

She nods, and I blink back in surprise, adding, "Okay, I know this one is going to sound weird and concerning. But if you're familiar with the area, you have to know the reputation Bluebone Ridge has." I let my words sink in, but she doesn't look perturbed by them, so I continue. "Have you ever seen anything weird here?"

"Anything weird? Like patients with concerning behaviors, or ghosts roaming the halls?" The touch of unexpected amusement in her words helps convince me she's not about to have me committed longer.

"The second. Ghosts, or monsters, or stuff like that. I've heard a lot of stories. Umm...I guess everyone has. I'm not talking about literal werewolves popping out of the trees or ghosts re-enacting their deaths in the halls. Just anything you can't explain?" I hope I sound casual and not too interested, but I'm not sure if I'm successful with that or not.

"No, unfortunately." She shrugs, looking almost apologetic at the words. "I can't say I've ever seen anything here that I can't explain. But that doesn't mean I'm ruling out the existence of such things. It's a big world after all, Fern." Dr. Radley turns to look out the window, and for a few moments, it seems like she's gotten distracted looking at the distorted view through the thick glass. "What about you?" she asks at last, surprising me after such a long silence.

"Me?" I repeat, my eyes meeting hers when she turns back to look at me. Her brown eyes seem interested, though not overly so. I force myself not to get worked up over the fair question. I'd asked first, after all.

For a moment, I consider telling her about the thing I saw outside on more than one occasion. About what Hattie said, her repeated warnings of *they're starving* and *they're coming, they're here*. I even consider mentioning the word *hi* on my window that Hattie somehow knew about.

I think about the possibility of sharing all that with the doctor, before shoving the notion away very firmly. There is no way in hell I'm going to volunteer any information that could get me stuck here for longer than the next seventeen hours. I'd rather stick scissors in my good hand, I decide in that moment.

So I look at her, eyes wide and plaintive, and with all the sincerity I can muster, I shake my head and give her an apologetic grin of my own. "No," I lie, and shake my head. "No, I can't say I've seen anything weird at all."

I walk past Cairo before I realize that I have, but once I register his presence, I stop in my tracks while considering if I want to start a conversation. Yesterday's interaction in the shed was the last time I saw him, and I'm still unsure of how I feel about it. But I can feel his attention, his gaze on me, even as I look up and study the high ceilings of this hallway that haven't been dusted in probably a decade.

It's a good thing I don't really have allergies.

When I turn, I'm unsurprised to see him looking at me, and the tilt of his head combined with the curiosity in his eyes makes him look almost like a lost puppy. It disarms me easily enough, but when I take a step back toward him, that open curiosity fades and he straightens a little, with his arms still folded loosely over his chest. He makes the powder-blue of our matching outfits look good, I decide, especially with a black long-sleeved shirt under it.

"Hi," I greet, moving to mirror his stance and lean against the tall window in front of him, though I'm definitely not obstructing his view. Cairo turns to look outside again, searching, before letting out a sigh and giving me an almost baleful look.

"Coming from therapy?" he asks, in a voice that sounds as tired as he looks. "Your last therapy session, right? Since you're getting broken out in the morning?" I swear I see a small smile on his face, and the fading surprise that I stopped to talk to him.

"Dr. Radley pronounced me all good to go."

"Did she really?"

"Well, no, but we all have problems."

He snorts at that, smiling in spite of himself, and turns to gaze out the window again. I look out the glass as well, wondering if there's something to see. But all I find is the courtyard one floor down, with a few patients milling around or talking. Two orderlies sit outside as well, deep in conversation while one gestures animatedly with the book she's holding. I can't see any of their faces clearly, of course. Not with the ancient window between us. "It'd be better if you could go tonight," he remarks offhandedly, and I huff out an agreement.

"It would be better if I was never forced to come here at all. But then I wouldn't have met you, and my life would be just a shade less interesting."

His eyes find mine, and Cairo gives me a once over. "You're brave today. It must be from the excitement and the fact you're almost out." He's surprisingly spot on, though I won't give him the satisfaction of knowing that. Still, it makes me check myself, and I don't respond. I only watch him, still leaning against the window like he is.

"How long have you been here?" The question is out before I really think about it, but I suppose the worst thing he can do is not answer.

Cairo rolls his shoulders in a shrug. "I don't know." The words are a breathy sigh. "I don't really keep track. Feels like I just showed up here one day, and that was that."

"Want me to smuggle you out with me?" The offer is a joke, but he looks at me with surprise on his face, like he wasn't expecting it, so I continue with a few nods. "Yeah, I've seen a few movies where someone gets smuggled out of jail. We could put you in a laundry hamper? Or, on a scale of one to ten, how would you rate your ability to hold on to the bottom of a bus all the way down the mountain?"

"Low." His voice is flat, and he rolls his eyes, but I swear I can see the humor in them from my words. "Very low, in fact. And we have laundry machines here, so why would they send it out on a bus?"

"Well, I don't hear you coming up with anything."

"Maybe I don't need to leave." He goes back to looking out the window again, and worries his lip between his teeth before adding, "Or maybe I don't need help to do it." His eyes dart back to my face, judging my reaction, and he finishes with, "Perhaps between us, I'm the one with a better rescue plan and if the roles were reversed, I'd be breaking you out with me."

"And Moro," I say instinctively, though my stomach twists when I think about the dog. "We'd have to get Moro out, too."

He doesn't answer that part, only shrugs and looks back out the window again.

"Do you have therapy?" I can't imagine why he'd be on this side of the building, unless he does. I rarely see anyone hanging out here for fun.

"No." His answer is absent as he stares out the window once more. "I don't have therapy, Fern." The way he says it seems more like he doesn't have therapy *at all* versus not having it right now. But I know that can't be the case.

"I won't say I'll miss you." The silence stretches between us after I say it, though once again I see the little hint of a smile on his lips. "Because I barely know you, and you're a little weird."

"Just a little?" His gaze flicks to mine, showing his amusement. "That's very kind of you."

"I know." We lapse into silence again before I push off of the window with a sigh. "See you later, then. Probably not, but —" He catches my arm suddenly, and my words trail off as I look at Cairo, even though he's not returning the attention. Instead, he's still gazing out the window.

But he doesn't say a word. He finally glances at me, with an expression I can't read for the life of me, before letting go of my arm and dropping his gaze back outside. "See you later, Fern," he agrees with a sigh. It's a clear dismissal, and I take it as one.

I walk a few steps backward before turning, trying not to notice the feeling of his eyes on me as I flee.

CHAPTER NINE

MY GOAL OF SLEEPING UNTIL I CAN SKIP DOWN THE STAIRS AND HOP ON the bus back to town is promptly shattered when my eyes open and it's still pitch black outside.

I sit up before I really know what I'm doing—and before I'm properly awake—though it's with a heavy sigh and the drag of sleep. "What..." I sigh and press my palm to my face, trying to figure out why I'm awake. Admittedly, I haven't slept very well here, which I'm shocked by, but given the fact my clock that's bolted to the nightstand shows it's barely after midnight, I can't help but feel dull surprise. I've only been asleep for a couple of hours, and this isn't my normal time of night to be restless.

Rubbing my face again, I sit on my bed with my legs crossed under me. I'm more awake than I have any right to be, and I wish I knew why I bolted up so fast, without a good reason—

"Fern?" I swear I hear my name from somewhere out in the hallway, though it's so soft and indistinct it could've been half a dozen other words. Still, I get to my feet, toes curling against

the cold hardwood beside my bed. Automatically, I slip on my laceless-shoes to fight the chill, though when I stand upright, my eyes catch movement outside of my window. Rather than heading to the door, I go there, pressing my nose against the glass as my eyes search the trees beyond.

I expect to find nothing. For three breaths, I stare at the ground and the darkness of the trees, lit only by the outside lights of Bluebone Ridge. But just when I'm about to turn away, I finally see movement as something stands up, right in front of me, at the edge of the trees where everything gets dark.

As it straightens, I can't look away.

It's not an elk.

My breathing stops, held in my chest, and my fingers clench against the windowsill under my hands.

It's definitely not a wolf.

The...thing is human-like, standing on two legs instead of four. It tilts its head one way in a jerky, strange motion and stares up at me with round eyes reflecting the dim lights.

"What..." My word seems to break the strange moment, and the thing lurches backward into the trees, disappearing from sight. My breath huffs out against the window, fogging it up, and when I step back just a little, something there catches my attention as well.

Hello.

The word is just under where I wrote my *hi,* and I go cold at the sight. But even as I look at it, the word fades as the foggy surface turns clear again, leaving me standing there confused, with my heart racing, and more than a little confused.

"What is going on?" I whisper to no one at all, reaching out with two fingers to the window. I breathe against it, making the word visible again, and streak my fingers across the *hello,* just to be sure.

And as I expect, there's a fresh line through the foggy glass, showing that this was written on the *inside* of the window, not outside.

It doesn't make me feel any better. If anything, it makes my stomach twist and sets my mind racing. I have no idea who could've written this, though the longer I think about it, the clearer the answer is. *Hattie.* She was the one to bring it up, after all. But she also said something else along with it that made it seem like she hadn't been the one in my room at all.

They've never had someone say hi to them before. They liked the message on your window.

Her words play in my head, and I twist my fingers together, pressing against my injured, still-stitched palm. This is ridiculous. It has to have been her, right?

And yet...

I walk back to the window once more, looking outside in the darkness. It's so quiet right now, with most everyone else asleep and no one causing a disturbance on this side of the sanitarium, at least.

I don't see anything, even though I stand there until the word with my mark through it fades again. The woods are just as silent as they had been before, and just as still. It's hard not to wonder if I imagined it, or blame whatever I saw on the fact I'm still half asleep. That's probably a better explanation.

A more rational one.

Taking a breath, then another, I force myself to settle down. A shiver goes through me, from the chilly air and the memory of what I saw, but again I tell myself that there was nothing there.

Everything is fine.

Right?

Before I can convince myself to go back to bed, I hear a shattering noise, like glass, from so far away that it would've been easy to miss if I were still asleep. I doubt it would've woken me, but since I'm already up, it's impossible to ignore.

I only hesitate for a moment, then I turn and head for the unlocked door that will take me out into the hallway. It's probably none of my business, sure, but—

Someone screams.

Then someone else follows suit, setting the hair on the back of my neck on end just as I reach the door. My movements become more urgent, and I reach out for the handle just as the door slams open, causing me to stagger backward into my room with a gasp.

And admitting *Hattie*.

"Hattie?!" I gasp, eyes wide as I catch myself on the end of the bed. "Hattie, what are you doing? Did you hear that? What —" As I step forward, she closes the door hard. She moves so quickly that she does that and has time to turn around and grab me by my sleeves, forcing me back until my back hits the window hard before I can even try to finish my question.

"You can't leave!" she hisses, eyes wide and panicked. "We can't *leave*, Fern."

"Why can't we—"

"Because they're here." She leans forward, her forehead pressed to mine. *"And they're starving."*

Another scream cuts through the air, making me jump, but Hattie seems unbothered and unsurprised. She just holds me here, forehead against mine, with her hands digging into my shoulders. Another scream, then another, and I can't help gasping as my hands come up to grip her wrists.

"What is going on?!" I demand, my words a cross between a shriek and a snarl. "And let go of me!" In my panic, I push her away gently, trying not to hurt her, and Hattie steps back without much of a struggle. There's confusion on her face as she watches me go to the door, but when I grab the handle and turn it...nothing happens.

"How—What—?" When I try the door again, I realize it really is jammed shut somehow. I whirl around to face Hattie, seeing her standing by the window with her face pressed almost against it. "Hattie!" I snap, managing to get her to look at me over her shoulder. "What happened to the door? And what the hell is going on here?"

She doesn't answer right away. I stare at her as she goes back to surveying the grounds outside, looking interested and curious rather than panicking like I am. *"Hattie!"* I finally shriek. My whole body is vibrating with tension, and I feel like a trapped rat.

"I told you." She turns to look at me, and for the first time I notice blood spattered across the front of her powder blue shirt. Unlike most of us, she's not wearing a long-sleeved shirt under it, and doesn't seem the least bit cold. "They're—"

"Here, starving, yeah. I heard you." I don't mean to be rude and cut her off, but I don't know what else to do. My heart races and I glance back to the door at the sounds of footsteps running in a nearby hallway and a door slamming. There are also raised, panicked voices that echo in the hallway, but I keep my attention on Hattie.

I can't open the door, so I'd rather focus on figuring out what Hattie knows. "Who's starving? *What* is here?" I walk toward her once more, trying not to seem threatening but also hoping I can get her to actually say something that will be helpful to me.

But really, I shouldn't be surprised by how she just watches me with mild interest before sitting down on my damn bed. She stares at me as I pace, like I'm an exhibit in a zoo and this is just some normal Tuesday.

"HATTIE!" I shriek again after I hear another set of

screams, this time closer to my room. "Hattie *please!* Tell me what's—"

Something slams against my door and I whirl around, unsure of what to expect. But when Sam's eyes meet mine and I catch sight of the blood spattered across her face, I freeze.

"Help me!" she gasps, grabbing at the handle of my door. "Fern, please, you have to help me!" She's shaking, wide-eyed with absolute terror, and I bolt to the door so I can see her more clearly through the small glass panel. The lights outside my room flicker on and off, like they've been partially knocked out, and with the tiny window, all I can really see is her face.

"Open the door!" I yell back, looking down to see the handle jiggling slightly, though it isn't turning all the way.

"It's stuck!" Her desperation is contagious, and she turns to look down the hallway, freezing as a soft whimper leaves her throat. "Fern...please..." she breathes out, and it looks to me as if she's paralyzed.

"Come on! You have to work on the door!" My distress is rising, and I jerk hard on the handle, trying to get it to do more than jiggle.

But Sam looks back at me, tears running down her face, and she just looks hopeless. It sends a visceral, painful reaction through me, and my stomach clenches just as she's jerked sideways without warning, hard enough for me to know it wasn't by her own will.

Then the screaming starts. I lean forward, trying so hard to see what's going on. But just as I catch sight of something that might be her hand, Hattie wraps her arms around me, dragging me away from the door with her head to my shoulder.

"He said not to look," she murmurs, hiding her face in my shoulder. She's surprisingly strong enough to easily keep me against her near the window, rather than letting me go back near the door.

"We have to help her!" I manage to choke out, fighting her half-heartedly. "Please! Hattie, we have to—"

Sam's screams come to a halt as Hattie shakes her head against my shoulder. "We can't help them." The words are a whisper in the sudden, deafening silence. It's dark in my room, and the lights out in the hall are still flickering wildly. I count my heartbeats in the quiet, until someone else screams further away, sending another shudder through me.

A sound I don't recognize finds my ears and I flinch, watching as the handle falls off the door then rolls across the hardwood. I can't move, I can't *breathe*. I can only watch the door swing open slowly, creaking on its hinges as I stand there frozen in place with Hattie wrapped around me.

Standing in my doorway is a monster.

The same monster I've seen in the woods since I got here.

CHAPTER TEN

I CAN'T SCREAM, BECAUSE THAT WOULD REQUIRE ME TO BE ABLE TO breathe. Instead, I stand on the spot, paralyzed, feeling completely aware and also like I'm not really in my body at the same time. It's not quite like when I dissociate, but it's close.

The creature rises to stand on its back legs, and I see that while it's vaguely human, there's no way I could ever mistake it for one entirely. Its skin is pale and grey-tinged, with hollow cheeks and round eyes that reflect the light flickering in the hallway behind it.

Hattie holds onto me tighter, and I hear her breathe something in my ear that sounds something like *just don't move.*

But seeing as I'm very clearly paralyzed, that isn't a problem.

When the thing opens its mouth, it reminds me of a crocodile. Its mouth is too wide, too long, and reveals a set of sharp, blood-stained, fang-like teeth that are dripping with thicker things I don't want to identify.

It takes one step inside, then another, before dropping to crouch on the floor of my room with its head tilted upward, as if it's trying to scent me. Its eyes flicker from one side of the room to the other, never quite focusing on me or Hattie, though I know we sure as hell aren't really hidden. Belatedly, I realize I'm trembling. I can't help it, and I move a little, just enough that the floorboards creak under me. Unfortunately, it's also enough to get the thing's attention back on me.

It *chirps*. A strange, animalistic sound, before opening its mouth wide to literally scream up at me. Then it's standing again, blocking out the doorway and rolling its shoulders like it's prepared to pounce.

I'm going to die.

There's no way I'm not going to die here tonight.

In a detached sort of way, I wonder if Dr. Radley will be disappointed that she missed this, given that she seemed interested in the idea of something supernatural going on here at Bluebone Ridge. But she's lucky, since she gets to go home at night.

The thing takes a step.

Then another. It's still so far across the room that it's not close to reaching distance, but I have nowhere to go in order to escape. But just when my heart seems ready to slam right out of the cage of my ribs, another sound comes from the hallway behind the monster.

It's a shriek, but a lower-pitched one, I think. The thing in my doorway turns at the sound, stepping right back toward the door in an almost frustrated manner. It opens its mouth wide again, hissing to show off those teeth, before it's dragged away suddenly with an indignant, panicked yowl that echoes in the hallway as it goes.

The sound lasts for much longer than Sam's screams had. But I remain there, frozen and terrified, with Hattie as still as a statue against my back except for her muttering. Finally, the noises die off, though the thing sounds mad as its voice fades away. It must be getting carried or dragged, since it hadn't seemed like it wanted to leave.

But I don't want to meet whatever could just pick it up and carry it off anymore than I wanted to meet that. The paralysis breaks at the thought of finding something scarier in my path, and I stagger away from Hattie with a bit of difficulty, shrugging her off despite her protests.

"Stop!" I snap, shaking off her hand when she reaches out for me. "I'm just going to look!" Though I wonder if sticking my nose out is maybe the worst possible thing I could do, truth be told. There's an excellent chance that the monster or something like it could still be out here, waiting for me to do just this.

On stiff legs, I make it to the door, and I'm slower than I'd like to admit to take that last step out into the hallway. Immediately, my eyes work to adjust to the flickering lights, and when I turn, my stomach clenches and nausea climbs up my throat at the sight beside my door.

Sam's body lies there, or what's left of it. Torn into more pieces than I'm letting myself count, she's very, very dead with her insides strewn about the hallway and parts of her torn away. Her face is the worst, and when I see what's left—her jaw cracked and eyes sightless and staring—that's what does it for me.

I lean the other way and retch, thankful I didn't really eat much at all for dinner, so all that comes up now is burning bile as my body heaves its protests against what I'm seeing. "I'm sorry," I murmur, eyes closed as a shudder goes through me. "Fuck, I'm so sorry, Sam." I barely knew her. I'd barely spoken to her three times, but I still can't help the stab of guilt that goes through me.

If only I had gotten the door open, maybe I could've saved her.

Or maybe all three of us would've ended up in pieces on the hardwood floors.

The unwelcome thought feels practical, but I don't want practical right now. Or rational. I don't want to let myself be grateful that I didn't end up like her. With her body so close, it feels wrong to be relieved that I'm still alive, at least for now.

Almost in punishment, I force myself to look at her body one more time. Whatever got a hold of her had been strong enough to quite literally wrench her apart into pieces, though it doesn't look like it actually broke her bones.

A cold part of my mind relates it to pulling apart a chicken at the weak points, which only makes me double over to heave all over again, disgusted with myself and horrified by the comparison. "Fuck," I groan, wiping my mouth on the back of my hand. "Fuck, get yourself together, Fern," I whisper, trying not to focus on the vaguely nauseating way the lights continue to blink on and off.

"Hattie!" I call back into my room once I've made as sure as I can that there's nothing still alive in the hallway. She's leaning against the window in my room, staring out with a thoughtful, slightly blank expression on her face. "Hattie, come on!" I try again. "I...I think we should go."

But she doesn't respond. She doesn't even look at me, and I only know she's somewhat aware because her eyes move, following whatever it is she's watching on the other side of the window. Frankly, I have no interest in learning what that is, and I'm not about to go back to the window to check. I hesitate for a moment longer, wondering if I should grab her and drag her out of here, even if she doesn't want to go. However, the memory of how easily she grabbed and held onto me is quick to flicker in my brain and I sigh, shaking my head.

"Hattie!" I try again, and I hope this time it's enough to jerk her out of her stupor. But it isn't. Once again, she doesn't even fucking look at me. "Fine, I...I can't stay here. I have to go. I have to—"

"*Fern?*" My name sounds in the hallway, from the direction of the stairwell where I met Cairo and Tyler only a few days ago, though it feels like a lifetime. The word seems to echo, a little eerie, and everything in me suddenly seems on edge.

"Hello?" I call back tentatively. "Did someone—"

"*Fern?*" the voice calls again. It doesn't say anything else, and still has that same eerie quality that doesn't sound quite right. But I'm sure the monster that growled and chirped wouldn't know my name, and with its mouth, wouldn't have been able to say it anyway.

I turn that way, the direction that's thankfully away from Sam, and take a few tentative steps. I don't hear anything close enough to be worrying—or at least any more worrying than this entire night has become. But I'm still as quiet as I can possibly be as I pass other women's rooms, trying not to look into the first few, since the doors are all open and some are hanging off their hinges. What remains of the other patients is visible out of the corner of my eye, and there are spatters of blood in the hallway, but by the fourth one, I can't help looking.

The two women inside are familiar in the way I'm sure I've seen them around the halls before. They're older than me, probably in their forties, and both of them are just as torn apart as Sam was. The job seems hasty; the teeth marks are voracious and feral. I don't let myself dwell on the fact there are definitely chunks of them missing, as if something hadn't just torn them apart, but *ate* what it took.

This seems like a lot for just one creature, but how am I supposed to know that for sure? I don't even know what was standing in my doorway, or what was able to drag it away.

They're starving.

Hattie's words echo in my head, and the realization that she knew, and that there's more than one, hits me with all the joy of a sledgehammer to my chest. Nausea claws at my insides, and it's so hard not to focus on one woman that was ripped apart with something that looks like glee, given how scattered her remains are in the room that I pass. Barely any of her seems to be missing, though I don't know the inside of a human body well enough to know what remains in the mess of gore that's spattered around the room.

At least my stomach isn't protesting quite as much now that I'm becoming a little numb to the situation.

The voice calls out again, my name garbled on their tongue, and it occurs to me the person might be injured. It doesn't sound like Cairo or Esther. In fact, the voice has a very neutral, unidentifiable quality to it that makes it impossible to place. But Sam's face in my mind weighs too heavily on me to even think of leaving them and finding my way out. Besides, the stairwell is just as good an escape as any, I hope. The stairs are the quickest way I know of to get to the first floor, and it will mean I don't have to cross the main areas of the building, where I can still hear screaming.

Finally, the stairwell is in sight, the open archway looming in a menacing, and not at all reassuring, way. The windows near it are broken, glass scattered all over the floor in thick shards, and I can't stop myself from looking out to the ground beyond, even though I don't know what I expect to see.

I'm not even shocked when I don't see anything. After all, with all the monsters inside, what's left outside except the trees? But a breeze makes me shiver, reminding me that we're near the top of a mountain in northern Washington, where it never really gets warm and I constantly need some type of jacket. My long-sleeved thermal under the powder-blue scrub top definitely isn't cutting it, and I rub my hands over my arms as I walk.

"Hello?" I call while standing just outside of the stairwell. The lights inside are off, and the door has been ripped clean off its hinges. I don't really want to run in there blindly, given that with my luck, I'll probably end up tripping and falling, breaking my neck on the staircase before any monster has the pleasure of ripping me apart.

Although all things considered, it would probably be a better death.

The moment I finally get the courage to take a step forward, there's a snarl and a scrabbling noise on the floor behind me that makes me whirl around. It takes me longer than it should to realize that the thing hurtling down the hallway behind me isn't one of the creepy, man-eating monsters that killed Sam and stood in the door of my room.

It's a dog?

It's Moro.

"Wait!" I put my hands up, heart racing and blood rushing through my veins. "Wait, don't—" I don't know what I've done to piss her off, but her lips are peeled back from her fangs and her eyes blaze with fear and aggression.

Distantly, my brain tells me that my hands aren't going to do a damn thing against a wolf dog attacking me head on. But I don't know what else to do. I don't know how to stop her—

She lunges right past me, not touching any part of me with her fangs or claws, and there's an inhuman, unnatural yowl from the darkness of the stairwell behind me that has me whirling around and nearly sliding in the still-wet blood on the floor. The sight behind me makes me gasp, one hand flying up to cover my face. One of the monsters is there, in a tangled, writhing heap with Moro, who's showing absolutely no mercy.

Part of me wants to yell something encouraging as my

hand finds the wall to brace myself. The other part of me is content to stand there, horrified and unable to look away as she snaps and snarls, fangs tearing into the monster's flesh. She's efficiently brutal, and twists away from every attack so its claws sink into her thick fur instead of finding any purchase on her body. I still cry out, terrified for her, but I can't look away.

At last the monster disentangles itself, dripping dark blood with skin ripped from its limbs and face. One of its eyes looks unsalvageable, but I find I don't have any pity for it. With one last chirping shriek, it glares at me and runs away with jerky movements, sometimes dropping to all fours as it skitters down the steps and disappears into the darkness below.

I don't move, and the only sound in the hallway is Moro's panting breaths. But when she turns and I see her glance up at me, almost expectantly, my inner dog-lover kicks in full force.

"Good girl!" I gasp, dropping to my knees on the blood-spattered floor of the hallway. She wags her tail and walks toward me, a little uncertain, and my heart twists in sympathy for her when she clearly hasn't gotten all the affection she deserves for being *such* a damned good girl.

"Come here, good girl. God, you're so good. You're perfect," I praise. When she's close enough, I let her sniff my fingers, watching as she seems to consider my scent before her tongue comes out to lap at my palm in what I'm hoping is her method of showing approval. It seems that way, at least, when she steps nearer to sniff at my face while I hold perfectly still.

Then her tail starts wagging in earnest, and even though all I want to do is throw my arms around her and cry, I only reach up to scratch at her ears, burying my hands in her long, thick fur. "How'd you get free?" I ask, knowing she won't answer and not really caring, anyway. The guard doesn't deserve her, and I'm more than happy to take her with me.

"Thank you, thank you so much." After another couple of affectionate scratches, I get to my feet, staring down at Moro as she watches me with expectant yellow eyes.

God, I've always wanted a dog. I'm not sure if I should complain to the dog distribution center for its timing, or wonder what I did to deserve Moro saving my life when I hadn't known there was danger in the stairwell, but I'm definitely okay with it. "Come on," I whisper, and turn to jog back down the hallway, trying to ignore the blood on my clothes.

"Hattie!" I call when I'm nearly at my door again. "Hattie, come on! We have to go. If we stay here any longer—" My words stop abruptly when I turn to look into my room, eyes searching, only to find it completely empty.

"...Hattie?" I ask, confused. The window is still in one piece, and there's no sign of a struggle. The lights in the hall are still flickering ominously, sure, but I hadn't heard anything other than Moro's fight with the strange thing in the stairwell.

Even though I look under the bed and in the armoire just in case, I can't find her. Hattie isn't in this room, and it's as if she's just disappeared.

I only waver for a second longer, however. There's no way I can stand here just waiting for something to come kill me. I *won't*.

"Let's go, Moro." My steps take me back out into the hall, and as much as I'd rather slip out through the stairwell instead of head down the main steps and have to go through the lobby, I'm too afraid of the absolute darkness and what could be hiding in it.

Something that knew my name.

It's hard not to run, but I'm able to keep my pace to a jog, working not to look at the dead bodies or listen to the screams that continue to echo through the halls from other parts of the building. My stomach churns, though it's definitely empty, so there's nothing for me to throw up. Not even when I'm confronted with Esther, who's half sprawled over the desk in the lobby with her body pulled into pieces, and what definitely looks like her spine shining through the blood. It's a close call, though.

I cover my mouth and nose while I try not to look, appreciating the way Moro stays right beside me or a few steps behind. She doesn't seem interested in the noises or the bodies, except for an occasional sniff or whine.

Maybe she's just as desperate to get out of here as I am.

Good for her.

The front door is flung open, and I shudder immediately once I'm outside in the chilly night air of Bluebone Ridge's parking lot. When it occurs to me I have no idea what to do, or how to get out of here, the realization that this is as far as my plan takes me hits hard.

Nausea bubbles up my throat again, leaving a bitter taste in my mouth. Sure, I doubt I can find a ride off the mountain, but if I can just get out of here and follow the road, I can hope that at some point, I'll find someone.

Right?

It's all I've got, at least. It's the only thing I can count on, or make myself consider doing.

Moro's growl is the only warning I get, and I turn around just as something knocks me down onto the asphalt. When I scream, it's met with a snarl, as my hands come up to shove at the angry, snapping teeth and clawed hands that grab for me. Wide eyes meet mine, though their humanity is questionable when they shine like a predator's in the dark, reflecting the lamps that are still lit.

This creature seems stronger than the others I've seen; it's more muscular instead of skeletal. It grabs and tries to pin me down, though within seconds it's fighting both me and Moro, not that it seems to mind so much.

"NO!" I scream when its fangs come dangerously close to my skin. "No! Let me go—" I scream in fear, frustration, and pain when its teeth catch my shoulder. Pain blooms against my skin as it jerks back, tearing the cotton of my shirt away. Thankfully, it got more shirt than skin, but it still hurts.

I can't do this forever. Even with Moro helping, trying to get it away from me, I can't keep fending off the impossibly strong monster.

I'm going to die here.

The realization hurts.

"Fern!"

My heart sinks, acceptance hitting painfully even as my body and mind roar with dissent. I don't *want* to die here, when I was so fucking close to getting out of Bluebone Ridge.

"Fern!"

I barely register the voice, but that's probably because at the same moment, the creature pulls me off the ground, only to slam me back hard enough that I see stars. The force makes my grip falter, and I hear Moro yelp as she's kicked away. My gaze manages to focus on fangs and a nasty, gory grin as the monster rears up over me, reminding me of a predator about to take the killing bite.

There's no way I'll make it through this.

I know it's true, but I can't watch it happen. My eyes slip closed just as something knocks the monster away. Then there's a new snarl in the mix, this one filled with rage and hatred, and a few shrill yowls before the sound of footsteps echoes on the pavement and Moro barks encouragingly for the monster to leave.

My head spins, and opening my eyes is hard, though I force

them to stare up at the swirling night sky that's suddenly obscured by something.

"Fern..." Something touches my face, and I hear a sigh I can't place. "You really don't know—"

I can't understand what the rest of the words are, or who in the world is talking to me. Nausea and the pain in my head team up to fight against me, and when I close my eyes again, darkness rushes up to pull me out of this horrible nightmare once and for all.

CHAPTER ELEVEN

I JOLT UPRIGHT WITH THE SENSATION OF CLAWS REACHING FOR ME, OF snarling lips peeled back from bleeding teeth that want to sink into my throat. My scream comes next, and my eyes aren't even open as I reach out, blindly fighting what I assume is there.

"Fern, Fern!" an unfamiliar voice calls. Arms grapple for mine, gently pushing me down, not against hard asphalt, but a soft bed. "Fern, it's okay! You're okay!"

My eyes finally snap open, and I don't see the dark sky full of stars over Bluebone Ridge, but the white fluorescent lights of a hospital room that nearly blind me. My scream dies to a whimper at the realization of where I am, and I let the nurse slowly push my arms back down to either side of me, though her hands remain on my wrists.

"I'm sorry," I breathe, my voice hoarse. Now that I'm awake, the ache in my head becomes less easy to ignore, as does the sharp pain in my shoulder. I realize belatedly it's where I got bit by the...the *thing* from Bluebone Ridge; I have the urge to look at it, though when I roll my shoulders I can feel that it's covered by bandages.

"Where's Moro?" The words are out of my mouth before I can stop them, and way before I realize the nurse beside me has no idea who in the world I'm talking about. "The...the dog," I add, feeling a little stupid.

"The dog?" The nurse shakes her head. "Sorry, but it was just you. I don't know anything about a dog." And by the tone of her voice, she doesn't really care all that much about her.

"She saved me." My chest tightens, the worry for Moro is heavy and weighing me down. I can feel the sting of tears already, but I push them back with the hope that maybe, somehow, Moro spooked and ran away, off into the woods of the mountain. Though I refuse to dwell on how slim the chances of her making it out alive are.

After all, there's really nothing I can do about it now.

"Can you tell me what happened?" I make myself ask, looking around the small, private room again. "What did the others say they remember?"

When the nurse doesn't answer right away, I glance back at her, watching her face go from doubt to concern, then finally to reluctant acceptance. It gives me the chance to study her, to note that she's probably only a few years older than me. She's pretty, and gives off a very comforting vibe, instead of my anxiously chaotic one, considering how I usually vibrate off the walls in my worry.

"There are no others," she admits finally, her voice quiet and unsure. "But that doesn't mean anything yet," she adds quickly, looking back up at my face to study my reaction. "Not all the patients are accounted for, and half of the staff leaves for the night, so they were already gone. The police are thinking some of the other patients spooked and—"

But I don't need to hear her explanation or lack thereof.

There are no others.

Because everyone else is dead.

The thought is horrifying, and a coldness creeps through me, allowing me to hear my speeding heart on the monitor beside the bed, which doesn't exactly help me calm down.

"Fern—"

The door opens before she can finish her thought. But I don't need the empty comfort, and we both turn to look at the door as it bangs back on its hinges to reveal my mother, pale and worried.

And definitely here just to make my day worse.

"You shouldn't have sent her to that place!" Her righteous indignation is impressive as she marches in, followed by a doctor who was unprepared for her temper. He slouches a little, shoulders hunched, and glances at the nurse plaintively for help as he stays in my mother's shadow. "She told me about tha-that hospital! Blueridge or whatever it is. And you!" She whirls suddenly on the doctor and I watch, impressed, without much pity for anyone here.

"You had her see a doctor *on an iPad* who deemed my daughter unfit to go home. What a joke." She's not normally this upset, and I can't help but wonder how much of it is for my wellbeing, and how much of it is just for the situation. After all, I'm sure this is even more of an inconvenience for her than it was to sit with me in the hospital for a few hours last week.

"How long have I been here?" I ask, interrupting the start of another tirade.

"Two days," the nurse tells me, also seeming pleased to ignore my mother. "Give or take a few hours."

"Which we will not be paying for," my mother is quick to cut in as she glowers at the doctor again. "How long does she have to stay? Last I heard, her shoulder didn't need stitches, and once she woke up, she would be fine to leave. Is that still the case?"

He's nodding before he can really answer, and the doctor

takes a nervous breath. "Yes, umm. I'd like to keep her here until the morning." A quick glance at the clock shows me it's almost eight. And if it's been two days, that would make today Tuesday, I think. Which I confirm when I see the digital clock has a date on it as well, thankfully answering my questions so that I don't have to ask them. Well, at least I can start working as soon as I get home, since there are always freelance jobs to get done for my agency.

I have to pay that mortgage, after all.

"And the police want to speak with her," the doctor adds, nervous as he looks between me and my mother. "They want to ask her about what happened since she's the only..." But he trails off, and I lay back down against the white sheets, listening to the steady beat of my heart on the monitor.

To my surprise, my mother comes to me instead of getting into his face, and tangles her fingers with mine in a way that could almost be called comforting. "Fine," she says, her attention fixed on me. "But I want to be here."

"Mom—"

"No, no *Mom*, no arguments." Her voice is firm, and when I look at her, I can see a glimmer of worry in her face that makes me wonder and hope that maybe I've been too hard on her. That perhaps she cares more than I've given her credit for.

Tentatively, I wrap my fingers back around hers, and give her a very small, very tired smile. "I want her to stay," I agree, barely glancing at the doctor. "I'll talk to whoever, but I want my mom to stay with me. That's okay, right?"

Honestly, I don't think the doctor could say no, even if it wasn't. Not with the way my mom is looking at him as if she's just waiting for a reason to fully go off and make his day worse.

He makes his escape quickly after assuring my mom she can stay, and in his absence and once the nurse departs, Mom pulls up a chair to the bed, though the sound of it scraping across the floor makes me wince.

"How do you feel?" Mom asks, her voice quieter and kinder now that no one else is in the room. She gives me an almost genuine smile, though it feels a little distracted.

Just like she usually is.

"Like crap," I mutter, closing my eyes. "Mom, I don't know what to tell the police."

"Do you remember what happened? If you don't, we can tell them that. We can just say—" But the door opens, allowing her time to just grip my hand a little tighter as two officers dressed in uniform come in, both of them looking like they'd rather be anywhere but here.

Honestly, they can just join the club at this point. Distantly, I dream of my damn bed, my clothes, and the way I can control the noise and what's going on at my house. If I want quiet, I can have quiet. Or I can have the TV on, or music, or whatever.

And I don't have to deal with people when I don't want to. Unlike now, and the last several days.

I take a breath as the cops both sit, introducing themselves as they do, but it's just white noise to me. I'm tired, though I won't admit it, and as I answer their questions and repeat what I remember of what happened, I leave out one very important, probably life-changing detail.

That the things that had killed everyone were monsters.

I really don't want to end up right back at some kind of sanitarium after going through everything I did just to get out of Bluebone Ridge alive.

The cops seem disappointed when they leave, and they seem to know that I'm not quite being honest with them. I barely sleep that night, even though I was given meds and my mom stays with me and promises me I can.

By the time I finally get back to my house the next afternoon and I convince my mom that I'm okay, that I really am fine, it's night and everything is quiet.

But it's not everything I'd hoped for. Even curled up on my couch with the television on just enough to be a source of white noise, it's not...*right*.

Nothing is right now that it's all sinking in.

Nothing is how it should be.

My mind races with the memory of the night at Bluebone clear and heavy in my head, no matter how many times I relive it or try to push it away.

I have no idea what's on the TV.

I have no idea how long I've been crying.

But tears slip down my face unbidden, and I remember the feeling of claws on my shoulders and the sound of those gnashing fangs so close to me. Part of me wonders if maybe I didn't make it out, that this is some kind of hallucination my brain is presenting me with before the acceptance of death really comes.

No, I tell myself with a snort against my pillow. No, because I hurt too much emotionally and physically for that. But I can feel myself drifting a little, like I do when I'm over-stimulated. Like I did the day that got me into this shit in the first place.

Maybe that wouldn't be so awful tonight, though. Not when—

My backdoor rattles. I know what it sounds like well enough to know the noise by heart, and when I bolt upright from the sofa, my bare feet hit the floor hard. "Hello?" I call, turning toward the kitchen. "H-hello?! Is someone—"

The sound comes again. A rattling, like someone is shaking my back door trying to come in.

For a moment, I just stand there. I don't know what to do, and tears continue to stream down my cheeks. The face of the monsters from Bluebone Ridge, Sam's screams, and the fact I'm the only one left—all these facts tear through me at the sound against my back door as it rattles.

But curiosity and dread propel me forward. I stumble across the laminate floor, palms clammy and numb, with my heart pounding so loudly I can't hear anything else.

Three steps to go until I turn the corner, and once I'm there, I won't be able to unsee it.

Two steps.

I stop at the last one, wondering if I should call the cops or do something even slightly smarter than going for the back door to see what's there. Nothing in me can rationalize it. It's barely windy, and there are no trees close enough to make this kind of noise.

No, the rattling is distinct. Purposeful.

Something wants to come in here.

It takes longer than it should, but as I finally take that last step, my heart clenches in my ribs and a small, soft exhale leaves me. A pep talk runs on repeat through my head, reminding me that whatever is there, however terrifying it is, I can handle it.

I can handle it.

The moment she sees me, Moro barks. She stops pawing at the door and stands up on my deck, tail waving, and I nearly collapse in relief, barely managing to make it to the door to shove it open and allow the wolf dog into my small house. I greet her with no shortage of relieved tears and lots of praise for the best dog that exists in Washington. Maybe anywhere, really.

CHAPTER TWELVE

For a dog who was clearly treated like shit for a while, it surprises me how easily Moro adapts to life indoors. Though perhaps this was her aspiration all along, and I'm just fulfilling her wishes in an overdue manner.

I scan the news channels, and the sofa trembles just a little as the large wolf dog lies stretched out, panting, half on the cushions and half on me. Absent-mindedly, I reach down and she stops panting to lick my hand affectionately, her head ducking so I can scratch her ears just how she likes. I was more than a little out of sorts the morning after she showed up at my door, and finally in a better mindset to actually address the surprise, at least in my mind. And while the week since has been incredibly uneventful, I still have questions.

The first, of course, that keeps going through my brain: how did Moro *get* here? Did she really wander off the mountain and somehow miraculously come straight to my house without ever having been here before?

No, I don't think so, I muse as a news anchor talks about some school's fundraiser a county over. Not just because that's unlikely —and something out of a kid's movie—but because when Moro got here, she was completely cleaned up. There was no monster blood or gore on her face like there had been that night. No dirt or anything. Even her fur had seemed soft, like it was just brushed out. There's no way she could've shown up like that on her own.

But I'm grateful, whatever the circumstances might be.

Blinking, I finally focus on the television, realizing they're actually talking about something I should care about. Even Moro seems interested, one ear flicking back, though it might just be because my hand has paused and I'm not actively petting her anymore.

"Bluebone ridge Sanitarium will be shut down, owners say, for at least the next year. After the incident last week, the damage is greater than they initially thought." The news anchor says it casually, brushing off the reality of the situation, like it really is just about property damage, and not the amount of people that died there.

Like Sam.

And Esther.

Hattie, Cairo, Tyler—

The doorbell rings just as my heart twists and Cairo's face in my mind hurts a little more than Sam's does. But I'm jolted to the present when Moro launches off of me, a paw in my gut, to trot toward the front door with her tail curled up over her back.

Cairo.

His smirk, his scent, his closeness...I didn't know him well, I remind myself. But it still hurts to know he's gone, even if I hadn't actually seen his body.

According to the cops, I'm the only survivor. The only living person found, though there are still a few unidentified bodies remaining and people whose bodies they think were dragged away by 'animals.'

Monsters, they meant. But I haven't been able to bring myself to say it.

Moro barks again and I slide to my feet on the laminate floor, shoving a hand through my hair. "It's probably the mailman, Moro," I tell her with a sigh. "With your stuff from the pet store. Don't be ungrateful." I tap her lightly on the head, though my lecture has little effect on the way she bristles defensively, clearly protecting what she now sees as her home.

Truthfully, I have no idea how she'll be around strangers. But when I open the heavy door and leave just the screen between me and the porch, she sees the mailman, who pauses and looks at her with a smile. "Well, aren't you pretty," he greets.

The comment mollifies Moro instantly. Her ruff lies flat, and her tail becomes more relaxed, wagging more naturally. Apparently, mailmen aren't threats in her world.

"I just got her," I say with a smile, still with my hand on her head. "Sort of unexpectedly. I...inherited her." That's a tactful way to say it, since Jeremy's obituary popped up online a few days ago with no mention of her. And he never deserved her, so I'm not looking to find out if his family has any interest in continuing her mistreatment.

"Pretty girl," the mailman praises. "She friendly?"

"Umm...I'm not so sure," I admit. "I think she is. I mean, she's looking like she is?" But I'm not sure the mailman really wants to be my guinea pig.

He proves me wrong, however, and agrees that she seems friendly enough, so when I crack the screen open, it's to him with a treat in one hand, standing perfectly still and waiting for her to make a move.

Moro proves us both right and my fears unfounded by

stepping forward and taking the treat without hesitation. She sniffs him and licks his hands, allowing him to pet her ears while I hoist up the box to hold it against one hip while he tells her she really is the best dog ever.

I couldn't agree more.

By the time he's gone and I have the box of dog toys, necessities, and a bed that was stuffed into a vacuum sealed bag but is now re-inflating on the floor, I feel more alive and willing to actually do things today. For the first time in days, I want to do more than be a lump on my couch, ordering in and sulking with my dog.

Not that I can tear my mind away from the monsters at Bluebone Ridge. But I know the cops won't be able to help me, and anyone I tell will just cart me off to the next-nearest sanitarium to talk about my trauma and delusions.

So the internet seems like my best bet. Especially when any segments on the news I've caught about the incidents have labeled it an animal attack, an accident, or brushed it off as being less traumatic than it is.

Maybe if any of those news anchors were actually there, they'd have a stronger opinion about it than they do now.

But I wouldn't wish that night on anyone.

Except maybe Moro's former owner, who I don't feel bad for in the least.

Armed with my laptop, I switch from surfing news channels to Animal Planet, figuring it'll work for white noise while I search. I don't expect to land on a documentary about the feeding habits and man-eating history of grizzly bears, however, though I watch for a few minutes in grim fascination.

"Yeah, not today," I mumble, flipping instead to the home cooking network. Finally, I'm granted a reprieve, with the sort-of attractive host of the cooking competition show reading off the list of ingredients the chefs will have to use in their dish.

Not that I can cook, so I can only grimace in sympathy at the idea of using pig tongue in any kind of recipe. Moro is back beside me on the couch once she finishes breakfast, stretched out like she owns the place, and makes me adjust so the computer is more on my ankles than my thigh, which is her prime real estate to sleep on.

One hand wanders as I search, ending up on her head and gently scratching behind her ears while she lets out a satisfied sigh.

Unfortunately, most of the articles about Bluebone Ridge just reference its longevity and offer accounts of people that worked or 'recovered' there. Though to me, it simply felt like an enclosure for those deemed too harmful to themselves, so that the medical staff of whatever place that sent us there wouldn't have to be responsible for any incident.

I don't feel cured. With or without the monster attack.

I try searching a few different phrases, including '*Bluebone Ridge monster*' and '*Bluebone Ridge attack*' without any luck. But finally, when I change the last words to *attack survivor*, I see an article pop up that hasn't appeared on any of my other searches.

Bluebone Ridge patient Laura Simms (43) says monsters are responsible for deaths on the mountain.

It's certainly a mouthful for the article title, and as I skim through it once, then again, something in me tingles with unease. It feels familiar, even though our situations aren't the same, and the woman, who was twenty years older than me at the time, stares at whoever took her picture with a quiet, accepting horror on her face.

After a successful escape attempt from the sanitarium in the middle of the night, Laura says monsters tore her friends apart in the woods. When she was found outside of the gates, bloody and nearly catatonic, Laura would only repeat the words "they're starving."

I have to stop at that, and the blood runs cold in my veins. My fingers curl in Moro's fur, and it feels like everything in me comes to a grinding halt.

They're starving.

That is enough proof to me that Laura Simms saw the same thing I had. I skim the rest of the article, but it's told from the view of someone who clearly hadn't believed her. Instead, I look her up, taking longer than it should to actually find any record of Laura Simms, who seems to have vanished into obscurity for a few years after the attack.

Not that I blame her.

But a picture of her finally surfaces, and with a jolt I find she's a clerk for the local courthouse. It seems insane to me that she's here, living so close to where it happened just a few towns over, but it's also my good luck that she does. It means I don't have to go on a road trip or give up on this idea entirely.

Still, I sit there, worrying my bottom lip, debating if this is the right thing to do. Part of me wonders if I should just try to move on. To let things go.

But all it takes is the whispered memory to change my mind, the sound of Hattie's voice in my ear when she said,

"They're starving."

Then Cairo's face tugs at something in me, and I know I can't let this go. Looking at Moro, I watch her drowse for a moment, noting the way her ears twitch, before I close my laptop and ask, "Want to go for a ride, girl?"

Laura Simms' house is...not at all welcoming. I stand in front of it with Moro in my car, the windows half down. It's cool enough that I'm definitely not worried about her, and I'm not sure Laura would want a wolf dog showing up at her door, so leaving her seems like the more polite option. But now that I'm standing on her stoop, with ivy and mold creeping up to frame the front door on all sides, I'm not so sure I should've left her.

This place feels...sad. I suppose that's the right word for it, and I bite my lower lip between my teeth as I debate if I should even ring the bell. She might not be home, even though there is a car in the short driveway of the little house.

She might be dead.

Or asleep.

Or deaf, for all I know.

But I *need* to know, or at least do all I can to figure out if we saw the same thing like I think we did. So I cautiously reach up to ring the bell, hearing it reverberate inside of the house in long, rhythmic chimes.

"She's definitely not secretly a murderer," I whisper to myself as I hear a door closing and approaching footsteps. The old wood of the house creaks, and I stand there, trying to look harmless, while wondering if Laura is glaring at me through the peephole.

That's what I would do, anyway. But then I also probably wouldn't open the door to someone standing here like me.

I wait for a few moments, shifting from one foot to the other, not sure what to expect, before finally the old door with its peeling and flaky paint cracks open just enough for me to see someone standing behind it.

"Who are you?" The woman sounds older, like she's in her mid-sixties, but that makes sense, given how long ago the 'incident' she was interviewed about happened.

"Hi, I'm Fern," I answer honestly, linking my hands behind my back. "Sorry. I'm not trying to bother you." Desperately hoping that politeness is the way to go here if I'm looking for answers. "I...I'm looking for Ms. Laura Simms?"

The woman doesn't reply at once, and I get the feeling

she's scrutinizing me. I hold as still as I can, trying not to look impatient or fidget. Not that I succeed.

"Why?" The question comes out snappy, almost like a demanding bark. But I expected this, rather than a warm welcome. I'm a stranger, after all, and I'm sure she's had a lot of people question or mock her over the article.

"Because last week at Bluebone Ridge Sanitarium something happened," I say quickly, hopefully before she slams the door in my face. "And I want to know if I'm crazy...or if I really saw monsters."

"So why come to *me?*"

"Because they were starving."

She slams the door in my face. Hard. I stand there blinking, a little surprised by the aggressive strength of her slam, and after a few seconds I turn to look around the old, rundown subdivision. No one else is outside, even though it's early afternoon and the weather is still holding up, if a bit cloudy. It's cool for late summer, and my sleeves are pushed up to my elbows in the mild air.

Moro hangs her head out of the driver's side window, tongue lolling as she watches me. She, at least, looks pretty at ease with the situation, and doesn't really seem anything except interested.

But I just wait, hoping that something will change...only for it not to. Finally I sigh, shoulders dropping, and turn to walk off the porch.

I'm three steps down the sidewalk when the door creaks open again, the same amount as it had the first time, judging by the sound.

"That your dog in the car?" Laura Simms asks, because really, it can't be anyone else.

"Yeah," I say without turning. "Her name is Moro."

"Don't leave her in there. She'll be bored. Get your dog and come in, if you're coming." There's no kindness in her sharp words, but my stomach unclenches anyway. I still don't turn to look at her, though. I don't want her to revoke this strange invitation she's suddenly given me. Besides, I realize as I clip Moro's leash on and let her jump out of the car to sniff along the grass. I'd rather have Moro with me if I'm going into a stranger's house than be there alone.

I worry a bit when I'm coming back up the concrete stairs and the door is still mostly closed. But whether she decides at the last minute to let me in or if it's Moro's happy charm, her tail wagging, once I'm on the landing with the wolf dog's leash in my hand, the door creaks open wider, revealing a hardwood floor entryway.

"Thank you." It feels appropriate to say the words as I step inside and the door closes behind me with a sound of musical chimes that makes me turn. A small instrument hangs on the door, wooden balls swinging over metal wires like a harp or a guitar. I've never seen anything like it, and I watch the circular contraption as the balls slow and the musical sound becomes quieter, before I even think to look at Laura herself.

"My father made them," she explains after seeing where I'm looking. "He was into woodworking, and he made those for all of us kids and his wife." She reaches up to trace her fingers along the metal wires, producing a very soft sound. It gives me a chance to really look at her, and my heart twists at what I see.

Life has not been kind to Laura Simms. She looks eighty, instead of sixty, with heavy lines on her face and dark circles under ghostly grey eyes that seem pale with age. Her hair is brittle and straw-like, thin enough that I can see her scalp through the white strands. She's hunched over a little, standing maybe five foot even with the decline, making me feel way taller than I ever have the right to.

I expected an intimidating, cold woman hardened by her experiences.

But I hadn't expected such a frail, fragile-looking woman.

When she sees me looking at her, the smile on her face turns cool and unsurprised. "Not what you were expecting?" she asks, though I can tell she's not looking for an answer. Her hand goes out to Moro, who sniffs her and then licks her thin, age-spotted palm.

"I don't know what I was expecting," I admit, shrugging my shoulders heavily. "This is Moro, by the way. She belonged to a guard up at Bluebone Ridge until a week ago."

Laura pins me with her gaze, curiosity rather than suspicion in her eyes. "Did you steal her?"

"She saved me and somehow found her way to my house. Her old owner is dead, though he didn't treat her well." I say it easily, without trying to sound defensive or like I'm expecting an interrogation about it. Honestly, I don't think Laura cares much about the circumstances of how I got her.

But she looks at Moro in a new light and runs a hand over her head again. "So you were the most recent alarm system, eh girl?" she asks, surprising me with the words. "Only one dog? There were two back when I was there. I bet they told you some bullshit about her scaring off the local wildlife, right?"

"Was that not true?"

"You tell me. Did you ever see anything get close enough for her to scare off? Other than the monsters that attacked on Sunday?"

I shift uncomfortably, somehow surprised at how much she seems to *know*. "No," I admit quietly. "All I ever saw was *them*. Those things, or whatever they are. But you saw them too, right? You—"

She walks away, leaving me a little nonplussed and standing in the foyer of the small house. But when Laura turns to look at me, I realize I'm supposed to follow her. So I do, letting her lead me to a small kitchen with room only for appliances, a few cabinets, and a two-person table squeezed into the breakfast nook. Laura gestures for me to take a seat, and I do, on the side of the table with less space. Moro doesn't need any coaxing, and stretches out on the floor beside me.

At least she's easy to please and doesn't seem to require much other than a few casual adventures, food, and a steady supply of belly rubs while we watch reality TV at home.

Laura walks over and sets down two glasses, both of them with tea and ice cubes that rattle delicately against the real crystal. Carefully, she levers herself into the seat across from me, taking her time and then looking up to study me the same way I'd studied her.

"I heard you were the only confirmed survivor," she says grimly, her gaze never leaving mine. "How'd you do it?"

"How did I..." I trail off at the question. Normally I'd lie or brush it off. But she knows what I saw, and I figure I can't gain anything from lying to her if I want her to tell me what happened all those years ago. "Moro saved me when I followed the sound of my name to the stairwell. It was strange. It sounded so familiar, but I couldn't quite place it, you know?"

"Oh, I know," she assures me quietly.

"She saved me, and we got out. I don't know what I was thinking, except that I needed to get off the mountain. But another one attacked me in the parking lot. I heard my name again, I think? This is where it gets a little foggy, actually." Absently, I press my fingers to my palm that's now healed. Still, there's a shiny new scar just below my thumb where I cut into my hand with scissors, and it still twinges as I run my fingers over it with more force than I should.

"It bit me, sort of. Moro was trying to get it off of me. But I passed out. I guess she must have gotten it off of me, or killed it." I nudge Moro with my foot, who thumps her tail on the floor. "Unless something else distracted it, maybe?" But I shake my head. "I really don't know anything else. Two days later, I woke up in the hospital. And lied to the cops," I add. "I didn't want to end up right back in another asylum."

"Good for you," Laura chuckles. "That's what I would've done too. What I *should've* done all those years ago." She goes quiet, her eyes distant. "Why did you say that outside? *'They're starving'*?"

The question catches me off guard, though I guess it shouldn't. It's our shared trauma, after all. The one detail we can both relate to, more than anything. "There was a girl in there with me. Her name is Hattie—was Hattie," I correct unhappily. "Somehow she knew about them, I think? She said that to me multiple times before they got there. And then that night, too. Really, I thought she was just rambling, and I have no idea how she knew." I toss my hands up in surrender, and then busy myself with picking up the glass of tea. The ice is already melting, and I swirl the crystal gently in one hand before taking a sip.

"This is amazing," I say, surprised at how it tastes. "Did you make this? Like, yourself?"

"It's sun tea." There's pride in Laura's voice that I can't miss, and she gives me a genuinely grateful smile. "I made it yesterday."

"It's amazing," I reiterate, though I don't even know what sun tea is. "Thank you." It's not every day that I get anything homemade."

"None of us knew," Laura tells me after a few moments of tracing her fingers over the crystal glass. "Even back then we heard the same stories as you, I'm sure. I made a couple of... friends." Her voice turns bitter on the word. "They talked me into trying to get out. It was summer, so they said the weather was mild enough that we'd be fine. They would've been there for a very long time otherwise. I would've been out in a few weeks. But still..." She sighs. "I was naïve. Escaping was the easy part. There were staff shortages back then, and we had their shifts memorized."

The idea of it being understaffed surprises me, given how many orderlies prowled the halls and courtyards at all hours of the day and especially night. But I don't interrupt her. I worry that if I interrupt her, she won't finish. Not that I'd blame her, since this isn't my favorite topic either.

"We escaped and made it to the woods, dressed in some stolen clothes we found. We thought that without the uniforms, no one would recognize us. And since none of us were there for criminal reasons, it wouldn't be a big deal so long as we made it off the mountain. Can you believe the ignorance in us thinking that?" Her laugh is not humorous. It's an ugly, derisive sound that has me biting my lower lip.

"Within an hour we were lost," she goes on. "Hopelessly so. I remember when we started seeing these things in the woods. Jen got scared first. She took off running at the sight of them, and it was so fast. Like she triggered their hunting instincts." In her eyes, I can see the same horror I felt. I don't need the details, and she doesn't seem interested in giving them.

"Alicia was next. I just stood there, watching. Didn't know what to do," she admits, shrugging her frail shoulders. "I don't remember much about it, just what I told you and what they printed in that damn article." She sits back then, mouth pressed flat. "Except for one other thing that I've never told anyone." Her gaze finds mine and holds it. "There was a woman out there, about your age. She wasn't afraid of them. I don't know where she came from, or who she was. I don't know if she was human, or maybe I made her up. But given what you said when you came to my door..." her voice trails off, eyes going unfocused.

"What did she say?" I prompt. "Or do, or—Did she help you?"

"She told me they were starving." The words send a shiver down my spine, and I sit upright in my chair. "She said I couldn't blame them, could I?" Her mouth twists in a sneer. *"They're starving. They can't help themselves. You shouldn't be out here, where they suffer."*

I don't know what most of that means.

"The only things Hattie ever said to me were 'they're starving,' 'they're coming,' and 'they're here,'" I admit, feeling like I've disappointed her. "She didn't know anything else. Or if she did, she didn't tell me." When Laura doesn't answer, just stares, I give her a few moments to see if that will change.

It doesn't.

Eventually, I get to my feet, feeling like I should leave. She seems almost catatonic now, and certainly has no interest in continuing this conversation with me. "I'm sorry I brought it up," I tell her quietly, drinking the last of my tea. "And I'm sorry for everything that happened to you. I just needed to know that I wasn't alone. I just..." But I trail off, because I don't know what else I want. Or what else I even *could* want.

With a nudge, Moro gets to her feet, but before I can go anywhere, Laura reaches out to grab my arm, her grip surprisingly strong. "I've seen them since, you know," she tells me, not looking up from her glass. "I see them in the woods around town sometimes. It always makes me wonder when someone goes missing if it really was just an accident. Then I wonder how they survive when they aren't attacking and killing humans. Because they aren't human." She finally looks up at me, her eyes sharp.

"But I think they were once. I saw them that night talking,

using the voices of my friends when they were looking for me. They're not normal. Not *natural*. But I think before they became whatever they are, they were human."

"Why?" I blurt out, confused.

"Because only humans know how to think like that. An animal wouldn't consider using another's voice to trick its prey, would it?" Her grin is humorless and dark, but it sends a shiver down my spine. I excuse myself quickly, unable to stay here, and I head to my car so quickly I barely notice the sound of the chimes on the door when I yank it open and close it behind me.

Only when I'm in my car, with my back against my seat, do I let out a breath and sigh. Of everything I've considered, this possibility bothers me the most. That these things, these *monsters,* could've ever been human.

What kind of human *eats* its own kind?

CHAPTER THIRTEEN

I CAN FEEL MORO'S BREATH ON MY FACE AND SMELL HER SURPRISINGLY inoffensive breath long before she gives a little *woof* to wake me.

"We cannot be doing this," I mutter, eyes still closed even with her paw planted on my shoulder. "Seriously, Moro, we've done so well before now. Please don't break our streak and start being a menace during the night."

She woofs again, making sure I know without a doubt that I *will* be getting my ass out of this bed for her. It's traumatizing, but I shove myself upward, gently shooing her away from me as I break free from my comfortable, enviable slumber. "I still love you, Moro. But maybe a little less if this becomes a thing." God, this really can't become a thing.

I stumble to my feet in my t-shirt and shorts; my need to sleep while basically freezing always wins out no matter what the temperature outdoors is. Tonight I also slide on my sneakers, and groan when I see that it's a little after two am. This is *prime* sleeping time, and I definitely don't stay asleep long enough on my own to deserve Moro disrupting what little of it I get.

The back glass door is a little heavy, especially when I'm still half asleep, but I yank it open, forcing it to slide open on its track. I flip on the deck light to squint out into my fenceless backyard that opens up into the forest behind the few houses on my road. "Just hurry up, okay?" I sigh. "I want—"

Unlike every other time I've let her out, Moro takes off, running lightly down the little deck's stairs and out into the yard. She circles a few times, then moves to sniff one of the nearest trees, her tail wagging. A quick yip of excitement comes from her mouth, and with that she's gone, disappearing outside of the range of my light.

"Moro?" I ask, and my stomach suddenly clenches nervously. "Moro!" Usually when I call her, she's quick to come. And I've never seen her actually leave the yard any of the times I've let her out before off of a leash.

But tonight she doesn't come back. I don't hear her in the trees, nor the sound of her paws brushing across the debris in my yard. "MORO!" Her name comes out as a scream from my lips, and before I know it, I'm off of the deck and jogging across my yard.

What if she gets lost? I can't help that thought, but the one that whispers through my mind next is even worse.

What if one of those monsters found her?

My steps pick up until I'm all out running, my feet carrying me faster into the chilly night air and away from the safety of my lit backyard. It's not until I'm ten steps into the woods, however, that I realize just how bad of an idea this is, and how I really need to go back to the house. There's a very real chance of me getting lost once the trees start getting thicker and I can't see even a speck of light from my deck.

A rush of movement catches my eye, and I whip my head

around with a gasp, feeling a strange sense of déjà vu from that night at Bluebone Ridge. "Oh, fuck," I whisper, stumbling back. "Oh, I fucked up real bad. Shit." Every curse word I know comes bubbling to my lips, and I flex my hands against the bark of a tree behind me.

Yeah, I really should've stayed in the house.

Suddenly Moro appears, barking, her tail wagging stiffly and her ears pricked forward. She runs past me, evading me easily as I grab for her collar, and I nearly hit the ground from overbalancing in the effort. "Damn it, Moro!" I whisper, staggering. "Come *on!*" She's ignoring me, darting and bounding at something I can't see.

Finally she stops moving, and I see her standing with her tail wagging, about twenty feet away by the base of a large tree, like she's trapped something against it. Surely if it is one of those monsters, it would be fighting her. Even if it's wounded already. But she's not exactly attacking either, I note, slowing my steps as I get closer to her.

"Moro?" I breathe, and my dog looks up at me briefly, her tail wagging again like she's found something worth showing off. I still can't help my apprehension though, even as I tell myself it's probably a stray cat or raccoon or some other poor, unsuspecting animal she's scaring to death. That's what gets me the rest of the way to her, and it's not until I'm rounding the last tree before reaching Moro that I realize cats and raccoons and opossums don't wear jeans and dirty sneakers that have seen better days.

"You're not a cat," is all I can say, as my gaze falls on Cairo's face where he sits, reclining against the large tree.

His eyes open, flashing in the night like an animal's reflecting light. My stomach clenches, and the feeling only gets worse when he grins and I see the hint of fangs between his lips.

"I'm definitely not a cat," he agrees in a tired, raw voice. "And I'm probably not as charming as one either. You should go back inside." He grimaces when he tries to move, prompting Moro to step closer and nudge at his arm.

"Why?" I ask, unmoving. But alarm bells are going off as I look at him and see the blood spattered on his clothes that aren't Bluebone Ridge issue at all.

"Because you weren't supposed to know I was out here in the first place." He grimaces at Moro's next nudge and finally relents. Cairo lifts a hand and settles it on her head, scratching behind her ears. "Thanks a lot for that, by the way," he tells her flatly. "I clean you up and bring you to her, and this is the thanks I get?"

Moro's tail only wags harder, but I've never been more confused.

"You *what?*" The words send a shock of surprise through me, and I feel so strange standing above him in the woods. Belatedly, as he looks up at me, I realize he's bleeding. "What the hell happened to you?" I murmur, kneeling beside him. "Was it—" But I snatch my hand back when he grins, once more showing me too-sharp teeth.

"It was," he tells me without hesitation in a voice that holds a soft, dark chuckle. "But not for the reason you think." He moves to scratch Moro's chest, though grimaces when she tries to lick at the blood running down the side of his face and gently pushes her back. "That's gross, Moro," he tells her disapprovingly.

"You saved me." It isn't a question as my mind puts together the pieces of that night. "The voice I heard before I passed out was yours. How did you get...it..." He looks up at me balefully, and my question dies on my lips.

Because it's obvious, and I don't need him to confirm it for me, with his reflective eyes and sharp teeth. "You're hurt," I force myself to repeat, trying to keep my mind on that.

"I've been hurt worse."

"I didn't ask."

He rolls his eyes at that, settling back against the tree. "Well, it's not fatal. And you shouldn't be out here, Fern."

"Why?"

But he doesn't answer me this time, only gets comfortable with his hand on Moro as his eyes slide shut. It gives me the opportunity to survey him from where I'm kneeling, though I can't see much in the light of the moon and the useless illumination from my deck in the distance.

I can't leave him out here.

Not when he's the reason I'm alive. "Come on." I gently kick his leg, being as careful as I can be to not hurt him. "Get up, Cairo. My house is over there."

"I know." He sighs airily, which doesn't make me feel any better.

"Which is weird." I lean a little bit closer without letting myself chicken out. "We should talk about how weird that is, because it makes you sound like a stalker."

"I'd have to be human to be a stalker, wouldn't I?"

The admission sends a shiver up my spine, and I freeze with my hand outstretched toward him. Cairo opens his eyes to slits, and I see the satisfaction there. It hits me that this was his intention; he *wants* me to be afraid of him.

"You look human enough to me." Before I can chicken out, I drag him to his feet, not that he really fights me on it. "Shut up," I add when he starts to say something.

I'm definitely putting on a facade of confidence, but I don't know what else to do. Cairo walks back toward my small house with me, mostly supporting his own weight except a few times when he has to stop and lean on me, letting out sharp, hissing breaths between his teeth.

Finally, I haul him up on my deck with Moro loping inside once I open the door, wagging her tail and turning like she's welcoming him into her home. The sight makes me snort, and I shake my head at her treating him like her friend.

"You really helped her?" I close the sliding glass door and lock it while he leans on my small table, panting.

"Well, yeah. I stuck around until I could hear the ambulance coming for you. She didn't want to leave you," he adds, grinning back at me. "She almost bit me every time I got close to you for a few minutes."

"Oh." I glance back at Moro, who only wags her tail at both of us and steps forward to nudge at Cairo's hand. "I'm happy you did that. I'm happy she's okay. And I'm also pretty thrilled that I'm okay."

Making a decision, I grab his arm and bring it over my shoulder, ignoring his undignified squawk of disapproval. "Are you hungry?" I don't know where he's been, or how he's doing other than being hurt, but for some reason my question gets a grating chuckle from him.

"I'm *starving.*"

The words make me stop. We're in my bedroom, just outside my bathroom door as I stare at him. Those words make everything inside me twist with anxiety. "Don't say that."

"Why?" His eyes flash in the light, doing that creepy reflecting thing again. "Because you've heard it before? It's kind of our thing, so I'm not surprised." God, I have no idea what he means, and I'm a little afraid to ask.

I finish dragging him into the bathroom, and he helpfully sits down hard on the toilet seat with a groan. "Your teeth weren't like that," I point out quietly. When I turn on the light, he squints, looking away from it. "And you weren't sensitive to light back at Bluebone Ridge."

"Yeah," he agrees. "Because I was starving, Fern." He rolls his eyes like it's obvious, but I certainly don't understand what he's saying.

"You just told me you *are* starving."

"I was exaggerating. I'm just a little hungry right now, compared to what I was when we met." He shifts on the porcelain, grimacing, and tugs off his long-sleeved shirt without my prompting. "And when I'm starving, things are different."

I'm barely listening. I can't look away from his chest that's marred by claw marks, with dried blood crusting his olive-toned skin. "Fuck," I breathe, one hand raised like I'm going to touch. "What happened to you?"

Cairo grimaces and stands up, having to support himself on the counter to turn and examine himself in the mirror. "It's not that bad," he muses, twisting to look at his back as well as he can. But he winces and adds, "I would heal faster if I ate."

"I can fix you something?" I ask, only to have him meet my gaze in the mirror and give me an unfriendly smile.

"You can't fix me what I need. And you don't want me to eat in front of you, I promise you that, Fern," Cairo assures me in his drawl.

"God, you're being annoying." Turning away from him and his annoying charm and sharply gorgeous features, I move to the shower, where I twist the knobs using muscle memory for what I would want in terms of heat. When I turn around, I see Cairo looking at me with raised brows and a surprised look.

"You want me to shower? With you in here? Are you going to wash my back for me, Fern?" he asks tauntingly.

I give him a very enthusiastic, thorough roll of my eyes. "I liked you better when you were trying to be charming and a little mysterious. It's like you're just hoping I'm scared enough of you not to talk back."

"Are you?"

"Clearly not." But I watch as he touches the scratches on his chest, wincing every time. The ones on his back look gnarlier, and there's blood and dirt caked on them, where his shirt was torn and he hit the ground. "I could help you, though. I could at least help clean you up."

"I've been in worse shape." His hissing reply is oddly flat, his voice changing in a way I can't comprehend. He sees me looking at him in the mirror and sighs, baring his teeth that are sharp, but not fangs like the things at Bluebone Ridge.

"Were you one of the ones in the dorm? Who killed Sam or Esther?" I ask. My words are barely audible over the shower, and I can't stop staring at him. The silence between us stretches until all I can hear is the shower and Moro's panting from the bed in the other room.

Finally, Cairo turns to look at me, surveying my face. He reaches out and reluctantly flips off the lights, immediately closing his eyes in relief as his shoulders fall. "No," he tells me, tilting his head back against the mirror over my sink. The action bares his throat and all of his upper body to me, but I remind myself it is *definitely* not polite to stare.

Not that it stops me.

At all.

Without the blood and the painful wounds, he would be gorgeous. Hell, even with them he's terrifyingly feral and beautiful. I know he isn't human. That thought runs over and over in my head. But for some reason, I can't liken him to the monsters from the dorm or the one that slammed me into the asphalt and bit my shoulder.

"But that shouldn't make you feel better." His eyes open, shining in the light from the small window. They reflect like moons in his face, shiny white like Moro's when she's outside and looking at me with the deck light reflecting in her gaze. "Because while I didn't kill them, I've killed others. I do what I have to in order to survive, Fern." He shows me his teeth when he says it, prompting me to bite my lip so I don't make the fearful noise he's looking for.

With just the bedroom light instead of the bathroom light, he looks different, somehow. Like he blends in with the shadows when he's still, and every time his eyes move, I catch a sliver of light reflected from them. "Why do your eyes do that?"

He blinks in the low light, and touches his chest, running his fingers over the wounds there. "Same reason Moro's do," he murmurs. "I'm not a biologist, Fern. I can't tell you the specifics. But I can see much better than you in the dark."

I swear I see him run his tongue over his teeth as he turns and surveys himself in the mirror, but I can't be sure. "Pretty sure a biologist would have a field day with you. Don't you need, like, a cryptozoologist to study whatever it is you are?" I notice him turn to glance at me, and feel suddenly self-conscious. "What?"

"I just wasn't expecting such a rational answer." He glances at the running shower, then at me. "I really don't *need* to shower, you know. The others in the woods and on the mountain don't care if I'm dirty or bloody or anything else. And I'll heal in a few days."

Biting my lip, I look over his chest at the gouged claw marks. I have no idea how he'll heal in a few days, but I say nothing. "Well, you're in my house, and I'm offended by you," I say. "So you're showering."

"Are you going to get my back for me?" I can practically hear him roll his eyes with the words, and I know he's expecting me to back out. To walk away and leave him here with Moro as his watchdog to make sure he doesn't drown.

And I almost do.

But I stop, because there's something about him, beneath the arrogance and the monstrous teeth and eyes.

Cairo saved my life.

"Yeah. So get in." I gesture at my shower, which is arguably my favorite part of the house and probably why I chose to go for it, apart from the seclusion and surrounding woods. "We're losing hot water, and I'm not scrubbing off blood in the cold."

He doesn't move at my words, but the moment I silently celebrate my victory for catching him off guard, Cairo gives a sudden scoff. He reaches for his jeans and, still facing me, unbuttons them. Right in front of me. While I'm watching.

I turn away just as he tugs them down his thighs, staring dutifully at the corner of the bathroom as my embarrassment sends a rush of heat through my veins. "Yeah, okay, I was not expecting you to do that," I admit, partially to myself.

"What did you think I was going to do? Get in the shower wearing denim?" I hear the glass door slide back, but he makes no noise as he steps inside. Suddenly, I'm not so sure about my bravado in offering to do his back for him.

"You can run away if you want," Cairo says over the spray. I'm glad for the darkness, because it means I can look *almost* anywhere without seeing all of him.

Quickly, however, I decide I won't run away. I may not be willing to waltz into the shower with the monster who saved my life, but that's more about my personal hangups about strange, naked men in my bathroom rather than what he is.

Whatever he is. Since he doesn't seem willing to give me a straight answer on that.

I sit down on the toilet lid, leaning back against the tank

and looking at the ceiling. "Are you going to tell me what you are exactly?" I ask, and my voice echoes in the small space.

He hums noncommittally, still not giving me a real answer. I hear something thicker than water hit my shower floor, and grimace. God, I am not looking forward to cleaning that up in the morning, since it sure as hell won't be tonight. "Fine, okay, if you won't tell me that, even though it seems like a weird secret to keep, I have another question."

"Of course you do." Cairo sounds resigned, but not at all surprised. "You're always so full of questions, especially when it would be better for you not to be."

For a few moments I sit with that, running my fingers over the top of my counter just for the feel of it. While this is my favorite bathroom in the house, it's also the one I was in when I drove a pair of scissors into my hand and got myself locked up in Bluebone Ridge in the first place.

"You know, I was here when it happened." I don't know why I say it. I doubt he cares, and it's a weird thing to bring up of my own free will, like it's a conversation point instead of traumatic and dramatic oversharing. "When I, you know..." Not knowing if he can see me, I still lift my other hand and make dramatic stabbing motions toward my hand on the counter, giving it a little creaky sound effect.

Cairo snorts, so I assume he's able to appreciate the full effect. "How poetic. What's your question, Fern?"

Part of me is sure he isn't going to answer, but the other part of me, the buried optimist who's normally smothered by doubt and overstimulation and whatever else I pile on myself, pokes her head up. "Back at Bluebone that night when...you know."

"I do."

I glare at his little quip, but if he notices, he doesn't speak. "When I was in my room... Actually, I have two questions.

There was one of those things—creatures," I amend. After all, he's the same thing, even if he doesn't look quite like them right now. "In my doorway. Coming inside. But it got distracted, and something else dragged it away."

This time I notice he's not moving, judging by the way the water spray sounds the same instead of like he's rinsing off.

"Was that you?"

The sound of the spray changes, but he doesn't answer for a few seconds. I'm not sure why it's such a complicated answer, but finally, carefully, he says, "Yeah. It was me."

"Thank you."

"But then you fucked it up by leaving," Cairo sighs, nearly cutting me off. "Hattie told you to stay, didn't she? You're lucky Moro—"

"Is Hattie dead?" I don't mean to interrupt him, but I can't help it. My face turns toward the shower, and something like hope strangles in my chest, for a girl I barely knew but who probably saved my life.

"I don't know."

"Oh."

"Was that your second question?"

I lean back again, the top of the tank digging uncomfortably into my upper back. "No."

His sigh is audible over everything, even Moro's panting. "Of course it wasn't."

I consider throwing something at him, though I'm sure it would lose its efficacy when I have to lob it over the glass shower door. Not only that, but I don't want to risk knocking over the mess of half-empty bottles in my shower I will undoubtedly have to deal with in the morning, along with the blood.

"Something was calling my name. But it sounded weird, you know? Sort of recognizable, but sort of not. That's why I went to the stairwell. But when I got there, it was just one of them. One of you." God, I don't know how to refer to them, when Cairo seems so different from the creatures that ripped Sam and the others apart. "I can't really explain it right to make it make sense, I guess. Sorry. That's not really a question."

There's silence in the bathroom, apart from the spray of water and Moro's panting. She's stretched out on the bed and mostly asleep now, not looking like she has any intention of going on another midnight jaunt in the woods.

"Fern?" The voice that comes from the shower makes the hair on the back of my neck stand on end, and I nearly choke on air. It's a strange mix of many voices and nothing all at once, just like that night.

"They're starving, Fern." Hattie's voice echoes in the shower, and I give a full-body shudder and bolt to my feet on the floor.

"How are you—"

"Any allergies?" It takes a few seconds for me to remember the voice of the cook in the staff kitchen.

"Stop."

"We're all sort of unwell here. I'll need a little more than that to know who you mean." I have no idea how he's mimicking my conversation with Sam so perfectly, or how he heard it, but my heart races in response.

"I said *stop!*" I all but yell. Every part of me is on edge, but thankfully, Cairo doesn't do it again. The shower door opens, hitting me with a face full of steam. Before I can go anywhere at all, Cairo is in front of me and his hands come up to cradle my face as he drips onto the bathmat below us.

"I'm a monster, Fern," he purrs, in a voice that's barely human. "No matter how you want to look at me and differentiate me from the others that night, I'm still just as much of a monster as them."

"But you look—"

"Mostly human?" He strokes his thumb over my lower lip, and my brain unhelpfully reminds me that he's naked, and all I'm wearing is my sleep shorts and thin t-shirt. "Don't you think that's the point? It's much easier to get close to you like this, to get close to any human, when we don't look like monsters."

I have so many questions, but the only one that comes out of my mouth is the one I didn't want to ask.

"Why did you save me?"

We stand there, with his hands on my face and my fingers coming up to grip his wrists, though I'm not pulling him away. My heart rushes in my chest, protesting and trying to get free from the monster in front of us, who has the most beautiful eyes I've ever seen. Especially in the dark, when they catch and reflect little bits of light.

"I don't know," Cairo admits finally, and there's a raw honesty in his words I can't help but believe. "I don't think I've decided yet. But you should be more careful, little bird." The nickname makes my stomach twist, and I tell myself it's from fear, even as he pushes me a step back so I'm pressed against my bathroom counter and Cairo is only inches from me.

"Why?"

"Because I haven't decided if I'm willing to save you again... or if next time, I'll be the one coming to kill you." Without warning, he lunges forward in a smooth and graceful motion that's too fast for me to even register, and his lips press against mine. It's sweet for all of a second until I feel the prick of his teeth on my bottom lip.

Cairo takes advantage of my small, surprised sound, by licking his tongue into my mouth like he's trying to taste me. The realization that *he is,* sends a shiver through me, and I grip his wrists tighter until my nails are digging into his skin—not that he seems to mind.

When he pulls away, it seems to be difficult for him, and he gives a little sound that's not entirely human while running a hand through his hair. "Go away, Fern," Cairo sighs, eyes flashing as he looks at me sidelong. "Let me get dressed and leave before I do something I'll probably regret."

"Like what?" I can't keep the words from coming out of my mouth, and his strangled scoff is half exasperation, half amusement.

"Like eat you."

The following click of his teeth is enough to send me walking out of the bathroom, though I do, at least, manage not to run as I stride past Moro with a quick, nervous touch to her fur. Then I head back to the living room, as if distance will protect me from the creature in my bathroom and his taste that lingers on my lips longer than it should.

CHAPTER FOURTEEN

Being woken up by my cellphone vibrating with a vendetta under my face is not pleasant, and I groan at the feeling, trying to ignore it. "Let me sleep," I groan when it goes off again. "Please, for the love of God..." I grab my phone and sit up, noticing the unfamiliar but local number before I answer.

"Hello?" All traces of irritation are gone, though most of my drowsiness remains. According to my phone, it's ten am, which is way later than I normally sleep, but today is a bit of a special occasion.

I wasn't able to fall asleep for hours after Cairo left silently, without a word to me, as he slipped out at some point while I was recovering on the couch and staring at the ceiling with the television on.

"Hello, Fern? Sorry to bother you. I didn't think you'd still be asleep." I feel like I should know the voice, but my brain isn't connecting the dots.

"Umm...good morning?" It comes out as a question, and I'm still frantically trying to figure out who it is. "Sorry, but may I ask who's calling? You sound familiar, but—"

"Oh! I'm so sorry. This is Dr. Radley." The relief at no longer being confused is quickly followed by a sinking, unhappy feeling in the pit of my stomach.

"Oh, hi!" I throw as much false positivity into my voice as I can, and Moro flops over onto her back on the bed, worming her way into my warm spot as I watch her do it. At least one of us is sure I'm actually getting up for the day. Then again, what does she really have to do other than look cute, eat, and not shit on my floor?

Maybe she thinks she put in a full night's work by finding Cairo.

Belatedly, I realize he never told me why he was in such bad shape to begin with. Though I don't know why I expect he would've answered me, even if I'd throttled him and tried to get the answer—

"What?" I blink, realizing Dr. Radley has been speaking and I have no idea what she's been saying. "I am so sorry. I'm really out of it. Uh, I didn't sleep well last night."

"I wouldn't be surprised if you're having quite a bit of difficulty sleeping now." Her voice is full of concern and care, but I don't want it. The reason she thinks I didn't sleep isn't accurate, but I can't tell her that. *"I spoke to your doctors at the hospital. I was concerned about you after what happened."*

I already don't like where this is going, but I don't say anything.

"I think it would be best if we continued your sessions. You won't owe me anything, of course. Since Bluebone's insurance is covering all of your care." Vaguely, I realize I knew that. Mom made the doctors promise I would not be paying a damn thing.

But that doesn't make me want to go to Dr. Radley any more than I already do. Still, I know I can't refuse without seeming weird about it. "I've actually been doing better than I thought I would. You know, all things considered," I continue, trying for a weak attempt at getting out of this. But I know it won't work even before she starts talking again.

"I'm glad about that, Fern. But I told you in your last session at Bluebone that I thought you would benefit from regular therapy sessions. I still feel that way, and not just because of the incident. There's time in my schedule for me to start seeing you as your regular therapist, and I want to make sure you heal from this." She lets out a soft breath, and her voice gentles. *"I feel responsible, in my own way. You're my patient, and none of that should have ever happened to you or anyone else. Please let me get you set with ways to cope, at least. I want to be there to help you. I want to see you come out of this stronger than before."*

Her pep talk is almost inspiring, and if I weren't so tired, I would be impressed. Running a hand through my blonde hair, I tug at tangles created by how restlessly I slept. "I...yeah," I acquiesce at last. I don't know how I could actually deny her, when I'm sure she could make this mandatory based on my time at Bluebone Ridge in the first place. Even my mom would agree, and with my luck, she'd drive out here just to throw me in the back of her car and dump me at Dr. Radley's office.

"Could you tell me where your office is? And, umm, my schedule is pretty open." Lately all I do is entertain monsters, walk my dog, and go see old ladies who had a similar experience in Bluebone that I did.

They're starving.

The words whisper on repeat in my mind, never quite leaving, though that is something I will not be telling Dr. Radley.

"How about today? Could you make this afternoon work?" I've never met a more eager therapist, and suddenly, I really wish she cared less about her job and her ethical responsibilities. Grimacing, I flop down on the bed beside Moro.

I don't exactly have a valid excuse to get out of this, though I wrinkle my nose in distaste. "Yeah, I could do that. Just tell me what time, and where and...whatever." God, I'll have to do laundry. I've been avoiding it for a week, and I guess this is my wake-up call. It's that, or dig through the hamper hanging on my door for clothes that don't stink and hope for the best.

No, I have more self-respect than that today, I decide, as Dr. Radley tells me she'll text me the address and a reminder. I have a few hours longer to suffer here in bed or get coffee, and I tell myself that by four this afternoon, I'll be a real person again, with motivation and goals and clean clothes.

To the surprise of no one, especially not myself, I am not a real person when four p.m. rolls around. But I have clean clothes, and that is something I'm counting as a win. I hadn't considered that I'd be leaving Moro here, and all I can hope for is that she doesn't destroy the house.

"Seriously," I tell her, checking that she has dry food and water along with the bone I'm giving her on my way out the door. I kneel in front of her, my hair up in a ponytail instead of being thoroughly brushed, and wearing a t-shirt and leggings along with my trusty sneakers that were in their prime some-time four years ago. "I can't afford a new couch. Or a new kitchen. I don't know if you've noticed, but I'm sort of doing odd freelance jobs online at the moment. So I need you to, you know, remember our living situation before you tear up anything. Okay?"

Moro just watches me, ears up, in that attentive way that she's good at. It's both a little unnerving and also very reassur-ing, so I give her one last scratch behind her left ear that has her head tilting to the side in appreciation, and then I pick up the filled, all natural bone from the counter to give to her as tribute.

The drive isn't bad, since Dr. Radley is just in town. But it does take me a few times of circling the small downtown roundabout before I see the building where her office takes up space on the third floor, and another circuit before I actually figure out where to park.

By then, I'm nearly late, so I bolt out of my car once it's parked, hoping I'm in the right place. I jog down the sidewalk with my phone and keys in hand, silently wishing I'd been able to say *no thank you* to more sessions with Dr. Radley.

Whirling around the corner of the building, I stumble to a stop, however, when I almost run into a woman coming my way.

Or...so I think until I take a better look at her. She isn't walking at all, just standing there, and her dark eyes watch as I try to regain my balance instead of hitting the sidewalk without offering to help.

"Sorry." I'm not sure I mean the apology, since it feels strange that she's *just standing there.* The woman only tilts her head the other way, her black hair like a shining curtain in the afternoon sun.

Yet again, she doesn't say anything. She just stands there, *looking* at me. A shiver goes up my spine at her weirdness, and I tell myself it's leftover from everything that's gone on. Some people are just weird.

Maybe she's drunk.

Or on drugs in the middle of the afternoon in town, surrounded by businesses and people.

Drunk is a little more likely...but she's probably just weird.

I watch her as I walk, not being particularly subtle about it, and I feel the need to give her a wide berth as I circle around her on the sidewalk. Still, she doesn't say a word. It isn't until I'm at the door that she speaks, and by then, I'm trying to focus on anything else.

"Good luck." Her voice is a little light, a little soft. But when I look up at her to ask if she's talking to me and why I would need *luck* to go see a therapist, the spot where she stood is empty.

It's just me, and the couple arguing down the block in front of one of the two diners in Whippoorwill Gap. Arguably the better one, too, and part of me really wants to reward my therapeutic efforts after this with a grilled cheese, onion rings, and a dreamsicle ice cream cone.

The building smells a little musty with age, but the too-sweet smell barely affects me, given that I've lived in old towns most of my life. It's a common smell for places like this, and I double-check the directory before heading up the stairs, deciding this is one of the few times I'd rather work out my excess energy by abusing my knees than taking the elevator and having the extra few seconds to panic.

There's nothing I can do now, and it's not like she can *do* anything to me. I hope. No more getting committed. No more Bluebone Ridge. No more *monsters* except the one in my woods. Going up the stairs also helps me focus on rehearsing the same story I told the cops in the hospital, when I pleaded innocence and amnesia instead of admitting that I saw monsters in the sanitarium, for all the good that did me.

By the time I reach her door and find an old-fashioned wooden frame with frosted glass, I'm out of breath and regretting my decision to take the stairs. Clearly, I overestimated myself. And my stamina. *Especially* my stamina, given the way I have to lean on the wall and pant for almost a minute before I can breathe like a normal person again. When finally I feel like I don't look like as much of a mess as I am, I tap lightly on the door, just as her text instructed.

Maybe she won't answer, I think to myself, crossing my fingers behind my back. But my hopes are dashed only seconds later when the door opens to show Dr. Radley standing there in a dark pantsuit, her hair pulled back into a bun and her glasses on a chain around her neck. "I was scared you got lost, Fern," she greets, a small smile curling over her lips. "You're late."

Surreptitiously, I check the clock on her desk as I walk in, surprised at her comment when I see it's literally two after four. "Oh, umm...sorry," I apologize, unsure. "I, uh, tripped outside. It was stupid." That's not the whole story, but I'm not about to tell her a weird woman stared at me and it freaked me out, and I needed to take the stairs to shake it off.

That seems like a stupid, fanciful excuse that she won't believe. Dr. Radley doesn't reply. She gestures for me to sit on the leather, overstuffed couch that looks more aesthetic than comfortable. But I'm not going to complain. I sit on it and scoot to the back, fighting the urge to use it as a Slip 'N Slide since it would be way too easy to just whip around on the leather.

Dr. Radley sits in an armchair that's just as structured and uncomfortable looking as the one from her Bluebone Ridge office. Looking around, I find that much of the decor is similar, and a bit dated. There are pictures of a family on one wall, kids smiling in the snow in front of a large lodge built in the woods. The family changes, kids getting older, until finally the two girls become one unsmiling blonde, who glares at the camera like she'd rather be anywhere else.

"That's me," Dr. Radley states, noticing where I'm looking. "I stopped liking pictures being taken of me when I was a teenager." But she smiles fondly at her wall of memories. "That's our lodge up in the mountains near here. My grandparents bought it dirt cheap, and my family spent all the time we could up there."

"That seems nice," I respond, wondering why in the later pictures, the family never seems together. But it's not my business, and I don't ask. "Were you born around here, then?"

"In Seattle, actually. My mom moved there for school, where she met my father. What about you?"

"Tacoma," I say. "My parents both lived there. Then my dad died and we moved. Not here, though. I bought a house out here just a couple of years ago."

There's the notepad again, appearing in her hands just like it had every time at Bluebone. She scratches down something in her quick handwriting, giving an interested nod. "Why all the way out here?"

"Because I like the quiet. I don't do too well in cities. I get, uh"—my smile becomes a small grimace—"overstimulated really easily. So, I like being alone out here. It's nice." My fingers tap my opposite palm, and my curiosity grows when she writes down more in her notepad.

"Did you ever go up into the mountains as a kid? A lot of the locals spent their summers in lodges or finding trouble in the Cascades," she inquires, giving me a small, familiar smile.

"No, Dad and I went hiking a few times a long, *long* time ago. I think maybe once or twice those hikes were in the Cascades? But..." I shrug my shoulders, unsure. "Dad died when I was twelve, and he wasn't doing so well for a year before that. I don't remember many of the hiking trails he took me on. Just that a few were cold and steep, and I could see what I thought was all of Washington at some trailhead when I was like, eight." I can't help but smile at the memory, and the way my dad was the opposite of my mom in every way.

A pang of sadness goes through me, and my heart twists like a washcloth being wrung out in my chest. I *miss* my dad, and that emptiness has never once gone away, only lessened a little with time, giving me so many other things to worry about.

If Dad were here, I never would've ended up in Bluebone Ridge.

"What?" Realizing she's asked me something else, I blink up at Dr. Radley with a frown. "Sorry. I'm a bit out of it today."

"I was just asking if you wanted to tell me what happened that night at Bluebone. The last night," she clarifies, as if she needs to. My shoulders stiffen, but I force myself to relax with a sigh. I knew she'd do this, so I can't be unhappy or surprised now. What other reason would she have to take an interest in me, when I'm sure insurance companies or some legal team is breathing down her neck just to make sure I don't sue for something? Though I don't know what I would sue for. Emotional trauma?

The words come out of my mouth like a monologue I've memorized, and I'm able to detach from the story to see when Dr. Radley writes anything down. I mention finding Sam's body, and Hattie being in my room. Just like I had to the police. I mention running outside, of course, and tell her how I yelled and screamed in the parking lot, which is obviously a lie. I don't say a word about Moro, either. If anyone could get her taken away from me, it would be an employee of the sanitarium. In the end, I explain that something hit me, and I fell onto the asphalt, hitting my head hard enough to knock me out.

"There are some parts I just don't remember." I sigh, putting my head in my hands. "I keep trying. I want to remember what happened to Hattie, or what was doing that to Sam."

"And you didn't hear anything? A certain kind of animal, maybe? Or a person?"

The question makes the hair at the back of my neck stand up, and I glance up at her with genuine confusion. "A person? Well, I mean, I heard people screaming—"

"Anything else? Weird voices?" She's paused in her writing now, and her attention is fixed on me. "Nothing strange at all?"

She's pushing me for something, and I try to scan my

words to make sure I didn't say anything I shouldn't have. My hands twist in front of me, fingers pushing into the fresh scar on my palm. I watch Dr. Radley carefully, and then just shake my head. "No? I don't think so. Just a lot of screaming."

Her pen taps on the notepad in her lap, but my therapist doesn't look upset. She looks interested, though I can't figure out what about my non-answer could serve to interest her, if she was looking for some other answer. I end up tapping my fingers along with her, copying the movement without a pen. Something about her silence puts me on edge, giving me the slightly hazy feeling I got the day I dramatically rammed scissors into my palm.

Suddenly, the room feels like too much. Every little sound between the walls, the hum of electricity, and even the soft whirring of the fan beats against my temples like machine-gun bullets. I want to leave. But more than that, I don't want her to see. She doesn't know me well enough, and I'm not quite bad enough for this to be obvious, but I know it will be if this goes on for much longer.

"I'd like to see you every week." I tune into her words, nodding along with them, my fingers still tapping even though her pen is now writing. "If that fits into your schedule?"

Again I nod, but when she looks up, I realize she's looking for a verbal answer instead. "Sure. Umm...yeah. Whatever you think. I want to move past this." My voice sounds hollow even to my ears, and I check my phone like I have some place to be.

Which I do. It's just anywhere but here.

A few more words of small talk filter in and out of my ears like a bad radio broadcast, and when Dr. Radley stands, I'm quick to lunge to my feet as well. That earns me a quick look, and I offer her an apologetic smile and an escort to the door while she asks, in her friendly and calm way, if I'm all right.

"I've just been tired." I sigh, trying to look like I mean it.

"Tired after...all of it. I want to move past it, but it's hard, you know?" I hate that I've opened myself up for more of a conversation, but luckily, she just nods and opens the door.

"I want to help you however I can, Fern," the therapist agrees. "But you have to *let* me. Otherwise..." She shrugs her shoulders and offers me a plaintive grin, tucking her hair behind her ear even though there's nothing out of place to tuck back. "Well, I can't help you if you won't let me. Have a safe week, all right? We'll talk more next Tuesday."

Somehow, I make it out of her office without triggering her suspicions, and down the stairs without falling over myself and tripping. I feel a lot like I did that day at the coffee shop, not that it was the first time, and today I hope there's no one waiting for me at home.

My hand is out and reaching for the door when it suddenly opens, causing me to stumble unexpectedly. But someone steadies me, their grip firm on my shoulder before I can trip over the threshold and hit my face on the sidewalk.

"You're all right." It's not a question coming from the woman who stood on the sidewalk earlier. Her dark eyes are flat as she looks me up and down, though I can't read what she could be thinking. "I've got you." The words feel more relevant than just holding me from falling, and she's slow to take her hand away.

She looks so familiar, though I can't figure out why. It's something about her face, but I know I've never met her in my life before...probably. "Do I know you?" I ask, still standing in the middle of the door.

Slowly, she shakes her head, eyes on me the entire time. "We've never met." But when I take a deep, shuddering breath, she steps back and pulls me out with her into the sunlight and the cool late summer afternoon. "But you're okay."

My soft laugh is derisive, and not particularly amused.

"Oh, I'm far from that most days of the week," I tell the strange lady. In the sun and this close, I guess she's around my age, if maybe a little older.

"But this day of the week you can be." She looks up toward the upper floors of the building, her eyes narrowed a little bit. Her mouth opens again, but she only closes it and gives a small shake of her head. "Go home, little bird," she says with a sigh, dropping my arm. "She can't follow you home."

"How do you—" But she doesn't stick around to answer. She only turns and walks away, her skirt billowing around her thighs and her steps so perfectly balanced and placed that she almost looks like she's on her own personal runway.

Only then do I realize she's barefoot on a sidewalk in the middle of town.

CHAPTER FIFTEEN

WHEN I MAKE IT HOME, IT'S TO THE SIGHT OF A THANKFULLY EMPTY driveway, and a house still standing. I shove myself out of the car and into the house without really seeing where I'm going. Overwhelmed is an understatement, and I can only be distantly grateful when I see no obvious damage to the house. Moro gets up when I come in, approaching me with soft whines and a few touches to my hands.

"I'm fine," I lie, closing my eyes. I reach up with one hand, pressing my palm to my face. The longer I stand here, the more I feel like I'm going to fall apart. And that's not acceptable right now, or preferably ever. A few more deep breaths don't do me much good, and I let out a sharp breath as I walk into the end table by my sofa.

"Fuck." Biting my lip, I toss my phone and keys onto the counter, though the clatter only makes me wince. It also makes me realize my house is too small, too *close* for me to stay inside right now. I need *out*, when I thought I needed *in*.

My fingers scrabble at the sliding door for a few seconds, until I realize I'm being stupid and that I have to unlock it first.

A low, derisive scoff leaves me at my stupidity, and finally I manage to yank it back, the glass slides open to hit the frame and bounce back just a little. But I barely remember to close it before I'm out on the tiny deck that's only big enough for the small, hardy plants I keep on the wooden railings.

Moro is the first one out onto the grass, but only barely. I'm right behind her and following around the yard, not really caring where we go as long as we're moving instead of standing still.

I'm okay, I tell myself, and wish I could believe it. I don't know what has me so worked up, so unwell, this evening, but I can't help it when I get like this.

Maybe Dr. Radley was worse for me than I thought, or the stress of lying to her finally made me snap for the day. My plans for going to the diner are long-ruined now, and instead of hunger, I just feel the churning of nausea in my gut while I follow Moro.

"I'm fine," I whisper, my hands twisting together in front of me, barely feeling it when my nails sink into the scar on my palm, and I only belatedly notice tripping over the root of an exposed tree as we walk into the woods. "It's okay, I'm fine—"

Moro's frantic barking edges into my consciousness, but isn't enough to pull me out of my thoughts. I keep walking, the bird noise strangely dying out from the trees, instead of increasing, until the canopy of leaves overhead makes it look like the sun is close to setting, instead of dusk being hours away. But I just need to move. I just need to keep doing stuff, keep making my legs work to keep my mind off of—

The thing that steps out from behind a tree in front of me isn't Moro. It rises on two legs instead of standing on four and surveys me with black eyes set in a hollow, sharp face. Its appearance is enough to break through my almost dissociation, and my lips fall open in a gasp, though I can't make a sound as my throat closes in fear, stopping anything that might come out.

"Moro?" I finally breathe, but when I don't hear her, I turn around, afraid that in my haze, she's been killed. If so, then it would be all my fault, and the thought causes my fingers to dig deeper into my palm until I hiss with pain. But I see her a second later, her eyes trained on the creature, hackles up in a silent snarl and her ruff raised, fur up all along her spine. Beside her, silent and watchful, is Cairo.

The relief is short-lived when he doesn't immediately do anything, but when I start to say something, he reaches up and presses a finger to his lips. When I press mine together, he moves forward, Moro coming with him, until he's standing beside me and looking much better than he did last night.

"You just wander around without thinking. Don't you, little bird?" he muses. The nickname isn't new, but something about it makes a part of my brain light up, as if I'm missing something.

"Are you going to—?"

"Chase him away? No." He glances down at my hands and makes a noise in his throat before reaching out to pry my hands away from one another. "Though if you bleed out here, he's going to be a little upset."

My gaze slides slowly back to the creature standing in front of us in the woods, who stares at me sullenly, like he's studying me. It hits me that he doesn't look exactly like the ones I saw at Bluebone Ridge, though I can't exactly pinpoint the differences, save for the way he looks just a little bit more human.

"Hi?" I offer, suddenly feeling rude. If Cairo is one of them, then that means they aren't animals. They're intelligent, and basically people when they want to be, unless Cairo is different. "Sorry, I umm, almost screamed at you."

He snorts and rolls his dark eyes to Cairo. "You would," the thing says, in a low voice that sounds *exactly* like the man next to me. But Cairo only grimaces back at him. "She'll break."

"She didn't," Cairo replies. "Now go away before I have to show you my teeth." There's a warning in his dark eyes, and he definitely doesn't seem as exhausted as last night. When the creature doesn't move right away, Cairo does just that; lifts his lip a little, to display the edges of his shiny, white fangs.

That does it, though I don't know how or why. The creature turns and strides away until he's invisible in the trees, and I can breathe normally. But when I try to tug my hand free of Cairo's, he doesn't let me.

"What have you done to yourself?" he scolds, glancing down at the red scratches on my palm that, now that I'm looking as well, make it look like I was trying to tear open my skin. "And how did you not notice him until you nearly walked right into him? Which, by the way, would've been unfortunate."

"For me?" I ask, shaking free to rub my thumb over the marks with a hiss.

"For him," Cairo corrects. But he pushes my hand away again, then grips my chin and pulls my face up to meet his gaze. "Oh, you're not doing so well, are you?" he asks while searching my eyes. "I thought I smelled it on you. But I wasn't sure. You always smell a little anxious."

His words are all so strange that I have to stand there to let them process. The idea that he can *smell* when I'm upset or anxious is unnerving, and I can't help the question that falls from my lips before I can shove the words back in. "Can you smell other moods too?"

Cairo blinks, one brow arching toward his bangs. "Yes," he answers simply. "Some are easier than others to differentiate, but I've had a lot of practice." Instead of asking more, I simply watch his face, hoping he'll give something away.

He doesn't, of course. He's just as hard to read as he was every time I've seen him, and with his attention fixed all on me, I feel more unnerved than certain about his intentions.

"Why are you in my woods?" I murmur at last, searching his face for any tiny clue. "I won't lie, Cairo. It still feels a little like you're stalking me." He just fixes me with that look, and my stomach clenches a little. "Holy shit, are you stalking me?"

The only answer I get is a little shrug, and Moro whines, prompting me to look down. "Ouch!" I gasp when Cairo runs his fingers a little harder over the scar that I've been messing with, his nail running along the mark. "What are you doing?"

"The same thing you were doing. Only I'm being nicer about it." He tugs me closer without explanation, his eyes on mine once more, brows furrowed. "You're not doing so well," he says again, his voice soft. But this time, it's not a question like it was before.

"I'm fine," I deny, though I still feel like I'm falling apart at the seams. Especially now, with the adrenaline from what we saw out here wearing off. Thinking of it makes me turn, and I can't help but look between the trees to see if there are any more of them, or if I can see anything out of the ordinary. "Where did it—he—come from? Why—?"

Cairo crushes me to his chest suddenly, and my brain goes blank. All of my thoughts snap right to him and this, as his touch grounds me and brings me back to this moment. Carefully I reach up, my hands twisting in the long-sleeved t-shirt that hugs his form. He's not dressed for late summer when it's particularly cool out here, but I'm not doing much better in my own lightweight shirt and loose pants.

It's...nice, I have to admit to myself. Somehow, his being right here and holding me this tightly keeps my mind in the present, instead of overworking itself. With my grip on his shirt and my nose pressed to his shoulder, it's easier to focus on things other than the universe and floating above the trees while I just try to go through the motions.

"I have problems, you know," I find myself murmuring into his shirt.

Cairo snorts. "Join the club, little bird."

"And I have questions. A lot of them, and if you're trapping yourself with me—" My words end in a very undignified squawk as I suddenly find myself up off the ground, dangling over his shoulder. "Cairo!" I howl, scrambling for purchase as he walks. "What are you doing?!"

"You're such a good girl, Moro," Cairo praises, totally ignoring me. "Even if you did start barking and wanted to rip up the couch today because you were bored without Fern. That's okay. I'm bored without her too."

A shudder goes through me, my fingers cold and gripping against his shirt. "How did you know that?" I breathe. "Seriously, are you stalking me? Watching my house? Are you—"

He pulls me down hard, causing my back to slam against a tree, though he doesn't let the back of my head come near it. Cairo tilts his head to look at me, his eyes seeming so dark that he almost has no iris. "You have so many questions, little bird," he muses, leaning close to me. "It's like you forget I could eat you and barely feel bad about it."

"Okay, but...you *would* feel bad about it. So you won't. Right?" I ask, hopeful, nervous, and anxious all at once. His warmth radiates against me, and when he reaches out to lightly grip my jaw with one hand, I force myself not to flinch. I want to prove that I'm not afraid of him, or at least die trying.

Cairo rolls his eyes, and before I can blink, I'm back over his shoulder. My view includes Moro as she walks at his side like a very loyal puppy and his ass in the well-fitted jeans he was wearing last night, still stained with blood. Well, at least he has a new shirt. Beggars can't be choosers when they're thrown over a man's shoulder, I tell myself, and try not to focus on the iron band of his arm across the backs of my thighs. I hear his feet on my deck stairs rather than see where we are, and he slides open the door to my small house with a quick, easy motion. Moro goes in first, like always, and I give a protesting struggle with an irritated groan on my lips.

"My legs aren't broken."

"Maybe I like carrying you."

"Maybe you're a stalker."

He sighs at that, and seconds later, Cairo grips the back of my shirt as he pulls me back down. But he doesn't let me stand up. Instead, he tosses me onto my sofa, dropping me there on my back so I can see my ceiling. At least until he leans over me, caging me in with his arms. "You don't smell right," he informs me, mouth open as he inhales. I can still see the tips of his fangs, and before he can walk away, I reach up to grab his hand.

"Why didn't you look like that at Bluebone Ridge?" I ask, getting to my feet when he tries to pull away. "Cairo!" I grab the back of his shirt with my other hand, refusing to let him go. Even with my heart racing and my brain churning overtime, I refuse to let him walk away. Not when I need to know. "Answer me!"

When he doesn't answer, I do something stupid. I whirl around in front of him and shove him back, or try to, hoping to surprise him into sitting down so I can have some kind of leverage, some kind of intimidation factor, while I'm on my feet and he isn't.

Even though he doesn't appear that muscular, he doesn't move an inch. But Cairo does snarl, his teeth on display, and I barely get a chance to regret my decision before my back is against the wall, lifted high enough that my feet dangle in the air at least six inches above the ground.

"Because, Fern," he snaps, his eyes seeming to get darker, pupils expanding like they'll pull me in and trap me in his gaze. "Because that night at the sanitarium, I was *starving*." He shows me his fangs, all of his teeth sharp like they've been filed to points. "I was so fucking hungry, and I worried that if I didn't eat, then I wouldn't be able to protect you. To save you from them." He sneers the words, getting closer to my face. His hand is tight around my throat, keeping me aloft, but when I give a soft noise of anxiety, he presses one thigh between both of mine so I'm no longer dangling from just my neck.

While the support is appreciated, part of my brain can't help thinking about just *where* his leg is, and how thin my leggings are.

"I don't understand," I breathe, my eyes never leaving his. "What did you do, Cairo?"

He leans forward until his lips brush my jaw and licks against my skin like he can't quite help himself. "I did what I had to do," he whispers, in a tone that tells me he doesn't regret one bit of whatever that is.

"While you ran around looking for an escape and attracting more of my kind to you, I sated my hunger. I tore Esther apart in the lobby while I kept an eye on you." He licks again, a little bit lower, and I shiver, suddenly regretting pissing him off.

"I was *starving*, so I ate as much of her as I could. And I don't regret it, Fern. Not one bit. Even if she didn't taste half as good as you."

CHAPTER SIXTEEN

I can't move, or breathe, or even *blink*. My fingers flex against the wall for a moment before I reach forward to curl them around his wrist, though I'm not trying to pull him off of me. I wouldn't be able to, even if I really wanted to, and I'm not stupid enough to think otherwise. Instead I squirm a little, trying to find a way not to be perched on his leg, but I can't move enough.

"Don't lie to me," I murmur, but I know somehow that this isn't a lie. He *is* telling me the truth this time, at least about this.

He really did eat Esther.

"You *ate* her?" I'm not sure how long we've been standing here, with him nosing along my jaw and me trying to accept the horror of what he said. The information doesn't help today's mental state at all, and I feel my fingers flex around his wrist as I become a little detached from my body.

After all, not being here would be easier than digesting all of this.

"Hey." Cairo's voice is suddenly normal, if a bit concerned. He leans away from me while keeping me pinned to the wall with his hand still around my throat. But his grip loosens, so he's not impacting my ability to breathe at all. "Hey, Fern." His fingers flex and release, then he takes a moment to just *watch* me, which is unnerving as hell.

"I'm fine," I breathe, closing my eyes and unconsciously digging my nails into his wrist. "Shit, I'm—" I ease my grip, but before I can let go, his other hand covers mine to keep my hand on his wrist.

"No, that's okay. You dig in, little bird." His voice is gentle rather than commanding. "You can't break my skin with your nails, I promise you that." Cairo holds me against the wall until I finally open my eyes to glare sullenly at him.

"I'm so sorry," I snap, self-conscious, "that I wasn't prepared for you to tell me you'd eaten someone that I met, that I talked to—"

Cairo growls to cut me off, his face close to mine again. "Don't try my kindness, pretty girl. I'm hungry, and the mouthier you get"—he breaks off and lunges forward, running his tongue up the side of my throat, up my jaw, and only stopping at my hairline—"the better you fucking taste. I'm trying to help you so you don't get lost on me. You wanted this confrontation so badly." His voice turns a little mocking.

"Frankly, I think you've gotten the wrong idea of me."

Before I can ask what he means, Cairo jerks me away from the wall. He doesn't put me down though; he lowers me just enough for my toes to occasionally brush the floor. With only one arm wrapped around me, he moves through my house, bringing me to my bedroom where Moro hops expectantly up on the bed, her tail wagging.

Clearly she doesn't give a damn about Cairo's threats of

eating me, and it makes me wonder if she'd let him do it in hopes of him giving her attention.

It's a shame my dog is ready to betray me for a man of all things.

"Not right now, Moro." I swear Cairo's nicer to her than he is to me, and he closes the door in her confused face, leaving her in the bedroom with us in the bathroom.

"What are you doing?" I snap, nervously digging my nails a little harder into his arm as if I'm offering some kind of threat. But that only gets me a withering, baleful look, and Cairo pushes me onto the counter before letting go.

"If you leave this room before I tell you that you can, I will eat you," he informs me oh-so-casually. As if he hadn't just threatened my life.

Honestly, I want to call his bluff. I want to get up right now and bolt for the door, locking him in the bathroom to create a barrier of safety between us. I even glance sidelong at my closed-off escape, though when I feel his gaze on me, I look back to see he is indeed giving me a shrewd glance from the corner of his eye.

"Try it," Cairo invites, opening his mouth enough to show me the tips of his fangs. "Try me. Do I really seem that benevolent?"

"What a stellar use of benevolent," I tease quietly, never looking away from his dark eyes in the bathroom where the only light comes from the nightlight over the sink. I still feel a little detached, and I hate the way I miss his wrist to clutch onto. Instead, as a fallback, I sink my nails into the fresh scar, hissing at the soreness of my abused skin.

The shower is on within seconds, and Cairo is back in a flash. Though considering my current state, I could've just blanked out for those ten seconds. He pries my fingers away from my palm, snorting disapprovingly. "Such a masochist, aren't you?" he murmurs. "Is that what helps ground you, little bird? If you want pain, I am more than happy to give it to you."

"By eating me?"

"No. I don't like to play with my food. I'd snap your neck if I were going to eat you." He says it so flatly, in such a clinical way, that I shudder against him. "I could find so many fun, pretty ways to hurt you, Fern. And maybe if I do, you'll realize I'm not human enough to be your friend."

"It has nothing to do with how human or not you are," I reply without giving myself a moment to consider staying quiet. "Human, dog, or monster, I'd be your friend. It has a lot more to do with you wanting to *eat me* and making threats about it."

Cairo bares his fangs, his grin surprised and sharp. It's the first real, surprised smile I've seen from him, and his mouth just *keeps opening* until I swear he's dislocated his damn jaw to show off all those shiny, terrifying teeth.

A shiver goes down my spine, and his eyes glitter. His tongue licks over one canine, then the other, and it takes a moment for me to realize he's showing me it's longer than a human's tongue, just as his jaw somehow opens further than a normal human's ever should.

And then there are his *teeth*. His canines have to be twice as long as mine, while his other teeth are a little slanted, so every single one could do me harm. When he finally closes his mouth properly, he leans close to me again, caging me in over the counter.

"Let me hurt you, little bird," Cairo purrs, sounding more like a cat than a person. There's a strange, terrifying light in his eyes, making them look like emeralds instead of just plain green. "I could make you want it and keep your mind off of anything else."

But I slowly shake my head, maintaining eye contact like I

can't look away, more like I'm looking around than actually
disagreeing.

The feeling in my stomach is mostly fear. At least eighty
percent is terror at the idea of him doing something terrible to
me. But the other twenty percent is, embarrassingly, anticipation. Secret, subtle *desire* to know what it is he'd do for me to
want him to hurt me.

My fingers flex against his, and he steps closer, leaning
down to growl against my hair. "Sit there and stop trying to
hurt yourself," Cairo tells me. "Or I'll be meaner, since that's
what it seems like you need."

"Says who?" I breathe, trying for confidence and missing
spectacularly as evidenced by Cairo's withering glance.

"Do you need to clean your wounds again?" I ask as my
confusion settles somewhere alongside the fear. There's a
touch of worry for him as well, no matter how much I try to
hide it, and as soon as he turns, I'm back to scraping my nails
along my scar. Though I switch to pinching it between my
forefinger and thumb a moment later, wincing at the sharp
sting of that particular abuse.

"Little bird..." His tone is something I haven't quite heard
before, almost like the way he says things in voices that aren't
his. Yet somehow, the sound is all Cairo, though it's part husky
purr that shouldn't be possible from a human throat. "You're
just determined to push me, aren't you? Fine. I'll give you what
you need to make your scent go back to normal."

"How do you know what I need?" I snap nervously,
watching him tug off his shirt. Immediately I'm caught by the
way his chest looks. It's healed, or nearly so. As if the wounds
there are weeks old instead of just a day or two. "Fuck, Cairo.
How did you—"

But he's on me before I can finish, eyes flashing to reflect
the illumination from the nightlight by the mirror.

"I don't know exactly what you need," he admits, not seeming put out by it in the least. "But I'm willing to experiment. You're shaking, Fern." When I only look at him, he picks up my hand in one of his, showing me the slight, persistent tremble in my fingers. "You stink like fear and anxiety. And..." but he trails off, then shakes his head like he's dismissing the thought.

"What happened today before you found me? Before you walked around in those woods and didn't realize you were being followed by not one, but *two* of us?"

"Nothing," I lie, not wanting to tell him about my day. Suddenly, I'm afraid of showing him weakness, and unsure of where I stand in this situation. I don't even know if he's being honest about not killing me, not eating me, or not feeding me to his friends. My muscles tense, thighs pressed tight, and my fingers twist in his hand, though he's got a death grip on the fingers I've been pressing to my scar, just shy of being actually painful.

"Little liar." Cairo clicks his tongue in disappointment. "You're so disobedient, and I can smell a lie on you a mile away. I don't like it when you smell of fear unless I'm the sole reason for it." Again he gives me that wolfish grin, and leans in against me. "You wanted to try me, didn't you?" he breathes, lapping at the skin of my jaw like it's candy. The idea of tasting good to him sends a shudder down my spine, and I flex my hands against him in an attempt to push him away.

"You wanted to bully me into answering your questions about me. About *us.*" When I feel the graze of his teeth, I nearly shriek. But only a soft whimper leaves me, and his grin is so wide I can sense it on my skin. "But now you're here. Trapped against your mirror and still dissociating from whatever got you so shaken up today. My poor little bird," he coos. "Your heart is pounding hard enough that if you were a rabbit, it might burst. Do you want to fly away, hmm? Instead of being here with me?"

It's the most he's ever said to me, but he seems to get bolder every time he licks my skin or after any noise I give him.

"I just need to ground myself," I breathe. "Just let me—"

"No, sweetheart, I've let you do enough tonight. I've spent the last six months in a fucking asylum. You think I don't know what dissociation looks like?" His voice twists on the word asylum, letting me know exactly how he feels about it. "Clothes off. Shower."

"With you?"

He rolls his eyes at me balefully, showing me his teeth as he does. "What's wrong, little bird? Scared of me seeing all of you? Scared I won't be able to control myself?"

"You weren't this talkative at Bluebone." I know he's right, that a shower will make me feel at least a little like a person again. But he's also right that I'm not sure I should be alone in the shower with him.

Cairo doesn't respond to my words. He just stands up, giving me a slightly softer expression. "Promise me you won't drown," he sighs. "Or fall and hit your head. That would be such a waste, Fern."

"Cross my heart and hope to die."

That doesn't seem to reassure him much. He snorts, but turns and opens the door of the bathroom, hesitating.

Like he's waiting for me to say something.

And I can feel the words on my tongue. Right there, asking him to stay rather than leave. I have to remind myself that he's a *monster* and, quite literally in every way, a killer.

He eats people.

He ate Esther.

"You aren't leaving." It's not a question when I say it

quickly, the words echoing in the bathroom. "Not for real. Right?"

"Depends on whether you want me to." There's a careful neutrality in his voice, like he's trying not to let me hear what he really thinks.

"Do you want to?"

"Do *you* want me to?"

God, he's so infuriating. I snort and get to my feet, some of my bravado coming back to life in my chest now that he's not pinning me against the wall or caging me in on the counter. "How did you heal so fast?" My eyes are fixed on his back, where the mostly healed marks are on full display.

He just sends me *that* look over his shoulder. "Do you want me to leave?" he asks again, this time slowly. Pointedly.

I don't.

But that's the problem.

Fuck it, I decide. My life is already so fucked lately, and I have no idea what I'm even doing with myself at the moment. I've felt off ever since stabbing myself in the hand. Though if I'm honest with myself, I've been doing not so great for a lot longer than that.

"No," I admit. Then before I can stop myself, I reach out and grab his hand. I drag Cairo back toward me, terrified and using my last little bit of bravery to do so. My heart flutters in my chest, making me wonder if I'll regret this in about ten seconds. "Please don't leave."

The surprise on his face is genuine and unfiltered. He doesn't even think to hide it.

He takes that last step toward me, closing the distance, and brings his hand up to cup my face. He's sweet, almost gentle, until Cairo lunges forward with a growl and presses his lips to mine in an all-consuming, demanding kiss.

He really isn't human.

That's all I can think of as his fangs brush against my lips, my tongue, and every time I move they're all I can feel. His tongue snakes into my mouth, tasting and touching. Exploring, maybe. There's nothing normal or boring about the kiss, or the way he cages me in on the counter. "Don't wanna shower," I breathe, my fingers gripping at his shoulders. "Not dissociating—" My words end in a yelp when Cairo suddenly picks me up, carrying me out of the bathroom to drop me unceremoniously onto the bed.

"Good," he agrees. "Because I don't want you to shower either, little bird. I don't have the patience for it. Not now." Cairo pounces—there's no other word for it—and pins me onto the bed under him. Luckily, Moro already escaped to trot back to the living room, her tail up like she's offended. I can't help but laugh a little, though it's immediately cut off when Cairo presses his hand to the base of my throat. He doesn't use enough pressure to hurt, but just enough to let me know he's there. Just enough to keep me in my place as he looms over me like a predator sizing up its prey.

My hand comes up, and I brush my fingers along the healed scars where his wounds were. He shivers under my touch, and in the faint light I see him bare his fangs as he leans close to me again, and Cairo's eyes pick up the light to reflect in a green-yellow glare.

"My little bird," he purrs in the voice that's both familiar and not. It's not his. That's for sure. But it sounds so empty, like it's nothing at all. He leans down again, his tongue out to lave over my face, drawing a line up to my jaw. "You taste so sweet for me. *Fuck.*" There's a note of impatience in his words, but as his claws skim down my shirt, his eyes meet mine in the dimness with a question plain in them.

I really should tell him to leave, seeing as he's a *monster.*

He ate Esther, my brain is quick to urgently remind me. The words echo and overlap until they're white noise, like the sound of birds in my ears drowning out anything else.

But when it becomes just nonsense, just more white noise in the static of my brain, I suddenly find I'm able to move again. I reach up and gently tug up on my shirt, my eyes locked with Cairo's as I do it.

He doesn't need another sign. His hand grips the loose material, yanking it over my head so quickly I'm stunned. My bra is next, and then Cairo stops, holding himself up to stare down at me.

"Don't," he murmurs, when I move to cover myself, feeling vulnerable and unnerved under the reflective gaze. "Don't you dare. I don't want you to hide yourself from me, little bird. Not now." Slowly, ever so slowly, he lowers himself until he can press his mouth against my throat. One hand smooths over my collarbones, down the hollow between my breasts, until he gently lays his fingers on the softness of my stomach.

"If only you knew how delicious you taste, Fern." Cairo sighs like he's both enjoying this and suffering. He licks at my throat with small, gentle kitten licks, before kissing over the spot, allowing his fangs to brush my skin. When I reach up to twine my fingers in his hair, he growls, and I hesitate, unsure.

But then he moves his hand up as well, encouraging me to sink my fingers into his hair. "You can't be afraid of my sharp edges, or the sounds I make," he huffs against my skin, leaning up just enough to meet my gaze. "Otherwise, this will never work."

"I'm not afraid of any of you," I say boldly.

Cairo tilts his head, fixing me with that look that says he doesn't quite believe me.

But then again, I don't quite believe me, either. "I'm

trying," I amend, hating that I have to do it. But he snorts and kisses me again, sitting up to gaze down at me.

"Such a *brave* little bird," he coos teasingly, absently unbuckling the front of his jeans that hang low on his hips. "And all mine." He doesn't push them down further, but then he's on me, biting and kissing at my lips like a desperate, dying man.

I don't expect the intensity, but I try to match it. Small sounds leave me as his hands come up to cup my breasts, like he just wants to feel them in his hands, before his thumbs move to tease at my nipples. That makes me a little louder, a little bolder, and I shove at the waistband of his jeans that I can reach while he kisses down my throat.

My efforts to get him naked come to a stop, however, when his sharp fangs find my nipple. I yelp, hands flying to his hair, but I don't pull him away. The white-hot, almost pain has me arching into him, grounded in the moment without an urge to be anywhere except here.

"Oh, fuck." I breathe sharply, hearing his soft, purring chuckle of contentment. He switches to my other breast, doing it again before licking over where he's bitten.

"You like that?" Cairo teases, using his hands on one, though he alternates where his mouth is so I never feel neglected for long. "You like my fangs on you like this? What if I stopped playing so nice with you, hmm?" He bites down on the curve of my breast, slowly, just enough, but the pressure increases as I writhe and squirm under him.

It doesn't hurt enough for me to want him to stop. Instead, I find myself breathily begging him for more, until my chest stings and burns with the aftermath of little bites that are sure to bruise, and he's again licking his way over my skin like he can soothe the burn.

Belatedly, I realize he's grinding against me, no longer content to just lay over my body. I raise one leg, knee up and toes curled against my mattress, to nudge him closer to where I'm starting to really ache for him. Cairo isn't stupid; he gives me a look and a soft chuckle for my actions. "Needy," he teases, but I level a look at him.

"So are you." I roll my hips up against him, and his hiss is answer enough. In seconds he's shoving his jeans down and off his legs, leaving him completely bare and me only in leggings. My eyes drop to the v of his hips, and to where his cock is already semi-hard between us.

I can't help but want to ask if *that* has changed with becoming what he is as well. But it feels rude and inappropriate for the situation. His fingers hook in my leggings, dragging them down, down...until he can hook them over my ankles and toss them to the floor.

With nothing between us, I feel much more vulnerable than I ever have before. It doesn't help that the light from my window hits his eyes *just right*, giving that inhuman, reflective quality to his stare as he studies me.

He takes his time, smoothing his hands down my sides, then my thighs, until I'm impatient and wiggling as my heart continues to flutter in my chest. "Cairo..." I protest, one hand reaching up between us. He grabs it, turning to kiss my wrist and run his fangs over the delicate skin there as well.

"Needy," he repeats, pressing both hands down over my head. He nudges my knee further up, giving him the space he wants. Without breaking eye contact, Cairo slides one finger along my slit. He watches my reactions as he adds another before letting them press between my folds. Just a little.

Just to be a fucking tease.

My arms twist above me, but I don't move them from where he placed them near my pillows. I don't look away from him, only arch my hips to encourage him to keep going, hoping he'll give me *more*.

Finally, he does. Two fingers sink into me, drawing an appreciative, deep breath from me as my hips come off the bed and he purrs his approval into the air between us. "You're so wet for me, aren't you?" he murmurs. "Such a sweet little bird. Maybe you won't like me though, here in a minute."

"Why?" I ask, eyebrows knit together in confusion.

Cairo leans downward, his lips brushing my ear just to say, "Because I'm too starved for you to be *gentle*." Two fingers become three instantly, and I suck in a breath as he thrusts them into me, curling them until my thighs are tense and there are protests on my lips.

But he doesn't give me the time to enjoy it. He pulls them free and slicks them over his cock, stroking himself with his wet fingers while I watch. It's *so* hot that for a moment, I don't remember to breathe.

Then Cairo is right there, looming over me, and he grabs one of my hands to hook it around his neck. "You can claw at me," he invites. "Pull my hair and sink your nails and teeth deep. I'll like it, Fern. I promise you I will."

Without waiting for an answer, he lines up and sinks into me, drawing a long, loud sound from my throat that's way past a gasp and somewhere closer to a moan than I'd like to admit. My back arches off the blanket, and my nails dig into his shoulder as I bring myself closer to him, but that just makes him shudder.

"Good girl," Cairo praises. "Mark me just like that. Come on," he urges, drawing back to slide into me again. The second time is just as intense as the first, and it's not until a good dizzying half-minute goes by that I feel like I can breathe almost normally.

My other hand comes up to grab his shoulder as well when

he fucks into me a little harder. The whines leaving my lips are needy, and maybe a little bit feral, but I don't care. He fills me up perfectly, stretching me in a way that's both wonderful and painful and therefore *perfect.*

I doubt anyone could ever fuck me like Cairo is right now, and I might quite literally be ruined for anyone else. Especially when he really starts fucking me in earnest, with filthy words of praise slipping from his lips that keep edging me closer and closer to my peak.

"Such a sweet voice you have, little bird."

"I'll mark you inside and out, so there's no mistake that you're mine."

"Claw me deeper, Fern. I want to wear your marks like you're going to wear *mine.*" He snarls the last part, and I cry out at a particularly sharp thrust. His free hand moves between us, but it only takes a few rough strokes of his fingers over my clit before I'm coming with my leg hooked over his arm and his name on my lips.

"Cairo!" I nearly howl the two-syllable sound that's barely a word in my mouth. *"Cairo!"* I try again, and I swear I feel my nails break skin, though he only fucks me deeper. My pussy flutters around him, clenching him, like my body is silently begging for him to stay while I ride out my release with my nails in his back and my mouth open so I can breathe.

It's not long before Cairo growls, releasing an impossibly feral sound, and he lunges forward to bury his teeth in my throat just hard enough I feel them break skin. His whole body is stiff, his thrusts are only small, rocking motions of his hips, and I feel him chase his release inside of me, though the sounds he makes are nothing short of animalistic against me.

A predator claiming what's his, I think to myself, and a shiver of delight and fear goes down my spine.

When he pulls away, I'm panting, but there's only a sheen

of sweat on his upper body to show that he's done any work at all. "Are you...?" My eyes narrow, and he grins, still seated inside me.

"What, little bird?" he teases with a satisfied, feline smile on his lips. "You thought that was all? Oh, no." His fingers curl around the base of my throat, and he leans down to nuzzle a line up my chest until his mouth is just above mine.

"We're just getting started."

CHAPTER SEVENTEEN

I'M PRETTY SURE I'VE NEVER SLEPT BETTER IN MY LIFE.

Waking up without being afraid that something is breaking in or from some shitty nightmare is a nice experience. And I fully expect to see Cairo gone now that the sun is up. It's what always happens to monsters and myths, after all, and he's a bit of both in my mind.

But when I turn over, my arm brushes against something warm and solid. I open my eyes to find him right beside me, his eyes on my face and his expression thoughtful. He reaches out to me, and just when I think he's going to do something sweet like brush my hair back from my face, he instead wraps his fingers around my throat and pulls me to him with a purr of possessive satisfaction.

"You look good like this," Cairo tells me in a husky, soft tone.

"Like what? Tired?" I murmur, not fighting his grip on my neck or particularly freaked out about it. "Post-panic and post-slightly dissociative?"

His mouth twitches in a grin, and he rolls his eyes. "No,

little bird. Marked as mine and worn out from what I did to you. Though I want to do so much *more* to you. I was keeping myself a little human, for you."

"What?" I ask, surprised and more than a little confused. "What do you mean?"

Cairo's eyes glint with amusement. "I'm a monster, Fern," he reminds me, seeming happy to point that out again. "If I were to indulge in what I really want with you, then you wouldn't be getting out of bed today. I wouldn't let you." He speaks with such confidence that my stomach twists and I feel like my chest is full of butterflies.

Before I can remark on it, Cairo glances toward the window, his eyes go serious and his smile fades. But he doesn't let go of me. Instead he shifts to wrap an arm around my shoulders, his chin resting against my hair with my face pressed to his shoulder. With anyone else, I would've called the move cute. Affectionate.

With Cairo, it screams possession. Like he sees me as *his* and is just proving it in any way he pleases.

"Is something wrong?" I ask, when all I feel is the too-fast beat of his heart and his slow breathing. He's warm against me, like always, and it's hard not to just close my eyes and drift back to sleep, even though my instincts won't let me completely forget he's neither human nor absolutely safe.

"Yes," he sighs suddenly. "Unfortunately. Lately there's always something wrong." He moves his hand, allowing his fingers to skim down my back, like he's trying to touch every bit of me he can. "They're restless."

"Who?"

"The others like me."

For a moment I only focus on the feeling of his fingers drawing senseless shapes on my back. But my curiosity gets the better of me, and I can't help it when questions bubble to my lips; my urge to know more about him is unstoppable. "What are you, exactly? And don't say a monster. That's incredibly vague."

Cairo huffs out a laugh, and I swear I can sense him rolling his eyes at my attempts at humor. "I didn't know you needed a label for everything, Fern. But to be honest with you, I'm not even sure what you'd call us. Some of the others say we're cursed, so I've always gone with that."

"Cursed like you pissed off a witch in a chicken-legged hut?" I can't keep the sarcasm out of my voice, and I pay for it when Cairo rolls me onto my back, caging me in when he rises above me on his hands and knees. His face is close enough to mine that his eyes look black, but a second later they reflect the light, becoming an illuminated green and incredibly unnatural.

It's creepy, in a way.

But I'm starting to be less afraid every time I see it. It's just *him.* Just a quirk about him that exists, rather than something necessarily bad. He bares those too-sharp teeth that he didn't have at the asylum, prompting more questions to line up in my head.

"No. Cursed like we did something awful in order to survive, then we paid the karmic price for it." He clicks his teeth near my face, pulling an involuntary shudder from me. "It gets cold in these mountains." His voice takes on that eerie, ambiguous quality again, where he doesn't sound like himself, but like a jumble of voices all at once.

"How do you do that? The voice thing?"

By now, my inappropriate curiosity barely phases Cairo. He just blinks, and I see his throat working as he considers it. But then a slightly less-than-friendly smile appears on his lips, and when he opens his mouth, he says, *"How do you do that? The voice thing?"* In a perfect copy of my voice and tone.

An involuntary shudder goes through me as fear coils like a

cold snake in my stomach. That's something I don't know how to get used to, and he doesn't act like he's bothered by my fear. "You ask so many questions, don't you?" Cairo laughs darkly, back to his own tone. He leans down, and before I can do anything other than give a quick, surprised inhale, his lips find mine.

He isn't sweet. But that doesn't surprise or disappoint me. He's voracious and hungry. His kiss is starving, like he wants to eat me from the inside out. Cairo's tongue is possessive, tasting every inch of space between my lips like he hasn't done it before. Once in a while I feel his teeth against my mouth, but he never bites down. When I try to sit up a little bit though, a hand is quickly splayed at the base of my throat, and a low growl drifts from his mouth to mine.

"*Stay*," he orders, in a voice that tells me it's not up for debate. "You *stay*." I do, expecting him to get up and pull his disappearing act. Instead, he goes right back to kissing me. Cairo is unhurried, and thorough. When he's done with the inside of my mouth, he moves to my face, then my throat; dragging his tongue up the side of my neck in long, savoring sweeps while a purr builds in him.

"Feels like you want to eat me," I say on a breath, pressing my thighs together as arousal flares to life in my stomach.

"Yeah," he agrees. "Well, that's because I do." He captures my mouth again, pinning me to the bed with his hand on my chest once more. Cairo doesn't offer an apology; he just spends a good five minutes licking and nipping at my mouth until my lips are sore and swollen before he finally sits up.

His eyes dip to where my thighs are pressed together, and a small smile twitches at his lips. He shoves the covers back and before I know what he's doing, reaches down to shove his hand between my thighs, easily getting between them.

"Poor thing," he purrs as he slides his fingers against my

slit and dips them inside teasingly. "My poor little bird." When he pulls them out, his fingers are slick and glistening with my arousal. I watch as he brings them to his mouth, his tongue laves against them and his eyes drift shut.

"Something to remember you by," he tells me, getting to his feet.

"You're leaving?" I sit up in my bed, aroused and frustrated. "You're actually, literally *leaving*?"

The grin Cairo throws my way tells me that he most definitely is, and I watch as he pulls on his jeans and the long-sleeved tee he came here in. "Yeah, I'm leaving. I have to go take care of this disquiet." His eyes flick to the window again. "It's better to snuff it out now, I suppose, than have to deal with the consequences later." He doesn't sound thrilled by the idea, and his voice is flat with disdain.

"You're *leaving*." I repeat, still flustered.

Finally, Cairo stops, understanding what I'm saying, and smugness radiates from him. "What's wrong, little bird?" he teases in a lilting tone. "Will you miss me? Will your fingers not be enough for you after last night? Poor thing." He moves back to the bed to twine his fingers in my hair, and urges me up on my knees until I'm kneeling against him.

"Maybe this way, you'll miss me," Cairo purrs, showing off his fangs. "And next time I show up, maybe you'll forget about your questions, hmm?" With that, he kisses me again, just enough to leave me panting when he lets me fall back onto the bed before turning and opening the bedroom door. He stays long enough to love on Moro, telling her what a good girl she is, before leaving so quietly I don't even know what door he's taken.

When I finally force myself up and out of bed, I remind myself that he is in fact the more dangerous one between us, and that I can't put a hit out on the man/monster I let fuck me last night.

But only because I don't want to go into debt to a hitman in this economy.

All I can think to do with my day is to get out of the house for a little while. With Moro in the car, I head back into town, deciding to get my food from the diner I missed out on yesterday thanks to panicking. "I'll get you a hot dog if you don't tear up my car or start a panic," I tell Moro, sitting in the lot behind both Dr. Radley's and the diner, only two spots away from where I parked yesterday. Given that it's Saturday, I've convinced myself that Dr. Radley isn't here. So she certainly wouldn't be plastered to the window staring me down or anything quite so ridiculous.

Which means I'm safe to get my grilled cheese in peace, I hope. But it's still difficult to force myself out of the car when she managed to set me off yesterday. Eventually, I roll down the windows for Moro, telling myself it's not nearly hot enough to feel like a bad dog owner, and since I've called in my order except for the ice cream, I'll only be gone for a few minutes.

Moro being in the car also lets me pretend that when I walk really fast across the sidewalk with a wary glance up at the window to Dr. Radley's office, I'm speeding up for my dog's sake instead of doing it to get away from my therapist's potential prying gaze a little more quickly.

My food is almost ready, and I pat myself on the back for my timing. I already ordered Moro a hot dog, so my threats of her only getting it if she'd behaved are empty. While my fries finish, I order a dreamsicle shake like I've been craving, and it takes only another minute for them to hand me the bulgy, white paper bag full of fried, cheesy goodness.

Now, all I have to do is make the quick drive home and

figure out what I want to watch while I eat. My few small free-lance jobs can be done later, I tell myself, *after* I've watched a few episodes of some questionably realistic court shows with high drama and not so high stakes.

But when I round the corner so my car is back in sight, I come to a stop. "Hey..." My words trail off, because the person standing at my car window where Moro is barking isn't a stranger like I initially thought.

It's Hattie.

"Hattie?!" I yelp, unbelieving. I nearly drop what I'm hold-ing, and only belatedly realize that Moro is acting like she is not a fan of the redhead from the asylum. She turns to me, looking at me with wide eyes, and suddenly smiles so much that it lights up her face.

"Fern!" She flies at me, practically knocking me down, and I barely maintain a hold on my food and milkshake while stag-gering back until my back hits a wall. "He said you were okay," she rambles. "But I worried. He isn't always truthful. Isn't always *right*."

I have no idea what she's saying, or how she's here. She looks a little worse for wear, with dirt streaked across her face and her shirt needing to be washed three wears ago. But she's alive and, from what I can see, unharmed.

"Do you mean Cairo?" I ask, confused, as she continues to hold me tight in her shaky embrace. "When did he tell you? How did you—"

She draws back, her eyebrows pulled together as she searches my face. "Not Cairo. No, no he didn't tell me." She shakes her head. "He's not my friend."

"Then who's your friend, Hattie?" She looks at me strangely, and again I look her over. She really does seem different, and a little more off than usual—which is really saying something. "Are you okay?"

"He said you were okay, and you are. He said you should've stayed with me. I told you to stay with me." Her eyes narrow as she chastises me, but I don't feel guilty about whatever she's upset about. Then again, I barely have any idea what's going on.

"Hattie, where have you been? Are you safe? I didn't think anyone else survived." Except for Cairo, but that's a bit different, given what he is. In my mind, I was the only *human* survivor. Until now.

She hugs me again rather than answering. Hattie rocks us back and forth, humming softly in her throat like I'm the one that's unwell, instead of her. "It's okay now." She sighs contentedly. "You're okay, like he said. Everything's okay."

"How'd you get out?" I ask, trying to match her strange calmness instead of bombarding her with anxious questions. "I came back for you. I was worried about you."

"So nice to worry about me. But you didn't have to. Tyler wouldn't let them hurt me," Hattie assures me.

Instantly I pull away from her, head tilted. "Tyler?" I repeat. "But how would he?"

A look of frustration crosses Hattie's face, and she shakes her head. "No, no, he told me not to talk to you about that. So you can't ask me, Fern," she tells me, irritated. She backs away, hugging her arms to her chest.

"I'm sorry," I say, confused. I take a step toward her, but she shakes her head, still backing away. "Hattie..."

My next step closer to her makes her tense, and my use of her name makes her turn and flee. I don't chase her—because I'm not a crazy lady who's going to chase a *crazier* lady through town—but I do stand where I am, confused. I resolve to get answers from Cairo the next time I see him, even if I have to do something drastic in order to pry the answers from his lips.

CHAPTER EIGHTEEN

The bodies are screaming.

Sam's torso with only one arm attached is moving like it can go somewhere, and her eyes are wide as she looks up at me with a whimper on her lips. "It ate me," she gasps, tears rolling down her cheeks. "Why did you get out, but it ate me?!"

I don't have an answer for her, but my focus gets pulled when I hear my name from the stairwell and turn to see the hallway is dark and spattered with blood. The floors are slick with it, and the walls are covered as the blood runs in rivulets from the ceiling, dripping in other places to create puddles on the floor below.

But my name sounds again in the loud, screaming hallway, though every sound except for my name is muffled and somehow in the background.

"Hello?" I call, my voice echoing in the hallway. "Can you hear me?"

But the only response I get is another sing-song variation of my name, drawing out the one syllable until the walls ring with it.

I know I shouldn't walk toward the stairwell—I remember what happened that night—but I do. As I go, I can't help but look into all the rooms on either side where dead or dying patients scream and wail.

In some rooms, the creatures are there; devouring body parts while the people watch and scream and beg.

My stomach twists, but my feet keep moving. I can't stop walking. Can't stop heading to where the same voice calls my name in different ways.

"Tell me who you are!" I demand, finally reaching that oppressive darkness. "Tell me what's happening!" This time, there's no Moro to stop me, or surprise me from going inside the blackness.

I step inside the stairwell, and the meager light from the hall vanishes. I'm in complete blackness with only my breathing and the whisper of my name that beats against my ears for company.

"Hello?" I whisper, but my voice makes no sound. Suddenly, something grabs me, throwing me against the wall. The lights flick on, then off, like they did in the hallway, and when the stairwell lights up, I see the feral, bloodied face of Cairo in front of me, twisted into a look of primal hunger.

"Cairo!" I gasp, voice still a whisper.

"I'm so hungry, Fern," he tells me, in that voice that sounds like everyone and no one at once. "You'll help me, right? You'll fix me?" He leans forward and licks a line up my throat, his mouth stopping near my ear. "I'm just so starving, and you taste so good."

"Cairo, please—"

I feel his teeth sink into my throat. Though there's no real sensation of pain, I still feel every inch, each flex of his jaw. I swear I can sense every layer of skin that gives beneath his too-sharp teeth and every vein that shreds between his fangs.

"I'm starving, Fern," he repeats with his mouth in my throat. He rips backward and I feel the horrible, gut-churning sensation of part of my throat going with him as he steps away, letting my body slide

to the floor while I stare up at him, watching him lick the traces of blood from his lips.

"You were never safe from me, little bird." His voice echoes, and he drops to his knees, fingers twining sweetly in my hair. "You should've known you can never trust a monster." He dives in again, eyes black with hunger, as his teeth glisten with my blood in the flickering light just before he—

My eyes snap open, and I sit up with a gasp. My hand goes immediately to my throat, fingers gripping hard around my skin. I'm shaking, and Moro sits up beside me to lick at my face, while concerned whines come from her throat.

"It was just a dream," I whisper. As if I'm trying to convince her when in fact it's my mind and body I'm talking to. But I can't sit still. Immediately I'm up and getting dressed before I even know what I'm doing. I can't sit here and do nothing with my mind racing and panic threatening to take over.

I know there's nothing wrong. That none of that actually happened, and the night at Bluebone Ridge went remarkably differently. Cairo saved me, not killed me. The bodies weren't screaming, and the walls hadn't been dripping blood.

But here I am, getting dressed in a hoodie and a pair of loose shorts that aren't appropriate for the chilly night. I find my sneakers and yank them on, then shove my phone into my pocket. I have no business going anywhere. Especially with my heart racing and my mind not quite where it needs to be. But I hesitate, glancing around the house.

"Cairo...?" I call, half-hoping he'll appear.

But he doesn't. It's just the darkness, me, and Moro behind me, looking eager for the inevitable car ride she knows is about to happen. Naturally. The one time I really want him to be here so I can bother him or *be* bothered by him, he's nowhere in sight.

"Well, we live in a tiny town, Moro," I tell her, pushing open the front door. "So there's nothing open at one in the morning, except maybe fast food? I guess we could get you a burger." She wags her tail at me, but that's probably just at the idea of getting to go out and explore.

"Yeah, okay. We'll get you a burger." She bounds into my car the moment I open the door, excitement all over her doggy features. For a moment, I just sit in the car in silence. My fingers flex around the steering wheel and I sigh, biting my lip.

I should go back to bed.

But my heart is still beating too fast from the nightmare. My hands still shake, and it feels like I'm being zapped by electricity, with a charge running through my veins that keeps me restless and anxious.

If I go back to bed now, I'll just lie there and panic until it gets worse and I'm a mess who can't function in the morning. Not that I'm doing great as it is. But if I can just give myself something to focus on, give myself a *task*, I should be able to work through my anxiety from the nightmare that isn't fading.

"Burger," I repeat, watching my grey and white wolf dog pant happily in the backseat. The collar around her neck interrupts her fluffy ruff, and the tag I got shines in the reflected headlights. "You, clearly, will starve without a burger."

I do get her burger, just as I promised. But naturally, the restaurant's coffee machine is broken, or being cleaned, or maybe just not on the premises at all. For all I know, both it and the ice cream machine were abducted by aliens five minutes before I got here.

So all I end up with is a Cherry Coke, and while I know I asked for a small, the cup currently taking up my console is anything but. And I know if I drink all of it before I get home, there's no way in hell I'll be sleeping tonight.

Somehow, I miss the turn to my road, then I miss the next

turn to make it *back* to my road. My fingers flex on the steering wheel, and I don't say anything over the low music playing in my car. I do finally turn onto the winding mountain road I've never taken on purpose.

But that doesn't mean I don't know how to get to Bluebone Ridge by myself.

The drive is long enough that I have plenty of time to wonder what the hell I'm doing, and if I'm going insane. This is the last place I should want to be, and certainly not in the middle of the night.

But I can't stop myself. I can't force myself to take any of the routes that would get me back to town and home. Though I do slow down to account for the narrow, winding mountain road. I'd really rather not end my night by plummeting off the side of a cliff in the Cascade Mountains after surviving a monster attack in the same place.

Though I suppose it would be poetic. And ironic.

When at last I end up at the parking lot in front of Blue-bone Ridge, it feels like the drive has been both too long and not long enough. My fingers tighten on the steering wheel once I park in front of the partially open gates, and I look over the dark building, lit only by the moon in the clear, cloudless sky above.

It's just as eerie as it was that night, but it looks...the same. I don't know what I expected. Maybe signs of nature taking it back already, as impossible as that would be. Maybe signs hanging, or police tape fluttering in the breeze...

Something to signify what happened here barely two weeks ago.

Moro whines behind me, and I glance back at her with a shaky smile. "You can stay in here if you want," I tell her, knowing she doesn't understand but needing to say it nevertheless. Still, she doesn't hesitate and surges out of the driver's side door behind me the moment I'm out of her way.

Thank God, I sigh to myself. I really don't want to be here alone.

Leaving my lights on is the smart move, and gives me some extra illumination as I slip between the gap in the heavy, bent gates. They're definitely not made to be moved manually, and I don't think the power is on to get them any further open so I could park near the door.

But that's fine. I have no idea what I'm doing here anyway. Not in the least.

The cold is the first pressing thought that finds me, and I cross my arms over my chest to try to preserve some warmth. Not that it helps my bare legs. Shorts were a bad idea.

Coming here was a bad idea.

Every noise makes me jump. Every ruffle of leaves in the trees outside of the parking lot has me tripping over myself, and I'm sure something is going to come out of the forest with the intent to eat me.

I even imagine I hear my name—like I had in my dream—coming from the darkest parts of the asylum. Though I force myself to admit in my head that it's my mind playing tricks on me. There's no one, and nothing here. Not now, not anymore.

There's no reason for them to be, I reason. If they were just here because they were hungry, there's no reason for them to stick around now that all the food is gone. I shudder as I walk up the stairs, having to push the word *food* out of my head when it's really people I'm talking about.

Moro doesn't stick by my side for long. She explores the courtyard, her tail waving like a flag when she pauses to investigate something of interest now and then. Stopping to watch her calms me down, since in my mind, there's nothing here to be afraid of if she's acting like everything is okay.

"Moro?" I call, standing at the top of the front stairs, where the large double doors were ripped off of their hinges. I have no idea how anyone explained this as an animal attack, unless an army of bears had shown up here to cause a coordinated scene.

I haven't looked for any news on what happened in days, though. Not since I talked to Laura Simms. What's the point? The truth isn't going to come out, anyway. Anyone who knows isn't saying anything, for fear of being called crazy and being locked up somewhere else with better security and less monsters.

The only other things that know what happened here aren't human.

The lobby is free of bodies, but I can see where blood had pooled and sat on the old hardwood before anyone attempted to clean it. Which wasn't done very well, judging by the dark stains. It was here I saw Hattie for the first time, and I curiously stride to the corner she'd been standing in that day, looking up to the ceiling high above us in the cathedral-like room like she did.

But there's nothing anywhere. Nothing now, anyway, though I suppose I can't rule out that back then there may have been something more interesting than dust. Moro's nails click on the hardwood, and as I walk around the room, I watch as she sniffs at pooled bloodstains, one after the other, her ears going back to lie against her head as the fur of her neck slowly rises.

Judging by her attitude, this place makes her uneasy, too. At least where the bodies were before they got cleaned up.

"Me too, Moro," I whisper. I walk over to the desk with one larger stain and streaks across the wood, and stare down at it, remembering this is where Esther had been. Where her sightless eyes stared up at me, wide with fear and confusion.

I hope she died fast, at least.

Before Cairo ate her.

Had he done it right here? Sat on the floor and ripped her apart, feeding on her flesh and marrow while waiting for something to attack me outside? Or did he drag her away, to a darker corner, like a leopard with its kill when it takes the bodies into trees to eat in peace?

I don't know what prompts me to, but I look up suddenly at the open doors, my gaze instantly going to the figure standing there, framed by the shattered doors and lit from my headlights that barely reach this far. The lobby is dark, for the most part, given the lack of electricity, so I can't tell who it is at first.

"Cairo?" I ask, unsure. It doesn't look him him, from what I can see. But Moro isn't growling or freaking out, so I'm unsure if it could be any of the other creatures that were here that night. Surely if whoever is standing there intended to do me harm, Moro would be doing more than just watching, her fur on end and one ear cocked forward like she's unsure.

"Not quite." The voice is familiar, but I still can't see the person's face. Judging by their tone, it's a woman, and I see her lift up a hand, finger beckoning to me. "There's nothing to find in here, little bird. Just the smell of old death and the start of decay."

"Who...?" I follow her out into the moonlight, where I can see it's the barefoot woman from town, when I first saw Dr. Radley outside of this place. "You," I breathe. When she turns her head, the moonlight reflects off of her eyes, giving them a greenish hue and making my heart jump in my chest. "You aren't human."

"No," she agrees, a smile touching her lips. "But I'm starving enough to pass as one." At my confusion, her brows lift, and a small, almost pitying smile appears on her full lips. "He really hasn't told you anything, has he? He's talked so much to me about you, about what he wants. But he's keeping you in the dark."

Her words send a chill down my spine. "I don't know what any of that means," I have to finally admit. "Do you mean Cairo?" She nods, so I think about my next question, or rather all the ones I want to ask, before continuing with, "What's your name? Were you here that night? When...you know."

"No." The word is decisive, and I can sense disgust in her tone. "*He* called them here, because he knew they were starving and wanted to make a point. But I cannot be called. My name is Agatha," she adds belatedly, like she almost forgot I asked.

Her answer is just as confusing as my question had been, and I don't feel any more informed on the subject than I did before.

"I'm sorry." I tuck my hair behind my ear as Moro edges toward her, looking intimidated for the first time since I've had her. Unsure, I reach down to wrap my fingers in her collar, only for Agatha to snort.

"I won't hurt your dog, little bird." It's so strange to hear Cairo's nickname coming from her. "And she knows better than to try to hurt me. You don't have to hold onto her."

Slowly I let go of Moro's collar, and my wolf dog edges forward to lightly, nervously sniff at Agatha's fingers before darting warily back.

"I didn't think she was afraid of anything," I admit as I watch her submissive tail wagging and head down as she circles me, though it's Agatha she's looking at.

"She's a predator. She knows when something is higher than her on the food chain." Agatha shrugs.

"But she's not afraid of Cairo," I comment, confused by her words. "If it were just that, why wouldn't she be afraid of him?"

Agatha doesn't answer. She just looks at me, searching my eyes with her dark gaze. In the moonlight, the shadows under her eyes look ghastly, though they don't take away from her beauty. She's dressed similar to me, in shorts and a t-shirt. Though she's barefoot, standing on the stone stairs perfectly balanced and seemingly unbothered by the cold, night air, unlike me.

"Aren't there other things you'd like to ask me? Maybe you'll find me a bit less evasive than Cairo if you ask what you really want to know," she invites unexpectedly. "Or are you just going to stand there and marvel at your dog wanting me to know she's not a threat?"

While I am amazed and confused at why Moro is acting the way she is, I make a conscious effort to let that go for now. "What are you?" I ask, though I asked Cairo the same thing. "Cairo told me you were cursed, but that seems vague. There has to be a better answer, right?"

Agatha tilts her head first one way, then the other. She looks thoughtful instead of irritated. Like she's figuring out what to say to me. "You're not asking for a name." I shake my head, though her words are a statement not a question. "And he won't tell you what you want to know. He wants to protect his little bird, how quaint." A smirk flickers over her lips, and she studies my face curiously.

"If you don't tell her, I will," she says suddenly, her voice a little louder, though not by much. She's not yelling, and the level of volume is still conversational. "I don't have the same interest in keeping her in the dark as you do."

"Who are you talking to?" I ask, wondering if she's just as crazy as Hattie and possibly me. But Agatha doesn't respond. Instead she looks over my shoulder, prompting me to turn, until I'm facing the lobby doors once more, even though we've walked far enough to be halfway to the parking lot.

Cairo stands there, brooding. His arms are crossed over his chest, and even in the dark, I can see the displeasure on his expression as he stares at Agatha, though there's no outward aggression or challenge in his body.

"She's talking to me, Fern," he says, voice quiet. "And you shouldn't be here."

CHAPTER NINETEEN

"Why won't you tell me?" I round on him, watching his brows rise like he's surprised at my boldness. But he looks over my shoulder again, likely meeting Agatha's eyes once more.

"Because he worries he's going to chase you away. He's trying to hide the worst parts of what we are from you, little bird—"

"Don't call her that," Cairo interrupts, showing her his teeth in a snarl. Though he drops the expression a second later and looks down at the ground. "Please," he adds, though the word is unnatural and grating in his throat.

"Possessive, aren't we?" Cairo doesn't reply to Agatha's teasing, and when I turn to look at her, I see that her eyes are on him, a little narrowed, like she's waiting for something. Though judging by the way Cairo is looking anywhere but at her, he's not going to give it to her if he can help it.

"Can one of you tell me *something?*" I hate how impatient I sound and feel. I hate that there's so much they aren't telling me. "Can you tell me how you became what you are? And if I hear 'we did what we had to do,' one more time, I'm driving off a cliff. Or why you can mimic voices? How do you look completely human, but he doesn't anymore, even though he did at Bluebone when we were there? And what you were doing there in the first place?" I add, this time looking directly at Cairo when I ask.

Agatha gives him all of five seconds before she snorts. "You're impossible," she tells the man behind me. "You want her more than you let on, but you're too afraid of her leaving to tell her what that means."" Cairo snarls a little, but it's directed at the ground instead of at her. "He's not lying, though. There's no name for what we are. And this?" Her voice changes, her next words sounding just like Cairo's voice.

"It's to help us lure in our prey. If I sound like someone you know..." she trails off, but hearing her speak with Cairo's voice, who doesn't look a bit surprised, is unnerving. It sends a tremor down my spine, causing me to clench my nails into my palms. *"Then I don't have to work as hard,"* she finishes in Dr. Radley's voice.

"That's unnerving." Is the only thing I can say, and it brings a snort from Cairo. "What about your eyes?"

"I told you we can see in the dark a lot better than you. Look, there aren't really any explanations that would make sense to you. None of us know how this started." Cairo's voice is hesitant. Like he doesn't want to explain all of this to me right now.

"So you guys just woke up one day and *bang*, you're not human anymore? That's really how this works?"

"No," Agatha says, not giving Cairo a chance to speak. When he makes a noise, she glances his way, gaze pointed, and he shuts up. "No, you don't get to lie to her about this one. If your *little bird* doesn't know, she can't make an informed decision on if she wants to see you again."

Something in her words makes me feel the cold even more

acutely, and I shiver in my hoodie, with my legs pressed together.

"She needs to go home, Agatha. Unless you've forgotten that humans still feel the cold," Cairo retorts weakly. "She's going to freeze to death by the time you get done explaining anything."

"Then you tell me." I'm tired of feeling like a ping pong ball. I whirl on Cairo, chin up as I advance on him, even though my heart flutters at talking to him like this. "I've asked you so many times. So come on, Cairo. Give me a real answer." I don't push him. That didn't work out how I thought it would the last time I tried to use physical force to catch him off guard.

"Fern..." He reaches out, his hand cupping my jaw and his thumb brushing over my lower lip. "Little bird, you don't know what you're asking for. Can't you let me have this? Let me have you not knowing, so you keep looking at me like that instead of how you'll look at me after?"

I search his face, wishing I understood what he was getting at, and shake my head. "I won't look at you any differently," I breathe. "You're still a terrifying, flesh-eating creature of the dark. And I'll always look at you like one."

His smile is small, but genuine. He taps my bottom lip, opens his mouth to answer, then suddenly hisses. His expression turns aggressive and Cairo shows his fangs in irritation, looking past me again. "Your timing is as terrible as always."

This time I don't think for a second he's talking to me. I turn around, looking for Agatha, who's still standing where she had been before. She taps the ball of her foot on the ground, but she's no longer looking at Cairo. Her eyes are narrowed, reflecting light more brightly than I've ever seen from one of them, and she's staring without amusement at the newcomer sitting on the railing of the stairs, perched there like he belongs.

"Oh, come on, Cai." Tyler laughs, twisting his hands over the metal. "You're not being very friendly. And it's so nice to see you, Fern." He grins, showing off fangs like Cairo's, though his mouth is bloody, not clean like the other two. "I was a little scared for you when you didn't stay with Hattie like she told you to. I tried to help you, too, with that," he adds, glancing back at Cairo.

"I don't need your help," Cairo insists, pushing away from the door. Then he curls an arm around me as Moro suddenly growls, her ruff bristling and her tail straight up over her back. "And neither does she. She's not like your crazy, broken doll who you keep locked away from the world."

Does he mean Hattie? I resolve to ask him about it later, but for the moment I just stare between them, unsure and confused.

"You need someone's help," Tyler taunts with a chuckle, in a rather unfriendly way. But then his gaze goes to Agatha, and I swear I see a hint of uncertainty in his eyes. "Are *you* giving him yours?" he asks, though it sounds more like an accusation than anything.

Agatha doesn't reply, though she gives Tyler a *look*, as her stance and gaze change subtly, though I can't tell exactly why or what she means by it. But either way, it makes Tyler drop his eyes to the ground, and his posture becomes less aggressive.

"You shouldn't make humans part of your game," is the only thing she says, with a quick glance in Cairo's direction as well, though she only seems a bit frustrated with him, rather than the look of actual dislike she gives Tyler. "You shouldn't let him have this game at all."

Tyler snorts at her words, pushing off the railing. "He ran to an asylum to hide from our 'game,' Agatha. What is it you think he's going to do, hmm?" He jerks his head in a sidelong motion, baring his fangs. "But I'm starting to get bored of the rules you play by, Cai. They're just as boring as hers."

Cairo makes a noise in his throat. "Don't call me that. We're not friends."

"No," Tyler agrees. "We never were, were we?" Without warning he lunges for me, causing Cairo to intercept him a bit awkwardly so he can't make contact. But protecting me lets Tyler have the advantage, and he grips Cairo by the throat, jerking him back to throw him over the railing of the front steps. When he turns back to me, Agatha suddenly snarls, and she's beside me in an instant.

"*I said no*," she sneers sharply, and the vehemence causes Tyler to stumble backward, but he recovers quickly. By the time Cairo is on his feet, Tyler lunges for him, another snarl on his lips and his claw-tipped fingers outstretched.

"Cairo!" I shout, jerking forward like I'm going to do anything. At least, until Agatha grabs me by the arm, holding me in place with another soft growl.

"*No*," she tells me in a voice that sounds like so many people and no one at the same time. "You are not going to make this easier for Tyler. If you go over there, I won't protect you from him ripping you apart."

Moro barks high and sharp, standing in front of me and dancing back and forth, looking for an opening. The sounds Cairo and Tyler make are primal, feral, and not very human. They grapple, with Cairo shoving Tyler back into one of the doors that shatters from the impact. But when Tyler lunges for him again, teeth sinking into Cairo's shoulder, I realize why it seems so one-sided.

Cairo is fighting to get Tyler to stop, to shove him away, and repel his attacks.

Tyler, on the other hand, is fighting to kill Cairo, or at least lethally wound him, judging by the way he's going for Cairo's throat and chest.

I don't know what to do. I don't know how to help him, when Cairo is being so hesitant about actually hurting Tyler for some unknown reason. "Cairo!" I shriek, reaching up to grip Agatha's arm for support, though I don't try to tug her off of me. Somehow, her hold is reassuring, and so is her solidness behind me.

Finally, Moro gets tired of dancing around. She jumps forward just as Cairo stumbles back, and in the small space between them she lunges at Tyler without any kind of fear. It's a good thing, I realize belatedly, because as blood arcs through the air from a wound in Cairo's shoulder, I know that he is definitely injured.

Moro takes additional offense at that, snarling and nipping at Tyler. It helps that he's already worn out, and Moro's quick, darting movements only serve to tire him out more as she blocks Tyler from getting closer to Cairo and causing him to spit in frustration. He looks at Agatha, then me, and bares his teeth when he meets my eyes.

"You're always so lucky," he spits at Cairo, who's curled up on the ground with a hand over the bleeding wound on his shoulder. "But you won't be forever!" He fends off another of Moro's quick lunges and growls at her, causing the dog to start backward momentarily in alarm. It gives him the chance to turn, and he quickly disappears around the wall of Bluebone Ridge's main building, with quick and graceful movements. But I only watch for a moment. As soon as I feel Agatha's arms loosening, I bolt for Cairo.

I'm too slow.

He's up and moving, ignoring my words and my cry of his name. With my hand reached out, I barely manage to brush his arm and feel his muscles jerk under my touch, before he flees into the woods in the opposite direction from where Tyler went.

"Where is he—" I turn to look at Agatha for answers, only to find that she's gone as well.

I'm alone with Moro at Bluebone Ridge, with only blood on the steps to prove that the others were ever here at all.

But I can't focus on wondering how they move so fast, or where Agatha and Tyler have gone. Frankly, I don't want anything to do with Tyler at all. Only one thought echoes in my head as I jog back to my car for my phone, following the bright headlights that are still the only real source of consistent light in the courtyard, except for the moon.

I have to find Cairo

CHAPTER TWENTY

AFTER NEARLY TWENTY MINUTES SEARCHING THE AREA WITH MY PHONE light and Moro, I realize Cairo is gone. That, or he's somehow hiding his scent from Moro, who seems just as eager to find him as I am.

"Come on," I call Moro with a sigh, leading the way back to the car. My hands are shaking, causing the light from the phone to waver a little, and it's cold enough that I'm really starting to feel it. Especially since I'm not exactly dressed for anything other than bed or a gentle late summer breeze. I turn the heat up the moment I sit in my car, giving an all over shiver as Moro pants and stretches out in the back seat.

She isn't as relaxed as usual, though. She whines on the drive back down the mountain, and fidgets more than her normal amount. But I can't blame her. I hate that we didn't find Cairo, and worry itches at me.

What if he isn't okay?

What if Tyler hurt him badly enough that he won't be able to heal like he did last time? The worry plagues me the whole way home, until it's a knotted pit in my stomach that I can't shake. When I finally pull into my driveway, I cut the engine and rest my head against the steering wheel with a sigh. There's nothing else I can do here.

Moro's bark startles me, making me jump. I sit up and look at her, twisting to glare at her over my shoulder. "What's your —" She cuts me off with another bark, her ears stiff and her eyes fixed on something I can't see. The wolf dog isn't paying me the least bit of attention, though I don't know why.

Fear creeps over me, along with the sudden worry that we aren't alone here. Hadn't it only been a few days ago that the creature was in the woods behind my house? What's to stop Tyler from figuring out where I live, and coming here to take revenge on Moro or me for getting in the way of him killing Cairo?

Sitting in the car isn't helping, though. I'd rather be in the house, where I have more to defend myself with, just in case. But when I open the driver's side door, Moro surprises me by lunging forward and over me, stepping on my thigh and my spleen hard enough to make me gasp and arch off of the seat, hampered only by the seatbelt. "Moro!" I gasp, voice breathy with pain. "Wait!" She doesn't. Even as I fight the seatbelt and almost clock myself in the face with it, she disappears behind my small house. At last I'm able to stumble after her, barely managing to slam the car door behind me.

Her barking is the only thing I can follow, but as I worry that she's disappeared into the woods, I see her grey and white coat illuminated in the moonlight shining into my cleared backyard. She prances worriedly around the stairs of the deck, her tail up and waving like a flag, her movements are almost concerned as a soft whine sounds in her throat.

Cairo groans and sits up from my bottom step, trying to fend off her affection. "You make it impossible to go anywhere without *everyone* knowing," he complains, his voice hoarse as he tries to hold her at arms' length and fails. "You know that, Moro?"

I can't help it. I take a sharp, surprised breath, quickening my steps until I'm all but running toward him. "Cairo!" I call, flushed with sudden relief at his presence. "Holy *shit!* We looked for you up on the mountain for—"

"Twenty minutes, give or take, judging by how long it's been," he cuts in sourly, rolling his gaze up to meet mine with a flat, pained look. It's then that I see the blood and the wound marring his shoulder and the base of his throat.

I don't stop jogging toward him, even when he bares his too-sharp teeth at me and his eyes flicker in the moonlight. While it should give me pause, it doesn't. Not at this point. I kneel in front of Cairo when Moro moves with a whine in her throat, but when I reach for him, he grips my wrists with a low, frustrated growl.

"I don't need your help, little bird," he tells me flatly.

"Maybe not, but you did show up on my back deck. In case you didn't notice." I shake his hands off of mine, my eyes fixed on the gouge in his shoulder that makes my stomach twist with nausea. "Cairo..." God, it looks bad, but I don't want to say that out loud.

He grumbles under his breath, but lets me sink down beside him on the steps, my teeth biting into my lower lip at all the blood. It's impossible to ignore, and I take a long, shuddering breath. "You're bleeding."

"Yeah," he agrees with a small smirk in my direction. "That's what happens when cursed things fight."

Cursed. It's the second time he's used that word, and again it sticks in my head like it's important.

"Yeah, but like, you're *really* bleeding. Is it—" I have to swallow the first three words that come into my head, before I take a breath and try again. "Is it fatal?"

Gently Cairo reaches up to prod at the wound, wincing as he does. He comes away with blood that he examines, then lets out a rough breath, looking more irritated than panicked. "No. It'll take a lot more than this to kill me."

"Not much more," I can't help but reply, and that makes Cairo turn, grabbing my wrist that had been heading to touch the wound.

"*Much* more," he disagrees, his eyes shining in the moonlight with that creepy, unnatural glimmer. "Here." He tugs me forward, until my hand is splayed across his chest, blood slick against my palm. "You feel how he tried to claw out my heart? We don't need to worry about bones as much as humans. He could reach in here and just grab it. That would do the trick, and I'd be just as dead as any human I've eaten."

Cairo's words don't exactly comfort me, and he shifts my hand until my fingers brush the unmarred side of his throat. "The only other way he could've done it was to tear off my head. Not just break my neck or slit my throat. He'd have to rip my spine and everything connecting it, until he could make sure my head and body weren't still connected by even one sinew." My stomach twists, clenching, and I make to move away, but he won't let me. Instead my fingers clutch lightly at his throat, and I feel him swallow under me.

"That's the only way you can die?" I breathe softly, not realizing how close I'm leaning. "Tear out your heart or cut off your head? That's very vampire-lore of you."

He snorts, shaking his head, and Cairo releases himself from my hand to settle back on my stairs, where he's definitely getting blood all over the wood. "I suppose setting me on fire would work. We are quite flammable. But because of that, it's not something we're willing to do to each other." When Cairo heaves himself to his feet, I'm up with him, immediately gripping his wrist even though I know I couldn't stop him if he wanted to shake me off.

"Wait," I breathe. "Please don't go."

He wavers. I can feel him consider my words even as he stares thoughtfully at the trees. But when I tug lightly on his arm, Cairo pauses, giving me a look over his shoulder. "Just for now," he agrees at last, seemingly unsure of the commitment. "I have to eat in the next day or so."

"I could fix..." I trail off when I realize how stupid that sounds, and his eyes narrow as he pins me with his amused gaze.

"No, little bird. I don't think you want to be involved in my meal plans." He rolls his shoulders with a grimace that only makes fresh blood soak into his shirt, and I hear the grating groan in his throat from pain.

"Come on." Before he can change his mind, I pull him up the stairs, though he's definitely putting in all the work for himself. He doesn't need to lean on me, or even really need to let me pull him along, as my blood-slick fingers fumble at the unlocked back door. I can hear his derisive scoff, and I'm sure he's burning to tell me something about my lack of common sense.

But honestly, it appears I forgot to lock it after letting Moro out for the last time before bed. "God, you're such a mess," I mumble, when I'm able to see him in the low light from the living room lamp. He turns away from it, eyes squinting shut, and it gives me time to catalogue his wounds.

"Your clothes are wrecked," I add. "I don't suppose you have some secret stash nearby? Surely you don't just roam naked in the woods when you aren't, I don't know, terrorizing people or living in asylums for fun?"

Cairo snorts. But let's me drag him back to my bathroom, the same place I first brought him when he showed up here injured and filthy. Though this time is definitely worse, and I'm not quite as afraid of his sharp edges as I had been then, though it's only been such a short amount of time.

"Cairo..." I sigh as I look at him in the light from my bedroom, having not turned on the bathroom light. He prefers the dark, and I would be able to tell even if he hadn't told me so. Unfortunately, I don't have magic—or cursed—glowy eyes, so I need at least a little light to see him by. Just like last time, Moro hops up onto my bed, stationing herself as lookout even though she's curled up in my usual spot instead of standing sentry duty.

"What's wrong, little bird?" He flashes his fangs at me in a grin, and obediently leans down so I can peel his mangled shirt off over his head. "Don't like what you see?"

"Of course I don't like seeing you all fucked up," I'm quick to snap, though my voice is light and without any real malice. "You don't think he'll come here, right? To like, finish you off?"

Cairo shakes his head. "Tyler doesn't know where you live, or I wouldn't be here. And he's never been a good enough tracker to find anything. Except for Hattie." He rolls his eyes. "I think she's some kind of magnet for him, but that's not important."

I want to ask more about it, but I file away my questions for later. He's right. It's unimportant right now, when I'm much more concerned for *him*. "Why didn't you do what he did?" Once I've got the shower on and heating up, I carefully unbutton the front of his jeans. Cairo stiffens, though I can't tell if it's from the question or my bold, unhesitant actions. His fingers find mine, and when I look up at him, I see a glint of surprised amusement in his face.

"What are you doing?"

"Getting you naked, obviously." I roll my eyes, and his smirk grows.

"Oh yeah? You're the one in charge now?" He's avoiding my question, and I tug on the front of his jeans, though he isn't exactly putting up any kind of fight. I swear I hear a purring sound in his throat, and his hands drop to my elbows, encouraging my actions as I peel his jeans down his bloody thighs, along with his underwear.

It's the first time I'm really seeing him, without the haze of heat and passion and tinge of fear the other night. My gaze flickers to every part of his olive skin, whether it's bloody or clean, and with his jeans at his knees I reach up to trail my fingers over the v of his hips and upward. "Why didn't you want to hurt him?" I ask, more direct this time.

"Last I checked, I wasn't just batting at him with sheathed claws," Cairo snorts indignantly, reaching out to tap my cheek with his fingers that end in sharp, bloody nails.

But I just look at him, undeterred. "Liar. I don't know a lot, but I'm not stupid. I watch Animal Planet." That gets an eye roll from him that speaks volumes. "He was trying to kill you." I gesture to his neck for emphasis, and then poke at his chest, beside the worst of the claw marks. "You said earlier that the two ways to kill you are decapitation or ripping out your heart."

He looks sullenly away from me, toward the shower, then back at me with all the innocence of a puppy who's just eaten my shoes. "Shower's gonna get cold," Cairo remarks weakly.

"Then let it. Why were you trying not to hurt him when he wanted to *kill you*?"

I don't know why I'm expecting an answer. Even standing there and glowering at him, he doesn't look like he's about to back down. Instead he sighs, casting his gaze up to the ceiling. In a sudden flurry of movements, he strips me out of my clothes just like I'd done him, amidst my yelps of disagreement and my hands trying to fend him off.

But I suppose fair is fair. Especially when he hoists me against his chest and steps into the shower, under the hot spray that immediately has dark blood cascading in rivulets down my drain. "You're gross," I tell him, staring down at the blood and water eddying around my feet. He just purrs a laugh, reaching out to comb his fingers through my loose, blonde hair. "Why won't you answer me?"

Cairo continues what he's doing, until he has me up against the wall with his face pressed to my neck and his hands on my hips. He reminds me of a giant cat trying to get closer, trying to touch every part of me he can. But this isn't about me, when he's so injured. It takes a few seconds for me to push him off, especially when I want him right here, with his body covering mine. I *want* his oppressive warmth, and his touch that's so different from anyone else's I've ever felt. I love his quiet ferocity, his feral nature, and everything about him I've come to know so far.

But I want to take care of him.

"Stop trying to distract me. If you aren't going to answer me, just, I don't know, purr more," I complain. I manage to push him lightly against the wall of the shower, conscious of his wounds even if he isn't. Cairo watches me, a question in his glinting eyes, as I smooth my hands over the uninjured planes of his hips.

"Let me help you." It isn't a question, and just barely a request.

"You don't have to," Cairo replies, in an echoing tone that sounds so much like my own voice it sends a shiver down my spine to hear it.

"But I want to." He doesn't reply, and the echo of my words die in the small space as I stand in front of him, waiting. I expect Cairo to push me away. I expect him to growl, and give me his usual level of roughness. It's clear he doesn't like being fussed over or being cared for, but here in the darkness of my shower, with hot water raining down on both of us and sluicing away the blood from his wounds and his claws, he seems to melt just a little.

I can't help my feeling of victory when his shoulders relax ever so slightly. So I lean up on my toes and brush my lips to his, though his hand comes up between us for him to grip the base of my throat with a low growl. "Don't push your luck," he purrs in my ear, though there's no anger in it. If I had to guess, he's like a wild animal right now. One who's wounded and afraid and fighting his urges to push everyone away so he can lick his wounds on his own.

But he doesn't need to push me away.

Though I don't know how to make him see that. I sigh and reach up to brush my fingers over his lower lip, feeling the flesh under the pads of my fingers. He turns with my movements, nipping lightly at my fingers with his sharp teeth, and again I hear that purring growl I'm starting to think isn't a sound of displeasure at all.

"Does it hurt?"

"All the time." But when Cairo meets my eyes, it hits me that he's not talking about his wounds.

"I meant—"

"I know what you meant, Fern. Yes." He rolls his shoulders with a grimace. "They don't exactly feel good. They'll heal in a few days, though. By morning they'll be more annoying than anything." But he leans back against the wall under the spray, eyes going half-lidded as a sigh leaves his barely parted lips.

I take that as the most permission I'm going to get. With a wet rag I wipe gently along his body, not getting too close to the ragged claw marks across his chest while wiping away the dried blood that water from the shower can't penetrate. He twitches under me every few seconds as I get closer to the wounds with the soft rag. But I'm careful not to hurt him, and after a few minutes I'm satisfied with my work. Next I move to the gouge on his neck, shivering at the muscle and bone I swear I can see.

"This is so bad," I breathe, not really wanting to be heard over the sound of the rushing water. "Cairo..." He reaches out to grip my elbow, stroking his thumb along my skin.

"I've had worse," he sighs. "This would be bad for you, but for me..." He rolls his shoulder with a pained grimace. *"I've had worse.* The rules are different when you're cursed, little bird. This is one of the few perks." His lips twitch in a rueful grin. "If you can call them that, anyway."

I snort, but don't answer. After all, I would definitely call healing this fast, and being able to just walk away with wounds like this, absolute perks. But without knowing why he's 'cursed' or what he did, I don't really want to comment. When I'm done, the wound on his shoulder and throat looks a little better, at least in my opinion. I swear I can't see quite as much bone, though it still makes me queasy to look at if I focus on it too much.

The rest of his body is mostly unmarred, save for a few scratches, but when I start to pull away, Cairo suddenly grasps my arm with a soft sound in his throat. "Wait," he murmurs, eyes shining with reflected light so eerily like a cat's.

"Yeah?" I breathe, heart in my chest.

"You missed one." His eyes flick downward, then back up. I'm confused for a moment, until he shifts pointedly, drawing my gaze down to the smallest possible graze on the front of his thigh. My mouth twitches in the hint of a grin, but I hold a straight face, gazing up at him with wide eyes.

"You're right," I agree softly. "I can't believe I missed that." The same half-hidden smile flickers on his lips as well, and I can see the amusement dancing in his eyes. Even on me, the scratch on his thigh would be minor at best. Like a scrape from a branch or something rough on bare legs.

When I drop to my knees, he draws in a surprised breath, like he hadn't expected that from me; it makes me smile slightly. I keep my eyes on his as he widens his stance a little so my knees fit between his ankles perfectly, the shower water raining onto my hair and cascading down my shoulders.

"Tell me how to make you feel better," I murmur, my voice quiet in the small, dark space.

"I'd rather show you." The rough purr is back in his voice, as one hand comes up to thread through my soaked hair and his nails scrape against my scalp. "You're too tempting down there, little bird." But he doesn't pull me to my feet. He guides my face closer to where his other hand is wrapped around the base of his cock that's swelling under the attention.

My eyes dip to it, and I gaze at the impressive length that's just as striking as the rest of him. I can't help but wonder if this part of him changed, too, whenever he became what he is. Or if he was always just very *gifted* as a human.

With the flat of my tongue I lap over his tip, hearing his soft intake of breath as I do it again. I tease him with little kitten licks and teasing flicks of my tongue, my eyes on him to watch every small reaction and micro-expression. He's so hard to read that I have to watch closely, but I'm getting better.

I know when he's getting frustrated, so it isn't a surprise at all when his fingers tighten in my hair and he hisses with impatience. "Little bird…" he warns in a voice that echoes off the tiles, becoming different halfway through and mimicking someone else's, though I don't know whose. His throat works as he trails off, tensing, and I wonder if he has any idea he's doing it at all.

"What's wrong?" I ask, turning my face to nuzzle at the

side of his length before kissing his tip with a smirk on my lips. "Am I not doing it right, Cairo?"

That brings a growl from him, and his eyes snap open so he can look at me, though all I see is the glimmering green reflective surface, instead of his pupils or irises around them. "You're getting too bold, for a human," Cairo warns, making my stomach flutter at the tone. "You'll regret it if I lose control and show you what you do to me."

"So you're saying I should take pity on you?" Without waiting for an answer, I lick over his tip again, sending another full body shudder through him.

"I'm *saying*...Either you get your mouth on my cock, or I'll fuck your face to show you the consequences of being such a fucking tease." He doesn't look at me, with his eyes shut again and head against the wall. So he can't see my challenging, teasing grin. Nor how I go back to little laps and licks, my tongue stroking, but not doing more than teasing his tip between my lips.

He tolerates it for about thirty more seconds. Long enough for my arrogance to grow, and for me to decide that he's bluffing about dishing out consequences whatsoever. At least, until suddenly he apparently snaps. I feel his body tense against me, and Cairo's fingers tighten in my hair. "I warned you," he growls softly, and then he's dragging the tip of his cock over my lips, no longer letting me set the pace.

"Did you?" I ask, knowing it'll just spur him onward. But I can't help wanting to see what he'll do. To know exactly what will happen if I push my flesh-eating monster when he's in my shower with my mouth so close to his cock.

Another growl is my answer, and he lets go of my hair to grip my jaw in his hand. Without a word, he presses at the hinges of my jaw, forcing my lips open unless I want it to hurt like a bitch. I do give him a bit of token resistance, which only makes him tilt his head in a way that causes my stomach to flutter. He doesn't press harder, he just *looks* at me.

But it's enough. I open my mouth, allowing his cock to slide over my lips. While I watch his face, he feeds me his length, an inch at a time, until he's heavy on my tongue and I have to breathe through my nose as I sit on my knees in front of him.

A soft whine leaves me when I feel his tip against the back of my throat, and I shiver, even as Cairo's hand moves back to my hair where he scrapes affectionately at my scalp. "That's my good little bird," he purrs, voice rumbling in his throat. "You look so good on your knees. I've wanted you there for so long. Come on, pretty girl." Leaning against the wall, he arches his hips until he can sink further into my mouth, making me thankful I don't have much of a gag reflex considering how big he is.

His hand tightens as he pulls back, holding me in place. Holding me *exactly* where he wants me. There's something hot about that. At being his toy here in the shower, where he's being oh-so-careful not to hurt me when we both know he could rip me apart without any effort at all.

Never in my life could I have imagined being a monster's toy like this.

Now I don't think I could find anything more satisfying.

I can feel the strength and control in his grip as he languidly rolls his hips forward to fuck my mouth. Cairo is so measured, even as his breath hisses through his teeth, and my thighs tense under me, heat pooling between my thighs at the weight of him on my tongue and the sheer control he has over everything.

"You like being down there." It isn't a question, and his words are slurred a little as they pass his fangs. "Fuck, you *love* being down there for me, little bird. You can't deny it when I can smell it. Come on," he goads. "Touch yourself for me. Do something useful with your hands." His eye contact is almost overwhelming, but I can't stop myself from doing as he says. Even though I'd rather have his hands, his mouth, or his cock, I slide my finger along my slit, releasing a soft whimper at the smooth glide from the shower and my arousal.

I've never been one to find this hot. But then again...no one can ever compare to Cairo. A soft sigh leaves me as I relax a little, teasing my clit with my fingers as he continues to thrust down my throat. Another sound leaves me when he thrusts harder, though he murmurs comfort and filthy praise with his eyes shining, glittering in the dark. There's nothing human about his face from this angle, with the glitter of his teeth and the shine of his inhuman eyes.

But that's absolutely part of the appeal. His claws continue to scrape against my scalp, not hurting me, but I still know it's a possibility. I can't do anything but be *his* with him looming over me like this, though he's so relaxed and languid against the wall. When he pulls out of my mouth with an appreciative sigh, I immediately shift on my knees, licking a trail of water up his inner thigh until I can nuzzle and lick at his cock playfully, teasingly.

"You're begging to get hurt, little bird," Cairo sighs softly, brushing his hands against the sides of my face, his thumbs trailing over my cheekbones. "You're going to make me lose control."

"Then lose control," I breathe, kissing the tip of his cock. "You think I mind?"

His grin turns a little less friendly, and he tilts his head to the side. "I think you're arrogant. You'd regret me taking you like the monster I am." That does nothing to cool down my body. If anything, it makes me arch my hips into my hand, causing my breath to hitch when I continue to tease my clit while he watches.

"Such a pretty, gorgeous thing," Cairo purrs. "Get your mouth back on my cock, Fern. I want to come in your mouth and watch you swallow all of it." It's not a request, and he doesn't give me a chance to consider it. With one hand at the base of his length and the other back in my hair, he slips his cock back into my willing, open mouth while I remember how to breathe through my nose.

Fuck, it's so much hotter than it has any right to be. He never slams down my throat, or speeds up his rhythm. He just fucks my face with the same controlled dominance and restrained power as he whispers and hisses half-slurred praises under the spray of the shower.

Cairo lasts until I'm arching my hips consistently against my fingers and making sounds of pleasure against him. Then, without warning, his fingers tighten against my scalp and he drags my face closer, until my nose is pressed to his skin and his cock is buried down my throat so far I feel tears in my eyes. I whimper, barely able to breathe, but he holds me there while growling and giving soft, snarled noises while he rocks his hips against my face.

I feel his cock swell and pulse, and though I can't taste it, I feel his release in my throat, prompting me to swallow around him. He shudders at that, head thrown back, and holds me there while he rides out his release. I want to tease him, to lick at his skin, but all I can do is hollow my cheeks and swallow around him again until he's snarling and suddenly yanking me to my feet, instead of keeping me on my knees.

"Such a fucking brat when you want to be," he chuffs, spinning me and dragging me against him so my back presses to his chest. I gasp at the quick motion, worried about his wounds as the water starts going cold. But he doesn't let me voice my concerns, just grabs my face in one hand, turning my head and forcing my face to his. He kisses me long and deep while two fingers plunge into my pussy so quickly my knees nearly buckle with pleasure. He's so good at knowing how to get me off. Just like the other night, within minutes I'm sagging against Cairo, and his arm is the only thing holding me up while he fingers me.

"Such a good girl for me," he murmurs in my ear, spreading my pussy with two fingers and using the other to run his fingers along my slit. "Will you come for me, little bird? On my fingers like you did on my cock?" His middle finger finds my clit unerringly, teasing and stroking, until I'm a mess in his arms. He kisses me again before I can say anything, and this time I can feel his tongue tasting and teeth nipping my mouth.

He's way too good at this.

I sob and thrash against him, wordless, and only manage a keen against his mouth as his fingers play with my nipples and I come without much more effort.

There's definitely something supernatural about *this* aspect of Cairo as well. That's the only thing I can think of as he rubs my slit and I pant my way back from oblivion. "You'll...stay..." I pant, leaning back against him and trying to stay away from the worst of his wounds, even if he doesn't seem to care about them. "You'll stay tonight, right?"

Before he can reply, I turn to meet his gaze, and something softens on his face as it becomes more human. He sighs and leans down to lick my cheek, one hand splayed across my stomach as he reaches out to turn off the water before it's completely cold instead of just tepid.

"Yeah, little bird," he huffs out. "I'll stay. For now."

CHAPTER TWENTY-ONE

I DON'T WANT TO LEAVE HIM.

Though I feel like such a creep right now.

Sitting on the bed with my legs crossed under me, I rest my weight on my elbows even while I roll Moro's ears between my fingers, thumbs stroking at the soft fur. She's still half asleep, breathing deeply while surreptitiously worming her way closer and closer to my warm spot that I'll be leaving behind when I commit to getting up.

But I can't stop staring at Cairo, who's well and truly sleeping for the first time that I've seen. Even when he stayed over before, I wasn't convinced he slept. But with his lips parted softly and his eyelashes fluttering with dreams, or maybe nightmares, he looks so *human* in my bed. His sharp teeth are barely visible, and his inhumanly dark, reflective eyes are hidden from me under the sweep of his long lashes.

I can't help watching him. While I don't consider myself some kind of creepy stalker who watches the guy I fucked while he sleeps the next morning, I still can't tear my eyes away. At least until he sighs, and his mouth quirks up into a soft, rueful grin.

"You're being weird, little bird," Cairo murmurs sleepily, reaching one arm out toward me across the bed until he can brush my thigh. "Don't you think it's a little obsessive of you to watch me while I sleep?" The white of the bandages I applied to the worst of his wounds is, at least, still pretty clean.

"I've only been doing it for like a minute," I lie, not wanting to admit it's been longer than that. His claws skim against my skin, and his smile widens.

"Sure you have." There's a purr in his voice, and when he finally opens his eyes, they're so dark that they're almost black. With a jolt, I realize that the dark circles under his eyes are back in full force, after they'd faded after the asylum attack.

But now they're worse than I've ever seen them.

"Cairo..." I lean toward him, invading his personal space without hesitation. "Holy shit, you look like you haven't slept in—"

He sighs and buries his face sullenly in my pillow. "Thanks for the compliment," he grumbles, cutting me off. "Really makes me think you like me."

"Probably about as much as you like me," I agree, pressing my hand to his shoulder, trying to get him to roll over. "Come on."

"No. Don't you have *therapy?*" He turns just enough to roll his eyes up at me and reaches one hand down to scratch Moro's ears. "Moro and I are completely fine here."

He's definitely in a mood, and it's more than just his usual sarcasm. But if I had a hole bitten in my throat, I probably wouldn't be in too great of a mood either. So I sigh, not particularly offended, and lean down to kiss his cheek lightly, feeling him melt a little with a soft purr at my affection. "I'm fine, Fern," he promises me.

"Yeah, I figure if you made it through the night, you must be telling the truth." Sitting up, I go to move, only to be surprised when he grabs my wrist and yanks me back down until I'm on my back on the bed, and release a small gasp.

Cairo hovers over me, searching my face. "You shouldn't get so attached," he breathes suddenly, gazing down at me from those dark eyes that seem like black holes. "You're already *too* attached."

"Then so are you," I'm quick to respond, trying to sit up. But he stops me with a hand at the base of my neck, and Cairo looms over me, hovering and looking over all of me he can see. It makes me feel vulnerable in a way I can't explain.

"Yeah," he agrees at last, a rueful smirk tugging at his lips. "Little bird..." His thumb strokes the hollow of my throat, as he seems to consider his words. "Don't come out to the woods tonight," he says at last, his eyes holding mine. "Because you won't find *me* there."

"What do you mean?" His words only stir more confusion in me, especially when he leans closer and I can feel his breath against my lips. Cairo kisses me sweetly, his teeth sharp against my mouth, and pulls back with a sigh.

"You'll find what I am when I'm not holding back for you."

With that he licks over my lower lip, and before I can reply he rolls off of me to curl up under the blankets again. This time, Moro abandons all signs of being subtle, and burrows herself under the covers with him with a huff of satisfaction once she's stretched out against Cairo.

"Ridiculous." I sigh, watching both of them do their best imitation of sentient lumps. "I don't know why you're trying to scare me, but you're being *ridiculous*." Cairo doesn't reply, and Moro doesn't come out. But it's a bit of a relief to leave her here with him, rather than having to worry about her being alone in the house.

With a groan, I'm out of bed, tugging off my t-shirt and boy shorts. But no matter how many remarks I make or unnecessary door slamming I do, they still don't come out of their blanket cocoon. Soon enough, it becomes apparent that Cairo is asleep again, which gives me pause.

If he's really asleep, does that mean he *needs* it to get better? I've never seen him so quick to surrender to unconsciousness, and I work to quiet my movements as I finish getting dressed in a new t-shirt and loose sweatpants. The whole time I run a brush through my hair, I stare at the lumps on my bed, leaning in the doorway of my bathroom.

You'll find what I am when I'm not holding back for you.

I'm not exactly sure what he means by that, but it's clear he doesn't think I should find out. With one last sigh, I push away from the wall to put my hair in a ponytail and head toward the front door with my phone in one hand and my keys in the other. Though I pause with my head pressed to the wood, listening for anything other than Moro's snores, and hear nothing.

"Bye," I murmur, knowing he can't hear me and not expecting an answer. I don't get one, but that's all right. It makes me feel better to say it, and makes something in me loosen a little, when I remind myself that I'll be back way before dark, and I'm sure he'll still be here.

I hope.

S tanding outside of Dr. Radley's office reminds me of how much I don't want to be here. The blonde is anything but my friend, and nothing in me wants to walk into her office and deal with her droning on for the next hour about my mental state.

Last time, she gave me a damn panic attack.

But I force myself into the room with a sigh, closing the door behind me when Dr. Radley looks up at me with a bright, natural smile on her face that makes me feel incredibly bad about my misgivings of her.

The hour even goes okay, considering I avoid most of her questions or at least work not to answer honestly. Though she doesn't seem to mind so much.

But that could be because she can't stop looking at her phone. It's like she's waiting for someone or for something to happen. It's rude, and I figure it's not very ethical for a doctor, not that I'm about to say a word about it. I'd rather she paid less attention to me, and it makes the minutes tick by faster when she barely remembers what she's asked.

The moment the clock's big hand on the wall hits the twelve, I'm up and out of my seat with excuses on my lips about needing to get home to my dog. "Sorry," I apologize, not for the first time. "I haven't had her for very long. So I worry that she'll tear down the house in my absence, you know?" I offer Dr. Radley a plaintive smile that she returns before getting up as well.

"I like dogs," she tells me kindly. "You could always bring her here if she's well behaved. Did you get her after what happened at Bluebone Ridge?"

There's no way I can bring Moro here.

Not when there's every chance that Dr. Radley will absolutely recognize Moro and where she came from. I shake my head with an apologetic grimace. "No, she's weird. She, uh, might vomit on your nice rug." I've never seen her vomit, but it's at least an easy excuse. "And yeah. I was looking at getting a dog before...that. But then afterward, I realized I didn't want to be alone."

Even though Cairo is usually lurking around enough that I wouldn't be alone, even without my dog. With a few more polite words to my therapist, I edge out of the room at last once she's again looking at her phone instead of at me.

I'm grateful for it, and I let out a sigh of relief while taking the stairs quickly, nearly tripping down them. Once I'm out the door, I glance at the diner, giving a few stray thoughts about ordering something. But with leftovers in the fridge, I decide it isn't worth it. I really should just go home and be a responsible adult who eats what's still in her kitchen.

"Could've gotten a shake," I grumble to myself, meandering down the sidewalk back toward the parking lot on the other side of the old brick building. "Could've gotten a fried bologna sandwich and a shake, and I would've been so—"

The moment I turn the corner, something grabs me, shoving me hard enough into the brick wall that I drop my keys to the ground and yelp out a sound of pain and surprise. "What—" For a terrifying moment, I'm sure that it's Tyler. This would be the perfect place to kill me, after all, when Agatha and Cairo are nowhere in sight.

But it's *Hattie*. She leans in, shoulders shaking, with her hands knotted in my shirt and trembling. *"Shhh,"* she croons, stepping so close our bodies are pressed together. *"Shhh,* Fern, don't yell. Don't scream, just..." She shudders again and buries her face against my shoulder, unmoving for so long I wonder wildly if she's fallen asleep.

"...Hattie?" My hand comes up, but my voice is enough to jerk her out of whatever trance she was in. She stands up straight with her gaze on mine, and then I notice the dark circles under her eyes are so bad that she looks like she has a pair of black eyes.

"Oh, *fuck.*" I drop my hand and lean against the wall behind me as my stomach knots itself tightly. "Oh, *fuck,* Hattie." I don't know what else to say.

"I won't hurt you," she's quick to promise. Her hands tense, gripping my sleeves more tightly. "Fern, I'd never hurt you. Not when you were nice to me." But she trails off and inhales deeply, her eyes sliding shut. She's perfectly still until a shiver goes through her, and her eyes open again.

"But Fern." Again she leans against me, embracing me like I'm the one that needs comfort instead of the one who desperately wants to get out of this situation. Clouds roll over the sun and a breeze picks up in the absence of a clear sky. It makes it hard to hear what she says, but somehow, I make it out anyway.

"I'm just so hungry."

Fuck.

The words repeat in my head, and I force myself not to run or push her away. I don't know that I could get away from her if she's as strong as Cairo is. And I don't want to upset her with any sudden movements. On the other hand, I know I need to get away from her before she hurts me. Or worse.

"Okay. Umm. I-I want to help you," I stammer, with my heart racing like a rabbit's in a snare. "Hattie—" Suddenly one of her hands moves and she presses her palm to my chest while locking her wide, dark eyes on mine.

She sucks in a breath, then lets it out. Hattie does it again, breathing in shaky, uneven motions that cause her whole body to jerk, like a marionette with an unsteady puppeteer. "You're afraid of me," she says at last, and it's like an unexpected revelation as the words leave her mouth in a breathy whisper. "You think I'm going to hurt you."

I think she's going to *eat me,* but I'm not about to say that out loud. So I take a few deep breaths to steady myself, hoping to maybe influence her gasps into something calmer and less panicked. But it doesn't help. "You have me pinned against a wall, Hattie," I point out softly. "You just startled me. I want to help you."

Hattie shakes her head and looks away, frustration on her face. "No...no, I didn't come here for your help," the redhead tells me, like she's confused and trying to remember exactly why she came here in the first place. "No, I came to help *you.*"

I don't know what she could help me with, when she's clearly the more unwell of the two of us. But I'm not about to say that either. "What are you trying to help me with?" I ask her very slowly, like I'm afraid of spooking a wild animal.

Her sudden, broken laugh seems desperate, and I flinch at the unexpected sound. All at once, Hattie lunges to cradle my face in her hands, and her wide, dark eyes hold mine as she comes close enough for me to feel her breath on my lips, intimate like a lover's.

"Don't let him do this to you, Fern," Hattie whispers. "Don't let him make you like *us.*"

"What?" My brain is struggling to put the words together in a way that fits. Cairo certainly hasn't tried to make me into anything. Carefully, I bring up my shaking hands to curl my fingers around Hattie's delicate wrists. "What did Tyler do to you, Hattie?" I ask in as steady a voice as I can manage.

But all she does is shudder, then smile while inclining her head, until our foreheads press together and I can feel the cool clamminess of her skin. "He told me I'd feel better, Fern. He said the hunger isn't so bad...that everything else is worth it." She gives another full-body shiver, and her nails scrape against my face, causing me to gasp and wince away from the sharp, sudden pain.

"But I'm just so *hungry.* And I don't think he loves me like I love him. Don't let Cairo do this to you. Don't let him change you, okay? Promise me." Her grip tightens, drawing a soft sound of pain from me as I try to pry her off, increasing my struggle to get free.

"Hattie, stop!" I whine, writhing. "You're hurting me!"

"Promise me, Fern!" Her voice isn't hers any longer. It's mine. An eerie replica that sounds so spot on, it's like listening to a perfect recording of myself.

Finally, I whisper, trying not to scream, "Yes, I promise! I promise! I won't let him—"

She releases me suddenly, and I crumple to my knees, hitting the sidewalk without noticing the rough scrape of it on my skin. When I look up, Hattie is gone, and the clouds roll away from the sun like none of it ever happened. Leaving me alone on the ground with my keys, only steps from my car.

CHAPTER TWENTY-TWO

"Cairo?" My voice echoes through my empty house, and when Moro meets me at the door, tail wagging and whining softly, I realize he isn't here.

With my heart still racing from my encounter with Hattie, I can't help thinking that he's picked a really shitty time to vanish. But I sigh and slide down against the closed door, allowing Moro to sniff and lick my face while doing her inspection of me. "Thanks," I breathe, reaching up to rub her ears. "At least I always have you."

But what if I didn't?

Panic claws at my throat. I kept my anxiety under control all the way home by telling myself that Cairo would be here, and he'd be the one to explain and make everything seem okay. But now that I'm alone, I have to remind myself that I've been dealing with life on my own for years.

I don't need a man—or a monster—to help me stay calm. As long as no first-aid scissors are within reach, I guess. The ironic, macabre humor of the thought makes me snort, and I lean back against the door as Moro worms her way into my lap like she's a Yorkie instead of a wolf dog. Not that I mind. I could *never* mind her affection. Gripping her fur helps to ground me and remind me that things other than my racing thoughts exist.

"Thank you," I tell her, though she obviously has no idea what I'm saying. Moro is just happy for the attention I'm more than willing to give. I take a deep breath. Then another. Just to be thorough, I count to ten, then back down to one, all the while running my fingers through Moro's thick ruff. "Okay. I can't sit on the floor forever, huh?" Pushing her off of my lap, I get to my feet; wavering just a little in the living room while listening once again for any other noise in the house.

I'm still nervous and anxious as hell. But I feel a little more grounded than I did when I first walked inside and Cairo was nowhere in sight. *He has a life too,* I remind myself. I can't expect him to just be here, waiting for me, whenever I need him.

It's not like he's particularly comforting anyway.

That's what I tell myself as I remind my brain of his sharp teeth, his inhuman eyes, and how much he's hiding from me. I barely know anything about him, or where he's come from. I can't trust him, I try to convince myself as I grab a box of cereal and dump a liberal amount into my favorite bowl, followed by some oat milk.

I can't trust a monster.

But the word feels like an insult, and my stomach curls unhappily when I try to relate him to the word. Even though I know he eats people, literally, and that he *ate Esther,* it's still impossible for me to put him in the same category as the thing that attacked me, the one that killed Sam, or even Tyler.

On the other hand, he and Agatha feel strangely similar to me. I know there's no way for me to look up anything about her, since typing in *Agatha monster* or any similar term on

Google will probably take me to a weird side of the internet really quickly. I don't even know how old she is, where she's from, or if Agatha is her real name. Something about her feels timeless. Like she's older than she looks.

I also can't help thinking about how differently Agatha and Cairo act than the others. Tyler too, in some ways, but he seems less in control. More feral, and more eager to hurt others. But Cairo and Agatha...

Well, I doubt I can summon Agatha with just wishes and by leaving a juicy steak outside of my door. I'd probably end up attracting a bear to my back deck instead. She seems more willing to tell me about the whole cursed thing than Cairo does, and in my opinion, I have a right to know.

"I really do," I tell Moro conversationally as I sit curled up on my couch eating my cereal. "He's part of my life. Doesn't that mean I should get to know about his?" Hattie's warning suddenly fills my ears, and I stop eating to give it some thought.

Don't let him change you.

There's no way around the fact that she's one of them now. But thanks to Cairo's evasiveness and Tyler's impeccable timing, I don't know what it takes to be changed.

"We can rule out biting," I mumble to my canine conversation partner. I still have the marks on my throat from Cairo's teeth, and I reach up unconsciously to brush my fingers over the bruises and the raw scrape. It doesn't hurt; the touch sends a shiver down my spine as I remember the feeling of his fangs on my skin. If he could turn me with a bite, then he'd surely be more careful where he puts his teeth. Obviously, it isn't sex, either.

But that leaves me completely at a loss as to what becoming like them entails.

When my cereal bowl is empty and I've poured the milk

down my throat, I get to my feet and absently wash it off in the sink. With Moro staring at me, I have no choice but to fill her bowl and grab a few treats out of the cabinet for her as well. She deserves breakfast too, after all. And that means I can leave her crunching happily on my bed as I walk to the bathroom to shower, even though I did so last night with Cairo.

But this time, it's not about getting clean, or washing blood off of his wounds. Though that thought only makes me worry more about him. I need the hot water to make me feel more like a person, and sometimes, hot showers do way more good than they have a right to. I'm hoping that's the effect today, plus it'll kill some time instead of me sitting and pining about Cairo being gone and putting off work.

Or at least, try not to think so much about how I'd rather him show up here. Or about how I want him to pin me to the shower wall and growl in my ear while he takes out his hunger on me in ways other than violence.

"Yeah, Mom, I'm fine. I promise." Sitting back on my couch with my laptop on my lap, I sigh up at my ceiling as shadows shift across the white paint. The sun is nearly set, and only a few rays show between the thick trees behind my house. Somehow, I've managed to stumble through more work today than I'd thought I would be able to do, but when I glance at my laptop again, I know that all of my motivation for it is gone.

"Maybe I could come down this weekend," she tells me, sounding unsure over the phone. *"I had a dream last night about you. I'm worried."*

"Oh, yeah?" Gently, I close my laptop and let it slide to the coffee table. "What did you dream about? Me in the shower with the *Psycho* music, dramatically stabbing myself with nail scissors or a letter opener?" I know she won't appreciate the flat humor in my voice, but I can't help myself.

Sure enough, I hear her intake of breath, and it's only a

moment before she's launched into her reproachful lecture. *"It isn't funny, Fern! You could've died. What if you hadn't made it out of that animal attack? What if the doctor sent you somewhere else on more than a three-day hold? You're not taking this seriously enough."*

I'm pretty sure I'm taking this just fine, but I don't reply. I don't want to encourage her to draw out this tirade any longer. Putting her on speaker, I get to my feet and head to the kitchen. She starts again while I get the dog treats out, and during her rant I decide to work on Moro's hand commands. Not that she needs much work. It's clear someone put a lot of time into her, though I have doubts about it being Jeremy.

Of all the people who got killed or eaten that night, he's the one I don't have any pity for.

"Are you listening to me?" she snaps, still in her tirade.

"Yeah, Mom, I'm listening." Barely. "Sorry, I didn't mean to upset you." She's never understood my sense of humor, or had much of one herself. So I don't know why I made the joke when I should've known it wouldn't be appreciated. It makes me feel even less...heard. She doesn't want my opinion. She wants to reassure herself I'm fine. "And I'm doing okay. Really. I've gotten a lot of work done this week, and—"

"Have you been going to your therapy appointments?" Though it shouldn't, the question catches me off guard. I pause with a treat hanging in the air over Moro's muzzle as she waits patiently with her tail thumping on the linoleum.

I take a breath and drop it into her mouth before picking up the phone, and rather than making Moro do any other commands, I give her the other three soft, sausage-shaped dog treats. "I didn't know you were aware I was going to see anyone," I reply carefully.

"She called to tell me. She said she was worried about you and wanted my support in getting you help." My mom is all business

now, and maybe a little smug to have caught me off guard. *"I don't know why you didn't tell me yourself, Fern. I think I deserve to know."*

"It's not like it's costing me anything," I say, before I can think better of it.

"You think I'd only care if this was about money?" I can hear her indignant tone coming through, and I know I'm in for it now. My anxiety rises, though I remind myself she can't do away. She's two hours away and I'm an adult, not a child who she can trap in the car and lecture into a coerced apology just to get the situation to stop.

I'm fine, I remind myself, leaning against the fridge. But that notion gets torn to shreds when her voice rises over the phone.

"You really must think I'm a shit parent, Fern. I don't care about what it costs. All I care about is you. I don't want to end up back at your house and this time find you dead because no one was there to prevent you from cutting yourself." There's no good way to stop her, so I blandly watch the sun as it finishes its disappearing act through the trees.

God, I don't want to be on the phone with her. But I can't do anything other than listen. She goes through the usual guilt trip, accusing me of calling her a bad, uncaring parent, and before I know it, the words I've been trying to avoid leave my mouth as a defense mechanism.

"I'm sorry, Mom." The apology is caustic on my tongue, burning up my throat like bile. "I didn't mean to say it. It's just that I'm tired, and a little stressed out. I shouldn't have made the joke, and I know you care."

A second apology mollifies her enough for her voice to go back to normal, though I feel like an old-world servant in supplication to a cruel king for having to repeat my words in a slightly different way to get the message across. She doesn't deserve my apology.

I don't deserve to feel this way.

"Therapy has been going well." It's my olive branch, and I spend a few minutes talking about some of the surface-level conversations I've had with my therapist. All the while, I think that they're *my* therapy sessions and she has no right to know what I talk about with Dr. Radley.

It takes another thirty minutes for me to completely subvert her anger, and I'm convinced I won't wake up to passive-aggressive posts about me on Facebook with comments from all of her almond mom friends reassuring her she's done nothing wrong. Yet again, I'm grateful I don't live with her anymore, and that she has her husband and step-kids to keep her too busy for frequent, spontaneous visits out to Whippoorwill Gap.

"I have to let you go, Fern." The announcement is everything I'm hoping for, and I sag against the fridge in tense relief. *"Nathaniel and I are going to that new Italian place I told you about for dinner. The kids are with Katherine."* I don't know who Katherine is, and I really don't care. She's probably told me before, but I generally listen just enough for her to think I'm interested when she raves about her life now that Dad is dead and I've 'left the nest' to be an adult.

"Oh! You'll have to tell me how it is!" I inject as much false enthusiasm into my voice as I can, keeping my tone light and friendly. "I don't know what I'm doing for dinner yet. Maybe I'll make pasta now that you've brought up Italian food." *I'm not making pasta...*My words are lighthearted enough, though, that it keeps her in a good mood, and finally after another minute, my mom hangs up with promises to try to call more often.

"Sure you will," I tell no one after I've hung up and pushed off the refrigerator door. "You'll totally remember to call more often." She won't. The resolution might last a week until she remembers I'm not similar enough to her to be entertaining. Then she'll go back to her mom groups and talk about how we've reconnected, and how involved she is in my life and recovery.

I'm so busy stewing in my frustration and self-loathing at how easily I caved and apologized for no good reason that it takes almost an hour for me to remember Cairo's words about not following him into the woods tonight. Which, naturally, only makes me even more curious about what exactly I'll find if I do.

Surely he can't be as much of a monster as he claims. There's no way he's out there doing something that would horrify me, after everything I've seen from him. He's not like Tyler or the others.

He's *Cairo.*

Gazing down at Moro, I sigh and scuff my bare foot on the floor. "I don't even know if I could find him without you," I admit, though I'm not sure I want to take her if there's some chance of her being in danger. If there really is something different about him tonight, I don't want Moro to pay the price for my recklessness. Though I doubt he'd hurt her considering how much affection he shows the dog, and the fact he saved her just as much as he saved me from Bluebone Ridge, then got her to my house afterward.

I *trust* him.

And yet...something about his warning feels off.

But I still feel bad as I assure Moro I'll be back, probably with her second favorite person on Earth since I'm not willing to give up my reigning title of favorite. But if not, I'll at least make her a hot dog when I'm back to soothe her disappointment.

I can't stop my hands from shaking a little as I pull on leggings and a loose hoodie that falls to mid-thigh. While it isn't winter here in Washington, this close to the mountains, the nights are almost always chilly, and I'm a delicate flower. Finally, I tug on a pair of my favorite sneakers, my ankles bare just enough to scandalize any Victorian preacher who might happen to be wandering the woods tonight.

For some reason, I hesitate at the deck stairs. Armed only with a flashlight and my phone, the night feels more dangerous than it usually does, even though it was less than twenty-four hours ago that I went up to Bluebone Ridge to look around after having a nightmare about that night. Surely if I can handle a haunted asylum crawling with monsters, then I can handle the woods behind my house.

"You're fine," I whisper to myself, while Moro whimpers and paws at the glass door behind me. In theory, any cursed I come across won't want to hurt me, as long as Cairo isn't too far away. That one I saw last week hadn't looked *so* bad, and didn't try to chomp on my innards at all.

But Cairo was right there, my brain reminds me sourly. *He's not here now.* Not that I can see, anyway. Still, I make myself walk down into the yard, feet crunching in the grass. I take a breath with my eyes on the dark trees in front of me. Considering my luck, I won't even be able to find Cairo. I'm just one person, and the forest back here is huge.

There's no trail for me to follow, and after about forty minutes of wandering around, some part of me relaxes. I'm sure now that there's no way I'm going to find him back here. No way I'll just magically stumble across him, or—

Something screams, sending a tremor up my spine and making me stumble to a stop. The trees loom ominously overhead, and I clench my teeth together until my jaws ache. The sound comes again, echoing through the trees, though I can't tell if the sound is human or animal.

Please, God, be an animal.

My mouth opens, and for a moment I think about calling out. But just as Cairo's name forms on my lips, I lose my confidence and the sound dies before it can truly form. The flashlight shakes in my hand, and I force myself to head toward where I think the echoing sound came from.

Again the creature cries out, a pained, agonized scream that bounces from tree to tree before sinking into me and pulling up a wave of nausea from my stomach. I breathe in through my nose, wanting to clasp my hands over my ears at the sound, for all the good it'll do. But the trees only seem to crowd closer to me as I walk, and when I look around, it occurs to me I have no clue about where I am. Worse still, when I check, my phone has no service this deep in the woods.

I've absolutely fucked up now, I realize, and I groan softly, a wounded sound in the back of my throat. I have no choice but to follow the noise, though the next cry wanes a little in the darkness. It hasn't quite finished ringing in my ears before something flashes in the illumination of my flashlight, and I dip the beam down to focus on dark black splashes on the grass in front of me.

Blood.

There's nothing else it can be, some rational part of me thinks. Only blood would look like this, the red color washed out in the darkness from the trees and the pale white lights of both my light and the moon shining down from above. Thankfully, the clouds from earlier have disappeared, because without the moon, I'd be a lot more panicked than I am. Even though the branches block out the majority, letting only eerie bars shine down on the underbrush to strike across it like bars, it's better than nothing.

But that's undoubtedly blood. The splashes get bigger, and closer together. When my light starts to shake, it takes a few seconds for me to realize that it's because my hand is shaking, not the light malfunctioning.

"You can do this," I breathe, though Cairo's warning replays over and over in my head. He won't hurt me...I hope. God, I hope my faith in him isn't misplaced, and that I'm not following something else entirely.

The scream comes again, cutting through my thoughts, and it's close enough that I jerk my flashlight up to scan the trees around me. "Cairo...?" What I wanted to be a loud call through the trees comes out as a whisper from my lips. But I don't stop moving; I continue to follow the blood trail that's now forming drag marks in the crushed grass. Even though my body is begging me to stop, to turn, to *run,* I tell myself that I'd know if what I was hearing is human.

So, it has to be an animal.

It has to be.

Gurgling noises find my ears, and I stop, too afraid to do anything but stare down at an illuminated patch of dirt. I can hear the sounds so close to me I know if I look too far ahead, I'll see whatever is making them.

Maybe it's not Cairo, I tell myself. *Maybe it's something else. Someone else.* While I wanted to find him, now I'm not so sure. Not now that the sounds are much less animalistic and so much more human.

I hear a soft, gasped plea, though it's broken off with a *snap* and one last breathy sound before the woods grow silent for only a moment. Then I hear the undeniable tearing and ripping of flesh; it takes everything in me to drag my gaze up from the dirt to look at the space between the trees in front of me.

Cairo is on his knees over a man's body, who I belatedly

recognize as Whippoorwill Gap's least favorite, most inappropriate drunk. He's not looking at the body, however. Cairo is staring at me with a snarl on his lips, and there's nothing human in the way his eyes reflect the glare from my flashlight.

He bares his teeth in a bloody snarl, as gore drips from his mouth, and he leans forward almost territorially across the body below him.

"You shouldn't have come here, little bird," he grates out, voice slurred from his fully extended fangs and what's in his mouth.

"Cairo..." my voice trails off, and my hand tightens on the flashlight as I take a step back, only to stupidly trip and fall on my ass on the dirt with a soft, pained gasp. "I didn't—I wasn't trying to—" When he sits up, I see his chest is bloody in the glow of my light, and once again he bares his sharp teeth. I've never seen him look less human.

Less safe.

"You should *never* have come here," he repeats as he leans down to the body of the man under him and tears into his chest.

And then, as I watch, Cairo eats.

CHAPTER TWENTY-THREE

My fingers go numb, causing the flashlight to hit the ground, and I scrabble back until I hit a tree behind me with a soft, breathy sound. The air escapes my lungs entirely, and I can't seem to draw more in as I watch him use his hands to tear into the man like a rotisserie chicken. Flesh parts like tissue paper under his sharp claws, and blood spurts upward, soaking Cairo's face and chest.

For a moment, when Cairo glances up at me before burying his face in his meal, I see the flash of his teeth and a glare in his eyes.

It wouldn't be so bad if I couldn't see the old drunk's face. But it jerks with every movement, his eyes sightless and staring up at nothing. His expression is fixed in a scream of fear, and I remind myself of all the times he stopped me in town, wanting money with alcohol on his breath and eyes that always wandered inappropriately.

No one will miss him.

There'd also been allegations, and reasons he never got hired, even at the local diner. I remember when he was in jail for three months, and everyone in Whippoorwill Gap was not so silently glad about it, so they could walk around at night without being accosted by him.

No one will miss him.

That's what I have to tell myself as I listen to his body get torn into smaller pieces for Cairo to eat. I make the mistake of looking at his face, of focusing on the way he tears away at the flesh over the man's ribs. One hand holds the body in place, like a dog's paw, and his mouth tears backward to rip away mouthfuls of his food.It's easier when I don't look at the dead man's face not to run away, but only a little.

"Oh, fuck," I whisper as I stand and take a step away from the tree behind me. Cairo growls low in his throat, territorial and soft, and his eyes roll up to find mine. "N-no, I'm not..." I don't know what to say, but I'm certainly not trying to fight him for his meal.

"I told you to stay home," he reminds me again in a guttural tone with his mouth full of blood. "I told you that you wouldn't like what you'd find out here."

His claws sink deeper when I take another step forward, and he growls again, pulling the corpse toward him possessively.

"Why?" I ask softly as I waver in place. "I thought you weren't like the others."

At that, he lets out a low, laughing growl. "I'm just like all of them deep down. I'm a *monster,* Fern. So many times I've tried to tell you to stay away. And I've tried to keep my distance from you. So go on then."

He looks at me, and as I watch, rips another strip of flesh off the man's chest. Blood and viscera drip from it, then his tongue comes out to taste as he lets it slip into his mouth.

"Ask me again."

I'm not sure what he means, so I just stare blankly until he gives a soft, frustrated chuff. "*Ask me* how I became *this*. I'll tell you this time, little bird."

Oh. Confronted with the reality of a cursed Cairo, I'm not so sure I want the answer. My hands clench at my sides as the forgotten flashlight lies on the ground and lights up the macabre scene in front of me with garish, uneven light. The angle never lets his eyes go back to normal, giving Cairo even more of a feral look than I've ever seen on him before. But even if curiosity killed the cat, I know somehow this is my only chance to ask.

"How did you become what you are, Cairo?" I ask in a voice barely more than a whisper.

He's silent for a moment, like he's surprised I had the courage to open my mouth and say it. That makes two of us, really, and I give myself an imaginary pat on the back for the boldness I didn't know I possessed.

"We used to go camping." His words snap me out of my thoughts, and I drag my eyes up from the corpse under him to meet Cairo's eyes. He licks his claws meticulously clean, sitting back with one hand still on the man's chest. "It was a long time ago. Before you were born." His grin is a flitting, flickering thing full of teeth and rueful amusement. "Before cellphones or GPS. We used to go camping in the mountains here. We weren't always so smart." He blinks, and I can finally take a breath when he looks away, his attention fixed somewhere in the past.

"I fell from a cliff on the north side of the mountain range. They looked for me, I think. But they couldn't find a way down, and help was days off. It should've been impossible for anyone to survive the fall, so they all went home and told my family I was dead." Here he lets out a snarl full of disgust. "I should've been dead, but I wasn't, and I hurt so much. I crawled around in the dirt and the mud and the *muck* with my legs broken and

the cold gnawing away at me until I couldn't feel my fingers."
Here his claws curl, sinking deep into the dead man's skin that
parts so easily.

"But how...?" To me, this sounds like a story of him *dying*.
Not coming back as something else.

He turns his face to me, his eyes green-yellow and no pupil
in sight. "Agatha was lonely back then. She was the only one
who was a little bit different." He clicks his teeth in frustration.
"She found me nearly dead, and wholly desperate. I was
starving, Fern. You can't imagine what it's like to be so hungry
you'll do anything. Not to mention the pain I was in from the
fall and the cold."

Unexpectedly, Cairo stands up, bloody and barely clothed.
His movements are quick and jerky, and when he grins at me,
his mouth seems to open unnaturally wide. "She knew what it
was like. She knew how hungry I was and offered me relief.
Then she told me she could kill me if I wanted. Or she could
save me." But there's a snarl on the word *save*. Like he's not
sure that's what really happened.

"You did what you had to do," I offer, unsure, but knowing
where this is heading.

"Yeah." His grin widens. "She brought me that hiker and
tore into him for me, as his blood steamed and she smeared it
on my face..." Then Cairo is in front of me, and I gasp when he
reaches up to grip my face in his bloody claws.

"I did *exactly* what I had to do in order to survive. And I've
never regretted eating him, or Esther, or this man." He gestures
at the drunk behind him. "Because, Fern, like I've been trying
to tell you?" He leans in suddenly and holds onto me while
nuzzling his bloody mouth along my jaw.

"*I'm a monster.*"

Something breaks inside me. Some flight, prey-like reaction I hadn't known existed in me, or maybe it didn't until this

moment. I stumble back from Cairo, seeing the surprise on his face. "Don't—" he begins. But I can't help it; I turn around and run.

My feet take me away from the clearing, away from the body cooling in the grass. I can feel the uncomfortable wetness of blood on my face, and I wipe it away as Cairo's curses fall in the distance. When I look over my shoulder, I'm surprised to see he isn't following me, but he's picked up the body in one hand while glaring at me.

But that's probably the best scenario for me. If I can get back to my house, I can lock the door against him, hide in the bathroom, and try to forget what I just saw. I don't know what else to do.

Unfortunately, I absolutely don't know where I am, and my flashlight is lying on the ground back beside the pool of blood from Cairo's prey. It's not quite dark enough that I'm running into trees, so I do my best to figure out where I came from, hoping to find some kind of trail or familiar landmark, even though I hadn't paid attention to any on my way out. Not to mention, I've never been this far out in the woods behind my house before. All I know, thanks to Google Maps and my neighbor who's a hiker, is that the trees extend for miles and miles, and there's a creek back here somewhere, with a little waterfall where he likes to watch wildlife.

None of that helps me, especially when the moon-bleached trees around me all look the same. Plus, soon enough I'm panting and out of breath; my body is definitely not used to this level of physical exertion. I slow my pace to a walk, heaving for air with my hands on my hips. Maybe I'm being stupid, I reason. Cairo was clearly more interested in his food than in me.

"Okay," I pant, finally coming to a stop and bending over to gasp and pant. "Okay, so, I fucked up." I don't know who I'm talking to, except maybe the trees that don't answer back. "I admit it. It would've been better if I had just stayed ignorant. This time, curiosity didn't kill the cat, but man, she feels almost dead right now."

Still bent over, I feel the brush of a claw against my face as it pulls my hair back from my eyes as I pant, and the purring chuckle by my ear is unmistakable.

"You're a very slow cat, little bird. Shouldn't you still be running?" A shiver goes down my spine at the words and his low growl when I stand up straight.

Cairo is still a gory, terrifying mess. Blood drips from his jaws, drying on his chest, and his hands are more stained than clean. Fear rises in my throat, and as he tilts his head up, the moonlight catches his gaze again, giving him that feral, dangerous look I'm so afraid of tonight.

I can't help myself. I bolt once more, adrenaline shooting through me and giving my legs the strength for another attempt at escape. This time when I turn, Cairo is nowhere in sight. He just seems to disappear into the shadows, until I see him between two trees, making me jolt in a different direction.

He does it twice more before I realize he's *herding me* like a sheepdog. Indignant frustration rises in my chest, and when I see him again, I make an attempt *not* to run in the direction he clearly wants me to go. But then he snarls, showing off all those teeth, and I stumble backward and trip, landing on my ass on the ground.

That brings a chuckle to Cairo's lips, and he stalks forward until he's standing over me, his head tilted in amusement. "You're not very good at this game," he informs me.

A jolt in my chest makes me realize he really *does* see this as a game. It's obvious in the way he's chasing me, plus the fact he hasn't taken me down and gutted me like a deer.

Like the man in the clearing.

"Fuck," I hiss, stumbling to my feet. "You are so not touching me right now. Not when you're this bloody."

"Why?" he steps closer, invading my space. "Because you're *clean*? No...You've lost all rights to complaints, little bird." There's a hint of reproach in his tone, and before I can take a step back, Cairo lunges forward to drag his tongue up my throat, then doing the same with the side of his face, undoubtedly leaving a trail of blood on my skin.

He straightens suddenly, looking around like he can hear something I can't. Letting go, Cairo tips his head the other way and surveys my face with one last flash of a grin. "I have to go move my kill," he informs me. "I'm saving it for later. If I catch you before you get back home, you're *mine,* Fern, because you didn't listen. And if there aren't consequences for your actions, how will you ever learn?" He sounds amused more than pissed, but there's a touch of a growling frustration in his voice I can't ignore.

I stand there, silent and shocked, as he turns and walks away. But finally I move with a start with a sound of confusion in my throat that makes him stop. "Wait! Cairo!" He stills and turns to look at me over his shoulder with a withering glare. "*I'm lost.*"

His smile is more than a little concerning, and the arrogant pride I see on his face hits me with the realization even before he opens his mouth to speak. "I know." Cairo chuckles. "You are so so lost in these woods. Good luck." Then he's gone, fading into the darkness again with an unnatural quickness that looks like magic when I'm watching. After all, there's no way he can just simply be *there* one moment and *gone* the next.

"God, I'm going to regret this," I murmur, fear and antici-pation curling together in my chest. But I scan the surrounding trees, noticing without hope that they all look the same. He actually got me lost in an area of the woods I don't think I've ever been in before.

But he wouldn't kill me...*right?*

I'm pretty sure he wouldn't, but I'm also not so willing to stake my life on it, if I can help it. I take off at a jog, being careful not to trip over roots or loose branches. Without knowing where I'm going or being able to see any landmarks, it's just a shot in the dark. Really, I just pick a direction and go.

The house I come to is definitely not mine. There's a light on the broken-down back porch, and I don't recognize the place at all. It's in a state of disrepair, that's for sure, and if I had to guess, no one has lived here in a while. But if I can find the road, I could likely find my house from there.

It's my best shot, and worth a try, at least. I have nothing better to do, so my steps slow and I walk to the back porch, wondering if I could hear Cairo show up if I try.

Probably not, truthfully. I hadn't heard him approach before. Hell, anytime he's wanted to sneak up on me, he's been more than able to do so. And with the way I'm panting and my heart is pounding almost painfully, I doubt I'm in any circumstance to hear him now.

My feet take me up onto the low back porch, where I stay standing for a few seconds to look around. I was mistaken before; there are signs of habitation in the still-living flowers in planter boxes and the door that's scraped free of dust.

But I don't get to admire anything else about the place.

A low growl makes me whip around. My hand lands on the railing of the porch, and my heart lurches into my throat when I see Cairo standing there. He's freshly bloody, with his mouth and hands dripping gore.

"Good girl," he praises, eyes dancing even in the darkness. "You ended up right where I wanted you to. I thought I'd have to do more work to get you here, but you really are the unluck-iest person alive."

His words take a moment to sink in, and only then do I turn to look more closely at the old hunting cabin. "You—Do you live here?" I gasp. "Did you herd me to where you *live?*"

Looking entirely too pleased with himself, Cairo licks his fingers like a cat cleaning its paws. "It's not much," he says smugly. "And I don't stay here very often. But when I'm not with you, yeah. I sort of call this place home."

"How far are we from my house?" My hands tighten on the rail of the porch, and I try to look bold instead of terrified and a little humiliated at how easily he pushed me to where he wanted me. "And..." I glance behind me. "Who owns this place?"

He glances at the cabin as well. "It's on some old guy's land. He and his son used to hunt here, but not anymore. And we're maybe"—he tilts his head, thinking—"three miles from your house."

My stomach sinks, and I look back toward the woods. "So, which direction is my house from here?" I ask weakly, but his eyes on mine tell me he's not giving that away so easily. He just walks up the stairs with a confident, dominating air, and his hand comes up to grip my throat, getting more blood on my skin.

"I told you not to come out here tonight."

"What did you do with the body?"

Cairo growls at that, showing off his teeth, and pulls me closer toward him. "I *told you*, little bird. I can't be human for you tonight. But"—his hand tightens, a warning against me speaking, as he surveys my face—"you think you don't need that. You're about to tell me I don't *have* to be human for you. Oh, Fern..." He clicks his tongue in disapproval. "I will take great joy in testing that resolve of yours tonight. You know,

Agatha will save you from Tyler and his...followers," he sneers.

"But there's no one alive who can save you from me."

Without warning, he picks me up, throwing me over his shoulder, as if I weigh little more than an inconvenient backpack. I squawk indignantly and kick at him, but he barely notices. The door slams open on its hinges before bouncing back, and even though we're inside the slightly warmer little cabin, he doesn't put me down.

"Cairo!" I shriek, trying and failing not to sound terrified. I kick again at him, not that he notices. But finally I feel myself coming off of his shoulder, and he tosses me onto a heavy rug in front of a long-dead fireplace. I don't know what I expected, but staring up into his face lit only by the moonlight outside is...terrifying.

"I can't see," I breathe when he moves to close the door. "Cairo—"

"I know." He cuts me off in a voice not entirely his. "But that's all right, little bird. Because I *can*." Without warning, he pounces, though I don't see or hear it coming. I only know because he's suddenly above me, shoving me to the floor on my back and snarling against my neck. "Show me your throat." It's not a request, and I barely stop to think before I shove my head back against the rug, my neck bare and on display for him.

Cairo wastes no time in nuzzling his teeth against my throat, his fangs are wet and smearing my skin with blood and something that feels thicker and more solid. I push against him with my hands as the fear in my chest rises, but he only snarls.

"If you're going to fight me, then *fight me*," Cairo urges. "Don't shove at me like a helpless little thing. Come on." He grabs my hand and brings it to his chest. "Curl your fingers. Claw at my skin. Fight me, Fern. I know you have it in you."

I shouldn't want to fight him. But something in his growl, in his words maybe, has me in fight-or-flight mode. I surge up against him and my other hand comes up to grope for his neck. He even lets me until my fingers tighten just below his jaw and I feel his pulse fluttering under my fingers.

"Oh, you could never kill me like that," Cairo goads. "But then again, a weak, clawless little thing couldn't kill me at all unless you find a flamethrower lying around."

I'm not focused on his words. I'm too intent on the feeling of his unmarred skin, and my hand slips down to his shoulder to be sure of what I hadn't noticed in the woods. "Holy shit," I breathe, gripping him tightly. "Cairo, you're completely healed! That's—"

He shoves me down again, once more burying his fangs against my throat. "That should terrify you," he tells me, frustration heady in his voice. "Don't you get it, Fern? If I get too hurt, if Tyler almost kills me, all I have to do is eat you." His mouth opens, and his fangs prick my skin. He's like a snake that can unhinge its jaws, and I swear I feel his teeth on either side of my throat, ready to snap shut and tear out my jugular.

Cairo could do it. It would be so *easy* for him.

"If I keep you around, what's stopping me from giving in, hmm? I'm a *monster,* Fern. But maybe I haven't been clear enough about that. Maybe I've been too human for you." Suddenly, he grabs my shirt and rips it, tearing the fabric until he can yank it off of me.

"Cairo!" I shriek, grabbing for it and missing. I'm not wearing a bra, since I'd just been at home, but when his hands go for my leggings, I grab his wrists. "Cairo, *stop!* I like these—" Instead of ripping them too, he quickly flips me over onto my hands and knees in the dark.

My heart beats more loudly while I can't see him. Especially as his nails trace down my sides, pricking and tickling in equal measure until I'm squirming and gripping the carpet hard. On a whim, I kick out, but he's fast enough that he just grabs my leg, yanking off my shoe before he does the same to the other. "So slow," Cairo taunts. "So *weak,* aren't you? I could do anything I want. I could have you in *all* the ways I want, little bird. All the ways I've been too afraid to show you."

When I don't answer, he takes it as curiosity. I hear his satisfied purr, and he presses himself against me, bare chest against my spine. "Come on, Fern. Do you really think fucking you in your bed while you gaze up at me with those sweet eyes of yours is enough for me? Now that you know what I am, can't you take a guess at some of the things I want? No?" he goads, and nips at my shoulder until I'm gasping, the skin stinging and raw.

"I want to *fuck you* until I'm satisfied I've ruined you, little bird. Until your body aches for me, and I'm sure that you'll never be satisfied by anyone else. I'm going to mold this sweet pussy of yours to my cock, before I do the same with your mouth and your ass. You're *mine."* He clicks his teeth near my face as he says it, and I wince.

"You had your chance to run away, to accept the version of me I was holding back and what I was giving you before." I wonder if his excitement is what's making him this talkative, or if it's the bloodlust from his hunt.

So I ask.

"You're very conversational. You aren't usually...like this," I admit, giving another halfhearted struggle as he trails claws down my body again. His claws are longer than usual, and the shadows are gone completely from under his eyes. Even his eyes seem darker, and the dark green iris has nearly swallowed the whites around them. Everything about him has shifted to *predatory,* and his words are accompanied by sounds that are more feral than usual.

"That's because I'm usually hungry." He chuckles. "So it takes a lot for me to think about anything else. But I'm not hungry now. You have all of my attention. All of my *affection.*" His claws dig into my hips until I yelp, and my back arches under him. "No matter if you want it or not. I hope you like me as I am, Fern. Because you aren't getting the other me back for a while. Not when you so willingly came out into my territory while I was hunting."

He pins me by the back of my neck, and before I can do anything at all, Cairo uses his nails to rip through my leggings at the seams. I yelp in protest, but he doesn't mind. Not when he's too busy tearing at them until the only fabric still on my body is a few shreds against my calves.

His tongue runs in a line up my spine, from my lower back all the way to the base of my neck. Cairo growls a little in my ear, and again opens his mouth wide enough that he can bite down on my shoulder, front and back. The feeling makes me shiver, but it's not exactly from fear. And when he bites down with his teeth at the junction of my neck and shoulder, I'm not asking him to stop.

I hear his jeans sliding down his hips, and he suddenly slides two bloody fingers against my lower lip with a purr. "Come on, little bird," Cairo goads when I jerk away from the gore he smeared on my mouth. "Get my fingers all nice and wet."

"Cairo, the blood—"

"Sorry." But he doesn't sound sorry at all. "He didn't taste very good. Fine. I'll do you a favor this once." His fingers disappear, and I don't know what he's doing until they reappear, dripping wet with his saliva and once again his claws prick my lower lip.

"I want to feel your mouth around my fingers. Distract me, so I don't just fuck your pretty cunt now until you're screaming on my cock." I shudder at the growled threat, and remind myself that it's a *bad* thing for him to just fuck me...even though I'm more than a little turned on and it probably wouldn't be very hard for him.

There's still the taste of copper on his skin when I let him press his fingers to my tongue. He thrusts them in and out, gripping my jaw with his thumb and ring finger to hold me in place while I taste his spit and traces of blood.

It should be *disgusting,* but I'm too fucked up and too far gone to do more than whine around his fingers while he leans over me, pinning me to the floor.

Even though we're inside, and it's relatively warm, it doesn't feel very human of us. Especially with how he purrs and huffs like a wild, uncontrolled thing at my back.

Finally, he pulls his fingers free and without another word, he slips three of them into me. It has me gasping, and my back arches at the surprise of having him spread them in my body instead of working up to them.

"There's my little bird," Cairo growls in my ear, his voice echoing and unnatural. Every few words he slips into it, sounding like different members of a choir, and sometimes no natural human tone at all. "Always so vocal for me." His fingers move impatiently inside of me, and just as I start pushing back against him, he slides them free to grip my hip and snarl against the protest bubbling to my lips.

"Mine," he purrs, lining himself up with me. "You are *mine."* He slides back into me possessively, with one hand on my hip and the other on the floor beside my face. The muscles in his arm flex, his claws dig into the carpet, and I stare at them as my body tries to adjust to his size.

"Oh, fuck," I whisper, when he slams into me. *"Fuck,* Cairo —" But he cuts me off with a purring growl and a little hiss when he continues with his relentless, brutal pace.

"I've never found anyone like you before," I hear him rambling breathily, though it's hard to hear him over the sound of my panting breaths and the noises between us. He isn't being gentle, and I don't want him to. I don't *need* him to be when this is perfect in its own way, making me hungry and needy for more.

"None of the others...No human..." He hisses out a breath, sinks into me, then jerks backward until I'm left empty.

A noise of discontent escapes my lips, but before I can ask why, I'm suddenly on my back on the thick rug, my vision spinning until it's filled with just *him* above me.

"I want to see your face this time," Cairo purrs, and sinks into me once more. "I want to see my little bird come apart on my cock."

"Cairo—" His name is a choked gasp on my lips, and unthinkingly I reach up to tangle my fingers in his black hair that's stiff with blood. It doesn't occur to me that it's disgusting as I jerk his face down to mine, and the surprise in his eyes is satisfying as hell just as I crush his lips to mine, giving a soft, experimental growl of my own against his lips.

It triggers something in him I hadn't expected, and Cairo's whole body shudders at the sound. At first, I'm sure I've done something wrong, especially since he isn't kissing me back. But then one hand goes to my hip and his other slams down on the rug beside me. Then he lunges forward to devour my mouth in a bruising, sharp-edged kiss.

When he thrusts into me again, I see stars. It's too much, and perfect, and so close to being painful that I arch my hips to both chase and escape the feeling. He swallows the noises I keep making, his mouth greedy on mine as his tongue teases and presses against my own.

Cairo tastes of blood, and death, and something *wild*.

But I can't get enough of it.

"Oh, you're asking for it, little bird," he chuckles in a rough, grating voice when I growl again. His hand on my hip tightens, his claws tight to my skin, before he shifts his grip to press against my stomach until I'm flat on the floor.

"Am I?" I gasp, but I only get a rueful look from his dark eyes in response. He's not fooled, though maybe amused, I hope.

His next thrust has me gasping, and my hips jerk into his hand, though he doesn't let me go anywhere. It jars my entire body, and I barely notice when his hand slips further down my body, until his claws are teasing at my clit, causing me to let out a choked whimper. "Cairo—"

"Your scent gets so sweet when you're about to come," the creature above me purrs, still holding himself up with one hand so he can watch my face. "And all it ever takes is this. You full of my cock and me playing with your sweet little clit. I wonder how many other ways I can find to make you lose control, little bird."

I want to say something, maybe something about him being just as predictable, but I can't. All I can do is close my eyes, as the feeling from his claws and his cock work to push me closer to my release. But I manage to jerk Cairo down to me again, and when I come with his name a choked cry on my lips, he swallows the sound greedily, licking every moment of it out of my mouth.

He's not far behind. I feel him pulsing, spilling inside of me, though his thrusts don't falter. It's a few seconds too long for me to realize he isn't *going anywhere,* and when I jerk him back a little by his hair, panting and already becoming overstimulated even without his fingers on my clit, he snickers openly at my expression.

"Yeah," Cairo agrees. "I know. And here you are, so perfect for me. I'm not going anywhere." He grinds into me when he's deep inside my pussy, and I throw my head back to gasp. Cairo lunges forward and sinks his teeth into the base of my throat, hard enough that I swear he draws blood.

"So it looks like you're going to have to suffer for me, pretty girl. All night long, until I'm satisfied. But don't say I didn't warn you." He licks over the mark and pulls out, only to drag me back to my hands and knees before sliding back between my folds.

"I told you not to follow me out here, Fern." Cairo drapes himself over me, already thrusting languidly, like he has all the time in the world even though my body is barely considering relenting for a second round. "I wonder how many times I can make you come, hmm?" He nuzzles the side of my throat.

"Maybe if you're good—after a few more times—I'll carry you home before I fuck you again. Doesn't that sound nice of me?"

"I think I hate you—" My words end in a yelp, and I jerk forward, only for Cairo to drag me back.

He laughs, a guttural chuckle. "Really? That's such a shame." His hand splays on my stomach, and I'm pressed against him so tightly I can almost feel his heartbeat against my back. "I'll have to see if I can change that before the sun comes up."

Cairo does try, to his credit. Before he carried me home wrapped in a stolen jacket from the cabin, he tore two more orgasms from me, and had me seeing stars. By the time he's let Moro out and I'm in bed, mostly asleep, I can barely remember my own name, let alone that I hate him.

But at his purr and the way he pulls me against him to lick and kiss at my neck while I drift off, I decide maybe I can try hating him for a little longer tonight. Just for show.

CHAPTER TWENTY-FOUR

THUNDER RUMBLING OVERHEAD MAKES THIS VISIT SEEM A LOT MORE ominous than normal. With my hand curled around the styrofoam cup, I stare upward at the cloud-covered sky, considering how long the storm might last while I'm here, in front of Dr. Radley's office, about to walk into my least favorite hour of the week.

At least the bruises have mostly faded. The ones on my neck are still a little present, but I no longer wince when I stretch too far. The claw marks are gone as well, not that she would've been able to see those, anyway.

Lightning flickers in the clouds, far away, and in a few seconds it's echoed by the call of thunder that hasn't quite committed to being more than a threat.

For some reason, I can't help wondering about Hattie. Cairo wasn't surprised when I finally got around to telling him about her, after...everything. I can't help rolling my eyes now at nothing when I think of his slight frustration, even though he hadn't given me any kind of real reaction.

Just stay away from her, little bird, he mumbled, already half asleep in my bed and covering my body with his.

Just...stay away.

As if *I* ever try to find *her*, rather than it being the other way around.

I shiver as the wind picks up, half-wishing I'd put on something more substantial than my t-shirt and running shorts. But there's no hiding from therapy. Especially from Dr. Radley. With a defeated sigh, I pull open the heavy glass door, stepping up into the old building and onto its creaky wooden floor.

I still don't know what's housed on the first floor, to be honest. A few signs and paintings litter the walls, along with the incomplete directory by the wooden staircase. But apart from smelling like wood cleaner, there's nothing down here to give me an idea of what it could be.

I've never seen anyone down here, either. No one to be found at the single antique desk by the back window, or by the filing cabinets tucked in the corner. For the first time, I don't hurry myself along. I'm early enough and trying to kill time, so I stride over the old wood and gaze down at the too-clean desk. It's almost...decorative, rather than functional. Like it's made to look like a reception area, without actually playing the part when anyone is looking.

But there is a scattering of pens on the clean desk, and a phone charger strewn across it. Surely *someone* has to work here, at least sometimes. A part of me wants to open the drawers to see what files are there just so I can figure out what this floor is used for, but I don't want to go to jail for a felony.

Or back to an asylum, which is arguably the worse option after the last time.

Exhausting my curiosity and my spare time, I turn and head up the stairs, wincing at the loud creaking that sounds like it's trying to give away my actions. Like there's someone here to tattle on me to, even though I've never seen anyone here other than Dr. Radley. But since there are multiple names on the directory, I know there are other medical professionals in the building.

So the sign says, anyway.

Her door looms once I'm on the second floor, and I stand in front of it, holding the styrofoam, half-full cup in my hand. Instead of a milkshake, I opted for a very retro Coke float, and now I swirl the thick liquid around the cup, feeling it tilt against my fingers unevenly. I don't know if she'll even let me have it in there, but if not, I'll toss it in the trash like an elementary school kid who brought her milk carton back from lunch like a squirrel hoarding acorns in her desk.

I knock as usual, waiting politely, but today I don't immediately hear her answer. I swear she's in there, since I can both see and hear her walking on the other side of the frosted glass. The sound of her voice is soft, and it occurs to me she's talking to someone other than me. Papers ruffle, a drawer closes, and when Dr. Radley pulls the door open, the look on her face is a little less friendly than usual.

Her eyes dart to the cup in my hand, but she doesn't say anything. Her expression only changes when she looks at the light bruises on my throat, and then her lips press flat into a disapproving line. It feels very judgmental and puts me on edge. My sex life is certainly none of *her* business.

"You're late," she tells me, and steps back into the room. I glance at the clock, noting that it's barely two after four. Not only that, if she had answered the door when I first knocked, I probably would've been on time. But I don't bring that up. Still, I lock my teeth together to prevent an apology that she doesn't deserve, and I follow her into the room while she closes the door behind me.

She's clearly not in a great mood today. Her movements

are less graceful and more fidgety than usual as she sifts through files on her desk that could be a sister to the one downstairs. While I take my normal seat and watch her, I continue swirling the cup in my hand without the urge to actually take a drink, though it's still about half full. "I hope everything is okay?" I venture at last, which finally draws her attention.

Dr. Radley studies my face from her space behind her desk. Today, she doesn't come to sit on the overstuffed armchair that she usually sits in like a throne. Instead, she sits on the desk chair, worn and dark, behind the large wooden desk and keeps her distance from me. Tense, quiet, she studies my face like there's something new about me she hasn't seen before.

I don't like it whatsoever. I feel itchy under her gaze, and restless enough that I almost can't sit still. "Umm..." I don't know what to say, and belatedly remember I'm the one who last asked a question. Not her. She can't be waiting for me to say anything, when she hasn't asked me anything.

Right?

"I'm really trying here, Fern." She leans back and turns the chair slightly to gaze out the window behind her, toward the darkening sky outside. The words put me on edge, and I set the styrofoam cup down on the table beside me. "I've been trying to let you go at your own pace. I don't want to push you, but you're not giving me anything to work with."

"Um, I don't know what you mean," I say, when she just stares out the window instead of continuing. "I've been doing what you say. I talk about what you want me to talk about, I—"

Here, Dr. Radley lets out an unfriendly laugh as the wind picks up outside. "We both know that's not true. You lie to me. Regularly avoid my questions. You evade telling me the truth at *every* turn." All at once, she turns to me, her eyes on mine.

"Where's Cairo Moore?" she demands sharply. "And Hattie Kenner? Tyler Wilson? Any of those names ring a bell?"

It dawns on me that all this time, I've underestimated her and her intentions. She doesn't want to help me, and it makes me wary of her every word.

It makes me wonder how much she knows.

"Cairo?" I blink, keeping a look of careful confusion on my face. "I met him at Bluebone Ridge. Did he make it out? Tyler was his friend, right? And I thought the official report on Hattie is that—"

"Stop it." Her lips twist into an unfriendly smile, and she stares sourly at me. "If you're going to lie, then I'd rather you said nothing at all." I watch as she forces herself to relax; Dr. Radley closes her eyes to sit back with some effort instead of looking like she's going to come over the desk and get in my face. "I know what happened that night, Fern," she says slowly. "I've always known what lives in the mountains. Starving, waiting, and trying to find anyone just as desperate as they are to join them."

A shiver travels up my spine, but I force myself not to look away, or to seem guilty. So I set both feet on the floor, leaning forward on my knees. "You'll have to explain what you mean to me," I reply just as slowly, articulating my words. "I don't know what you're trying to say, Dr. Radley. What lives in the mountains? Who's starving? What's—"

"Has he told you how it happens?" She cuts me off smoothly as if I hadn't said anything at all. "Have any of them? By now I'm sure you know there's more than one. I was never sure about Tyler, though with Cairo it was obvious. How could it not be?" Dr. Radley opens a small notebook, flipping through the pages as she studies the words on each. "Cairo Moore was actually born Cairo Merritt. He lived here in the fifties." She runs her finger down the page, reading from it. "Tyler Wilson.

Born 1978. Went missing in the late 90's." When she closes it, I notice more names. Other details. Though I'm too far away to actually read any of her scrawled writing.

"So I'll ask again. Have any of them told you how they do it?"

I refuse to admit knowing anything. There's no way I'll let her draw me into telling her something she doesn't know, and I force myself to stay on my guard as I shrug my shoulders cluelessly. "I don't know what you mean. How they do what?"

Her glare is withering, and I remind myself that she can't stop me if I get up and just leave. She can't call the cops and tell them I know about monsters and simply won't admit it to her. Even I know that.

"It would be better to just stop playing this game," Dr. Radley tells me coolly. "But I can't force you." Suddenly she's on her feet, and I jerk to mine as she strides past, though she doesn't stop. She just goes to the wall, pulling off one of the framed photos I noticed before. Coming back to me, she shows the photo to me, all but thrusting it under my nose.

It's the same one I looked at before, and it only confuses me more as I wonder why she's showing me a happy photo of her, her sister, and their parents outside of a cabin in the woods. "This was the last summer I ever got to spend with my sister Mikaela," Dr. Radley tells me in a soft, serious voice. "She's eighteen here. I'm twenty. We stayed at this cabin with our parents every year; this was the last one." Pulling the photo back, she drags her fingers over it affectionately, eyes dulling as she's lost in the memory.

"She developed a crush on some boy she met on the trails. He was so charming, she said. Mysterious, too, she never found out where he lived." For a few moments she's silent, and it scares me to think of all the directions this could go. Somehow, I doubt I'll be surprised.

"And then he wanted her to stay. They always want you to stay once they get attached, Fern." She sets down the photo, and her eyes pin mine before I can look away. "Do you know what it means to stay? Mikaela didn't. Not until it was too late. They don't take no for an answer." Her voice turns grim, and my heart sinks. When Dr. Radley steps forward, I step back and my knees hit the chair, causing me to sit unsteadily.

"The last thing she ever told me was how he wanted her to eat someone with him. Just *once*. How if she were hungry, really hungry, she'd understand. Does that ring a bell?" Dr. Radley's voice is tight, and I have to fight back any kind of comprehension on my face, considering what Cairo told me last week.

She's too close to his story to be wrong, but he certainly hasn't done that with me. I take a breath and clutch the arms of the chair. "You're scaring me, Dr. Radley," I murmur quietly. "I don't know what you're talking about, but—"

"He took her," she goes on, like I haven't tried to stop her. She leans over me, one hand on the armrest and her other on mine to keep me in place. "He took her and *kept her* until she was starving. But she wouldn't do it. She couldn't. I found her when she was dying, with a broken hip and having not eaten in days. She told me she was *starving*," the therapist whispers, too close to my face. "But when she wouldn't join him, he left her there to die. Now tell me, Fern." Her gaze holds mine, angry and fevered.

"What makes you think it'll go any better for you?"

"Because I know what I'm doing, and I know what he is." The words are out of my mouth before I can stop them, and Dr. Radley jerks upright, her look morphing to confident pleasure at the confirmation.

Fuck.

I walked right into that, and now all I can do is kick myself for not realizing where her words were leading.

"Oh, you do?" she challenges, and moves to put the photo back on the wall with meticulous care so it lines up perfectly. "Do you think Mikaela didn't? Do you think a monster can ever love you unselfishly? Or is he just looking for an end to his own loneliness? I don't think they're made to be alone. They're always hunting, always hoping. But you've heard them mimic human voices with their throats. You've seen the way they can look like us. But has it ever occurred to you...?" she trails off and walks back to lean against her desk, gazing once more out the window.

"What if he's also mimicking your affection for him? Who's to say it stops at voices and looks? My sister was a lot like you, Fern. Stubborn, independent. Anxious." She eyes me and I look away at the accusation. "Always needing approval and reassurance. She needed someone to tell her it was alright. Is that what he does for you? Does he keep you in the dark, only showing you what he wants? Does he disappear when it's no longer convenient for him and give you just enough to keep you interested? Tell me."

Again she gazes out the window, and I struggle to find an answer for her, thinking she's done.

"He told you he's the one who saved you that night, didn't he? But if he was really interested in your wellbeing, wouldn't he have warned you in the first place?"

The question hits something raw and sharp in me. A weakness I didn't know I had until right now. All of a sudden, my doubts unleash themselves, and I struggle to my feet across from her in the room, though I don't say a word. This time, she doesn't push me.

She doesn't need to.

Dr. Radley has finally found the thing to shake me to my

core, to open up Pandora's Box of doubts about Cairo's intentions. But that was her intention all along, I try to remind myself. She's not doing this *for me*. She's doing this to confirm what she already knows. I have to keep telling myself that, otherwise I'm going to do something stupid like fall apart in her office and tell her all the things she's looking for.

I won't be the one to do that to Cairo. Or Agatha.

Or even Hattie.

"I'm sorry about your sister." My words come out measured and soft. I pick up my styrofoam cup, shaking the liquid around inside with nervous, jerky movements. My heart is racing just as if I've run a mile from one of the cursed, and my adrenaline is going the same way. This woman is dangerous, and I shouldn't spend a second longer here than I have to. "And I appreciate everything you've done to help me through what happened that night. It really urged me to come a long way."

She doesn't respond or even look at me. She doesn't need to, and that frustrates me more than it should.

"Goodbye, Dr. Radley." My words are full of finality and forced calm, but when I get to the door, she finally speaks again.

"They're starving, Fern." Defeat laces her voice, and when I glance at her, she's still watching the storm. "But don't mistake that as a hunger just for food. He'll do anything to get you to join him, to sate his hunger." Finally she turns, meeting my gaze with flat, tired resentment. "Even kill you."

I don't say a word. There's nothing to say to her, really. But I hold her gaze, studying the look there, before turning and fleeing. Allowing the heavy door to slam behind me as thunder rumbles closer outside, a herald of the impending storm.

CHAPTER TWENTY-FIVE

WHILE I HAVEN'T SEEN CAIRO IN A FEW DAYS, I FIGURE THAT'LL probably change soon. Maybe.

Hopefully.

But my day can't get worse, I tell myself, so I grab Moro's leash and jog through the drizzle of rain back to my car. The wolf dog doesn't mind one bit. She happily trots along and jumps into the backseat, ready to go for an adventure.

Though today's adventure is a lot less exciting than the one we had last week. The night we went to Bluebone Ridge to search the place for any clues and eventually went hunting for Cairo after his fight.

Yeah, I'm definitely not looking for that kind of adventure today, I assure myself, and just head to the park. Considering the drizzle doesn't really bother me, it just means the park is empty of anyone in Whippoorwill Gap who doesn't want to deal with the weather when they could be literally anywhere else.

Which today ends up being everyone, to my surprise. I forgo the leash, letting Moro out of the back of the car for her to run in happy circles around me with her tail up and curled over her back. She never goes far from me, even after she's done her business in the wet grass while I wait with my hood drawn up over my head. It's not cold enough for more than leggings, though the rain soaks through to my skin after a few minutes, giving me a bit of a chill.

Still, I'd rather be out here than at home worrying. My anxiety is there, waiting to get the rest of me, and on the way home from Dr. Radley's, I felt the signs of dissociation gently tugging at my consciousness.

Cairo could help, I think, but I immediately shove that thought away, guilty. I shouldn't be. It's not like I've done anything to feel guilty about, and he didn't do anything wrong to me. He hasn't tried to make me like him. He hasn't broken my bones in the woods to force me to eat human flesh.

He's not like the boy Dr. Radley's sister knew.

Yet somehow, I can't get the story, or the anxious feelings, out of my head. I can't stop thinking about them. I can't help wondering if she was like me. If her cursed was just as charming as mine.

But even worse, I can't stop thinking about the idea that he's not only mimicking human *voices.* There was something in her words that stuck with me; about how he looks so human when he wants to, and how he can sound like anyone I want to hear, or no one at all.

Moro barks, making me jump, and I give her a guilty look. "Sorry, yeah. I'm being stupid," I agree with a soft sigh under my breath. She woofs as if agreeing, and I walk away from the small parking lot of the local park, out of the cover of the trees. The rain isn't bad. Even though I'm cold and almost regretting this little adventure of mine as water runs down under my hoodie, in the roots of my hair.

I don't *need* Cairo to feel better. Even if feeling better means playing in the rain with my dog.

Moro barks again, but this time it's different. There's less of a playful note, and more warning. Confused, I turn to look at her, seeing her fur bristling as she looks toward the trees at the edge of the park. "What's wrong?" I call, knowing I won't actually get an answer. "Are you okay?" I lay a hand on her shoulders, surprised at her bristled fur and the way she tenses under my hand. As I watch, she peels her lips back from her teeth, and her eyes stay fixed on the small group of trees between me and the parking lot.

Surely she wouldn't be doing this over another dog, though suddenly I'm worried about some local's little toy poodle being eaten by my big, bad wolf dog.

Those fears are dispelled, however, when Moro barks again, and it's answered by an unfriendly scoff. Footsteps crunch on the ground, and from the darkness of the trees appears a tall, lanky figure that I recognize instantly. Tyler leans back against a large trunk, arms folded over his chest and a lazy grin on his face. "I don't think she likes me," he remarks, not really seeming to care. "Strange, since she likes Cairo well enough. And I don't remember her having a problem with Agatha."

"She's an excellent judge of character," I say stiffly, curling my fingers in Moro's fur. I'm afraid she's going to lunge for him, and even more afraid that if she does, he'll kill her. "Stay, girl," I whisper, encouraged when she doesn't try going for him, and stays where she is in front of me.

"That's not very nice of you."

"You're right." I blink at him, not offering anything else. He breaks our standoff first, displaying his boredom with a roll of his eyes. "You're ridiculous, you know that? You're supposed to be more afraid of me than this. But whatever." Flicking a hand into the air, he pushes off the tree and inhales. "Cairo isn't here." It isn't a question, which unnerves me. My fingers flex in Moro's fur, and I decide to take a chance to satisfy my curiosity with someone whose opinion I don't care about.

"Do you remember Dr. Radley?" I ask before he can keep talking. It's clear he wasn't expecting the question, and Tyler's eyes narrow as he looks at me with his lips parted just enough so that I can see his fangs. "From—"

"Yeah," he cuts in. "I do. Why?"

"She knows about you. She knows *all* about you." Belatedly, I wonder if maybe I shouldn't have said anything. I might feel a little bad if he goes off to murder her. "She always has, since way before you and the massacre last month," I add hastily, just in case I can sway him.

"Oh, yeah?" He doesn't seem very moved by the notion, and it gives me hope that he's not planning Dr. Radley's death, even if she isn't my favorite person ever. "And what are you looking to achieve with this revelation?"

"Well, if you'd let me get that far—"

"I've already let you get pretty far, Fern. Much farther than I should've. I tried to have Hattie protect you, for *him*." He sneers the word. "And what did I get out of it?"

Ignoring that train of conversation, I shake my head, heart fluttering in my chest. "She said her sister was killed by one of you. Not like"—I swallow hard—"not eaten. She said all of you are looking for someone to turn. Like you did to Hattie. Is that true?"

Unfortunately, it seems Tyler is a little smarter than I gave him credit for. His lips twist into an unfriendly smile, and he gives a soft snarl, sneering at me. "Oh, *I see.* You want to know if that's what Cairo's trying to do to you. If he's laying the breadcrumbs on some trail for you to fall in love with him. What's wrong, Fern?" His voice morphs, throat working unnaturally, so his next words come out in Cairo's voice instead of his own. *"Afraid there's human flesh waiting for you at the end of that trail?"*

"Shut up." That's exactly what I'd been worried about, and I hate how he caught on so quickly. I shiver at the unnaturalness of hearing Cairo's voice from his lips, and my fingers curl more tightly in Moro's ruff. "That's—"

"Well, you don't need to worry about that." I can see the bunching of his muscles, and Tyler's grin widens until I can see his fangs clearly, shining and clean of blood. "Because I don't intend to give him the chance to turn you."

Before I can react, he lunges forward. In my shock, I trip backward, just as Moro surges forward, and with a cry I lose my grip on her. The wolf dog meets Tyler mid-lunge, snapping at any part of him she can reach. When she bites down on his leg, he snarls and jerks back from her, causing her fangs to tear through his skin, drawing ribbons of blood.

Unfortunately, without Cairo here to help her, Tyler's attention is fixed fully on Moro. He grabs her when she lunges again, kicking at her and sending her to the ground. I scramble to my feet, but I'm frozen in place, unable to do anything but watch as she gets to her paws a little unsteadily, snarling and barking with her fur stiff and her teeth bloody and bared.

"No!" I shriek in protest, but it's too late. He grabs her by the throat, causing her growls to turn into yelps as his claws sink past her fur, into the skin underneath, causing blood to stain her fur. Her cries make me move, and I stupidly throw myself at Tyler, who easily drops Moro to the ground where she collapses. He kicks her away and grabs me with his claws instead.

"Poor *little bird,*" Tyler sneers, barely panting with effort. "What will he say when I show him your head, hmm? And what will he do"—he drags me closer, my feet scrambling over the grass under me trying to get purchase as the rain picks up, and the thunder rumbles like an ominous herald of my death —"when I tell him I *ate* the rest of you?"

His other hand comes up to stroke my face, and I shudder, trying to shove at him. I taste bile in my throat, and my heart races, as if it can somehow escape the gory, grisly fate he's offering.

I don't want to die.

I *really* don't want Tyler to eat me.

"I won't make it quick," Tyler assures me in a mockingly sweet voice. "I'm too fucking tired of this game to make it—" He stops and turns his head, eyes narrowed in a look of utter confusion as his nostrils flare.

I hear something, but I can't even think of turning before something slams into Tyler, prying him off of me and sending him to the ground. For a moment, I'm sure it's Cairo. Or maybe Agatha. But apart from them, I don't know who would care enough to save me from the creature threatening to eat me slowly and show my head to my lover.

It has to be—

"Hattie?!" I gasp when I look up from the grass where I'm crumpled. Wild-eyed and with her hair in knots, Hattie looks like a monster, or some witch who's never seen civilization. She snarls at Tyler, pinning him down.

"*Not Fern,*" she growls, displaying teeth just as sharp as his. She's trembling, her eyes darting, and she shakes her head as she glares at him.

"Hattie..." Tyler's voice is placating. When he reaches up with one hand, she shoves him back down with a growl and a click of her teeth, though she doesn't seem interested in hurting him. "You're being ridiculous. She's not your friend!" He glares at me, dark eyes full of hate, which helps me get the nerve to shove to my feet, though my legs still shake.

The redhead doesn't answer. She looks at me, her eyes wide. "Go," she urges. *"Go* away, Fern." When Tyler tries to shove her off of him again, she slams him back to the ground, straddling him more completely to keep him pinned under her.

"T-thank you—" Moro's whimper cuts me off and I whirl around, dropping to my knees once more beside my dog. "Oh, God..." Her neck is bloody, but her eyes are open, though they shine with pain. "Oh, Moro, you're alive. Okay. I've got you, pretty girl. Don't worry, I've got you." Absolutely not caring that I'm probably going to regret carrying the sixty-pound dog later, I gather her up against me, having to all but toss her over my shoulder in order to stagger back to my car with her.

I don't look back as I lay her in the back seat, no matter that I can hear Tyler's snarls of protest and the not-so-quiet conversation as he demands for Hattie to let him go. All I can do is focus on not crying, and silently beg Moro not to die as I get in the driver's seat and pull out of the parking lot to find the nearest emergency vet clinic. Trying to ignore how my face and shirt are stained with my dog's blood while she whines softly in the backseat.

CHAPTER TWENTY-SIX

For a moment, once I'm parked in my driveway and the only sound is the drizzle of rain outside, I just...sit.

I'm exhausted, not only from what happened at the park and with Dr. Radley, but also from being at the animal hospital for five hours while Moro had scans, stitches, and enough pain meds for her to be drowsing in the back seat instead of whimpering like she was on the way there.

Warm wetness on my cheeks surprises me, and I reach up to wipe at the tears trailing down my face. "I'm sorry, Moro," I breathe quietly, though she doesn't do more than tilt her head a little on the seat in acknowledgment of my words. She'd been better than I could've ever expected her to be, when she was obviously in so much pain until they gave her an injection of something they promised would make her more comfortable.

Instead of getting out of the car, I lean forward, my forehead pressed to the steering wheel as I listen to the rain. Suddenly, the last few weeks seem darker, less innocuous. Less...*fun*. Maybe I'd been treating this like a game too, or at least not giving it the amount of caution that it deserved.

All I can wonder as I sit there, after having nearly lost my dog, is how could I have just accepted all of this so easily after finding out what Cairo is? More than that, after learning about what exists in the Cascade Mountains.

But what else am I supposed to do?

I can feel myself spiraling as I close my eyes, and I know all the grounding breaths in the world aren't enough to get me where I need to be. There's nothing I can do but let my mind run away with me, and allow the horrors of Bluebone Ridge, of Tyler, of *Cairo* to flood my brain.

Is it only luck that I'm still here?

Worse still is that in some ways I feel like Dr. Radley was right. I don't take this seriously enough, and I'm not willing to see what Cairo is, or what he wants. Tyler certainly hadn't denied anything when I brought it up to him.

Maybe I'm just an idiot.

It wouldn't be the first time I've had that thought, and my mom certainly has said as much to me on more than one occasion by remarking on my 'lack of common sense' or 'bad life skills.' If everyone else is saying it, and my brain and body are convinced of it, is it true?

My heart sinks like a stone in my chest, and nausea sits heavy in my stomach, insidious and bloating instead of the sharp, clawing feelings I've had before. This kind of dread is oppressive in its own way, and I'm not sure I can make myself get out of the car, when no part of me feels capable of doing more than this.

I can't move.

I can barely *breathe.*

I need—

The driver's door opens suddenly, and I turn my head to see Cairo, soaked from the rain and staring down at me. He just looks at me, though Moro's soft whine of greeting and the thump of her tail get his attention quickly. I can see the hesitation and the confusion on his face before he lets out a breath of his own and leans in to press his lips to my cheek in a surprisingly affectionate kiss. "I'll take care of you, little bird," he murmurs, without asking what's wrong. He doesn't even hesitate in opening the back door, and Moro lets him pick her up with only a weak whimper of protest.

"Just...be careful with her, okay?" I say in a too-small whisper that barely makes it past my lips. "Her neck and h-her ribs—"

"I've got her," Cairo promises me, striding through the rain after he closes the door to the back seat. My door remains open, and the rain mists in enough to slowly re-soak my hair and clothes, leaving me shivering even though I can't find the strength to do anything to stop it. My eyes drift closed again, and I listen to my breathing that I can barely hear amidst the rain.

As usual, I don't hear Cairo approach. Instead, I only realize he's beside me when the rain stops hitting the side of my face and my hand that's resting on the steering wheel. Opening one eye, I look up at him dully. "I'm coming."

"I know." But he leans down and, with about as much effort as he used to pick up Moro from the back seat, he pulls me into his arms until I'm cradled against his chest. His shirt is just as wet as mine, and he closes my door with his hip before turning and trudging toward my front door.

"I can walk."

"I know," he repeats calmly. There's no judgment in his tone. No disbelief. Just acceptance, and maybe a touch of relief. My fingers curl in his wet shirt, and even though part of me wants to wiggle free and prove that I'm fine, I don't. I let him carry me up the stairs to my front porch, cracked and faded and a little questionable, before he easily pushes open the door and then closes it behind him once we're in the living room. But even then, he doesn't put me down. Cairo carries me to the bedroom and past it, setting me down on the edge of the counter.

"You're freezing." Gently, he reaches up and pushes my wet hair back behind my ears to examine my face. "Little bird..." But Cairo trails off, like he's not quite sure what to say.

"I need to talk to you."

"I need to get you warmed up."

I feel so numb as he tugs off my shirt, my bra, and my leggings, until I'm left only in my underwear on the counter and staring up at his gorgeous, dark-eyed face. Cairo smiles sweetly at me and turns away just to twist the knobs in the shower before coming back to lean against me.

"You're okay, little bird," he promises. "Everything is okay."

"But—"

"No, whatever it is"—he turns to nose my cheek affection-ately —"it's okay. It can wait until after I warm you up. Moro's right there," he adds, drawing my attention to my bed outside the door, where she's sprawled out across the mattress like she owns it. As I watch, Cairo strips off his wet shirt and jeans, leaving him naked and barefoot.

He looks so human.

The thought makes something curl inside me, and when he reaches for me I draw back a little, though I'm ashamed at the motion. Cairo's lips only twitch in a soft smile, and he leans over me with his hands on the counter.

"I see I was wrong. We should talk now," he observes, his dark eyes on mine. "What happened, little bird?"

"In chronological order, or order of severity?" I can't help the sarcastic, witty response, and it earns a softer smile from him. A more genuine one.

"Either."

"Chronological, then. No—" I close my eyes, hands gripping the counter next to both of his. "Just...I need to ask you something."

He waits. Patiently, though I can almost feel a kind of tremor in him, like he's expecting the worst and trying to brace himself for it.

"Are you trying to turn me into what you are?"

The question falls between us, and when he looks away, I wish I could take it back. More than anything, I want to grab the words out of the air and swallow them back down. I'd rather live with the uncertainty, I decide at that moment, than hear the answer when I'm not sure I'm going to like it.

But it's too late for that now.

Cairo's eyes flick toward Moro, and he tilts his head as if putting together the events of the day in his head, without my help. "I knew you'd ask, eventually. Whether because you came up with it on your own, or..." He touches my face again, lightly, with just the tips of his fingers. This time, I don't flinch.

He's still *Cairo*, after all.

"That's a complicated answer. Because if I say no, then that would mean I don't want to keep you forever. But I'm not like *him.*" It's clear who he means. "I won't trick you, or force you. I won't kidnap you and make you dependent on me. Or take you away from your life to make it seem like the one I can give you is the only option you have. So...no, Fern. I'm not looking for ways to trick you or make you love me enough to give up anything and everything else. But if something happened, and you did become like me, you became *cursed* like I am, well..." His smile turns a little mischievous, and his dark eyes flicker with inner brilliance.

"I'd be lying if I said the thought made me unhappy."

His honesty is enough. My shoulders drop, and without warning, I lean into him, throwing my arms around his shoulders and burying my face in his shoulder. I inhale his scent, every bit of his skin smelling like *Cairo* and not some indescribably horrible monster.

Because he's still *Cairo,* even if he is *cursed.*

"We can go chronologically now," I breathe. "But shower first. Please." The coldness is creeping into my nerve endings, and even his radiator-like heat isn't enough to chase away the chill. Without a word, Cairo picks me up, opens the shower door, and once I'm completely nude, he sets me down so I'm leaning against the wall under the spray. When I try to move, however, he gives a soft noise of disapproval, gripping my hands and pushing them to the wall on either side of my hips.

"Stay," Cairo breathes. "Let me take care of you, little bird. Let me show you all the ways I want you to be mine."

"You have," I remind him in a soft whisper as he crowds close to me, running his fingers through my hair so the hot water sinks to my scalp, chasing away the cold. "In the woods, in the cabin—"

"There are so many ways I want to have you," he interrupts. "Just because I'm a monster, doesn't mean they're all like that. Some of them..." He cups my face in his hands, pressing his face to mine. "Some of them are gentle, and sweet. Because you are a thing to be cherished and kept warm."

My arms come up to twine around his neck, and he lets me. I sigh as Cairo kisses me, and I find I really don't mind his fangs as long as I'm careful with my tongue. As sweet as he is, this kiss, like every other, is devouring. He tastes every inch of space between my lips, swiping his tongue over mine and purring in delight.

Kissing him turns out to be a very effective way to warm up, I decide after a few minutes of this, when it becomes obvious my grip on him is the only thing holding me up. My legs certainly aren't doing it. I sigh into his mouth, and the sound after that is a little more needy. Cairo's purr grows in response, and his hands span my hips, nails pricking at my skin.

"I've got you, little bird," he tells me. His hands shift, roaming upward, until he's sweetly, teasingly touching me just as greedily as he kisses me. "Just let me take care of you." One hand disappears, and I watch as he drizzles shampoo onto his palm.

"I just washed my hair yesterday," I point out, but I'm not really complaining. Cairo fixes me with a plaintive look, and doesn't deign to respond before he's gently scrubbing my hair, his claws tingling against my scalp.

My skin prickles, and I close my eyes, letting him urge me against his chest while he rinses out the shampoo and then takes his time to work conditioner through my long, blonde hair thoroughly as though it's his job. The purr in his chest is reassuring and sweet, and it's so easy to drift, though this time it's less from panic and more because this is just so...*nice*.

No one's ever taken care of me like this before, and I decide I'm ruined for anyone else, if this is how Cairo is going to treat me. I don't feel broken, or fragile, or as though he's treating me like a child. I just feel cared for and important.

I know I can't say the words stuck in my throat. That would make me insane. But I have to bite them back as he gently uses my soft cloth washcloth to wipe down my entire body with soap. "What are you...?" The words are out instantly when he drops to his knees in front of me, but Cairo grins up from the floor of the shower.

"Returning the favor," he purrs. "You don't mind, right? It's not exactly a chore." His gaze flicks to the front of my body, and he leans in to lick a strip up to my navel. "Not when you taste this good."

Swallowing a gasp, I press my hands against the wall

behind me, fingers sliding over the grout between the tiles to ground myself. "That could be taken in a vaguely cannibalistic way, coming from you," I point out, though there's no fear in me at all.

"Yeah," he agrees without argument. "I guess it can." He does it again, the flat of his tongue strokes up over my skin, and he starts moving lower, until he reaches up to part my thighs and on his next lap, his tongue presses firmly to my clit, not going anywhere at all.

I have to take a breath not to move, not to speak, and I can barely even blink as I watch him continue his movements. His next lick is a long, teasing stroke. Cairo goes from my slit to my belly, then back again on only a slightly different path. This time, a needy whimper leaves me, and Cairo glances up at me from the floor of the shower with satisfaction in his dark eyes.

"You're enjoying this," I accuse. "Making me want it."

"Oh, yeah." His arms wrap around my thighs, holding them parted and perfectly still. Considering his strength, I'm not going anywhere. "And I'm going to take my time, little bird. You have nowhere else to be."

I don't.

I never do, not really. The only things holding me here are him and Moro, plus this house that I owe money on. But if he and Moro were to disappear, I don't know where I'd be.

It scares me when I think about it like that.

Thankfully, his tongue is an effective distraction. Especially when he centers his attention on my folds, and the frequent lapping of my clit, until I can't help but curl my fingers in his hair.

"Is this okay?" I breathe.

"You are always welcome to hold on to me," he promises.

I shouldn't want to cry from that. But I'm glad he can't see my expression so well when I tip my head back against the wall behind me, face turned up toward the spray. He's dedicated and unhurried enough that the pleasure in my belly is a low, building surge instead of the rush of a flame. I feel every inch of it, every added flicker of heat.

"You know, for a cannibalistic monster who lives in the woods, you're really good at this," I huff, my hips rocking in his grip, though only by degrees with how well he's holding me in place.

His chuckle reaches my ears, but Cairo doesn't reply. He seems too fixated on his task, and he suddenly growls in appreciation when his tongue swipes through my folds.

"I love how you taste when you're wet for me." Shivers wrack through me, and a touch of embarrassment at how easily he can tell only makes this hotter. "Your taste changes on my tongue. Did you know that, Fern?" Obviously I didn't, but I can't help listening to every word that falls from his lips.

"I always love how you taste, but when you get close, you get sweeter. You're like candy on my tongue. I've never tasted anything like you." To make his point, he thrusts his tongue into me, drawing a sound of surprise from my lips as he tastes all of me he can from this new angle. His nose bumps against my clit as he fucks me with his mouth, and my fingers tighten in his hair until I'm whimpering and squirming helplessly against the wall.

No amount of praise could ever come close to doing him justice when he's like this and I'm on my toes. But I certainly beg him for it anyway. "Cairo..." his name is a gasp on my lips, and my fingers scrape against his scalp in a way that makes him purr.

"Will you come on my mouth, gorgeous girl?" he asks, barely moving his face away from the apex of my thighs. "I want to taste every second of your release. I want you right here." He licks my slit again, and swirls his tongue around my clit. "All I want is my tongue buried in your pussy while you come for me."

Without another word, he lets go of one thigh to use his thumb to play with my clit. The double sensations—his long tongue wet and hot inside of me and his finger expertly toying with me—are more than enough to send me over the edge with his name on my tongue while my toes curl against the tile floor.

But my tightening body only makes him more indulgent. Cairo growls, his face buried between my thighs and his tongue licking inside of me, stroking my walls with velvety heat. It's a new, foreign sensation that has me panting and struggling against him, even as he drags my orgasm out with the way he's still teasing my clit.

Finally, I can see straight again, and I relax with weak knees and a hand still buried in Cairo's hair as he continues to lick me. But now it's not just my folds, but also my inner thighs and my stomach as well. The strokes of his tongue are languid, and when my knees fold, he lets me slide down the wall until I'm sitting in front of him on the floor of the shower, thighs around his.

Cairo purrs and captures my mouth in a kiss, letting me taste my release on him. He guides my hands toward him, until he's using my grip to stroke his cock with sure, measured strokes. It doesn't take long, and I'm surprised by just how much he enjoyed eating me out. When he comes, I'm leaning back enough that white, pearly drops spill over my chest and stomach, only to be washed away by the still warm spray before he leans over me possessively, protecting me from the softness of my bathroom if nothing else.

"Dr. Radley knows about you," I whisper, when I can breathe again.

"Yeah." He sighs, taking the wet washcloth to my stomach

to be thorough. "I sort of figured she did. She's not exactly subtle. "

"She's the one who said you're just lying to me, just pretending to be human to get me to love you." It's easier to say the L-word like that, instead of how I really want to.

Instead of coming from *me*.

"She says you just want to make me cursed like you." I take a breath, not needing to linger on that. Her sister's sad tale isn't as important to me as it is to her, and there's nothing Cairo or I can do to assuage her grief.

"Tyler found me when I was in the park with Moro." That makes him stiffen, though he glances up at me with a sallow-eyed look that lacks any real surprise.

"He hurt her," he states without question.

"Yeah, he wanted to kill me. He said he's tired of this game you're playing. He said..." But I trail off, shaking my head. "Obviously, he didn't kill me. And Moro will be okay. She protected me."

"She's how you got away from him?" Cairo guesses, but immediately I shake my head.

"No, he hurt her pretty badly, and she couldn't get up. Then Hattie was there. It was so strange. He should be stronger than she is, right? So why could she pin him down like she did? Was it just that he didn't want to hurt her?" Already Cairo is shaking his head, a wry grin on his face.

"I suppose I should be grateful to her, since she's apparently so attached to you." Smoothly he gets to his feet, and pulls me up with him before I can protest that I am *not* broken and can definitely do it myself. "She's new," he adds when I look at him askance. "For the first month or so, when we're *new*, we're strong. Stronger than we should be. Apparently strong enough to take down Tyler for a little while. It'll fade." He sighs, turning off the water and nuzzling against my jaw.

"What does he want from you?" I try not to protest as he carries me in his arms out of the shower, only to wrap me in a towel and set me down on the counter again. "Also, I really can walk, Cairo."

"And I really like to carry you." He leans on the counter again, kissing me sweetly, until my hands come up to play with his wet hair and run through the strands. He lets me, purring against my lips, and finally leans in to nose at my jaw like an affectionate cat.

When I shift a little, ready to ask again, he sighs against my skin and licks teasingly at the water trailing below my ear. "I know you won't be denied tonight, little bird. You can at least let me brood a little." After a quick nip to my jaw, he pulls away, his eyes finding mine in the dim light from the bedroom on the other side of the semi-open door.

"Everything," Cairo tells me in an empty, echoing voice. "He wants everything from me. And there's only one way to get that." His hand comes up, fingers wrapping around my throat.

My blood goes cold, and already I know I won't like the answer, though I can't guess what it is, except... "He wants to kill you?" My voice is soft, barely a whisper. Like admitting it out loud will make the idea more real somehow.

But Cairo chuckles. "But he doesn't just need to kill me for that to happen, Fern. He needs to devour me, down to my marrow. He wants to take everything I am for himself, and only then will he be satisfied with what he has. Or at least, he thinks he'll be satisfied."

CHAPTER TWENTY-SEVEN

He doesn't know I'm awake.

It's obvious, judging by how quiet he's being. If I weren't already up and going over his words and Tyler's in my head, I never would've known that he's trying to sneak away from me. But when he leans over and brushes his lips very gently on my cheek, I can't stay silent anymore.

"Where are you going?" I murmur, reaching up to grip his arm before he can pull away. I'm warm and perfect, though less perfect now that he's removed himself from our blanket cocoon on my bed, and I don't want to get up.

Cairo sighs and kisses me in earnest.

The bed dips, and he lifts the arm I'm holding to run his fingers through my hair, affection in every motion. "You should be asleep."

"Yeah. But so should you."

He gives a soft scoff at that, and tugs teasingly at the roots of my hair. "I'm only up in the daytime for you, little bird. And I don't need as much sleep as you do."

"Still doesn't answer my question. Where are you going?" I

roll onto my back to look up at him, to study his face. Even before he opens his mouth, I have a feeling I won't like the answer.

"To make sure this doesn't get even more out of hand. Don't ask me again, little bird." His fangs flash in an unfriendly, dry grin. "Because you're not going, and I'm not bringing you along. Stay *home* this time. This isn't for humans. Especially mine."

Mine.

I wonder if he knows how possessive he sounds when he says it. How intimate, and absolute. My stomach flutters with a cloud of butterflies at the word, and when he kisses me again, his low purr tastes better than any milkshake I've ever gotten in town.

Again, I almost say it. The words get stuck in my throat, though, and I can't say anything at all when Cairo stands up. "I'll be back later," he promises, and turns to leave without another word, and certainly without hearing mine.

I think I love you, Cairo.

I only last an hour lying in bed and doomscrolling on my phone. And that's an overly generous estimate. The storm has finally passed, and the silence is deafening with Moro so completely asleep on the bed, instead of worming her way up to ask for affection.

Once midnight hits, I can't do it anymore. The blankets and the bed are oppressive without Cairo. Especially when I'm so worried about him and a little indignant with curiosity. If I'm *his* then he's *mine.* That's how it works in my head, and how I justify it as I yank on a pair of sweatpants and a hoodie to fight the post-rain chill of the mountains.

While I'm not sure where to go, I certainly have an idea of where to start, though it's quickly becoming my least favorite place to be.

Nothing good ever happens at Bluebone Ridge, after all. And I doubt tonight will be any different.

The drive takes me the better part of forty-five minutes. This late at night, I don't expect to hit any traffic once I turn onto the winding mountain road, and I don't. But I still have to be careful not to drive myself off a cliff.

Leaving Moro at home was hard. She so obviously wanted to come, even though she's drowsy from her pain meds and very clearly still hurting. But I gently explained to her that she needs a day off from being the fierce protector, then I closed the door in her face.

Like a monster.

I'll cook her a hot dog, I tell myself as I get closer to the top of the hill. At the last minute, however, I pull off the road instead of driving all the way to the parking lot of the old asylum. I don't want to announce my arrival if I'm not alone. I doubt Cairo would appreciate it, for one, and in case there's something else here, I'd rather not be seen straight away.

"Fuck, please don't let this be the worst idea I've ever had," I murmur, turning off the engine of my car. Getting out, I jam my keys into my pocket, but I keep my phone in my hand. With the clouds from the storm lingering, it's almost completely dark out here on the mountain. This definitely feels like an awful idea, even as I tone down the light of my phone and drag my hood up over my head.

But I refuse to suggest I should've stayed home. I will *not* stay home when he's doing something potentially dangerous. Even though I have no idea what sort of help I could be.

"Well, it's probably not your best." The amused, dry voice practically makes me levitate, and I whirl around with my light up, looking back toward my car. My heart lurches at the glare of light in the person's eyes, when I know for a fact it isn't Cairo.

"Agatha?!" I gasp, dropping the light so it's not reflecting in her eyes.

"What *is* the plan exactly?" she drawls, still leaning there, barefoot and dressed in a mid-thigh length dark dress with a handkerchief hem skirt. It looks old, easily from at least a decade ago, but who am I to question her fashion choices, when my closet is full of hoodies, leggings, and sweats?

"I don't know. Umm…" I glare down at the ground, though I do surreptitiously look around, just in case other cursed are in the area. "It depends on whether I'm even in the right place. I guess judging by your being here, I am?"

She doesn't answer the question, though I hear her shift a little, and I wonder if the noise is for my benefit, since she hadn't made a sound approaching me. "Not everyone here is afraid of him, little bird. There are some who would kill you just to see him hurt."

"Like Tyler?"

Again she doesn't answer, and I add quietly, "But you aren't afraid of him either." And yet, I know what I saw before. Tyler *is* afraid of Agatha, and Cairo at the very least respects her. I have so many questions for and about her, but none of them matter right now when my priority is Cairo and making sure he's okay.

And if I'm honest with myself, being nosy about what he's doing, and where he fits in up here with the others. "How many of you are there?"

"In the world? I have no idea. We become territorial after it happens. In these mountains…?" she trails off, but when I look at her, she looks contemplative, rather than like she's ignoring me. "More than twenty. Less than fifty. There are some I haven't seen in years, decades, but that doesn't mean they're dead."

"*Decades?*" But I shut up, remembering suddenly what Dr.

Radley said about both Cairo and Tyler. They've been here for *decades*.

So what does that make Agatha?

I definitely don't have the courage to ask, and I don't know how forthcoming she's willing to be. But my light catches a small, crooked grin on her lips and the flash of fang, before she says, "Maybe I'll tell you a story about it soon." Who knows when *soon* is, though.

A long, keening howl followed by shrieks somewhere in the distance makes me jerk around, and I shine my flashlight into the darkness of the trees, as if that'll do me any good. When I turn around again, a yelp escapes me, and I stumble backward from Agatha, who's suddenly right there. She reaches out to steady me, gripping my forearm, and stares at me while I catch my balance.

"Don't go that way. As soon as any of them see you, they'll stop. Cairo will make you leave. So come on." Her clawed fingers slide down my arm, to my wrist, and finally twine with mine. With a small tug, she pulls me after her, following an invisible path through the trees that takes us further into the darkness.

My phone light is nothing out here, and only good enough to illuminate the space where I'm going to take my next step. Agatha is graceful and confident. Even barefoot, she never steps wrong once. It seems instinctual for her to dodge around obstacles without looking like she's doing so.

I could never be like her, and it makes me a little envious. How old is she, and how long has she been wandering these mountains, for her to look like such a natural part of them? Her dress never catches on anything, and I swear it's almost like watching her glide through the woods with consideration for my clumsiness and the way I stumble over everything that doesn't dare touch her or get in her way.

She stops suddenly, so fast that I nearly run into her. Her arm keeps me up, and I can see her glance back at me before she puts a hand over mine that grips my phone.

"Light off, little bird. Or everyone will know you're here before we take another few steps." When I hesitate, she adds, "Trust me. I'll keep you from falling off a cliff." Her words are teasing, but that doesn't make me feel better. If any of the cursed are masters of sounding however they want to, it's definitely Agatha.

But I don't have another choice. I suck in a breath of air and turn off my phone light, putting it in my pocket with a small sigh. "Okay." When I do that and she takes my hand again, I'm left completely at her mercy to take me where I need to be.

Thankfully, she really doesn't throw me off the mountain. My steps are loud compared to her silent ones, and all I can do is count them one by one in the dark, surrounded by the trees pressing against me like reaching hands.

"Can you really see like this?" I murmur, as quietly as I can manage. "Even though it's pitch black?"

"Better than you can see in the light," Agatha whispers in reply. A few more steps shows that we're closer to Bluebone Ridge than I thought we were, but we're in the woods along the back courtyard, where I was unable to watch Jeremy ignoring and neglecting Moro on my second day here. Belatedly, I realize that we're not far from the small garden shed where I read about the accidents, but I no longer need old newspapers to tell me what's going on out here.

Agatha tugs me down beside a fallen tree, where I have just enough space between limbs to see the people in the courtyard, but not enough to really tell what's going on in the corners. "There," she murmurs, directing me with a motion toward the stairs. I have to move a little bit, but when I can finally see clearly, I find Cairo at the top of the stairs, leaning against the empty doorframe as he surveys the others in the courtyard.

There's something different about him here. Something unapproachable and cold as he stands at the top of the stairs just watching. The others must all be cursed as well. They look human, or nearly. Many of them aren't wearing anything at all, and some of them snarl or sneer at each other.

"They look so..." I don't know how to phrase it. "They aren't like Cairo, or you, or Tyler."

"It happens like that sometimes. Some might change. Some might stay like this. They're not unhappy, and many of them weren't exactly pillars of society while they were alive." I see the flash of her grin from the corner of my eye. "Cairo was never like this."

"Were you?"

"No." Her tone is flat and doesn't really invite argument or further curiosity into her origins, even though I'm incredibly curious.

"Tyler was." I don't have to ask. Somehow I know that with his impatience and his aggression, he's closer to them than he is to Cairo or Agatha, whatever that might mean.

"Tyler was," Agatha agrees. "It's why some of them prefer him to Cairo."

I watch for another few minutes, seeing a few of those that remind me more of Agatha and Cairo walking around to break up petty squabbles or just maintain some sense of calm.

"Why aren't you down there?" Quickly I realize it sounds a bit like an accusation, and I glance sidelong at Agatha. But she only meets my gaze in the near-dark, though thankfully the moon is out enough now for me to see by. "I just mean...If they respect Cairo and Tyler, and both of them are afraid of you. Wouldn't you be able to make them do whatever you wanted?"

A smile ghosts across her lips. "And where's the fun in that, Fern?"

I don't know what to say in response to such an answer. What *is* there to say, when she could rip me apart and eat me like popcorn if she wanted to while watching whatever's going on down there. But thankfully a snarl breaks through the din, and when I look up again, Cairo's stepped down from the top of the stairs though he's still standing above the others.

One who reminds me of him sits on the steps below him, arms draped across her knees. She doesn't look up at Cairo, but something in her face makes it seem like she's just waiting for the others to make a move to shove them back into their place.

I can't hear all that Cairo says, though it's not like he gives some massive speech. I hear Tyler's name a few times, and a few questions that snap out like growls from the gathered creatures in front of him. But none of them try him.

"Then go," he finally says to one, stepping down until he's in her face. "If you want him instead of what you have, if you think his promises will really take you that far—" The cursed lunges for him, but Cairo is effortlessly faster. It's not like his fight with Tyler, but then again, it's not a fight at all.

Within seconds, the woman is on her back on the ground, throat bared to him, and Cairo just looks down coldly into her face with his lips peeled back from his fangs. *"Go,"* he repeats, stepping back. When she gets up, I can see her waver. I can tell that she doesn't know what to do. But instead of leaving, she slinks back to the others, hiding among them.

"I'm tired of his games," Cairo says, and now that he's closer to me, I can actually understand what he says. The wind picks up and he pauses, glancing toward my hiding spot, but he looks away a second later.

"Does he know we're here?" I ask, but Agatha doesn't answer.

"Involving humans off the mountain is too far. *She* made that rule, and we've all lived with it since before most of you were born." He snarls at another cursed who growls a little at him, sending that one trembling backward as well. "If you don't like me, that's fine. I've left you all alone for the most part. But do *not* go down into town—"

"Like you?" The voice comes from a guy who appears to be in his late forties. He stands far back from the others, arms crossed, and stares flatly at Cairo instead of looking down. "You've been down in Whippoorwill most nights for weeks."

"And I can control myself," Cairo hisses in reply, turning on him. "You can as well, and you don't involve humans in your games. My warning is for those who can't." At the almost praise, the man seems mollified, and he drops his shoulders.

"What about Tyler?" The question comes from somewhere in the group, but I don't know from where.

"*Tyler* has had his warnings. And now you have too. I'm done with his games, and anyone else who wants to play them can either go to him, or face me right now for the privilege of playing them for another night." His challenge and the warning in it echo through the silent courtyard, but none of them say a word.

As if an unspoken dismissal was given, the cursed start disappearing. A few at first, wander out of the courtyard, before more and more until finally it's only Cairo and two of those who look the most human. I can't hear their conversation, though one of them is the man who half-challenged him before.

The older man smiles suddenly, a dry grin on his lips, and claps him on the shoulder with a soft laugh.

"That's Elijah," Agatha murmurs in my ear, her voice almost inaudible. "He's a little older than Cairo, but he prefers to stay by himself most of the time. They're talking about you," she adds, sounding amused.

"Me?" I jerk back in surprise to look at her, trying to meet her eyes in the dark. "What *about* me?"

"Well..." She looks back at them and stands up, holding her hand out to me. I lean back on my hands, confused, since the whole point of us being here was to hide, or so I'd thought. "Ever since the wind changed, a few of them have known we were here. Come on." She takes my nervous hand, pulls me to my feet, and subsequently helps me over the log before we make it down to the courtyard.

Elijah snorts when he looks at me, then glances back at Cairo. His eyes are dark, and in the moonlight, they look almost black. "Well, that's definitely your problem, then. She's too curious for you to keep in the dark, Cai."

Cairo rolls his eyes at the man, and the woman beside him just gives me a look and a nod, before turning and leaving without another word.

"I'm Fern," I introduce, trying to sound confident as I hop the broken back wall into the courtyard, though I nearly hit the dirt when my feet slip on some stones. Thankfully, no one laughs, but I'm feeling a lot less sure of anything.

Cairo sighs, and when I glance up at him, I see him roll his eyes up toward the moonlit sky over Bluebone Ridge. "Why can't you do what I say, even once?" he asks, and then drops his chin to look at Agatha. "And do you have to be so helpful?"

"When she wants to be," Elijah puts in. He raises his hands in surrender when Agatha glances his way, though I don't see anything cruel or threatening in her look. "All right, all right. I'm gone. Just..." He turns back to Cairo, a look of concern etched into his features. "Be careful, you hear me? You're too soft, and he knows it. Otherwise, *she* wouldn't be here." He nods at me. "And she wouldn't be here like *that.*"

"Like..." I trail off, as the answer to my unfinished question hits me in the face.

I wouldn't be here as a *human*.

Elijah disappears just as quietly and quickly as Cairo can, which leaves me with the two of them, feeling like a child caught staying up past their bedtime as Cairo gives me the *look* from his narrowed eyes.

"I can't even be surprised," he admits, rolling his shoulders wearily. "Not when you're so interested in making this your business. *Both* of you," he amends. Though his next words are all for Agatha as he adds, "I don't suppose you'd like to step in to solve this problem?"

"Not at all," she assures him. "I'm tired of playing babysitter. It's someone else's turn for a while." Again I wonder just how long Agatha has been around, but I file the question away to ask Cairo later.

"What are you going to do?" I ask, striding the rest of the way to Cairo, who reaches up to cup my face in his hands. His claws brush my skin, and he leans forward with a soft purr to brush his lips against mine affectionately and easily.

"I'm going to end Tyler's game. It's gone on long enough."

"Too long," Agatha remarks. "You've let him get away with too much." There's a note of something in her voice that might be concern, but if it is, then Cairo ignores it. He just shrugs, barely looking at her before giving me his full attention once again.

"I'm going right now, and I'll be home by morning. Okay?" His purr meets my ears, and when he kisses me again, I clutch the front of his shirt to drag him against me.

"Do you promise?" I murmur, feeling dread coil in the first signs of a knot in my stomach. This doesn't feel right. It feels like it won't be okay, though I don't know why.

"Yeah, little bird." Cairo chuckles, nipping softly at my

lower lip. "I promise. I just need you to stay home, where I know you're safe. Wait for me, all right? Twelve hours. That's all I need."

"Twelve hours," I repeat, letting him step away. It still doesn't feel right. I want to stay with him. "Wait, no—Cairo. Can I stay, please? Let me go with you—"

"And do what?" he cuts me off, his voice sharp. "What can you do to help me, Fern?" The plaintive meaning in his words makes me flinch, and he looks away. "You're human. He would rip you apart just to spite me."

Some part of me has the audacity to think that maybe he's wrong. Maybe I *could* help him, if only he'd let me. But he must see that on my face, because Cairo's quick to reach out, and he tips my chin up so I meet his gaze. "I'm fine, okay?" he murmurs, and his eyes find mine in the moonlight, in the courtyard of the mental hospital where all of this began.

"I'll be home tomorrow. *Wait* for me." He gives Agatha a look as well, like he's trying to warn her off more of her help, and without another look, he disappears into Bluebone Ridge, fading into the shadows with an unnatural amount of stealth.

"He's right, you know," Agatha remarks, once he's gone and the moon is back behind the clouds, no longer out now that the show is over. It's stupid to think that the moon is its own kind of audience, but as the breeze in the courtyard blows my hair around my face and I shiver, it's the only thing I can think of with the timing of it.

Agatha tucks my hair behind my ear companionably, jerking her head toward the side of the building. "You wouldn't be able to help him as you are. You'd just get in his way, and he'd probably die having to protect you." The matter of fact nature of her words isn't helpful, and I flinch from them.

"But he'll be okay, right?" I ask, footsteps crunching on gravel. "Tyler can't really hurt him?"

She doesn't answer until we're at the front parking lot, and she stops to stare upward at the clouded sky while I dig my phone out of my pocket, figuring now it doesn't matter if the others know I'm here.

"Go home, little bird," Agatha tells me, and her voice is a mixture of so many others, yet nothing at all. "Go home to your safe, warm bed, and try not to think about problems that can't be solved by humans."

CHAPTER TWENTY-EIGHT

DESPITE THE MANY PROMISES I MADE TO MYSELF ABOUT STAYING awake all night on the whole ride home, they are put to shame pretty quickly. I barely make it through letting Moro outside, giving her a hot dog, before collapsing in my bed with my hoodie still on and my leggings somewhere half on the floor. Moro snuggles up with me, finally feeling a little bit better after her brush with Tyler yesterday and no longer so sedated from the vet.

"I'm sorry," I murmur against her fur, feeling like I owe her the apology. She only wiggles closer, and I wrap an arm over her before passing out into a deep, dreamless sleep.

I figure I won't sleep that long. But even if I do, surely Cairo will wake me up in ten hours, since that's when he promised to be home by. All I have to do is sleep, and wait, and try not to worry about him.

The phone vibrating against my face is what does it, though. I jerk upward, sitting straight up in bed and bothering Moro enough that she hops down to the floor. It's bright outside and with a glance at the phone's screen, I'm horrified to see I've slept for *eleven* hours.

"Fuck," I mumble, running my fingers through my hair. The call is from Dr. Radley, and I have no intention of answering it. "Cairo?" Surely he has to be home by now. But no one answers, and when I pick up my still-vibrating phone to walk through the house, I don't see any signs of him being here. Just my empty living room and my kitchen, and an empty hot dog wrapper still on my counter, crumpled up, with gross hot dog juice on the fake granite that I need to wipe up.

On a whim I open the back door, though it was still locked, and Moro trots out of the house to walk around the yard while my eyes search the trees for any sign of something that doesn't belong. I don't know why he'd be out here lurking instead of in my house or better yet—in my bed. But I'm not willing to rule anything out.

Not only that, but I figure that if Moro could smell or hear him, she'd be acting more excited, instead of just doing her normal circles around the yard in a patrol pattern clearly meant to keep away strange cursed and unwelcome squirrels. She comes back to me with a slowly wagging tail and I let her in, closing the door and setting my phone down on the table. It stops ringing after Dr. Radley's second call, but I can see that she's in the middle of leaving a message.

A petty, vindictive part of me wants to hit the red X that would stop her from doing so. But I'm an adult, and I don't want to give her any reason to think I'm not okay. Though, I'm sure I've given her enough of that already. To busy myself, I go to clean up the hot dog remains, tossing the package and paper towels in the trash when I'm done.

I can't fault him for being an hour late. That would be stupid of me. Things come up, things *happen*, and I can't assume that a disaster's afoot just because he's not back by when he said he would be. If I go driving up to Bluebone Ridge now, wild-eyed and crying with my wolf dog in the passenger seat, I'd be the stereotype of the overbearing, controlling girlfriend.

Or rather, soon to be *ex*-girlfriend. I couldn't blame him for never wanting to see me again if I acted like a helicopter parent instead of trusting him to be the adult cryptid that he is.

While I don't need to shower, there's something familiar in the routine. The water is hot and helps melt away some of the tension in my shoulders, along with the chill in my fingers from being outside with Moro. I definitely take longer than I need to, and even though I'm doing my best not to count the minutes, that's exactly what I'm doing in my head while I wash and rinse my hair with shampoo, then with conditioner, and finally scrub my skin with my body wash. My fingers trail over the places Cairo left marks. My hips are now mostly free of bruises, save a few faded yellow splotches just above the tops of my thighs. But I wrap my hand around the base of my throat, even though it doesn't give me the same feeling of possessive protection as it does when Cairo does it.

Still, it helps me remember the feeling of his touch, and his purrs in my ears while he calls me *little bird*.

It hasn't even been a day, and yet I know I'm too wrapped up in him for my own good. The feeling is like a hunger in my body, hollowing out my chest and stomach with no way to fill it without him. God, I'm pathetic, I realize as I'm toweling off my hair and glaring at myself in the mirror. Lovestruck for a monster I haven't even known for a month.

"Sad," I sigh to my reflection. "You should be ashamed of—"

My phone vibrates again, and I look down expecting to see Dr. Radley's name flashing across my screen. But I instinctively pick it up when I see it's my mother, pressing the phone to my ear once I've tapped the screen to answer. "Hey, Mom, what's—"

"*You cannot act this way.*" Her voice is impatient and irritated. In the background, I can hear the noise of conversation, so I know she's not at home. "*What is wrong with you, Fern?*"

Her words cause my chest to tighten, and suddenly I'm a teenager again, afraid of her wrath and trying to find a way to connect with her to avoid getting lectured for what she considered my bad behavior.

"I..." I trail off with my fingers tightening around the phone and my eyes wide on my reflection, like she can do something other than stand there looking dumb. "What are you talking about? Did I miss your call earlier? I just got out of the shower, and—"

"*Your therapist called me. You're ignoring her calls? She's worried about you. She told me you've been showing some worrying patterns recently, and that you've started falling in with some people who want to hurt you.*" My mom sounds mad instead of worried. But that's always been her thing.

"So much for HIPAA," I mutter petulantly, only half-joking. But it's the wrong thing to say.

"*HIPAA?*" my mother hisses. "*You're going to make a joke about privacy laws now? I'm glad she called me. You tried to kill yourself a month ago, and now you're trying to go off the grid.*"

My eyes narrow in the mirror, and frustration wells, burning in my throat. "That's not true," I say, almost cutting her off. "I did *not* try to kill myself, Mom. I told you I was dissociating. It wasn't—"

"*Same thing.*" I flinch back at her words. I don't know why I'm surprised, when she's never been interested in understanding my issues before. "*Whatever your mental issues are, you need help to get them under control. Call her back. Now. She brought up having you move back in with us.*"

The words catch me off guard. "No," I say flatly. "No, I don't need to move back in with you. I have a house, a job, and a *dog*. You're allergic to dogs," I remind her, looking for any excuse.

"Then it can be an outside dog, or we can look for a better home for it. Call her back, but I think this is something we should talk about more, Fern." While I'm sure she'll get over this, and technically she can't make me, her threat still sends a rising wave of panic to burn through me.

"Yeah, umm...yeah. Okay. Look, I didn't mean to ignore her calls. My phone was off until I went to shower. I've been—"

"I'm not looking for your excuses. I'm out with Nathaniel and the kids, and this isn't what I wanted to happen today." She sighs, obviously looking to guilt-trip me for ruining her outing with her *new* family. *"Just call your therapist back. She also brought up scheduling an appointment for me to be there as well, to start. I think that's a great idea."*

I don't.

But I won't cry, so I blink back the hot, angry tears that threaten to escape while I look at myself in the mirror. How *dare* Dr. Radley call my mother? How dare she look for reasons to get me away from Whippoorwill Gap?

Away from Cairo.

It dawns on me that that's her real angle here. She thinks getting me back to my mother two hours away will 'save' me from the cursed Cairo's attachment to me.

I'm not like Dr. Radley's sister, however, and now I feel stupid for feeling guilty at the idea of her being killed by Tyler. "Yeah," I say stiffly, barely registering the woods. "Yeah, I'll...I'll call her back. Talk to you later, Mom."

"The weekend," my mom insists. *"You'll call me by the weekend so we can discuss next steps."* Her voice softens, but I can hear the effort it takes for her to make it sound something

other than annoyed. *"I'm only doing this because I care about you, Fern. You're my daughter, and I love you."*

"I love you too." But the words are hollow on my tongue, and when I hang up on her, there's not an ounce of love in me for the woman who gave birth to me and raised me until I could feasibly move out and get my own place. Even if it is a small, older house in the middle of the woods that needs some work. That's never mattered to me, though. All I wanted was a place to call my own, and this house fit exactly what I needed.

Now, though, I'm realizing I'm less attached to it than I was before. With Moro and Cairo, I don't need a house to hide in to escape my mother.

The realization makes the bathroom feel cold, and I hurry through brushing and drying my hair. I barely notice what clothes I grab from the closet, just that they're warm against the chill of my empty house. Finally, staring down at my phone with blank eyes and an empty feeling, I press play on the message from Dr. Radley.

"I know you're ignoring me, Fern. I know you didn't like what I had to say yesterday." Here she sighs, almost regretfully, but I don't believe it. *"You're young. You don't understand what it looks like when a monster is trying to take you. That's what he wants. That's all he wants. You're vulnerable, and you need help. I'm going to help you however I have to. You probably won't like me for it, but I won't let you die the same way my sister did."*

There's a long pause, and I look up at Moro, who's stretching and shaking herself like she knows we're about to go on an adventure.

"You won't like me for what I do, but it doesn't matter as long as I can save you. You're going to leave Whippoorwill Gap on your own, or I'll make you. It won't be difficult, given your history and what happened at Bluebone Ridge. Call me back, Fern. Help me

help you. We'll figure this out together so you can be happy. Really,
truly happy."

The message stops, but I don't pick up my phone. I should
feel enraged, terrified, or at the very least frustrated. Instead
,I'm just...disappointed. A little empty, maybe, as I run the
zipper of my hoodie through my fingers.

I'm not her sister.

I'm not my mother's fragile daughter.

And if Cairo can't come to me, I'd much rather be with him
than here, even if that puts me in danger for being human.

CHAPTER TWENTY-NINE

IN HINDSIGHT, I DON'T KNOW IF BRINGING MORO AND LEAVING MY
phone was the right call, but I'm not sure what other choice
there was to make. My phone won't help me up here, and Moro
will. Even her emotional support is a lot more than nothing,
and she probably wouldn't have let me leave her home again.

"Please don't get killed," I whisper to my dog, parking in
the empty lot of Bluebone Ridge. The caution tape on the gates
is shredded and mostly gone now, and the place is really
starting to look abandoned with weeds and debris from the
woods around.

I'd been hoping for the whole drive up here that Cairo
would just *be* here, sitting on the steps pensively and staring
up at the moon. But he isn't. If there's anyone here, I can't see
or hear, or otherwise sense them.

The entire place just feels...*empty*. For the first time in
forever, it feels like Bluebone Ridge has been abandoned by any
and every living thing in a ten mile radius, though I know that
can't be right.

A sense of dread settles over me as I walk up the stairs, but

I don't bother going inside. This is starting to feel stupid of me, since I have no idea where to look or where Cairo might be. Unfortunately, my Bat Signal is broken, and I'm not sure how to fix it in a timely manner. Usually, Cairo just *finds* me whenever he wants, or whenever I need him to. Moro isn't helping much, since she's just sniffing around the stairs with mild interest and her fur raised like this place is just as appealing to her as it is to me.

"Maybe we fucked up," I breathe, sitting down hard on the stairs. I want to cry, thanks to my mom and Dr. Radley. I need Cairo to help me figure out what to do, even though he's not really any help with human matters.

Sometimes, I wish I didn't have to deal with my more human problems at all. Tonight, they can't be on my mind. Not when Cairo has been gone for closer to twenty hours than the twelve he promised.

Because he had *promised.*

Moro comes close to nudge my face, sniffing my hair like it might be holding some secret. But when she sneezes and walks away, all I can do is watch her go. Too bad she's not trained as a search and rescue dog, I think to myself. Maybe then I could give some kind of cue for her to find his scent and run with it.

Not that I have his scent just lying around on a hairbrush or toothbrush. Even though he stayed with me, Cairo's home was never *with* me, I realize. Not even for the past couple of weeks. His home is here, in the mountains.

Maybe this will never work after all, my brain whispers to me, only darkening my mood further. I can't see how I could ever introduce him to my mom, though my few online friends would probably accept him way better than her, even if I told them what he is. He can't exactly fit into normal society, since when he's starving he's very clearly not human.

And I can't live up here with him.

My stomach twists around the thought, and all of those hopeful butterflies that took flight in me only yesterday all wither and die, falling to their graves somewhere near my ribs that squeeze painfully around my insides.

The sound of dragging makes me look up, as does Moro's sudden interest in the courtyard on the other side of the stairs. "Cairo?" I ask, when Moro wags her tail instead of growling.

But the shape that appears around the stairs dragging a body isn't Cairo, and my heart clenches painfully in my chest.

"You look disappointed," Agatha observes, dropping the body like it's merely an inconvenience that weighs as much as a sheet. *"Sorry I'm not who you're looking for."* Her voice comes out as Cairo's instead of hers, and it sends an unpleasant shiver up my spine to hear it come from her lips.

"Please don't do that," I breathe, trying to sound polite and not like I'm making a demand, but rather a plea. "Do you know where he is? Or, I guess, what's taking him so long? I'm not trying to be overbearing," I add, my words coming out fast as I try to explain. "It's just that it's been a lot longer than twelve hours, and my day was kind of shit, and—"

Moro growls suddenly, her fur standing on end. While she wasn't willing to walk straight up to Agatha, this new reaction has me stunned and staring, even as she whirls away from the female cursed and looks back up at me, then past me.

Agatha is faster than Moro, and faster than I've ever seen Cairo move. One moment she's in front of me and the next she's behind me, having moved more quickly than I can see. I stumble to my feet, nearly falling down the stairs and turn to see her slam a male, naked cursed back into the doorframe, though he doesn't have the good sense to submit to her while she holds him there.

"That's not very nice. And you should watch what you say to me, sweetheart," Agatha observes, unimpressed. The man tears at pieces of the doorframe, sending debris raining down the steps, but he doesn't listen to her warning. His eyes are on me and he hisses, showing off his fangs, before Agatha rapidly plunges her free hand into his chest, pulling a gasp from my throat and a choked-off gargle from his lips.

Blood leaks from his mouth as he looks at her, but Agatha's hand is still inside of the bleeding cavity of his upper body. "You'll find I'm too old to put up with bad manners. And I'm not interested in second chances." While he watches and as a soft, desperate sound coming from between his teeth, Agatha yanks her hand outward in one smooth, quick motion, revealing her fingers wrapped around a mass of red and black.

It takes too long for me to realize she's holding the man's *heart,* and everything it was once attached to. He gurgles, blood bubbling to his lips, and both the man and I stare at the messy, gory thing she holds before she crushes it easily between her fingers, sending blood and tissue raining to the ground below. He falls a second later, and Agatha smears her hand on her dress, the fabric dark enough to not show the blood, not that she seems to mind.

"What was he doing?" I gasp, my eyes on the dead man. Dressed only in old, rotted pants, he's not one that I would consider to be like Cairo or Agatha herself. But my hands tremble, and I don't know whether to congratulate her or puke at the sight of what once was a living thing. "Why did you do that?"

Agatha sighs and walks toward me, stopping one stair up and reaching out to trail her still bloody fingers through my hair. "You are so young not to see what's happening here," she observes, and I can't even be offended. "I can't remember what that's like. He was going to kill you, little bird."

The words make me go cold. I look up at her, eyes wide and dumb. "Kill...me?" I repeat. "But Cairo—He wouldn't let—"

Her brow arches as I break off, a gasp on my lips. "No. No, he's not—"

"I'll ask." The words are so casual that they don't register right away. Moro doesn't even have time to look up from where she's licking at the blood seeping from the body before Agatha is gone again. Another man screams, and when I turn around I find her beside the stairs, holding him up even as he struggles in her grip.

"I'll leave." This one is smarter than his dead friend. His eyes are on Agatha, terrified and wide while reflecting the moon above. "I saw you. I didn't attack—I wouldn't, no matter what he said." The man's eyes flick to mine, then back to her. "Please, Agatha. Don't do this."

"Tell me what happened," Agatha commands in a calm, measured voice. Casually, she reaches up and tucks her hair behind her ear, exerting no more effort than if she were holding a squirming kitten off the ground, almost making me sigh with envy. If this were any other circumstance, I probably would.

Instead, I look at Moro, who's still lapping at the blood, and consider calling her off of it. But what the hell, I have bigger problems than my dog becoming a bloodthirsty killer by the light of the semi-full moon.

"He told us to kill her." The man nods at me, more afraid of Agatha than anything. He's still struggling, though it really is hopeless. There's no way he can get away from her, considering how effortlessly she's holding him by the throat.

"Tyler?" Agatha assumes, glancing at me with a look of warning in her eyes, like she expects me to do something stupid. I don't think I will, but that's not saying anything, given my recent life choices. Instead of adding in my opinion or commentary, I curl my fingers against my palms, digging my nails into my skin to ground myself as anxiety prickles up my spine, then try to take deep, centering breaths like my meditation app tells me to do.

Agatha shifts her grip, causing the man to hiss in discomfort, and for his feet to dangle a little higher above the ground. He's too afraid to fight her, and that doesn't give him many options for escape. "Where is Cairo?" she asks, and her tone makes it known that she expects to be answered.

But the man still hesitates, his eyes wide. "Please don't make me...I'm just doing what I was told," he murmurs, his fangs bared in fear rather than aggression. But the idea that she'll kill him for his answer makes my blood run cold, and I take a step toward her, barely noticing her warning glance in my direction.

"Where's Cairo?" I breathe, needing the answer.

The man takes a breath, swallowing under Agatha's grip. "He's dead," the cursed states, a tremble in his voice that probably has nothing to do with his feelings on Cairo's fate. "He came to confront Tyler...and he underestimated him. Cairo is dead, and killing me won't change that."

CHAPTER THIRTY

THE WORDS DON'T QUITE COMPUTE IN MY HEAD. I STAND THERE ON the steps, wavering, while my heart pounds in my ears in the otherwise silent night.

He's dead.

Cairo is dead.

"No..." Every part of me feels suddenly cold, and my nerve endings tingle.

He's.

Dead.

After all this, and all the things I hadn't said to him—

"Liar." Agatha's tone is flat, unimpressed, and definitely a little dismissive. "Smart, though, trying to hurt her like that."

My head jerks upward, eyes finding the man's as he writhes in Agatha's tightening grip. "What?" I breathe. "He's not—"

"He will be," the man spits in frustration, showing off his fangs as his eyes reflect the moonlight in garish greens and yellows. "Now or in two days, who gives a damn? What's *she* going to do about it?" he sneers the words, showing off dirty fangs, spit dribbling down his chin as he heaves and tries again to get away from Agatha's hand.

But she just sighs and sets him down, surprisingly carefully. "Where are they?" she asks, in a tone that sends a shiver down my spine, though on the surface she sounds friendly enough.

He looks at her, frozen, like a rabbit too stupid or stunned to move. "The old logging camp," he tells her quietly. "They're —" Agatha doesn't let him finish. Just like with the other cursed earlier, she plunges her free hand into his chest and twists, before ripping backward and dragging his heart through his ribs with a sickening, wet crunch.

The cursed gives a little sound in the back of his throat akin to a whine or a protest. He drops to his knees on the stairs, not caring that the concrete must be uncomfortable, and downright painful. But then again, he has bigger problems, seeing as there's a hole in his chest where his heart should be.

Without an ounce of pity in her eyes Agatha drops his heart and steps away from him, once more wiping her hand on her dress, though she doesn't get nearly all the blood off with just the simple action.

"He's not dead?" I follow her as she drags both men's bodies down the stairs, hovering close while Moro moves to sniff at the new organ offering she was given. "So you can help him, right?"

"He's not dead. I doubted he was," Agatha remarks coolly, dropping both of them in a heap like putting garbage out on the street. "But he will be. Tyler will keep him alive for a little while, just to prove a point. Just to let some of the others see, and so he can hurt him." She sounds so nonchalant about the whole thing, meanwhile my heart is twisting itself into knots.

"So you can help him," I repeat, standing on the stairs above her while she stares up at the moon. "You could—"

"No," Agatha says simply. She doesn't elaborate, and all I can do is watch her.

"*No?*" I repeat. "You could, though! They're all afraid of you!"

"Fine." She looks at me, her eyes slightly narrowed and a strange look in them. "I *could* help him. But I won't."

"But you like him!"

She shrugs her shoulders daintily, while adrenaline pumps through my body.

"Agatha please!" I stumble down the last two steps, not knowing what I can do, but willing to try anything. Panic surges through me, and I get close enough to her that every warning signal in my brain fires off, like I'm standing in the face of a polar bear. *"Please!"*

"No."

"Why not?!" I nearly scream, getting so close to Agatha that I can feel her body heat and smell the old blood on her dress. "He's—" I break off when she reaches up, bloody fingers moving to wipe at my cheek before showing me her wet nail.

"Crying for a monster who's eaten so many of your kind over the years," she remarks, studying my tears as if there's something interesting in them. "That doesn't seem very human of you, little bird. Shouldn't you be glad about his death? That's one less creature to prey on hikers or the desperate humans who mistakenly show up here in our mountains." Her voice takes on that echoing quality once more, but I don't flinch from her.

"I don't care. It's *Cairo*."

She studies her nail again before brushing away the tear, then Agatha's eyes flick up to mine, unnaturally dark in the pale light. "You help him, then."

The words take me by surprise, and I stare at her in absolute shock, like she's just grown a second head. "What?"

"It's Cairo," she repeats, in a voice that's the perfect mimicry of mine, down to the intonation of his name. "So why don't *you* help him?"

Shaking my head, I don't look away from her, still confused and wondering if Agatha's gone mad. "I can't," I say slowly. "How would I even begin to? I can't find him, and Tyler would rip me apart the moment I showed my face. I'm just a human."

Her grin tells me that's the right thing to say. Agatha reaches out again, cupping my chin in one hand. "That's always the problem, isn't it? You're just a human. Even if you could save him, what then? You're *just a human.*" I hate it when she mimics my voice. "You can't live in his world when you're *just a human.* But what if you...weren't?"

My mouth opens, then closes, though no sound has escaped. I stare at her eyes, digest her words, and try to figure out how to respond to them. "I don't understand," I admit finally. "He told me the only way to become what you are is to be starving. And to be, you know..." I trail off awkwardly, unsure why the word bothers me so much.

"A cannibal." Agatha says without flinching. "Which is the crux of the curse. That you're so *desperate* to do the unthinkable. That you're willing to consume one of your kind, just to keep living."

"To be starving," I add. "To be so starved and desperate that you have no other choice. But I'm not starving." But I am desperate.

"Aren't you?" Agatha slips away, striding back to the stairs where she dropped the burden she carried here earlier. As I watch, she kneels on the concrete and shoves her hand into the man's chest, being much more careful than she was with the cured men as she slowly extricates both her hand and the cold, dead heart she's cradling in her nails.

My heart races in my chest as I stare at her, both horrified and darkly fascinated. Time seems to slow as she comes back to me, and the wind picks up ominously around us as Agatha stands in front of me, taller and more imposing than before. I've never seen her look monstrous, and even though nothing has changed, somehow *everything* has.

"You brought a human body here?" I ask, staring down at the heart between us that she's holding up in her hand, fingers curled around it as coagulating blood slowly drips down her wrist. "Why?"

She doesn't reply, and the answer suddenly hits me in the face as my stomach plummets to the ground. Immediately I jerk my eyes up to meet hers, eyes wide and incredulous.

"Because you knew," I accuse, looking between the body and her. It's too convenient. Too *easy* for her to just have a human corpse lying around, unless this was her plan.

She doesn't deny it. Agatha tilts her head to the side, eyes narrowed, as the wind blows her black hair around her face, her dress ruffling with it as well.

"You *knew*," I say again. "Why are you doing this? Cairo said he wouldn't force me, or even ask me. He said—"

"But I'm not Cairo." Agatha's voice is cold, and less friendly than before. "I see the way he looks at you. His *little bird*." She so easily mimics his tone and I jerk back from it. "You're right. He'd never ask. He'd never take you from the sad state of your life, never do to you what so many of the others do to humans. What Tyler did to that broken thing he has with him. I'm certainly not like Tyler, but I am also not Cairo." She crowds closer, not letting me step out of her space. "You were right before. I do like him, though I think he is soft in some ways. I'm the one who saved him all those years ago, at the bottom of a cliff with his legs broken and blood filling his lungs, slowly drowning him." Her eyes flicker with something other than the moonlight.

"I'm not starving," I whisper, like that makes any difference, and I glance down at the heart before back up at her. The idea of biting into it is revolting at best.

She jumps on my words eagerly. "Aren't you?" Agatha asks again, feigning surprise. "If you aren't *starved*, then why do you cling to the creature who gives you unfiltered affection? Why is it you're willing to drop everything for him, and for her? You don't have your phone, so there must be no one for you to call for help. Every time I've seen you, all the times I've watched you, you've been alone. Your mother's child who she'd rather forget. The girl who drove scissors into her hand when the world became too much—"

"Stop it." I can't handle the truth of her words, though I have no idea how she knows so much about me. Tears roll down my face as I gaze at her, eyes wide and desperate. "Stop—"

"You *are* desperate, Fern," she coos, pressing herself closer. "And the reason this hurts so badly is because you know that if Cairo really does die, you will *starve*."

Her words echo with a kind of finality that shakes me, and an honesty I can't deny. My feet feel rooted to the ground, and when I gaze up at Agatha's face, there's a hint of triumph in her gaze, even though I haven't said or done anything.

"Could I really save him?"

"Yes."

She pushes the heart toward me, as her other hand lifts one of mine until my fingers meet the slightly warm, slick surface.

"Will it hurt?"

"Yes."

With her urging, I gently grip the cooling organ between my hands, cradling it like I could somehow damage it, even though it has no purpose now except as a piece of meat.

"Do you love him?" Agatha asks, her voice a chorus of so many others.

I look up at her, the desperation bubbling free of the doubt in my chest. *"Yes,"* I whisper, and I watch her lips curl into a satisfied, victorious smile as I lift the heart to my mouth and sink my teeth into the tough, grisly muscle.

CHAPTER THIRTY-ONE

I CHOKE WHEN THICK, COPPERY BLOOD FLOODS MY MOUTH, AND I nearly lose my nerve. My teeth work to cut through the tissue of the human heart, and the taste is revolting enough that I want to gag. But I manage to tear a strip of it off, chewing the tough sinew while holding Agatha's gaze. My shoulders heave with disgust, and I nearly spit it out before hastily swallowing.

But the feeling of the flesh sliding down my throat certainly isn't any better. Another shudder goes through me, and I heave with a hand over my mouth. "H-how much do I—" I'm not sure I can do this.

"More than that," Agatha tells me coolly, and watches as I force myself to bite into it again, and again. Moro senses my distress, whining and brushing against my leg. I'm sure this wouldn't be at all difficult for her, but I don't have sharp teeth or a taste for raw flesh.

"Oh, *fuck*—" I manage to swallow two more pieces before my body rebels, and I clap a hand over my mouth again, breathing through my nose and swallowing down nausea. "I don't know how you eat this," I can't help mumbling, and my eyes tear up as my body does whatever it can to convince me to expel the raw heart in my stomach.

Agatha chuckles and gently pulls the heart from my fingers. "Easily," she assures me, and as I watch, she bites into the heart with fangs that shear through the muscles. She barely chews before swallowing, and looking at her face, I realize mine must be just as gory as she drops the heart between us onto the stairs, where it lands with a wet thud for Moro's inspection.

"How long does it take?" I ask, still feeling like I'm going to puke while my hand hovers near my face, like that's going to do anything to keep the bits of human heart in my stomach. "Do I just—"

A streak of pain goes up my spine, and I gasp at the over-whelming, painful nausea that claws up my throat. I heave a little, lips still pressed together, my eyes watering, and I look up at Agatha again, who isn't at all surprised by this turn of events.

"I told you it would hurt." She watches impassively as I drop to my knees on the steps, the concrete hard and painful beneath my legs. Moro is there instantly, whimpering and nosing my face, but I barely notice when Agatha gently guides her away by her collar, saying something to her I can't hear over the pounding of my heart in my ears.

Every breath brings a new wave of pain. My mouth waters until I have to spit the excess saliva onto the ground, and when I lean over, I find I can't straighten back up. Every inch of me hurts. All my nerve endings, and every strand of hair screams at me, all too aware and begging for me to stop, to puke, to do anything except this.

Still, I force myself not to let what's in my stomach creep

up my throat. I swallow once, then again. I groan around the coppery taste still in my mouth, but the pain just gets worse. "How long—" I gasp again, trying to drag air into my contorted lungs. "How long does it—" But I can't finish any of my questions. An intense shiver works its way up my throat; my body's final attempt at aborting this terrible endeavor. But when I clap a hand over my mouth and swallow back what's coming up my throat, the feeling turns to pain that rises like a flame, searing every centimeter of my body and causing me to feel like I'm burning from the inside out.

When I black out from the pain moments later, it's a relief, and I don't even try to fight it. Nor do I mind that the last thing I feel is the soothingly cold concrete of the steps on my cheek, with Moro's concerned whines in my ears.

Something isn't right.

I follow the sound of voices further into the cave, whispers that I can't understand, while my legs keep moving of their own accord. When I try to stop, I can't.

I'm not in control.

Rounding the corner, I turn into a large chamber, hollowed out in a way that makes me think it's manmade, rather than natural. Two women sit across from each other on either side of a low fire, and behind them are bodies, strewn this way and that.

They both look at me, their eyes shining unnaturally in the light from the flames.

"You're starving," one of them observes, poking at the fire with a stick. Her clothes look like something out of a history book, and both are wrapped in furs with red, streaking lines painted on their faces. "So were we."

The other woman doesn't speak. She just picks something up off of the ground and bites into it, filling the cave with wet, squelching noises and her loud chewing. I stare at them both in the light of their fire, unable to say anything.

Finally, the woman eating stands up with the remains of her meal in her hand. Her fangs aren't quite as refined as Cairo's, and her eyes only barely reflect the light. She's cursed, I realize, but not the same. Like an earlier sketch of what they are now, as if they somehow evolved over the centuries.

Their voices pick up again, though I can't make out what they're saying in the echoing space. The woman in front of me surveys my face and reaches out to trail her bloody fingers across my bottom lip. The liquid is still warm and drips down my chin even as she makes another pass over the top.

"You will never leave this place," she whispers, her eyes wide, a touch of regret in her tone. "None of us will."

"May your survival be worth the sacrifice," adds the other, and their fire goes out. I'm falling, sinking into blackness that's both empty and thick, but when I open my mouth to scream, no sound comes out. My body feels strange, and sound pounds against my ears, but just when I think the sound will overwhelm me, everything stops, and my fall ends with a jolt.

I open my eyes with a gasp, though my head is spinning so much that I can't move. The first thing I realize is that I'm no longer outside, with my head on the concrete, and the second is that Agatha is here.

She trails her fingers over my face comfortingly while I search the ceiling above me, trying to figure out why it looks so familiar. The bed under me creaks when she shifts slightly, and I take a breath only to choke on the myriad of scents in my nose ranging from old blood, to dog, and finally to the scent of pine and spice emanating from the figure sitting beside me.

"They used to live here too, though even I never saw them outside of that cave," she murmurs, her voice softer than ever but still perfectly audible to my ears. I reach one hand up to gaze at my splayed fingers, and I can't stop staring at the claws tipping each finger before running the pad of my thumb across the razor-sharp edges. "There was a woman who claimed to be one of their daughters when I was young. She told me about them. How they did terrible things to survive, and because of that, they slowly changed while they were trapped in that cave. It's not exactly like us now. But back then, the curse was a very new thing, or so she said."

Agatha moves to look down at me, and in the darkness I can see her perfectly. "But I disagree. I think the curse has always been here, in these mountains. You know, I heard another story once. From a man I met on a trail. Once he learned what I was, he told me a story of others like me, though different in their own ways. Instead of being *starved* like us, they were overcome by *thirst*. He said the last one he saw was far from here, where there are fewer mountains, no pine trees, and the winters don't come with six feet of snow."

She sits up on the bed and reaches out to grip my hand, pulling me into a seated position as well. "Not that you or I will ever go that far from the mountains," she adds almost ruefully.

"Why?" My voice sounds strange to my ears, and I barely whisper the words. "Cairo leaves the mountains. Can't we?"

"To an extent. You can go anywhere you want in these mountains, and around the bases of them. But at some point, things stop feeling right. You'll start getting hungrier, and animals won't be enough. Here, we know what we are. We control it. But out there? With humans surrounding us and the mountains far behind?" She shakes her head.

It occurs to me that I should be bothered by the revelation I can never really leave. It certainly wasn't part of what I signed up for, not that I got a lot of say in exactly what this is. Silently I get to my feet, turning at the sound of paw steps on the floor to see Moro in the doorway. For a second, I worry that she'll growl, or run from me. I can smell her in ways I've never been able to before, the same with Agatha, but after Agatha's comments, I'm relieved she doesn't smell like *food*.

She just smells like the woods, and vaguely wet dog.

"Hi girl," I murmur, holding my breath as she walks toward me. Her tail wags, sending the soft *swish-swish* of the sound to my ears, which I've never been able to hear before. She noses my hands and licks at the dried blood there, before her tail wags quicker. She woofs, almost like she's admonishing me, and my shoulders fall in relief.

I don't know what I would've done if my dog hated me for what I've become.

"This is...the room I stayed in," I observe, taking another breath. It's pitch black in here, though I can see nearly perfectly into the darkened corners. I can smell Hattie, and Sam, and a million other scents, but I ignore them and walk into the small bathroom without a locking door, though even the door it had now hangs from its top hinge.

I can still smell the blood outside, along with scents similar to Agatha's that I assume have to be the remnants of other cursed who came through here. Leaning on the sink, I gaze at myself in the mirror, noting the new darkness in my once light blue eyes that now seem to glow back at me like sapphires.

I'm still the same, but I'm so, *so* different. Baring my teeth, I lick over them and wince when I cut myself on the edges. So I reach up to touch them with the pads of my clawed fingers instead.

Agatha appears in the doorway behind me, arms crossed as she observes me. "Any complaints?"

"I'm hungry." The words are out before I can stop them, before I even realize it. I shouldn't be hungry. Not when I was so close to vomiting up the sticky, tough gristle from the heart I managed to swallow pieces of. "Not starving, not really. Just..."

"Hungry," Agatha agrees. "Get used to it, Fern. That's our curse. You will always, for the rest of your hopefully very long life, be *hungry.*"

"Cairo." I breathe his name while still meeting my gaze in the mirror. My fingers tighten on the porcelain sink, and it cracks under my hands, making me jerk back. "How—"

"You know how strong we are. But you are also new."

Pieces of her actions click together in my brain, finally understanding her motivation, and I turn to give her a sallow look. "That's why you did this now. So I could save him." It's not a question, and she doesn't give me an answer.

Agatha just steps away from the door, gesturing for me to follow through the asylum. "You can find him if you look hard enough. The old logging camp is east of here." She points through the courtyard, toward the sea of trees that used to look like a black mass. Now I can see the details of the bark of every tree, and my vision penetrates the darkness easily.

"How do I search for him?" I look up at the sky and, judging by the moon, I was out for a few hours. "Can I even make it to him in time?"

"Yes," Agatha tells me, linking her hands loosely behind her back. "But you have to run. You'll catch his scent when you get close."

My eyes drift to the remains of the body she brought, which now smells like the best food I could ever eat. My mouth waters, and for a moment my attention is caught between the two options. Agatha doesn't say a word, but I can feel her watching, observing my fight with the temptation.

But Cairo is more important than a piece of meat. I step away from it and smooth my hand over Moro's fur as she circles me like she knows we're about to do something exciting. "I'm not going to thank you," I tell Agatha, though now I can *feel* the dominance and foreboding aura she exudes, and everything in me whispers not to piss her off.

She only grins, unfriendly and cold. "Good. I haven't done anything for you to thank me over. Fly away, little bird. Before it's too late and you're stuck starving for the rest of eternity without him."

CHAPTER THIRTY-TWO

I DON'T REALIZE I'M LEAVING MORO BEHIND UNTIL HER BARKS OF protest meet my ears. I slow down, though it would be so easy to just keep running when I'm not tired in the least. My breathing stays easy, and my legs feel like I could run for miles more.

Moro pants as she bounds up beside me, her tongue lolling from her mouth. "Sorry, pretty girl," I breathe, and reach out to scratch her ears. "Normally, I'm the one who can't keep up with you." I still don't know where I'm going, and when I turn in a circle, all the trees look the same. But then I take a deep breath, even though I don't need to, as I'm not panting or tired.

The scents that flood my lungs are varied, confusing, and *new*.

Except for one. I focus on it, and I search my brain trying to remember its source, even though I know I've never been able to differentiate scents this acutely before.

Spice, musk, and the coppery tinge of blood.

Cairo.

It's deeper now, more complex than all the times I pressed my face to his skin and inhaled. But his warmth is there, and I can almost taste him on my tongue when I turn toward where his scent is strongest.

"Can you smell like this?" I whisper to Moro, though I know she's not about to answer me anytime soon. When I walk into the trees, she follows, occasionally moving away to investigate something, though never going so far that I can't hear her. My steps quicken when I'm sure of where I'm going, and I break into a slower run, wondering if I should purposefully leave Moro behind so Tyler can't finish the job.

Not that I'll let him.

I won't let him hurt her, or touch her, and whatever he's done to Cairo, I'll repay him tenfold. My speed picks up again, and I can't slow myself down this time, because the smell of fresh blood has joined Cairo's signature scent.

He's hurt.

But I had to expect that, so I don't let it shake me.

Stopping suddenly, I let myself breathe normally, smelling old, rotted wood and hearing the din of voices from somewhere up ahead. When I take another step, my shoes make too much noise in the detritus, and I wince, realizing suddenly why Agatha prefers going barefoot, since her favorite hobby seems to be sneaking up on people. Very carefully I remove my sneakers, leaving them in the dirt and gingerly standing barefoot, expecting it to hurt.

It doesn't, to my surprise. I feel the earth, the pine needles, and the debris under my feet, but it doesn't hurt. It just...*feels*. There's no better way to describe it. It's easier to walk forward after that, and I'm always sure to place my feet in ways to keep myself silent, though I probably don't look particularly graceful when doing so.

Carefully, I keep walking until I find myself at the edge of a clearing where nature has worked to reclaim the land with saplings, vines, and bushes taking over much of what was probably dirt for a long time. The logging camp is old, and all the buildings I can see are decrepit. Most of the roofs have fallen in, and the ones still up look like one strong breeze would take them out. Belatedly, I realize the wind is blowing towards me, which is how I could follow Cairo's scent, and when it picks up again, I can identify at least two others here as well, though their scents are wholly unfamiliar to me.

Moro barks from somewhere far away, and I hope the wind keeps the sound from anyone here. I don't know much about how being downwind or upwind works, except what I've seen in movies, but all of my memories of the media I consumed in my life seem...fuzzy. Like a dream, or like white noise that doesn't quite matter as much as it should.

Cairo is what matters, and I feel my lips peel back from my fangs as anger sweeps through me, heady and strong, at the thought of Tyler hurting him for his own gain.

It's a testament to how new I am at this that Hattie is able to sneak up on me, and when I move around one of the old buildings that smell of death and decay, she's suddenly in front of me, pushing me back with one hand over my mouth.

Her wide eyes are displeased, but unsurprised. Her clawed hand shakes, and she hisses in my face, causing an answering growl to sound in my throat. *"Stop,"* she whispers when my back hits the wall. I tense, muscles tight under her, and realize that if I wanted to, I could push her off of me.

It's not like that time at Dr. Radley's office. She can't stop me if I don't want her to. But I'm not looking for a fight with her, and my hand comes up slowly to grip her wrist before I peel her hand away. "Where's Cairo?" I ask, my voice just as soft as hers was. Like me, she's barefoot in the dirt, though she's smeared with grime and blood, her clothes having seen much better days.

She looks over her shoulder, eyes flicking from me to the other side of the building, but when I go to move, she shoves me back against the building, causing my anger to spike. I hiss again, baring my teeth, but Hattie just presses a finger to her lips.

"Not so loud, Fern. Not so *loud*. He'll hear you."

"You mean Tyler."

She blinks, but doesn't reply, and it hits me that she's helping me again, when she has every right to be loyal to him like I am to Cairo.

Which only begs the question—what did he do to lose the loyalty of the girl who was so devoted to him back at Bluebone Ridge?

"You promised me." Her words are sullen, sulking, and impatience flares in my chest.

"Hattie—"

"You *promised* me you wouldn't let him change you!" Now I'm the one reminding her to shush, and I reach out to gently grab her arms.

"He didn't change me. Not like Tyler changed you." It's a guess, but one that hits its mark when she jerks backward, looking down with her face clouded over in remembered pain. "I *chose* this for him." With Agatha's 'assistance,' but she doesn't need to know that. "I'm not trapped with him. I don't owe him anything...and you don't owe Tyler anything, Hattie. You never have, and you never will." I'm not sure how she takes my words, but she backs away, looking conflicted.

"Just tell me where he is," I plead, wanting the information before I spring out and reveal myself. "I'm not asking you to turn against him." Though it would be nice.

Hattie sighs and glances around us, looking for someone

who isn't there. "On the other side of the buildings, there are piles of logs. Where they used to load them onto trucks. That's where Cairo is." When I move to walk around her, she grabs my wrist, with a warning in her eyes. "I'm sorry, Fern," Hattie whispers with her shoulders hunched. "I didn't know."

It's surprisingly lucid for her, not that I'm complaining. On a whim, I hug her, wrapping my arms around her shoulders and sparing precious seconds that I hope won't cost me Cairo. "It's okay," I breathe. "You've done nothing wrong." She stiffens when I let go, and I feel her eyes on me as I walk silently around the building, heading to where she pointed.

Beyond the next building, the logging camp opens up, and I see the stacks of logs that Hattie mentioned, along with a few stray ones that lie strewn across the ground, half rotted back into the dirt. The smell of blood strengthens, filling my nose until it's overwhelming. But when I find Cairo strewn across two of the logs on the ground, I have to clap a hand over my mouth to stop myself from screaming.

There's no way he's alive.

That's my first thought until I remember what he told me about the ways to kill him. There's no hole in his chest, though it's covered with raking claw marks that mar his skin and left his shirt torn to shreds. His head is still attached as well, and he's certainly not on fire.

These are the things I have to focus on, rather than surrendering to the fury-driven panic raging through me. Looking closely, I can see the shallow rise and fall of his chest, but he doesn't look like he's conscious where he lies. Did Tyler really do this to him?

As if summoned by my thoughts, the cursed in question suddenly appears from between the two buildings behind me, talking quietly to Hattie. She glances my way, making eye contact as I duck into a doorway, but she doesn't say a word, and keeps his attention focused on her. But there's no way I'll be able to stay hidden for long. The moment the wind changes, or he just looks around, I'll lose my advantage.

With my heart racing in my chest and Moro's barking sounding closer, I watch as he strides toward Cairo with arrogance in every step. I see the tug of his grin on the side of his face, and notice the healing wounds on his bare chest and throat, probably where Cairo got him before whatever happened that went wrong.

"Poor *thing*," he sneers when he's close enough, and reaches out to kick Cairo's leg. From here I can just see Cairo's eyes open to slits, and he bares his teeth weakly up at Tyler, a rueful grin on his lips.

"Pathetic," Cairo drawls from where he lies. "So afraid of me you couldn't face me alone." His words are soft and slurred with pain, but it sends some measure of relief through me to know he's alive, at least. "You think anyone will respect you when they learn how you did this?"

"Who's going to tell them?" Tyler hums. "Agatha? She only crawls out of her den once every decade or so, and she doesn't care enough to save you. Your *little bird?*" He's suddenly mimicking my voice with the next words, and instead of scaring me, it simply infuriates me. "Teague and Fletcher left hours ago to find her and bring back her head." He kneels beside Cairo and reaches out to run his claws mockingly through his hair.

"I even asked Teague to bring me her heart," he whispers conspiratorially in Cairo's ear. "I thought about eating it while you watch, right before you *die.*"

Three things happen at once.

Cairo lunges and Tyler grabs for him, a grin on his face that tells me he was expecting it. But my temper snaps at the sight of his claws going for Cairo's chest, and I'm moving before I can stop myself. And Hattie lunges backward, moving away and disappearing instantly. She's not my concern, however. I tackle Tyler to the ground, my fangs on display as I pin him under me and a long, low growl leaves my lips.

"Fern?!" he gasps, just as Cairo echoes the sentiment and struggles to sit up.

"I have some bad news about your friends," I sneer. "They didn't make it." He surges upward, and I let him, tossing him away from me while raking my claws into the skin of his stomach, going for what my instincts tell me would be the softest.

"Fern..." Cairo pants, trying to get his balance on the logs that give a little under him. "Fuck..." When I turn to him, his wide eyes show surprise and utter shock. "*Little bird,*" he purrs, with both approval and surprise. But then his face falls, and he lets out a hiss, wrapping his arm around his body.

"Don't turn your back on him," he pants. "Don't underestimate him. I know you're strong. I know you feel invincible. But he's been alive a lot longer than you."

"He hurt you." I start towards him with the single-minded intention of checking him over, but Cairo shakes his head.

"I'll live...unless he kills you. Stand *up*, Fern," he growls with an authority that has me on my feet and willing to obey him like it's second nature, which is something to look more into later.

Tyler snarls a laugh as I turn on him, and he gets to his feet to wipe blood off of his torso. "That *bitch!*" He laughs. "I should've known she had a plan. That she wasn't willing to stay out of this like she promised."

"Don't insult yourself," I sneer. "For you to realize that would've required a lot more brainpower than you've ever shown around me."

Shock causes his eyes to widen, and the open indignation

makes me snort while Cairo lets out a rueful snicker. "You little bitch. You're too cocky for what you are, and I'll rip you apart while he watches."

He lunges for me, but it's not like that night at Bluebone Ridge. I can see his movements now, like he's just any other human, though realistically I know he hasn't slowed down.

I've just gotten faster.

I meet his lunge, though Tyler manages to score his claws down my arm, sending a white-hot shock of pain through me that has me stumbling backward in surprise. His experience lends him an advantage, and he keeps coming, knocking me to my back, his teeth bloody as he spits his fury in my face.

This is going to hurt, my brain tells me in a cool, detached way. I lift my arm up between us, knowing it won't help, but the rush of paws and a loud, furious snarling have both of us looking back over his shoulder, just as Moro tackles him off of me.

It allows me to roll to my feet, and I do so, one hand on the ground and fingers sinking into the dirt. The longer this goes on, the more Tyler can use his experience against me. I'm not afraid to kill him, though the lingering pain from the claw marks in my arm is sharper than I could've anticipated.

When Moro leaps away from his grasping hand, I move in again, gripping his arm and breaking it soundly. He howls, but it doesn't put him on the ground, even though the pain must be severe. His other hand moves in a blur, and Tyler grabs my hair to spin me around and slam me into the front of a cabin. The wood splinters against my face from the blow, and I can feel the trickle of blood as I shove backward and headbutt him in a graceless, slightly desperate move.

"*Bitch*," he spits, stumbling back with one hand over his face to guard his freely bleeding nose. But it's like he's forgotten about Moro, who closes her fangs around his leg and tears backward before dancing away to avoid his kick.

"I want to know why," I pant, rounding on him. My heart pounds with hate and adrenaline, and my focus on him is something I've never experienced before. "Why do you want to kill him so badly?"

Tyler scoffs and spits out a mouthful of blood that lands near my foot. "It's really not obvious to you, is it? You really don't get it." He feints left, and I react, making it easier for him to snap his hand out and rake his claws down my neck, tearing through my shirt. I hiss at the hot pain of his claws in my skin, and feel blood welling to soak into the ruined fabric. The pain doesn't make me want to run away, however. It only fuels my anger, and a sort of rage I've never known.

Cairo is *mine*.

The possessiveness surprises me, and it's my good fortune that Tyler is too preoccupied with my question to take advantage of my momentary distraction.

"They respect him. They follow him," he sneers. "He doesn't even have to try. And yet he doesn't want it!" The last words are thrown at Cairo, who is somehow on his feet, glaring sullenly at the cursed between us. "He could have everything —he could be like Agatha, but he doesn't just take it. What's wrong with you?!" He sounds desperate, and at his wit's end. "Why won't you just take what you could have?"

I don't feel like playing fair, and when he looks at Cario again, I lunge forward, eyes fixed on his throat. But it's clear I've miscalculated when Cairo snaps a warning and Tyler's hand comes out quick as lightning to grip my throat, his claws sinking into my flesh in a way that would've killed me twelve hours ago.

"Stupid little bird," he parrots, his eyes dark and full of hate. "Stupid, *stupid* little thing. You could've had her. You could've had everything." When Moro tries to nip at him, he shoves her away, easily sending her sprawling, though she gets to her feet, wary of him and panting.

My heart races as his grip tightens, and I struggle in his grip as my feet leave the ground. His claws are sharp, and the pain is blinding as he digs them deeper and deeper into my neck, making it clear what his intentions are.

"But now you can watch her die, and we'll see if that kills you too." My eyes find Cairo's, and I see his hand tighten on the worst of his wounds, his eyes are desperate and pleading. But full of a dark kind of acceptance.

He won't make it.

He can't save me.

Suddenly, Tyler is no longer holding me, and I drop to the ground when he is thrown to the dirt beside me. Hattie screams in his face, slashing wildly at him.

"You *promised!*" she hisses, tears streaming down her face. "You promised you wouldn't hurt her, that you wouldn't hurt *me!*"

Horrified, I watch as she swipes at him, and at how Tyler's surprise and affection for her make him slow to respond.

"And you promised me you loved me!" he screams back, getting his leg between them to kick her away, causing her to land in a shuddering, sobbing heap at Cairo's feet. He helps her to stand, even though it must pain him to do so.

Seeing all three of them there makes something click in me.

The broken girl who'd been so betrayed.

My dog, who's saved my life now so many times, I owe her a century's worth of filets.

And *Cairo.*

My body moves automatically, and I barely think to question it. In seconds I'm pinning Tyler to the ground, one hand around his throat and sinking my claws into his neck the same way he did to me. The blood is cold in my veins, and when I open my mouth, the sound that comes from between my teeth could never, ever be human.

But then again, I've never felt like this before.

Like a monster.

"It's time for this to end," I breathe, the words trickling from between my lips as my throat works in an unfamiliar way. I don't sound like myself, and he jerks back from me, eyes wide and staring. Tyler tries to surge upward, but I push him back down, slamming him into the dirt so hard he sinks into it a couple of inches.

"This is for Hattie." Without warning, I plunge my hand into his chest, feeling his ribs snap under my fingers as I reach for what I'm searching for. "For what you did to her, knowing she couldn't understand." He squalls like a wounded animal, fighting and bucking against me. But I'm immovable.

"This is for my *dog*." My fingers curl around his heart, and I'm still holding him down with my other hand as I drive my claws into his heart, piercing the muscle as easily as if it were butter. "My *dog*, who you almost killed for protecting me."

"This is for Cairo." I twist like I'm pulling weeds from my dad's vegetable garden, severing the vessels, the nerves, and the connective tissue. "Because he is *mine*." My claws in his throat have nearly met, and he tries to gurgle a response, but blood just bubbles on his lips.

"But most importantly, Tyler?" I lean forward until my face is just above his, our lips nearly brushing. My lips part in a grin, and somehow I know that the smile on my face is unnaturally wide, and bearing more of my teeth than should be possible. The horror reflected in his eyes certainly tells me as much, but all I feel is a sick, dark joy at his fear and his pain.

"This is for me." With one quick jerk, I rip upward, pulling his heart out of his chest and crushing it between my fingers.

The pulpy, gory mess leaks down my fingers while he watches, and his struggles get weaker and weaker.

I'm so close to him I can feel it as he dies. I can feel his breath escape his ruined body for the last time, whistling through his teeth. And I know I will never forget the way his eyes darken, going blank, as Tyler finally lies dead in the dirt beneath me with his heart and blood leaking from my hands.

CHAPTER THIRTY-THREE

THE WORLD IS SILENT FOR A LONG MOMENT. EVEN THE BIRDS AND THE wind stand still around us, or so it seems. But a sharp, sorrowful cry breaks through the stillness, and Hattie stumbles over to collapse on the ground beside me, leaning over Tyler and cradling his face in her hands.

At first, I can't understand why, or what she's saying in mumbled, breathy words. How could she mourn him, when all signs point toward him turning her against her will and certainly not treating her well after?

But when the words click, I reach out to place my hand on her shoulder when I realize what she's saying to his corpse.

"How could you do this to me? You told me you loved me, you promised—you said—you swore you would always love me."

She doesn't respond to my touch, and I push myself to my feet, startling her. She looks up at me with a wide, doe-eyed expression and springs to her feet to bolt into the woods beyond the edges of the old logging camp. "Hattie..." With one hand out toward her, I watch her go, but I can't bring myself to chase after her.

Not when everything I need is right behind me, bleeding, and probably about to hit the ground again.

When Cairo makes a pained noise in his throat, I'm on him instantly, smoothing my bloody hands over his face, down his neck, and hovering over his injuries. "Oh my God," I breathe, stomach clenching around the fear that this really might be fatal, no matter what he said. "Holy shit, Cairo. You're fucked up. How did he even do this? I thought—"

"Fern." He grips my wrists, his voice calm, but he willingly submits to more of my examination as I touch every bit of unmarred skin I can find, no matter if it's stained with blood or not. His jeans remain, and his boots, but nothing can be saved. We might as well burn it on a pyre made of Tyler's limbs for good measure.

"I thought you were dead. One of the cursed Tyler sent said that you were dead, and I was terrified. Holy fuck, are you sure you aren't dying?" Panic makes my vision blur at the edges, and my hands shake as I touch him.

"Fern..." Cairo sighs again, waiting until I'm done talking. "I need to tell you something." God, he sounds so calm. He shouldn't sound this calm, and it only fuels my panic.

"Are you dying? Are you just like, dying slowly?" Moro whines, circling both of us, and noses at his leg like she's worried about the same thing. "I'm so sorry I didn't get here sooner. I didn't have a plan, and I didn't know what I was doing. Agatha told me to follow your scent, but that took me awhile, and she's really vague and cryptic and—"

"*Little bird.*" The growl that leaves him has the immediate effect of shutting me up. My fingers clench, making my claws bite into my palms, and I look up at Cairo with wide eyes and my muscles tense, waiting for him to tell me he's dying or something equally awful.

"What?" My voice comes out as barely a whisper, and Cairo lets out a breath when he has my attention.

"I need you to stop panicking over me for maybe two seconds, all right?" A smile twitches on his lips, and I relax by degrees. Surely if he were dying—

"Because I'm trying to tell you I love you."

My brain takes too long to process the words. I just stare at him, mouth open slightly, as the sounds of birdsong and breeze echo in my ears along with the statement that burrows itself into my memories.

"No," I say flatly, and Cairo looks suddenly taken aback. "No, absolutely not! I was going to say that! What the *fuck*, Cairo?" I smack lightly at his chest, being incredibly careful not to touch any of the ugly wounds. "I did all of this, and killed some loser for you, and you can't even let me be the one to say 'I love you' first?! Way to steal my moment!"

Cairo's laugh is sharp and clear. There's nothing contrived or scripted, and his smile is wide enough that I'd say he's beaming. "I am so sorry, little bird," he apologizes, though I have a feeling he isn't sorry at all. "But maybe you should've led with that, instead of panicking over my wounds."

"You could be dying!"

"I'm not dying." He grabs my throat and pulls me close, purring in the back of his throat as he crushes his lips to mine hungrily.

It's nothing like his kisses before. Now I can tell just how much he was holding back, as he uses his teeth and tongue to his advantage. My inexperience with them makes me feel clumsy, and he easily has me against the wall of a cabin, breathless and gasping against his mouth.

"Wait…" I huff, palms pressed to his chest. "You're really

fucked up right now. I don't want to hurt you—" He growls again, and a wave of submission washes over me, ending my protest. "What was that?" I ask when I can speak again.

Cairo's grin is almost apologetic, and he sighs. "That was why Tyler wanted to get rid of me. Though he also would have had to kill Elijah and Vivienne before getting what he wanted."

"That's unhelpfully vague."

His grimace is cute, and bloody, and he kisses the tip of my nose when I glower at him in reply. "It's...dominance, I guess. Like wolves, or dogs, or any animal that lives in a group."

"Oh." I have to let that sink in for a minute, and my fingers trace over his chest. "That's hot," I admit finally, earning a snort and a shake of his head. "Are you *sure* you aren't dying?" God, I can't help being worried for him, but I'm surprised into releasing a yelp when he suddenly grabs me, picks me up and throws me over his shoulder.

"Allow me to demonstrate how much I'm *not* dying," Cairo laughs, walking between the buildings and tossing me down on a mostly clear patch of grass. I scramble to sit up, but he's there immediately, pinning me on my back and leaning over me with a growl that I give right back. This time I'm the one lunging upward to lick up his throat, tasting his skin under the blood and purring at the spicy-sweetness.

"Is this how I taste?" I murmur and then do it again.

"No." He shoves me back down and rips off the remains of my shirt and bra, leaving me half naked like him. His eyes darken as he looms over me on his hands and knees, not needing to have a hand on me to keep me in place. "You taste so much better." Leaning down, he runs his tongue up my body, from my navel, up between my breasts, and finally to the hollow of my throat. But when he tries to do it again, my control snaps, and I yank him up for a kiss that's more snarls and teeth than actual kissing.

Judging by his reaction and the way he ruts against me, however, Cairo doesn't mind. I help him shove off the shredded pieces of denim still covering his legs, but he doesn't bother trying to peel my sweatpants off of me. He simply rips the fabric at the seams, making my hips jerk with the rough, sudden movements.

"You shouldn't have turned yourself for me," he pants, one hand on the ground beside my head as he kisses my throat. It's hard for me to touch him only where he isn't wounded, but I manage to grip his hips as I arch into him.

"Agatha helped," I admit, and that earns a growl from him. "She's not exactly a benevolent fairy godmother, is she?"

He sighs against my throat, and jerks against me when I grind my hips up against his body. "No. She's not. I knew she had ulterior motives for helping you, but..." He sits up just enough to stare down at me, eyes hungry and nearly feral. "You'll have to forgive me, little bird. I can't be mad at her for this."

"I'm not mad at her either," I'm quick to agree, and at his urging I wrap my leg around his uninjured hip. "I just—" He sinks into me suddenly, and the combination of *too much* and *not enough* has me throwing my head back and howling.

Cairo purrs encouragingly and dives to bury his fangs in my throat; marking and licking over where Tyler dug his nails in. "I just wish she could've been more upfront about it!" I gasp and urge him into motion with a roll of my hips.

He doesn't need convincing. Cairo slams into me, not bothering to be gentle, but I don't want him to be. The raw, predatory claim of him inside me and the way he slams into me with every stroke stokes a fire in my chest that didn't exist until now.

"She isn't upfront about anything. *Fuck*, little bird." He

arches off of me, eyes closing as I drag him closer with my leg around him. "You're so tight. So fucking perfect for me."

"Well, I hope so. Because I think you're going to be stuck with me for a while." Reaching out for him, I wait until he's lowered himself to me before shifting to roll Cairo over so I'm straddling him in the dirt and gazing down at my lover.

He could flip us back if he really wanted to. I have no doubt he could snarl me back into submission or just pin me with his strength. But he gasps approvingly, keeping his eyes on my face as I place my palms on his abdomen and lift myself up, only to sink back down on his cock.

Both of us let out appreciative hisses, though his has more of a natural, practiced purr to it than mine does. He grips my hips in both hands, his claws pricking me just enough to send a shiver through my body.

"I love you," I say, tasting the words on my tongue as I feel myself getting closer. The statement also drives me to ride him in earnest, rocking my hips and taking a second to feel him as deep inside me as he can be before lifting myself up again.

"Not as much as I love you, little bird," Cairo retorts. "You saved my life."

"Yeah." I grin down at him. "And you saved mine. I didn't understand before, but Agatha was right." I gasp again, head thrown back, and focus on rocking my hips until Cairo drags me down against him and shoves his hips upward so he's meeting every movement. Our teeth continue nipping and biting at each other in a fake battle for dominance.

"What was she right about?" he whispers, getting just as breathy and uncontrolled as I am.

"That I was starving," I snarl against his lips, kissing him just as hungrily as he kisses me. "I was *starving* before you, Cairo. I just didn't really know it."

When he comes, it's with a soft gasp and a moan I've never

heard from him before. I push him down again, watching his face as I grind my hips so his cock slides against that spot inside of me. His hand gropes for the apex of my thighs as he spills inside of me, and it only takes a few quick swipes of his thumb before I'm coming as well, my thighs tight around his hips and my body clenched tight around him, greedy and demanding for him to stay right here with me.

My arms tremble, and my elbows buckle, though I try not to collapse on top of him. I manage to roll onto the grass beside him as a purr builds in my throat, and I can't keep my hands off of him. Though I glance down at myself with a small frown at how much of his and Tyler's blood is now smeared over my skin.

"I'm gross," I state, twining my fingers with his as I watch the rise and fall of his chest. He doesn't reply, and my eyes never leave him, just to be sure.

Cairo snorts and opens one eye to look at me, then closes it again. "I won't stop breathing just because you fucked me so well, Fern," he promises with a chuckle. "I'm just tired."

"And almost dying," I point out, not letting go of his hand. Moro's paw steps make me look up, and I see her licking at the cooling blood around Tyler's body.

I really should worry more about her becoming a blood-thirsty cryptid-companion of legend...but not today. That's tomorrow's concern.

"How did he do it, anyway?"

"He wasn't alone." Cairo sighs, sounding particularly disappointed about it. "I don't know why I thought he would be. It's our way; we're supposed to fight alone when we're fighting for dominance. When he brought me here, I didn't realize he wasn't alone until Teague and Fletcher jumped me. I thought..." Cairo trails off. "I still didn't want to kill him," he admits. "And that was wrong of me. Good thing I have my feral little bird to protect me from my own moments of weakness, hmm?" he teases, opening his eyes and gingerly turning onto his side.

"And don't you forget it. You're my..." I trail off, thinking. "Okay, well, obviously I need a nickname for you. I'll have to think about it." Sitting up, I wince at the growing pain and stiffness from my fight with Tyler, and glare down at all of our ruined clothes. We can't go back into town like this, since I have no desire to be locked up in the nearest asylum for a perceived mental break.

Cairo sits up as well and gets to his feet before dragging me up. He's much more comfortable in his nudity than I am, though belatedly I consider he's probably used to it after being up here for so long. Especially since he can't feel the cold in an uncomfortable way.

And now, neither can I. *Huh*...I'm now realizing the air just feels comfortable, like the ground. I run my hands over the already healing wounds on my arms, listening to Cairo lecture Moro about her meal choices, and trying to get her to drop Tyler's aorta, before looking up at both of them as the breeze brings their scent to my nose.

Never before—in my mother's house or my own—have I ever felt like this.

Like I'm *home*.

EPILOGUE

THE TICKING OF THE CLOCK IS OPPRESSIVE, AND I KNOW CAIRO WILL be less than pleased when he finds out I'm here. But I'm sitting in the same chair where I sat for weeks listening to Dr. Radley, looking out the window as the sun crests the edge of the mountain.

I still don't feel the *wrongness* Agatha mentioned that night at Bluebone Ridge, which seems like so long ago and yet was only a week. But then again, Whippoorwill Gap is basically in the mountains, anyway. My nails tap against the arm of the chair, and I tilt my head to listen to the sound of the front door opening and closing, then footsteps on the stairs making their way up to the office.

"I should've known you were an alcoholic," I remark, just as the door closes behind my ex-therapist. I can feel her tense even without looking, and her keys shiver in her hand, making the softest of metallic jingling noises. "But I guess you hide it well."

Slowly she walks around the room, giving the chair a wide berth. In the dim light of early morning, she gropes for the light on the desk, finally finding it and making it flare to life, surprising me into blinking a few times.

Dr. Radley's sharp intake of breath is soft, and she searches my face before setting down her keys and phone to press her hands against the top of her desk. "They got you," she breathes, resignation and fear in the set of her shoulders. "They took you before I could help you, they—"

"No." I don't get up, but I run my nails over the fabric of the armchair, gazing down at it. "I'm sorry about your sister. Really, I think it's awful what happened to her." I do, in a way, though the fate of a random human isn't at the top of my priority list anymore, if it ever was. I care about them in the way I care about a butterfly getting stepped on by Moro when she's playing in the woods.

Which is to say, not very much at all.

"Do you hate the wolves that live in the mountains? Or the bears?" I go on. "We're the same thing."

"No," Dr. Radley disagrees sharply. "You're *not*. You eat—"

"Animals." I show her a wry, sharp-fanged grin, and something in me twists with joy at the way she recoils from me. "I ate a deer this morning. But I didn't come here to debate with you. I very much doubt I can change your mind, Dr. Radley."

"Then why are you here?" I let the question hang in the air and take a breath to scent her fear, working through the different, bitter notes in my nose.

"You won't tell my mom about this. I doubt she'd come looking for me, but..." I trail off, hating the tickle of anxiety over my mother wandering too close to something she shouldn't in the mountains. "I'd rather that she think I'm dead, and she'll be happy to believe you if you lead her down that path."

"You're not coming back."

I shake my head, a little bit rueful as I get to my feet. "No, it...I can't," I say. "I don't know if you ever really cared, or if you just wanted to get vengeance for your sister on anyone you thought was similar. But I just needed you to see that this isn't the worst fate. Not when the alternative was what it was." When I look at her now, the malice and imagined revenge that I dreamed about on my way here fades out of me and trickles into the floorboards. She can't hurt me anymore. There's no point in holding a grudge, so I give her a half smile that she flinches back from.

"I don't believe you," she murmurs as I walk to the door, prompting me to glance back at her rigid posture, fear bleeding off of her in waves. "They're monsters, and they've made you one too."

I study her, and her words just roll right off of me. What once would've hurt me or caused me to panic, required me to ground myself or at the very least find a way to shake it off, now just washes off of me.

Neither she nor my mother can hurt me anymore.

The revelation is cathartic, and my smile widens. "That's okay." I shrug. "That's your choice. But I hope you can get some peace." Without another word, I leave, closing the door behind me. I hear her loud, explosive exhale, and the way she sits down hard in her chair, thinking she's safe from me now that the door is between us. But if I were the monster she thinks I am, then that flimsy piece of wood wouldn't be nearly enough to protect her.

Thankfully for her, I'm not.

M oro drops the stick she's carrying when she hears me, and she barks in greeting, though I know Cairo has been watching me through the trees for the last ten or so seconds. Sitting on the steps of Bluebone Ridge, he has a duffel bag and a backpack at his side. He looks better finally, and not so much like a victim of a violent crime now that his wounds are healed and the bruises have faded. Even the scars are shiny and thin instead of marring his body with red claw and teeth marks.

"Did you get Moro's medicine?" I ask, glancing down at the backpack.

"Yep," he confirms, rising to his feet. "Did you accomplish what you needed to?"

I meet his gaze as he steps forward to tuck my hair back from my ear, and Moro pushes between us, as if reminding us to leave room for her. Cairo reaches down to tangle his fingers in her ruff, and the wolf dog wags her tail happily.

"She's supposed to be *my* dog, you know," I huff, though that's not really true. She's ours, and her favorite between us seems to change every day, with this morning being Cairo's turn. "And yeah. I did."

Cairo studies my face before cupping my jaw in his hand, bringing his face close to press his forehead to mine. "Are you okay? I doubt she gave you what you needed, little bird. Which I could've told you, if you hadn't snuck away and left me with Hattie." His voice twists on her name, and I can't help but grin. The woman seems to have gotten a little better hold of her mental state since becoming cursed, but I doubt Cairo enjoys being followed around like a mother duck with his awkward duckling child.

I reach up to run my claws over the back of his hand, and lean in to nose his cheek. "She didn't," I admit. "Actually, I had plans. I thought I might scare her, or get her to apologize for intentionally triggering me. I thought maybe I'd give some speech that would make her see we aren't the monsters she thinks we are."

"Even though we are," Cairo points out dryly, prompting

me to scoff. "I take it she wasn't very receptive to the fiery speech full of passion and dreams?"

"Shut up!" I laugh. "Don't make me pull the 'I saved your ass' card again."

"Right, because you've only used it six times this week." But he gently shoos Moro away to drag me against him. Now that the strength of the curse taking hold is losing its effect, Cairo is stronger than me again, thanks to his years of experience.

Not that I mind. I like it when he drags me around, and I like it even more that he no longer has to be so careful not to break me. Which I'm able to appreciate now that I know how strong he is when he isn't holding back.

"I realized I didn't need it," I admit at last, burying my face in his throat with a purr I never could've vocalized before. But now my throat is different, and the sounds I make are less than human most of the time, and I'm even realizing I can understand and interpret those sounds when I hear them from the others. "I don't need her to accept this, or me, or to approve of it. She doesn't understand."

"Oh, yeah?" Cairo tilts my head up to his. "Does that mean we can leave this particular mountain for a while? It's sort of my least favorite, and I think I'd like to take you north for a while." His lips brush mine, and I lean up on the balls of my feet to kiss him in earnest. He kisses just as he had before, but with less restraint. My growls are met with his, and my teeth never find purchase in his bottom lip as he chases back with equal fervor.

By the time we break apart, I'm panting and grasping at the front of his shirt, not letting him go anywhere. When I purr up at him, he mimics the sound, licking at my lower lip. "We can go wherever you want...but you know Hattie is going to come too," I tease with a laugh, making him groan.

"I don't remember agreeing to adopt a feral child recently." There's no heat in his voice, and I know that while he's sometimes exasperated, neither of us wants her to wander off and get killed or hurt by one of the others who might take advantage of her. He just sighs, and licks at my lower lip, his attention back on me and his focus here, in this moment. "Are you hungry, little bird?"

My answering grin is equal parts feral and voracious, and when I drag him to me, I bare my teeth happily to say, "I'm *starving*," before kissing him again.

ABOUT THE AUTHOR

AJ Merlin would rather write epic love stories than live them. I mean, who wants to limit themselves to only falling in love once? She is obsessed with dark fantasy, true crime, and also dogs. From serial killers to voyeurs all the way down to the devil himself, AJ's specialty is in writing irredeemable heroes who somehow still manage to captivate their heroines (and her readers).

Connect with her on Facebook or Instagram to see updates, giveaways, and be bombarded with dog, cat, and horse pictures.

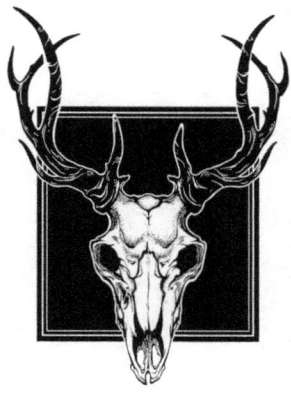

www.ingramcontent.com/pod-product-compliance
Lightning Source LLC
Chambersburg PA
CBHW072026020726
47501CB00006B/1975